PJ Grondin

Under the Blood Tree

PD House Books

PD House Holdings, LLC
910 S Meadow Drive
Sandusky, Ohio   44870

www.pjgrondin.com

pjgron@pjgrondin.com

Library of Congress Control Number: 2017943701

ISBN: 978-0-9984644-8-0

Dedication

This story is dedicated to children who are forced to grow up too fast, who are unable to enjoy their childhood because of circumstances forced on them by others. Kids should have the opportunity to just be kids.

Acknowledgements

My dear wife, Debbie, deserves an indulgence medal for her patience with me while this story developed from just a thought to a finished product. She is a saint. I am truly blessed.

Next, the idea for the Blood Tree was born from the childhood stories of my good friend and colleague, Randy Dively. Randy and I shared a kinship, being U.S. Navy Submariners. While we never worked together in the Navy, we worked side-by-side in the electric shop at Davis-Besse Nuclear Power Station, Oak Harbor, Ohio. Randy was one of the most knowledgeable people I have ever known. He was also a hard worker, willing to take on the most challenging tasks. Away from work, he pursued leisure activities with a passion. He was a loving husband, father, brother, and son. He succumbed to cancer on September 23, 2015 after a long, tough battle. He was 50 years young.

My sincere thanks to Bonnie Lukcso for her proofreading skills in reviewing this novel.. I am forever grateful.

Under the Blood Tree

Prologue

Thursday, August 26, 1999
10:55 PM

A distant lightning flash lit up the western night sky as four boys frantically ran through the wooded acreage bordering Cypress Lake Mobile Home Park. The stagnant, humid, summer air, combined with a temperature near ninety degrees, drenched their skin with sweat. Adrenaline flooded their young bodies, heightening the fear that caused them to race through the woods. To the northwest, along the storm front, thunder rumbled. Directly overhead, a full moon and an array of stars were visible. They headed towards the place they knew as their home base, their hiding place, their outdoor club. They knew they could take refuge under their tree.

Billy Ray Duke, the youngest of the four by just a year, yelled in his high-pitched, panicked, southern drawl, "Wait up! Hey, wait up!"

Tommy Alexander, the unofficial leader of the group, yelled back, "We're almost there! Come on, keep runnin'!"

The lightning flashes were roughly half a minute apart. The booming sounds of thunder rumbled off in the distance. Tommy hoped that the storm was headed their way, praying that a heavy rain would wash away any signs that he and his friends had been to Cypress Lake that evening.

Just fifty more yards now and Tommy would be the first to arrive safely at the tree. Andy Pepperdine was close behind, followed by Curtis Hardy. Billy Ray brought up the rear.

Tommy arrived first at the tree. He wiped his face with his arm and noticed blood mixed with his sweat. He felt his nose, then along his cheek, and found the spot where he had caught a branch in the face, a small cut oozing red. His lungs burned from exertion after running full tilt for a quarter-mile.

Andy Pepperdine arrived at the tree as Tommy worked to catch his breath. He noticed the trickle of blood on Tommy's face. "Looks like ya got whipped with a branch." He paused, taking deep, sucking breaths. "It don't look too bad."

Tommy leaned against the tree, his sweat mixed with blood. "You got a couple cuts on your arms."

As Andy took more deep breaths, he looked down at both arms, inspecting the minor damage. There was no flowing blood, but he had numerous scratches. He motioned towards Tommy's arms and said, "So do you."

Curtis Hardy ran up and dropped to his knees on the damp leaves that covered the ground near their tree. He put one hand on the tree and continued to breathe deep, sweat dripping from his chin. He kept looking down, his eyes unfocused, deep in thought. He said nothing and didn't appear to notice the scratches on his arms and another on his forehead. Like Andy, nothing was bleeding, but the scratches would sting over the next few days. He didn't look up at Tommy or Andy, but just kept up the deep, sucking gasps, fighting to get as much oxygen into his lungs as possible.

Finally, Billy Ray Duke broke into the clearing under the tree. He fell to his hands and knees, trying to catch his breath. As he watched the ground in front of him, he saw blood drip from his nose onto a leaf…then another, and seconds later, another. He screamed, "I'm bleeding! Daggummit, I'm bleeding!"

Tommy, whose breathing was now less labored, squatted down next to him and put his left hand on his back. "Billy Ray, calm down. Y'all's gonna be fine. Lemme see what's bleedin'."

Billy Ray leaned back on his haunches and looked up at his friend. A short gash, about three-quarters of an inch long, was right between his eyebrows. The cut was at a slight angle, higher on the left side. It bled steadily, a drop of blood hitting the ground every second.

Tommy said, "Take off yer tee shirt. Hold it against yer hard-assed head. It'll stop in a few minutes."

The boys fell silent, replaying the last half hour over in their heads. They all knew it was going to change their lives – perhaps forever.

* * *

Nearly thirty-five minutes earlier, Tommy was the first to hear the cries. The night air had been still, just as it was now. The only sounds heard at their hide-out were crickets, the occasional passing car on Cypress Lake Road, and faint country music coming from a trailer at the mobile home park over two hundred yards to the northeast. Tommy had hushed his friends.

"Y'all be quiet." After a long pause, Tommy cocked his head so his right ear was towards the lake. He heard it again. "Didj'all hear it?"

Andy Pepperdine asked, "What're ya talking about? I didn't hear nuthin'."

"Me neither." Billy Ray stood, cupping his hands around his ears, straining to hear anything out of the ordinary.

Then they all heard it; someone crying, the sobs carrying a long distance over the quiet, night air. As they listened, lightning again flashed in the distance followed nearly ten seconds later by distant, rolling thunder. When the low-level boom from the thunder subsided, they heard the crying again.

Tommy said, "We got to see whose cryin'. Come on, follow me."

The four boys headed out towards the lake. As they made their way through the woods, the crying grew louder. They had gone some five hundred yards, through thickets of trees and brush, when they came to Cypress Lake Road, which separated the woods and the trailer park from Cypress Lake. They crouched low, looking up and down the road for any traffic. There were no headlights in sight. It was past 10:00 PM. The sunset was long gone, but a full moon cast an eerie, silver film over the lake's glass-like surface. The distant storm contrasted with the clear sky overhead.

The crying was very clear now. There were no homes within two hundred yards. A crude access road led down to the lake's shore. A gate that had previously been closed and secured with a chain and padlock, sat wide open. The padlock had been broken for as long as the boys could remember. They had regularly used the road to access the lake and catch tadpoles and frogs.

Tommy's three friends looked to him for direction. Sensing their apprehension, Tommy had stood up. "Let's go."

They trotted down the path towards the edge of the lake, the sobs now mixed with whimpering. "Help me. Please, help me."

The path ended at a stand of trees by the lake's edge. The trees hid any view of this stretch of shoreline from the road. The bright, full moon cast eerie shadows from the trees onto the water's surface.

The foursome approached the trees slowly. When they were within fifty feet, they saw a young girl, about their age, leaning against a car's rear bumper. The front end of the car faced the lake and was near the water's edge. They couldn't tell the make or model of the car, but all four boys had immediately recognized the girl.

Carly Sue Saxon had not noticed the boys approaching until they were within fifteen feet. Even in the dark of night, with the moonlight blocked by the trees, Tommy saw her anguish. Her clothes and face were a dirty mess. The boys stopped just ten feet away.

When there was a brief break in her crying, Tommy spoke. "Carly Sue?"

She jumped to her feet and covered her mouth.

Tommy said, "It's just us, Carly Sue. We heard ya cryin'. Are ya alright?"

She knew the four boys, though she knew Billy Ray best because his trailer was just one hundred feet from Carly Sue's.

She stood, turned towards the car, then back at the boys. In a quivering, scared voice, she said, "Help me, please."

Tommy, confusion written on his face, took a few tentative steps towards her and asked, "What do ya want us ta do?"

She turned to the car and paused. "Push it into the lake."

Tommy frowned. He thought *What?* With disbelief in his voice, he asked, "Push what into the lake? That car?" The other three boys laughed, then stopped when they realized that she was dead serious.

Carly Sue said nothing, but nodded her head. She had her hands folded in front of her as if praying to the boys or to God. Tommy couldn't tell which. Even though the temperature had to be near ninety degrees, she was shivering.

Tommy scratched his head then turned to his friends. After a pause he said, "Y'all heard the lady. Let's push this wreck into the lake."

The four boys got behind the bumper and started to push as hard as they could, but the car wouldn't budge. Carly Sue moved in between Tommy and Andy and began pushing with all her might. The body of the car rose then settled back on the frame, but remained stationary. Tommy thought, *This thing's still in gear. I'll fix that.*

He walked around to the driver's side door. The window was down and the powerful odor of urine and feces overwhelmed his nostrils . He held his nose and looked through the open window. The body of a man was in the driver's seat, blood crusted on the side of his head.

He turned away from the car, nausea hammering his stomach. He wretched twice and threw up his dinner next to the front of the car.

Andy ran to his side. "What's the matter, Tommy?" Then his nose was assaulted by the odor and he saw the body. Curtis and Billy Ray came around the car and saw what caused Tommy to lose his dinner. They all stood in fear, then looked back at Carly Sue who started to cry loudly again. Tommy knew that he had to quiet her or they would all be in big trouble.

He wiped his face off with his arm and raced around the car to the crying young girl. He grabbed her shoulders and turned her square to face him. He begged her to quiet down, assuring her that they'd help her. He didn't know why she needed to hide that body, but trusted that it had to be important.

After half a minute, Carly Sue quieted down. Tommy put the car in neutral, and the five children pushed with all their might. At first the car moved slowly. Once the front end was in the water, it seemed to float and pushing the car became easier. Finally, the car was fully into the lake. They gave the vehicle a final push. It floated for fifty, seventy, one hundred feet.

Carly Sue started crying again. Tommy asked, "What's the matter now, Carly Sue?"

"It ain't sinkin'. Somebody's gonna see it floatin' out there."

As if on cue, bubbles started coming up around the sides of the car. It drifted out another fifty feet then disappeared from sight. All five children gave a big sigh of relief. The gravity of what they had just done began to dawn on them.

Tommy turned to Carly Sue and said, "Y'all go on home now. We'll walk ya to the road, then yer on yer own."

When Carly Sue left them and headed towards Cypress Lake Mobile Home Park, Tommy turned to his friends and said, "We gotta get outta here."

As they rose to head across the road, the headlights of a car shown as it came around a curve. The boys crouched back down, staying out of sight. As the car passed, they saw the rack lights on top of the car and the shield of the Bulloch County Sheriff's Department on the door. The car passed, but it seemed to take forever. When the tail lights were finally out of sight, they ran. And they kept running until they gathered at the tree.

* * *

"What're we gonna do?"

Curtis Hardy asked the question that was on each of their minds. He was still on his knees, looking at the ground in front of him, trying to catch his breath.

They all looked at Tommy. He was supposed to have all the answers. Tommy had decided they should find the source of the crying. Tommy decided they should help Carly Sue, without question or hesitation. Tommy found the body in the car. And Tommy always knew what to do in tough situations, like when they threw a baseball and broke old lady Crider's trailer window.

But this…this was something completely different, and they all knew it.

Tommy looked at his friends, noted the fear in their eyes, the anticipation of hearing his solution to their situation.

In that moment, Tommy knew that their days of innocence were over.

He drew out his knife. He told his friends to get their knives out as well. He scraped a section of bark from their tree. The fresh wood oozed sticky sap.

He turned to his friends. They all had their knives in hand. He said, "We ain't never gonna to talk 'bout this again. That's what we're gonna do. And we're gonna pledge with our blood, right here on our tree."

He looked hard at his friends. He saw fear and doubt. There were questions in their eyes, but none on their lips. Then he saw resolve.

Tommy said, "Take y'all's knives and make a cut on yer hand then place yer hand on the tree in that spot." He pointed to the bare spot that he had just created on the tree. "When ya do, say *I pledge that I ain't sayin' nuthin' 'bout this night the rest of my life.* And ya darn sure better mean it." He looked at his friends again. "Are y'all ready?"

The three boys took a deep breath and nodded.

Tommy started. He placed the tip of his knife in the palm of his hand and applied a little pressure. A bead of blood popped up. He placed his palm on the tree then pulled it back. A one-inch circle of blood remained.

Next, Andy Pepperdine repeated what Tommy had done. Then Curtis Hardy.

It was Billy Ray Duke's turn. Billy Ray was nervous. When he put the tip of his knife to his palm, he put too much pressure on his knife and cut into his palm, leaving a one-inch gash. Blood flowed freely from the wound. Even so, he placed his hand on the bare spot on the tree over top of the other's blood.

Tommy gave Billy Ray a nervous smile. "Between yer head and yer hand, ya might bleed to death. Use yer shirt on yer hand now. I think yer head's about sealed up."

Billy Ray didn't laugh or smile. Unlike his three friends, he was pretty sure that he knew why there was a dead body in the car that was now at the bottom of Cypress Lake. He looked up at the mixed blood on the tree and hoped the body would remain there for eternity.

Chapter 1

Sixteen Years Later
Friday, May 29, 2015
7:45 AM

Tommy Alexander stood in front of the kitchen sink, staring out the window but seeing nothing in his back yard. He was in a trance, a hot cup of black coffee in his right hand. Worry exaggerated the lines on his face. He wrapped his left hand around the mug, its warmth soothing to the small scar on his left palm. He did not see his children's fancy wooden play set that would rival some city parks, or the patio, or the shed, where he stored his top-of-the-line lawn equipment. He also didn't see his white privacy fence, or the second floor of his closest neighbor's home. It was like he was staring at a movie screen, the images running through his mind.

The kitchen television droned in the background, one of the national network's morning news programs reporting the drought's severity in the southeast. They mentioned Central Georgia as being hit particularly hard, the screen filled with images of parched earth, dead crops, and farmers tilling under the dry, brown, vegetation that remained. Reporters interviewed a number of family-farm owners, discussing the financial dire straits that they faced because of the total loss of crops this year. This year's drought, coupled with last year's crop loss due to torrential rain, left many farmers near bankruptcy. Some already faced foreclosure, their land and equipment auctioned off. In some cases, the land had been in the family for generations. The heartbreak was punctuated by tears flowing from grown men's eyes, facing extraordinary pressure to keep their farms, and their families, afloat.

Tommy didn't hear any of it. He wasn't concerned about money. At twenty-eight years old, he was quite successful as an independent insurance salesman. His family's net worth surpassed one million dollars, all of it through hard work and dedication to his business. Their home, a thirty-nine hundred square foot, two-story gem in the Irongate subdivision, was among the nicer homes in the upscale neighborhood southwest of Statesboro, Georgia.

He wasn't concerned about his family's health. His beautiful wife, Cheryl, and two young daughters, age six and four, were in excellent health. Life was good, and improving, as long as he kept his mind on work at the office, kept his family happy at home, and kept the two separate.

Tommy worked long hours, ensuring that his customers were properly insured. He used every tool at his disposal to recruit new customers. The growing business was largely based on referrals. His excellent reputation in the community, and his business ties through a number of civic organizations, also helped him connect with new leads.

His wife entered the kitchen and noticed him staring off into nothingness…again. Something was on his mind, which wasn't unusual. He was a deep thinker, his thoughts frequently wandering to the next great idea. She snuck up behind him and cautiously got his attention by clearing her throat while placing a hand on his left shoulder.

Tommy tensed but didn't flinch. His mug of coffee remained steady. He smiled, the back yard coming into focus, as the trance disappeared. From behind him, Cheryl's arms looped around his waist and she planted her head between his shoulder blades.

She commented, "The girls are dressed and ready for school. They should be down in a few minutes."

Tommy put his left arm over his wife's arms and squeezed lightly, then took a sip of coffee. He set the cup on the ceramic countertop and turned around, taking his wife in a warm embrace.

She looked up into his eyes. "Hey, sweetie, what's got y'all twisted up?"

She knew him too well, read him like a cheap airplane novel. He gave her a weak smile. "This drought. I mean, look at the lawn. It's baked to a crispy brown. I hate to walk on it, the dirt's so hard underneath. Gonna be another scorcher today, and tomorrow, and Sunday."

"It can't last forever, baby. I know we haven't had a good rain since…well, it's been a while. But, like the Good Book says, this too shall pass."

"Yeah, but it's already done a lot of damage. Insurance companies are paying out a lot of claims. I'm worried."

He hugged Cheryl tight and kissed her lightly on the lips until he heard his older daughter say, "Yuck. Don't come in here, Mommy and Daddy are kissin'."

The younger daughter smiled, then mimicked her sister. "Yuck." The girls laughed. It made Tommy smile, despite his mood.

Cheryl said, "Okay girls. Get your book bags and lunches and head out to your dad's car. Just another week of school, then you get a break for summer." She raised her arms in the air and yelled, "Yea!" Her girls joined her in the cheer.

Cheryl turned back to Tommy and put her arms back around his waist. "Try to relax, dear. No matter what, we have the girls and we have each other." She smiled at the man who had been her high school hunk, her college study partner, her best friend, and her lover. She loved him deeply to this day. "See you around six?"

"Wouldn't miss dinner with my favorite girls. Where would you like to go?"

"Why don't we stay in and order a pizza? I'll pick up a movie. Any preference?"

Tommy thought for a moment. "Not really. You and the girls pick. Lady's choice tonight."

They kissed again. Tommy and the girls headed for the garage.

* * *

Tommy dropped the girls off at Trinity Episcopal School. As they exited his gold Lexus, he told them to study hard even though the year was nearly over. He added that their mother would pick them up at the end of the day. He hugged them and kissed them. The girls turned and headed to the building, meeting up with a couple friends at the door. He smiled as he turned and got back in his car to head for the office near the intersection of South Main Street and Fair Road.

On the ten-minute drive from the school to the office, his mind wandered. He thought about the drought. He hated lying to his wife about anything and in reality, he had not lied. He really was worried about the drought, but not because of his company or its stock value or his clients. He was worried about shrinking lake levels…actually, just one lake level – Cypress Lake. He knew Cheryl was right, the drought would pass. The big question was *When.* The second question was *Would it be soon enough.* He believed the answers to his questions were *No time soon* and *No, it won't.*

* * *

By 7:30 AM, Andy Pepperdine was already at Low Country Seed and Supply Company, his farm supply store and warehouse. He liked to be the first to arrive and greet his employees with a smile and breakfast; usually doughnuts or bagels, sometimes egg-bacon-and-cheese sandwiches, or roll-ups, and coffee. He didn't have to do it, he just did it. What didn't get devoured by his employees was immediately taken to a homeless shelter down the street. It was a tradition that his father started years before. When his father decided that, at age fifty-five, he and his wife should retire, move to Naples, Florida, and turn the business over to their son, Andy decided to continue the daily ritual.

His employees weren't too sure how the transition would go. They loved working for Marvin Pepperdine. They found that little changed when Andy took the reins of the company. In fact, things improved slightly, if that was possible. Andy started a profit sharing program and a voluntary service program, where employees could work up to four hours each week at a charitable organization of their choice and get paid by the company. They just had to show proof of participation for the charity. It was a win-win for the company and the community.

Andy sat at his desk, reviewing the month-to-date totals, but found that he could not concentrate. He subconsciously rubbed the palm of his left hand where a scar had developed some sixteen years ago. A small cut, made with his pocket knife, had initially not healed well. He played with the cut with dirty hands, not allowing the wound to scab over and heal naturally. At the time, it didn't look like much, but over the next two days, the wound got infected. Before he finally told his mother, it was open and oozing.

The trip to the doctor was more painful than the treatment as his mother lectured him the entire time about taking care of himself. After a deep cleaning, treatment with some kind of antibacterial salve, and repeated admonishments to keep the wound clean and covered, the healing took about two weeks. The resulting scar was about an inch long by a quarter-inch wide. That wasn't so bad, except that the skin was harder and less flexible than the rest of the skin on his palm, making it difficult to grip anything.

As he continued to rub the scar, he thought about the extended drought. He drove past Cypress Lake the previous Friday. The level was down significantly, the drought-enhanced shoreline extending out, twenty to thirty feet beyond historical norms. He was so distracted that he almost clipped a car coming in the opposite direction.

When he got home that evening, his wife noticed his glum expression. They spoke about the drought and what it was doing to local farmers – their customers. It would no doubt hurt business, but they would weather the storm. They would even provide whatever assistance they could to help others in their time of need. Their ten-million-dollar net worth would take a hit, but it would be nothing compared to some farmers who lived year to year, relying on a good harvest, and decent crop prices for their survival.

As he had many times over the years, he thought about how expensive a good criminal lawyer might be. After all, they hadn't reported a crime when they knew one had been committed. Tommy said that they needed to just forget about it, as if they had not been to the lake that night, they had not seen the dead man in the car, and they had not helped Carly Sue push it into the lake. They had not even taken the time to ask Carly Sue how a dead body came to be in the car. It all happened so fast...

"Mornin', Andy."

Andy jumped, having been jolted out of his thoughts by his General Foreman. Lucas Grieves walked into his office with a bagel lathered in blueberry cream cheese in one hand, and a steaming, hot cup of coffee in the other.

"Mornin', Lucas."

"Drought gotcha in a fog this morning?"

"That easy to tell?"

"Oh yeah. I think everybody's got the funk over it. Gonna put lots of folks in the poor house, that's for sure. We need the government to step in and give us some guarantees that we're not all gonna go broke."

"Yeah, well, don't hold your breath with that bunch up in Washington. They can't even agree to disagree. I think we ought to toss 'em all out and start over."

Lucas grinned. People screamed about it every election cycle. Throw out the bums and put in a new set of bums. But the old bums always seem to win.

Lucas said, "Our best bet is to keep praying. That's got as good a chance as any to end this drought and put our customers back in business. I guess that's why the good Lord said to stock up when there's plenty, and ration when things are tight. Something like that." Lucas took another big bite of his bagel, then washed it down with a swig of coffee.

Andy gave a weak smile. "Would you mind looking over these month-to-date reports when you get a few minutes? I'm going to take a look around, greet everybody as they come in. I've got to get my mind in a right place, get outta this gloom and doom. Maybe a chat with the crew will help me think positive. What do you think?"

"It can't hurt. This drought, the heat, I know it's on everybody's mind. Anything we can do to keep us and the crew thinkin' positive is good. We've got it pretty darn good here. Maybe if we think about how much better off we are than some folks out there, it might help."

"You got that right." He smiled. "Did you leave any bagels for anyone else?"

Lucas smiled back. "I think there's a crumb or two."

Andy walked out and stood by the table that had the daily breakfast spread. He smiled as he greeted his employees and spoke with them about their families, their hobbies, their children and grandchildren – anything but the weather. The men and women appeared to appreciate their boss being so interested in their lives. If they came in with a bit of the blues, they left the breakfast table uplifted, if even just a little, before they started their workday.

Andy headed back to the office. Lucas was talking on the phone when he stepped in.

He heard only one-half of the conversation, but Lucas' face was tense. When he was done, Lucas said, "That was Curt Hardy with the City Water Department. They said they're calling all their commercial customers to let us know first, before they announce it to the residents. Their gonna start rationing water. We have to reduce usage by forty percent."

Andy's heart sank. Hearing Curtis Hardy's name, he wondered if Curtis was feeling the pressure from the drought. Apparently, the city believed that the drought would continue, unabated. After talking with his employees, he felt pretty good. Now the room seemed to close in around him.

He said a prayer to himself. *Lord, please protect my family from the coming storm. They had no part in this. And*

Lord, I don't know how deep that lake is, but we could sure use some rain...a lot of rain if you don't mind.

Chapter 2

Twenty-eight-year-old Curtis Hardy called the staff meeting to order. Eighteen of the twenty-one staff members of the Statesboro Water Department were on hand. Two other staff members were on afternoon and evening shifts, and the other employee was on sick leave. Everyone knew the topic: the unrelenting drought, and what was expected of the staff in the coming days and weeks.

Statesboro City Council, during its last session, very loudly and publicly demanded that city staff do everything within its power and budget to make sure that water supplies remained adequate and safe. Without a reason for concern, other than the drought had been going on for much longer than anyone expected, the council wanted positive and visible action. In other words, they wanted proof that city employees were carrying out their duties to the best of their abilities.

Curtis had worked for the City of Statesboro since his graduation from Georgia Southern University with a degree in Chemistry and a minor in Business Management. With just six years' experience, he was among the more junior employees in the department, but he was a quick study. He put in extra, unpaid hours learning the testing procedures, records requirements, and reporting requirements to local, state, and federal government agencies. He told his boss that he did it so that he could provide the best possible service to the citizens of Statesboro. The story was very convincing.

The real reason for his constant efforts was that the extra work kept him busy, both in mind and body. It kept his mind from wandering back to that night at Cypress Lake. He turned fear and despair into positive energy. All his free time was devoted to learning his job and implementing changes to improve the staff's day-to-day activities. It paid off for him in recognition and a promotion to management.

On occasion, he would think back to the reason he studied so hard in school and why he dedicated his time to learning the ins and outs of water treatment. The reason was more evident with each rainless day, with each news broadcast showing dry, dusty fields with wilted crops, and with every shot of lakes with drastically depleted levels. He studied to keep his mind off his past. He kept his nose to the grindstone, wishing that the car in Cypress Lake would just rust away and become part of the lake bottom. With each rainless day, he knew that there would soon be a day of reckoning.

"Hey, Curtis, we gonna get this meeting going? We all got work to do."

A low chuckle worked its way around the room. The team needed something to pop the anxiety bubble that hung in the room like a cloud of smoke.

"Okay, okay. Sorry. I zoned out." Curtis looked around the room and gave his department a weak smile. He knew that they had read the newspapers, and listened to the news, so they were well aware of the edict from City Council. He just had to make sure that they all heard it from him. He had the respect of most of the staff, but there were a few old-timers who felt the need to show their wealth of experience at his expense. It was true that they had years on him. It was also true that they were his employees. He wanted to make sure he used them appropriately, but it was a tenuous relationship.

Curtis started out saying, "If I say something that y'all already know, humor me. I need to make sure this gets said so that y'all hear the same message through me. The City Council..."

Curtis repeated everything that the council members had stated in their meeting. There were just a handful of questions, some related to overtime, which would be required. It was a good-news, bad-news scenario. It was good that the city was paying overtime and that the staff would get a chance to fatten their wallets. It was also good for the guys who liked to come to work and take it easy, because there wouldn't be much in the way of actual work. This was more or less a way to show the residents that the city was doing everything in its power to guarantee that they would turn on their taps and get plenty of good quality water despite the drought. It was bad news because all time-off, including scheduled vacations, was cancelled at a time when kids were completing the school year, and family vacations were high on many employees' priority lists. For Curtis, the good news was that he wouldn't get blamed for the cancelled vacations.

But there was plenty of bad news waiting for him at the bottom of Cypress Lake.

* * *

Billy Ray Duke had cursed to himself when he found out his latest work assignment. He and eleven other inmates from the Bulloch County Correctional Institute were hauled across the county from the jail to clean up along the shore of a lake west of Statesboro. It was an area he knew all too well.

Unlike his old, childhood friends, who all worked long hours to focus their attention, Billy Ray forgot all his problems by drinking too much. He had dabbled in pills and cocaine, but found them too costly, though he did sell marijuana from time to time for extra cash. He liked beer and whiskey a lot, the latter being his preference. But the hard liquor went to his head quicker, wiping out any moral compass that existed in that thick skull of his. Typically not a mean drunk, his lack of control put him in a number of precarious situations over the years.

Before he turned twenty, he had married. It lasted all of four months. That was when the young woman realized that he was intoxicated more than he was sober. He spent more time at the county jail than with her at his broken-down trailer in Cypress Lake Mobile Home Park. When asked if she wanted the trailer as part of the divorce settlement, she replied, "That rusted piece of crap? No thanks."

Time had not been kind to Billy Ray. The three-quarter-inch scar on his forehead between his eyebrows had stayed a creamy white while the rest of his skin was tan and wrinkled from too much time outdoors, too much hard drinking, heavy smoking, and years of constant worry. He did odd jobs for neighbors at the mobile home park, and he was employed from time to time, but he never held a job for a stretch longer than a few months. Whenever he was given a task by an employer, his mind wandered. He couldn't concentrate longer than a few minutes unless he was reading a good novel. It wasn't that he was bored. It was that his anxiety level was off the charts. He considered suicide a number of times but always chickened out. Now, as he stepped out of the prison van onto the shores of Cypress Lake, he wished that he had followed through on any one of his attempts.

The van pulled off Cypress Lake Road at the very path that Billy Ray and his friends used some sixteen years earlier. The gate had been repaired, but there was no lock in place. The sky was crystal clear, as it had been for well over a month now. A powerful high-pressure system hung over the southeast keeping any hint of moisture at bay. Even with scant humidity in the air, a temperature over ninety degrees guaranteed the chain gang would break a sweat today.

The driver pulled alongside the stand of trees that had been on the edge of the water. The drought had moved the water's edge some forty feet back. The exposed shoreline that had once been under water was parched and cracked. He couldn't remember the direction the car had floated that night, but he was pretty sure that the trees were blocking his view of the lake where the car finally sank.

The two deputies in charge ordered the inmates to fan out and pick up any trash that littered the shore as well as the exposed, dry lake bottom. There was a lot of trash. The shore was littered with soda and beer cans, glass and plastic bottles, plastic shopping bags, and a host of other debris. There were old tires that had been dumped into the lake but were now exposed. An old water heater was now stuck in dried mud.

The men moved along the shore keeping their eyes down, picking up the small items. Everyone was busy.

Everyone except Billy Ray. As soon as he rounded the stand of trees, he saw the car's roof poking out of the water. It was like a beacon drawing his attention and locking it in. Once again, he was given instructions to perform a simple task, but the horror that had held his mind captive for sixteen years came into focus. Now, for the first time since that dreadful night, the past was right there, visible to him, and visible to all.

The deputies instructed the men to put anything that wouldn't fit into a trash bag in a pile. A county truck would be brought in to collect those items.

One of the inmates asked, "What we s'posed to do with dat?" He pointed out into the lake.

Everyone stopped what they were doing and looked at the car's roof poking out of the shallow lake. Billy Ray tensed noticeably. Any hope that he was the only one to see the car was dashed.

The deputy in charge of the work detail spotted the car's roof. It was nearly forty yards into the lake away from the current shoreline. One thing was certain: it was going to take special equipment to pull the car in.

The two deputies huddled together and decided that they better call in the find and ask for the assistance of divers and a tow truck. In the meantime, they instructed the men on the chain gang to keep working. One of the deputies noticed Billy Ray still staring out at the car. He found it odd that the inmate was so mesmerized at the sight.

He walked over to Billy Ray and asked, "Ain't never seen a car in a lake before?"

Billy Ray flinched. He turned to the deputy and said, "Nah. I was just thinkin' of somethin'. No big deal."

"Get back to work. Alright?"

Billy Ray continued picking up trash, but kept glancing out at the car's top as if the vehicle would come ashore on its own. When he came alongside another inmate, a man he had known for some time, the man asked, "Hey, Billy Ray, ain't you lived in that trailer park there?" He nodded towards Cypress Lake Mobile Home Park.

"Yup. Still do, when I ain't in the drunk tank. Why?"

"Just wondered. You and your old man ever fish in this lake?"

"Nah. My old man was killed when I was just a kid. Never fished a day in my life. But we used to hang out in those woods across the way. Me and my old buds. When we was ten we used to steal cigarettes and go in the woods and smoke."

"Well, at least we're cleaning up yer ole stompin' grounds. Can't hurt, right?"

Billy Ray looked out at the roof of the car and said, "Right. Can't hurt."

Chapter 3

Carly Sue Hardy was still in her pajamas, drinking coffee. She hated being alone. It gave her too much time to think, and she always thought about her youth. Most women who were twenty-nine years old enjoyed reminiscing about the innocent days; the good years when friends bonded, when worries were few, and you were the apple of daddy's eye.

Carly Sue didn't have that kind of childhood. She never knew her father. He was gone from her life before she was born. No one knew, or cared, where he was. Her mother, MaryJo Saxon, dropped out of high school. A continuous parade of boyfriends came calling after Carly Sue was born, none lasting more than a few months. They had only one thing in mind. They figured that, since MaryJo was a young, single mother, she was easy, willing, and able to satisfy their needs and desires. That usually didn't work out well for them because MaryJo learned a hard lesson. When you slept with a guy, there was a good chance that you'd get pregnant, and she wasn't about to get strapped with another kid. She would tease them for a while until they got wise to her game. They would call her names: a tease, a prude, or worse. Once they knew she wasn't going to "put out," they simply left.

According to MaryJo, Carly Sue's grandmother died from lung cancer before she turned four and left all her worldly belongings to her daughter. That consisted of the beat-up trailer and furnishings where they lived, and an old Toyota Corolla that barely ran.

By the time Carly Sue had started elementary school, she was a cute little girl, but with some rough edges. Instead of playing with the girls from her class, she liked hanging out and rough-housing with the boys. When she turned ten, her body started its natural development. She went from a tough, cute girl, to a very pretty girl. The boys began to take notice that their rough and tumble buddy was less of a buddy and more of a girl.

Her friends weren't the only ones taking notice. Her mother's boyfriends began making eyes at her, making comments that were inappropriate. MaryJo turned a blind eye to the comments, at least while her boyfriends were around. When Carly Sue and her mother were alone, MaryJo acted like a jealous girlfriend instead of a protective mother. Even worse, when one of her boyfriends would break up, she would blame her daughter, claiming that she was acting too provocative around them.

By the time Carly Sue turned twelve, her mother had let herself go, gaining eighty pounds, never dressing up. She had a tough time getting and keeping a job or a boyfriend. The class of her already questionable suitors went dramatically downhill. She continually whined about the way the world had treated her, how men were pigs, and how her life was in the crapper...and she blamed her twelve-year-old daughter.

The day after Carly Sue's twelfth birthday, MaryJo came home with a new boyfriend named Dallas Peterson. For three nights straight, he stayed with MaryJo, watching television, drinking beer, and eating popcorn. Carly Sue knew that he was trying to seduce her mother. Through the paperthin trailer walls, she heard her mother rebuff the man's advances. Carly Sue fell asleep thinking that it wouldn't be long before this latest creep was gone from their lives.

Later that night, she heard the floor of the trailer creak loudly, followed by her bedroom door's screeching hinges. Before she was fully aware, Dallas Peterson lay down beside her, placing his rough hand over her mouth, whispering a threat in her ear to not make a sound.

Carly Sue had begged him to leave her aolone. He didn't rape her, but he molested her until he couldn't stand it any longer. Spent, he left her room and went back to her mother's bed.

Carly Sue couldn't sleep after the assault. She had shivered with fear the rest of the night, having no idea what had just happened. Confused by the dampness left on the bed, she put her covers on the floor where she remained for the rest of the night. When she heard Dallas Peterson leave the next morning, she stayed still until her mother called for her and asked if she was spending all day in her room. She wanted to tell her mother what had happened, but she knew that it would fall on deaf ears. Besides, she wasn't exactly sure what had happened.

That evening, Peterson came back to visit MaryJo, or so he said. Again, he and MaryJo drank beer well into the evening. Carly Sue watched as he kept offering to get more beer for her mom, while pacing his own drinking. Soon, her mom was fast asleep on the chair in the living room. Peterson told Carly Sue to go to bed. When she said no, Peterson picked her up and carried her into her bedroom and molested her again. He was more forceful this time and he hurt Carly Sue while holding her wrists tight. She knew that she had to put a stop to his advances, or she would wind up seriously injured.

The following night when Peterson came over and sat down next to her mother, she pointed her finger directly at him and said to her mother, "Mom, he's touching me after you go to sleep. He hurt me last night."

Dallas Peterson's face had turned bright red with a look of shock and surprise. In a surge of anger, he shouted, "You lying little bitch. I never laid a hand on you."

She held up her arms where his grip caused bruising. Courageously defiant, she hissed, "You did this. She won't do it with you so you think you can do it to me. You touch me again and I'll call the police."

She ran to her room, closed the door and locked it. She heard Peterson yelling at her mother that he never touched her, but that if she didn't believe him, he was leaving. He had shouted, "I don't need this shit. Y'all can go to hell for all I care."

Instead of telling the bastard, the guy who hurt and molested her daughter, to go to hell himself, she cried to him, begging him to stay, that Carly Sue would not tell anyone her lies.

My lies? My lies? Oh my God, she doesn't believe me.

Over the next year and a half, Carly Sue would encounter her mother's denial nearly a dozen times. Fearing that one of her mother's boyfriends would force her to have intercourse, she got birth control pills. The abuse continued from a number of her mother's boyfriends until Carly Sue had had enough.

The last straw was a guy named Allen Jason Scott. From the moment Scott walked into her mother's trailer, Carly Sue knew that she had to stay away from him. When her mother introduced him to her, Scott looked Carly Sue over from head to toe. She read the lust on his face.

The first night, he didn't make any advances, but she remained awake, fearing the worst. On the second night, almost as soon as MaryJo fell asleep, Allen Scott snuck into Carly Sue's room. He tried to sweet talk her out of her clothes, trying to kiss her with his rough, unshaven face, his foul-smelling breath assaulting her senses, but she refused. That didn't stop him. He forced her down flat on the bed and straddled her small frame. He pinned her arms down and whispered in her ear that they were going to have some fun. She tried to fight to get free, but he was much too powerful.

She had been afraid that she was, at best, going to lose her virginity by force and be badly hurt in the process. Then she remembered that she had a plan in case it appeared that one of her mother's boyfriends would go too far. The moment to use her plan had arrived.

She had whispered to Allen Scott, "Stop, please. If you want to do me, okay, but not here. I don't want my mom to walk in on us."

Suddenly, he had stopped struggling, smiled, and said, "Well, ain't that nice. Where y'all want to go?"

"Down by the lake. I know a spot where it's private. Nobody'll know."

"I'll bet you do." He thought for a moment, then agreed. "Okay. You head out to my car."

She hesitated. "Wait. I have to get some protection from my mom's room."

He had grabbed her by the wrists again and said, "Don't you try anything stupid. You wake yer mom and I'll beat y'all's ass. Go fetch it and meet me in the car. Remember, don't mess with me."

He let her up slowly, then led her into the living room where MaryJo was snoring loudly. She had motioned to Allen Scott to wait in the car. He pointed his finger at her and gave her a nasty look as if to say, *Don't forget what I told you*, and headed out the trailer door. Carly Sue turned and went to her mother's room. She opened the nightstand drawer and grabbed a pack of condoms…and her mother's thirty-eight special. She checked that the tumbler had shells in each slot and tucked it into the back pocket of her shorts.

Carly Sue opened the door to Allen Scott's aging Ford Tempo and closed it quietly. Scott put his cold, rough hand on her leg above the knee and asked, "Where to, pretty lady?"

"Go to the park entrance and turn left. There's a dirt road on the right about a hundred feet up the road from the entrance. It leads down to the lake."

He smiled and started the car. As the car headed for the park's entrance, Carly Sue looked back at her mother's trailer. MaryJo had pulled the curtain back and watched as her boyfriend drove away with her baby girl in the passenger seat.

* * *

Carly Sue's cell phone blurted out a Blake Shelton tune, startling her out of her trance. She was thankful for the interruption, glad that she didn't have to relive that next ten minutes of her past for the thousandth time. The cell phone was on its second verse when she picked up.

"Hey, baby, whatcha doin'?"

Curtis Hardy was purposely cheerful, knowing that his wife needed a midmorning push to get her going and keep her from falling into depression. It was a daily ritual that they had developed after Carly Sue was diagnosed with bipolar disorder. Curtis had gladly adopted the routine knowing that, without it, his wife would sink into a deep, psychological abyss.

Shortly after they were married, Carly Sue feared that Curtis suspected her of cheating on him. He said to her on several occasions that she looked guilty of something. He had said it in a joking manner, but she took his comments seriously, and her mood turned dark. After several episodes of her sinking into deep depression, Curtis insisted that she get professional help. And she did.

"Hi, Babe. I just finished a cup of coffee, then I'm gettin' into the shower."

"Everything going okay? Did you take your meds today?"

"Yeah, sweetie. Thanks for checkin' on me."

"Want to have lunch? I'll pick somethin' up and stop at home."

Carly Sue smiled. Curtis was always so thoughtful. She said, "Sure, sweetie. You know what I like. I'll be waitin'."

"Alright. I'll see you around noon. Love ya, baby."

"Love you, too."

Carly Sue hit the disconnect icon. She looked around the living room of her modest home. She couldn't believe that fate had smiled down on her after such a crappy childhood. Marrying Curtis Hardy had been the luckiest day of her life. He looked past her faults, was tolerant of her outbursts, even comforting during their infrequent sexual relations. He was kind and protective to a fault. And he kept her away from her manipulative mother.

* * *

Carly Sue and Curtis had a nice, quiet lunch together. He had kissed her gently before heading back to work. She sat and thought about how fortunate she was that she had such a loving and caring husband. Her thoughts were interrupted by Toby Keith belting out "I Ain't as Good as I Once Was" from her cell phone. She looked at the number on the display and immediately frowned. She hesitated, wanting to let it go to voicemail, but decided to answer.

In a most unpleasant voice, she said, "What do you want?"

MaryJo Saxon said, "That ain't no way to greet your momma. Why the nasty tone?"

"You know why, Momma. What do you want?"

"Carly Sue, can't I just call to talk and find out how my baby girl is doing? I worry about you."

Carly Sue's mood turned south. She wished that she hadn't answered her mother's call. She knew that no good would come from it. She replied, "You never worried about me a day in your life. Why now? What do you really want?"

There was silence on the line for several seconds, then her mother revealed the real reason for her call. "Carly Sue, I need to borrow some money. I lost my job…"

"Again!? Momma, why can't you keep a job? What did you do this time?"

"Don't talk to me that way, young lady. I'm still your momma." She paused, but Carly Sue didn't respond.

"The manager – he's an asshole, by the way – he accused me of comin' to work drunk. Then he accused me of stealing money from the register."

"Well, did ya?"

"Of course not! I would never take what ain't mine. You know me better than that. I had a little sip of beer for lunch before I went in, but that ain't bein' drunk on the job."

Carly Sue again remained quiet. She did know her mother and what she knew disgusted her. She had no doubt that the manager's accusations were true. Curtis had told her to not answer the phone when her mother called. He told his wife that it only pushed her into depression. He was right. It was happening again.

"Momma, I don't have any money to loan you. I wouldn't do it even if I did. Go get sober and get another job, or maybe two jobs. Just don't call here anymore."

"Carly Sue, I'm your flesh and blood. Why do you treat me like this?"

Anger flushed through Carly Sue's whole body. She felt the heat rise, the pressure building, like a bomb counting down the seconds to detonation. Instead of shouting, she hissed through clenched teeth, "You know exactly why, Momma."

She disconnected the call and threw the phone across the room, then wept for over half an hour. She finally made her way to the bathroom. When in the shower, she vigorously scrubbed her skin with a soapy sponge, then rinsed. She repeated the process multiple times, trying desperately to wash the pain and guilt away.

No matter how hard she scrubbed, she still felt dirty.

Chapter 4

The cloudless sky continued the string of days where there was no hint of rain. Not even a slight breeze. The sun shimmered off the surface of Cypress Lake as the divers in the lake caused ripples on what otherwise would have been a glass-like surface. The grim faces of the men on the shore spoke volumes regarding the mood surrounding the old Ford Tempo's discovery. It wasn't just that a car had been discovered submerged in the lake, it was the body in the car that had everyone's attention, especially the hole in the right temple. There was no confirmation, but the two divers who saw the hole knew it was the right size for a small caliber bullet. That information was making its way around the law enforcement team on shore.

The divers were in the water ensuring that a tow cable was attached securely to the car's frame. The lead diver gave the thumbs-up signal that the tow truck driver should engage the winch. As the cable tightened, the divers backed a safe distance away from the car to avoid getting sucked into the muddy water in the car's wake. The tow truck's motor grunted in protest as the cable tightened. Freeing the car from the mud's grip at the lake's bottom would be no easy task.

The truck's motor strained further, then relaxed some as the car broke free from the muck. The divers noticed the car move towards the shore ever so slightly, leaving swirls on the surface of the water. Soon, mud clouded the water behind the hulk.

The car was making noticeable headway towards shore. After forty minutes and considerable effort, it was completely free from the water, the intact skeleton still sitting in the remnants of the driver's seat, the skull resting on the edge of the open window frame. In the early afternoon sun, the neat hole in the temple was evident. Everyone who viewed the body concluded that it was murder.

Gerald R. Brannen, Captain of the Investigative Unit for the Bulloch County Sheriff's Department, had the area cordoned off with crime scene tape. He was on the phone with Sheriff Evelyn Adkins, providing as many details as possible on the find.

"This body's been in the lake so long, we don't know the sex, race, or anything else 'bout it. The skeleton, and car, are covered in slime, and we don't want to disturb anything until Cedric gets here." Cedric Malone was the aging County Coroner. "The only thing we can see is a hole in the right temple. Looks like he was shot from the passenger seat or through the passenger side window. There's no gun in the car, and we haven't found one in the area, but we just started looking. We're setting up search zones now. Searchin' the lake's gonna be a challenge. How the car ended up in the lake is anybody's guess."

"Thanks, Gerry. Make sure the crime scene folks do a thorough job. Just because this happened a long time ago doesn't make it any less important."

"Yes, ma'am, will do. I'll call if we find anything new."

Brannen went back to work with the crime scene crew. The two CSIs, a young man and a young woman, both of whom looked like high school kids, were busy taking photos of everything, from the skeleton, the car's interior and exterior, to the surface of the lake, and the tire grooves left by hauling the car ashore. They hadn't said a word since receiving their instructions.

At the same time, the two divers who were called to inspect the car and hook up the tow truck cable were back in the lake inspecting the lake bottom near the area the car came to rest many years ago. They were looking for a gun, and anything else relative to what was now officially considered a homicide.

Brannen took off his hat and wiped the sweat from his forehead with a cloth that he carried in his back pocket. His close-cropped, salt and pepper hair contrasted with his dark black skin. It highlighted the hairline that receded on either side of the top of his scalp, leaving a peninsula of hair over the center of his forehead.

One of those foreign hybrid cars pulled off Cypress Lake Road and parked next to one of the sheriff's vehicles. A man jumped out and headed for the trunk, which had already been popped opened, apparently by a button inside the car. The man pulled out a metal detector, a small shovel, and what appeared to be a burlap bag. He shut the trunk and headed towards Brannen.

When he ducked under the crime scene tape without asking permission, Brannen said, "Boy, you can't just ignore that boundary."

The man looked around, seeming confused. He looked back, seeing the yellow tape, then turned back to Captain Brannen. "Oh! I'm so sorry. I didn't realize what the tape meant." He smiled as if nothing was wrong. "Oh, I'm Dennis Flippin. The sheriff sent me to help with the search."

Brannen looked skeptically at the man. "I just spoke with Sheriff Adkins. She didn't mention that you would be coming, Mr. ..."

"Flippin. Dennis Flippin. I'm kind of an expert on metallurgy, particularly as it relates to artifacts. Mostly ancient artifacts, but I do shallow ground searches for law enforcement types around this part of the state."

Brannen's cell phone rang. He looked at the number. It was Sheriff Adkins again. "Hang tight, Mr. Flippin."

Into his phone, he said, "Hey, Sheriff."

"Hi, Gerry. I forgot to tell ya that there's a..."

"Dennis Flippin."

"Yes. I take it he's there?"

"Yes, ma'am. He has his metal detector, too."

"Great. Sorry I forgot to give you the heads up. Put him to work. Make sure you set boundaries for him because he gets carried away at times."

"Yes, ma'am. We're already talking about boundaries." He gave Flippin a serious stare. "Thanks, Sheriff. This may actually help with an old crime scene like this."

After the call was disconnected, he turned to Dennis Flippin who was already testing his detector on the ground near where he stood.

Brannen approached the man. "Mr. Flippin, that was the sheriff. She confirmed that you're supposed to be here. So, here's what we need."

Brannen laid out the plan to search the old shoreline and the dried lake bed for anything that might be related to the algae-covered car that still sat on the shore. Flippin asked what he should be looking for and Brannen said, "A gun, shell casings, jewelry, cigarette lighters, any kind of personal effects."

Flippin's eyes lit up as if he'd just received the greatest birthday gift of his life. "Is this a murder scene?"

Brannen frowned and said, "Yes. Yes, it is."

"Alright! I'll start a grid search. Where do you think the murder happened?"

Brannen looked behind Flippin and pointed. "Right over there, next to that stand of trees, along the old shoreline. This is just speculation, but we think the shooting may have taken place there, then the car was pushed into the lake."

Brannen watched as Flippin took his gear and mapped out an informal search grid, using his feet as approximating one foot. He moved twenty feet inland from the trees, then stepped twenty feet to the west. He pulled a bright orange plastic spike out of the burlap bag and pounded it into the ground. He repeated the sequence in the opposite direction. Brannen noted that the spikes stood over a foot high after being pounded into the ground, making them easy to see. After twenty minutes, his search grid was set, and he went to work, donning a headset and methodically waving the detector over the ground. He didn't change his pace, but made a few adjustments to the detector as he went.

Brannen went back to his CSI team and asked for a progress report. They didn't stop their work, but the young man said, "There isn't much left of the body but there will be dental records and maybe some medical evidence. If you look at the left arm, it was broken at some point. There may be more, but we can't disturb the body until the coroner gets here."

The young woman jumped in. "We have a partial number on the license plate. It's a South Carolina plate from the late 1990's." She read off as much of the plate number that she could decipher. "I think we can narrow it down to a handful of owners from that information."

"Thanks. I'll send this in so we can get the records search going."

As he turned and pulled out his cell phone, the coroner's van pulled off the road and parked next to Flippin's hybrid. Another young, slender woman, this one with sun-bleached red hair, stepped out of the van and stepped around to the back. Brannen saw the back doors open, then close again. To him, the young lady looked like a teenager. From the van's passenger side, an older gentleman ambled around the front of the van and met up with the young woman. The Coroner, Cedric Malone, moved slowly, pacing himself with each step. The young woman took his arm and assisted him to the crime scene.

As the two approached, Brannen said, "Howdy, Cedric. Thought you'd retired. Glad you're not." He tipped his hat at the young woman.

When they stopped in front of Brannen, Malone commented, "I don't think you've met my new Deputy Coroner, Ginger Evans."

Brannen smiled. "I have not. Nice to meet you, Miss Evans."

Malone went on, "She's eighteen years old. I'm pretty sure she's is the youngest Deputy Coroner in the State of Georgia."

Brannen's eyebrows went up as he looked towards the young woman. "Very impressive. I can assure you that Cedric is the best coroner in Georgia. You'll learn more from this man in a year than you would with other coroners over a lifetime.

Malone waved a hand. "Enough with the bull, Gerry. What have you got here?"

For the second time in less than ten minutes, Gerald Brannen explained the situation: a skeletal body, probably a bullet hole in the right temple, sitting in a car that may have purposely been pushed into the lake. He explained the relative location of the car and the search that was underway on the shore and in the water.

"Has the body been moved?" Cedric asked.

"No, sir. No one has touched the body at all. We pulled the car out of the lake real slow. Not a lot of water swirlin' either."

"Excellent." He patted down his forehead with a handkerchief, then turned to the Deputy Coroner. "Well, dear, let's get to work."

The two slowly approached the car, not to protect evidence, but more because Cedric was frail and simply took his time. They approached the driver's side window.

As Brannen watched, Cedric began his lesson. "The process of evaluating a crime scene should be a patient one. Never rush to conclusions, always observe and record everything, not necessarily on paper, or in pictures, but with your mind. Also, think about time. This body has been in this car, submerged in a freshwater environment, for many years. So, take yourself back and try to recreate the crime scene in your mind. The car was found in the lake some one hundred twenty feet from the current shoreline. When you add the forty or fifty feet of shoreline shrinkage from the drought, that's over half a football field's travel from shore, to where it came to rest. That seems like a long way, but maybe it isn't so far."

Ginger Evans nodded, her attention focused completely on Cedric. Brannen could tell that she was anxious to learn from the old man.

He continued, "Now, let's look at what we have here."

They moved closer to the driver's side window. There was very little body to observe, but Cedric moved closer, leaning into the open window. He maintained that position for nearly a full minute. When he withdrew, he told Ginger to take a look. She did, looking around the interior of the car, looking the skeleton over from head to toe. The interior of the car, with the exception of the metal components, was completely gone. The vinyl seats, the interior door panels, the carpeting, and the cloth ceiling liner had completely deteriorated.

When she finally withdrew her head, he asked, "Now, tell me, dear, what did you observe?"

Ginger closed her eyes and thought for a moment, before she said a word. Brannen stayed close so he could hear her evaluation. He also wanted to hear whether Cedric agreed and if he had more to add.

She said, "The hole in the skull is from a small caliber weapon. It looks like the shot was taken at a downward angle. You can tell that by the angle of the bone at the wound site. Either the victim was leaning over towards the passenger side, or the shooter was standing outside the car, shooting at a downward angle."

"Very good. Go on."

"We should be able to ID the victim through dental records. The teeth are in decent condition. Also, there are several identifying traits. The victim had several broken bones over the years. So, if there are medical records out there, that may help in identifying the victim. And I believe the victim is…I mean, was a male."

"Very good. Anything else?"

"Yes. There is a bullet in the bottom of the car, below the victim. I'm thinking that it has a high probability of being the bullet that killed our victim."

Cedric raised his eyebrows at that. He hadn't seen the bullet. When he poked his head back in the car, he saw it in a shallow groove on the metal floor of the car. It was barely noticeable since it was covered with a fine layer of mud and algae.

"One other thing. The car is in neutral. Since the car was so far off shore, the driver didn't drive the car into the lake. Somebody, or more than one somebody, pushed the car into the lake. It floated for a bit, but had momentum behind the push to get it out into the lake for a distance before it sank. That's why I think more than one person did the pushing. Only one person pulled the trigger, but they had help hiding the body.

He smiled at Ginger. "Excellent."

Cedric turned to Brannen and said, "She's a keeper."

Chapter 5

Tommy Alexander sat in his office with his last client of the afternoon before the weekend. He wished that he could work right on through until Monday, but Cheryl and the girls wouldn't allow it. Work was one of the few things that kept his mind free of the horrific scene that regularly popped up, seemingly out of nowhere: a man with a hole in his head, literally dead to the world.

"Hey, Tom, I can come back next week if you like."

Tom had fallen into a trance while reviewing a client's homeowner's policy. In his entire seven-year career, it had never happened before. He shook his head to clear the fog. "No, Norm, I'm okay. Just this clause about coverage for flooding struck me as ironic, all things considered."

Norm Stiller had been a client of Tom's for over five years and considered him a good a friend. "Yeah, this year. But last year we nearly had to use it. What a difference a year makes." Norm shook his head. "So, what happens next year?"

He paused for a moment, then his expression changed. "I almost forgot. Just down the road from where you live, you know that lake? Rumor has it they found a body. I was talking to Denny Adkins, the sheriff's husband. He said the body's been in the lake for years. Nothing left but a skeleton."

Tom's face must have been ghostlike because Norm asked, "You okay, Tom? You look like you're gonna faint."

So, it finally happened. As he sat there with his client, he rubbed the scar on his left hand as if he could rub the memories away. He had to keep his emotions under control, not only for his sake, but for the sake of his wife and his girls.

"Oh Lord! I'll have to call Denny. You know, he's Cheryl's brother. What else did he say?"

"Nothin' much at all. They just found the car this morning when a chain gang from county lockup was pickin' up trash along the lake. They saw a car in the water and decided to pull it to shore. I guess the divers nearly crapped their wetsuits when they saw the skeleton in the car."

"I bet. Did he say if they had any leads on how it happened?"

"Nope. Too early to tell. They sent a team of crime scene guys up there, but it ain't like there's a bunch of scientists here in Bulloch County. Probably a couple of college kids. I guess we'll know more in a few days."

"Yeah. Man, that's crazy." He paused, then changed the subject. "About your policy, you have any other questions? I think you're pretty well covered, without going overboard."

Norm looked at Tom for a second then asked, "Aren't you gonna try and up-sell me to something more expensive?"

Tom smiled. "Maybe next year. In the meantime, save your money."

The men laughed as they stood and shook hands. When Norm turned to leave, he stopped at the front door. "One other thing. Denny's wife said the skull had a bullet hole in the right temple."

"Holy smokes. The guy was murdered?"

"Well, if it was a guy."

After Norm closed the door behind him, Tom cursed himself for the slip-up. The body was skeletal. They probably wouldn't know the sex for some time.

But he knew. So did Andy, Curtis, and Billy Ray.

And Carly Sue.

* * *

"Hey, Andy, just made that seed stock delivery out to Adabelle at the Williams' farm. It goes without sayin' they won't be plantin' anytime soon, dry as it is. And there's a big commotion at Cypress Lake across from that trailer park. You know where I'm talkin' 'bout?"

"Yeah, I know the place. What's goin' on?"

"There's a bunch of cops and a coroner's van down by the lake. It looked like there was some guys in orange jumpsuits. Maybe they had problems with a chain gang or something."

Andy Pepperdine was paying close attention as soon as he heard the words Cypress Lake. Since the crowd was at the lake across from the trailer park, it most likely meant the car had been found. With the coroner's van present, a body had also been found.

"I wonder what's goin' on."

"With a group like that, there'll be reporters all over it."

Andy's driver dropped his paperwork in the office inbox, turned and left. It was all Andy could do to shift his mind back to the stack of work on his desk. The impulse to pick up the phone and call Tommy Alexander was strong, but the scar on his hand, the constant reminder of their lifetime vow of silence, was even stronger. He had to keep his promise.

But would they all follow through? Andy began thinking about who was most likely to break down and reveal their secret.

A knock on his door brought him back to the present. When he looked up, his wife, Cornelia, was standing in the doorway. He smiled. "Hey, sweetheart. This is a pleasant surprise."

Cornelia looked at her husband with a sly smile. "Whatever you were lookin' at must be real important. I thought you were gonna rub that scar right off your hand."

"Ah. It's nothin'. What brings you here? You coulda called."

"I was down the street at church. Dropped off a couple pies for a wake that's happenin' tomorrow after Thelma Jean's husband's funeral. I thought I'd drop by and ask what you wanted to do for dinner tonight. The kids said hamburgers. I'd prefer something a little more...adult. What do you think?"

"Can we get a sitter? They can have burgers. Then we can go have a nice evening at a steakhouse, or something like that."

"It's kinda short notice for a sitter, but maybe Mom and Dad could watch them for a couple hours. I can call and ask."

"Sounds good. If it doesn't work out for tonight, I think that we should plan a nice long evening next weekend. Maybe we could go into Savannah and try out one of the restaurants where we used to go, you know, BK?"

"BK?"

"Before kids." He smiled.

Cornelia put her arms around her husband's neck and smiled. "Are you trying to seduce me, mister?"

He smiled back and kissed her lightly on the lips and said, "Why, yes, I am. Is it workin'?"

"I better get outta here before we find ourselves in trouble."

"Hey, we own the place. Who's gonna tell?"

A gruff voice from the doorway said, "That'd be me."

Andy's General Foreman, Lucas Grieves, walked in. He smiled. "If y'all want a head start on your evening, I can finish up this afternoon."

"Thanks, Luke, but Cornelia was just headin' to pick up Wendy from pre-school. Maybe next Friday, though."

"I'd better let you get back to work then." She kissed her husband's cheek and headed for the door. "Bye, Lucas."

Lucas tipped his ball cap and said, "Ma'am," and followed her out with his eyes. When he turned back around, Andy saw a change in his foreman's expression. He looked confused.

"What's up, Lucas?"

"You. I've noticed that you've been having a hard time concentrating lately. I know the drought's been on everybody's mind, but you usually keep everyone else focused. Anything you want to talk about?"

"Nah, nothing specific. I don't know, Luke. This drought's really distractin' me. Maybe I just need a vacation."

"Why don't you take the family and go to Florida, visit your folks, take your daughter to Disney? You deserve a break. I know your folks would love to see their grandbaby."

Andy thought about what his foreman said. It might be a good idea to break away for a week or so with the police investigation in progress. Lucas could handle the business. Their daughter would be out of school a week from today. And he wouldn't be tempted to call his childhood friends and break their pact.

Great idea...maybe.

* * *

Eugene Morris heard the chatter on the police scanner about a body being discovered off Cypress Lake Road. To him, this was great news. He was bored to tears covering the City of Statesboro's concerns about the drought, and what effect that it might have on the Floridan Aquifer, the primary source of drinking water for the citizens of Bulloch County and beyond. He just wasn't interested in the science or the environmental laws surrounding potable water.

But murder? That was interesting, especially a murder from years ago, where the body is pulled from a local lake. Maybe it was a drug deal gone bust. Maybe a jealous husband popped his wife's lover. Could it be a suicide? The possibilities were endless, and a real challenge for an old reporter like himself.

Morris worked for the Statesboro Herald. He was officially the Lifestyles reporter, but that was just a title, one that he loathed. At fifty-seven, he was the senior reporter at the paper. Hell, he was the senior employee at the paper, having lasted longer than six editors, eight publishers, and everyone on the board by at least five years. Only one delivery man, who started his paper route at the age of ten, had more years at the *Herald*.

Twelve years ago, he had turned in a story for publication that had an error. At the time, it didn't seem like a big deal, but the story was used to bust a college student at Georgia Southern University on child molestation charges. It turned out that the information was close enough to the truth that the young man committed suicide, rather than face prosecution. His parents sued the paper for several million dollars – and won. Rather than drag out an appeal, the paper settled out of court for a significant, but secret, sum. In turn, the *Herald* demoted Morris and kept him away from sensitive news stories. Over the years, he slowly received more colorful assignments. Now, he was back covering hard-core news.

Morris pulled off Cypress Lake Road and parked next to the coroner's van. He stepped up to the edge of the crime scene tape and yelled to Captain Brannen.

When Brannen saw Morris with his pad and pen in his hand, he rolled his eyes, but he walked towards the reporter. It surprised him that it took this long for any media folks to happen on the scene.

"Howdy, Gerry."

Brannen tipped his hat and said, "Gene. I'm surprised they sent you out here," he smiled.

"I'm gettin' back in their good graces, little by little. So, what can ya tell the taxpayin' public?"

"Not too much, 'cept that we got a potential homicide. And it's an old homicide. We won't know how old until we can get some testing done."

"Has the victim been identified?"

"Nope, but we may have enough information to figure that out."

"So, is the victim a man or woman?"

"Can't say."

"Come on, Gerry. That ain't goin' to compromise the investigation, is it?"

Brannen took his handkerchief out, took off his hat and wiped the sweat from his brow and the top of his head. "No, but the body's been in the lake so long, we can't tell. Not too much left, except bones."

"Oh."

Morris' look of surprise made Brannen smile.

Morris asked, "So how do you know it's murder if there isn't much of the body left?"

"It has to do with the bullet hole in the victim's skull. The killer, or killers, went to a lot of trouble to get that car out into the lake. Beyond that, we have a lot more testing to do."

As they talked across the crime scene boundary tape, the van for WSAV Channel 3 news pulled off the road and parked next to Eugene Morris' car. Three people immediately jumped out of the van. A man and a woman went to work extending the van's antenna, preparing for a live broadcast from the scene.

Morris turned to Brannen. "So much for an exclusive."

"You win some, you lose some. I'll tell you what, Gene, you call me later, say, 6:30 PM, and I'll give you an update."

"Great, I'll do that. One last thing: What kind of gun was used?"

"I can tell you it was a small caliber weapon. I can't say anything more."

He started to walk away just as a young woman, the field reporter for WSAV, approached, waving her hands and shouting, "Captain Brannen, do you have a moment for a brief on-camera interview?"

"Give me a minute. I'll be right back."

The reporter turned to Morris. "So, are the rumors true?"

"Depends. What rumors?"

"That there's a dead body in that car?"

Just as she finished her question, one of the crime scene technicians opened the driver's side door. The young man reached in while the door opened just a crack and tried to support the skeleton by the shoulders. As the door opened further, he lost his grip, and the upper torso section of the skeleton fell to the ground, in full view of Morris and the TV reporter.

Morris smiled. "I'd say that's a yes."

He turned, just as the color drained from her face and she collapsed to the ground.

Chapter 6

At 1:30 PM, the crowd was small, just three ladies, one old man, and a preschool-aged child. After a few hours, it seemed that the entire population of Cypress Lake Mobile Home Park was standing across the road from the area roped off with yellow crime scene tape. The only thing larger than the crowd was the rumor mill.

Millie Crider, the park's eldest resident, stayed at her trailer until she heard a group of kids yelling that the police had found a body in the lake. Millie looked at her ancient housecat, Dusty. "I knew it. I toldja they'd find him, sooner or later."

Dusty looked back at his owner and meowed loudly, as if acknowledging the old woman's genius. Dusty slowly got up on all fours and hobbled towards his food dish, looked at the few bits of dried food, then looked at Millie, and meowed again.

"Alright, Dusty. Just hold yer horses. I'll feed ya, then I'm headin' out with the crowd. I'm gonna let 'em know who's in that lake."

Dusty meowed again as Millie picked up a bag of cat food and made her way to his dish. Her arthritic knees creaked as she bent over and added a quarter cup of food to Dusty's meager rations. The old cat rubbed against her legs in appreciation.

Millie pulled an old pink shawl over her threadbare, flowered, house dress and made her way out the side door, then eased herself down the straining metal steps. The hot air took her breath away. She slowly headed towards the crowd at the edge of Cypress Lake Road.

As she stepped up to the crowd, she listened to the chatter from her neighbors. Younger kids spun tall tales about aliens, and the adults speculated about a drug deal gone bad. Others just listened to the talk, while watching across the road, their morbid curiosity piqued, hoping for a glimpse of a dead body.

Millie looked the crowd over, taking an unofficial poll of who was there and who was missing. One face that she didn't see anywhere was MaryJo Saxon.

In a loud, gruff voice she said, "I can tell y'all who's dead down there."

Those in the crowd closest to her stopped talking and turned to see who made such a bold claim. When they saw that it was Millie, they smiled, rolled their eyes, and returned to their chatter with whoever was at their side.

A small girl clung to her mother's leg while she stared up at Millie. She tugged on her mother's arm. When the woman leaned over, her daughter, not so quietly, said, "Mommy, that lady scares me." She wrinkled up her nose and added, "And she smells bad."

Her mother turned and saw Millie, a look of shock across her coloring face, knowing that Millie had heard every word. She scolded her daughter for saying such nasty things, then turned and apologized to Millie. Millie didn't respond, and the woman turned back towards the lake and the crime scene. Her child continued to cling to her leg and stare at Millie.

Everyone at the trailer park knew Millie Crider. She was known as the crazy old lady with the mangy cat that must be as old as her. She was one of those ladies who had always been old no matter how old you were. Parents at the park warned their kids to stay away from her trailer, which led to rumors that, years ago, she made children disappear from the park, or that she was a witch. Some of the children had seen her looking out her trailer windows with binoculars, spying on neighbors. None had witnessed anything sinister. Once they grew older, they knew that she was just an old woman with nothing better to do.

Millie spoke again. This time she said, "You know what else? MaryJo knows who's in that lake. You just ask her. She ain't here because she knows somebody's gonna figure it all out. Mark my words."

When the folks closest to her shook their heads and seemed to ease away from her, she moved closer to the road, trying to get a better view of the crime scene. Over the top of the weeds that lined the road, she could see the Ford Tempo, still covered in slime. Thinking back over fifteen years, she remembered the night that she saw the man who was at MaryJo's trailer, the driver of that Ford Tempo.

It had been a quiet, humid night. She had all of her windows open trying to get some air circulating. MaryJo's boyfriend came out of her trailer and started the Tempo. It had a noisy muffler. Moments later, MaryJo's little girl, Carly Sue, had come out of the trailer and got in the car. The car pulled away and turned left on Cypress Lake Road. She was surprised when the car hardly sped up on the road, then went quiet again. It hadn't gone far. Once the engine was off, she never heard it again.

But ten or fifteen minutes later, she did hear the cries of a young girl between the distant rumbles of thunder. She had nearly dozed off when she heard footsteps coming up the trailer park's gravel road. With her binoculars up to her eyes, she saw Carly Sue heading for her mother's trailer. The young girl appeared to be wiping her eyes, but it was hard to see in the dim lighting of the park. She opened the door to her momma's trailer, ducked inside, and closed the door quietly behind her. Immediately after that, Millie heard the boys yelling as they ran through the woods. They were heading for their hideout. That's what she heard them call it one time. After that, the trailer park was silent, except for the faint sound of country music playing and rolling thunder in the distance.

That was many years ago. Now, as Millie watched the scene at the lake, a young man with a metal detector walked ever so slowly, back and forth, near the stand of trees. He looked as if he was enjoying himself. There were two young folks taking pictures of everything. And there was the chain gang picking up trash further along the lake shore. They looked like they had been there all day, their orange jumpsuits covered in sweat and dirt.

A news van extended a tall antenna for a live broadcast as a young woman held a microphone for a sound check. She handed the microphone over to her camera crew and moved quickly towards the crime scene, trying to get the attention of the officer who had been talking with another man. Millie figured the man talking with the officer was probably a reporter by the way he was writing in his notebook. A few seconds after the young woman got to the taped off area, the officer walked away. Millie saw the woman fall in a heap. She looked at the slime covered Tempo and saw why. The skeletal remains of a body had fallen out of the car. A loud cry, applause, and whistles erupted from the crowd.

Millie thought, *This is one sick bunch out here.*

* * *

WSAV Channel 3 aired the story as breaking news. The news anchor introduced the story with a brief monologue about an old murder that recently surfaced due to the drought. She introduced the field reporter, Mellissa Amano, who had recovered from her fainting spell in time to get cleaned up and prepared for the live broadcast.

Amano looked into the camera with a microphone in one hand. She read from notes that she held in her other hand.

Channel 3 News is following breaking news on the shores of Cypress Lake, just west of Statesboro. Inmates, on a cleanup crew from the Bulloch County Corrections Center in Statesboro, discovered a car submerged in the lake, the roof visible from shore. According to the Bulloch County Sheriff's Office, the car had been in the lake for an extended period of time.

Divers were dispatched to hook up a cable to pull the car from the lake. That's when they found the body. Police are not releasing details of the find to the public, but sources close to the investigation described the body as skeletal. A small hole in the right temple of the skull was noted and appears to be from a small caliber gun. The police are treating the case as a homicide.

Asked about how long the car has been in the lake, Captain Gerald Brannen would only say, "Quite a long time." The car is an early 1990s model Ford Tempo with South Carolina license plates.

The camera panned out across the crime scene, zooming in on the man searching the area along the shore with a metal detector. He shifted to the young crime scene investigators, as they continued to look for clues and snap pictures every few seconds. The camera then zoomed in on the coroner and his assistant as they placed the skeletal remains in a black body bag.

The reporter continued:

Though the alleged murder apparently occurred many years ago, this case won't go on the back burner anytime soon. Captain Brannen stated that this case will be a top priority for the department.

Mellissa Amano, WSAV Channel 3 News, reporting. Back to you.

Thank you, Mellissa. We know you'll stay on top of this developing story. In other news...

At 6:05 PM, Captain Gerald Brannen saw the bright lights from the live broadcast go out and the news team relax. He made his way towards the edge of the crime scene tape, intending to discuss what was said during the broadcast when Dennis Flippin, the man with the metal detector, started yelling, "Alright! Alright, alright, alright! Hey, Captain, over here!"

Brannen did an about face and headed towards Flippin. He was standing about twenty-five feet from the water's edge. This part of the shore would have been near the water's edge just six months ago. When Brannen stepped up next to the excited young man, he looked around, but didn't see anything. He looked at the obviously pumped-up Dennis Flippin, his face asking the question: *What are you all excited about?*

"I found the gun."

Brannen looked around. "Okay, where is it?"

"Oh. It's right here." As he said it, he waved the metal detector over an area of baked, dried clay. He glanced at the display on the detector and noticed a large spike in the lines on the screen. He looked at Flippin. "Are you sure?"

"Well, it may not be 'the' gun, but it is definitely a hunk of metal that is the right size for a gun."

Brannen rubbed his forehead with both hands, then pulled his hat off and rubbed the top of his close-cropped hair. "Dennis, it doesn't do us any good if the gun is still buried. Can you dig it up for us?"

"You betcha, Captain. Give me about twenty minutes. I don't want to scratch it up."

"Dennis, it isn't dinosaur bones, it's an old, rusty gun. Be cautious, but we need it up. Leave some of the dirt attached to it and bag the whole mess. They can clean it up better at the lab."

"You got it, boss. I'll let you know as soon as it's bagged."

"When you're done, turn it over to the two crime scene kids…I mean technicians."

Flippin laid his metal detector down and squatted. He took his small shovel and probed the ground, making a circle at the planned dig boundaries. He methodically removed dirt and placed it on a growing pile a few feet from where he was digging. Brannen watched in fascination at the level of patience Flippin displayed. The man enjoyed his work but took it quite seriously. After twenty minutes, he reached into the hole and extracted a large glob of what looked like an orange ball of clay. He dropped the glob into an evidence bag.

"Are you sure that's a gun?"

"Yes, sir. Once it's cleaned in the lab, you'll see more clearly. I'm not sure how much use it will be as evidence, but at least you have a gun. It's definitely small caliber. Since it is so close to where the body was found, you can be pretty sure that it's the murder weapon."

Brannen raised an eyebrow. He had hoped that they'd find the weapon in working order, but then realized that the years out in the environment would surely take a toll.

Flippin asked Brannen to keep an eye on his metal detector. He delivered the blob to the crime scene techs, had a brief conversation with the two, then returned to retrieve his equipment.

"I'm going to continue with the search, but when your techs go to the lab, I'm going to go with them if you don't mind."

"That's fine, Dennis. Good work. I see now why the sheriff uses you for this kind of work. You have a passion for the work."

"Thanks, Captain. You're right. I love this stuff."

Dennis moved a few feet to the right of where the gun was found and continued his search. He hadn't gone three feet when he said, "Alright! Bonus time!"

"Whatcha got?"

"I don't know for sure, but it looks like it might be a bracelet. I'll dig it up and let you know."

"Good man, Dennis."

Chapter 7

As she watched and listened to the young woman on Channel 3 News describe the discovery of a body in Cypress Lake, Carly Sue's mind broke free from the daily stabilizing drug regimen that kept her bipolar condition at bay. Her mind was transported into its own version of reality. She stared at the fifty-five-inch flat panel television but saw only the unshaven face of a man as he groped her, trying to remove her blouse, touching her all over. The foul odor of his breath was suffocating her. She struggled to fight off the imaginary attacker in the front seat of an old Ford Tempo, while terror invaded her entire body. It all felt so real that her body jerked involuntarily with every move made by her assailant.

The living room in the house that she shared with her husband, Curtis Hardy, was dark and quiet, except for the newscast. The curtains for the living room window that looked out at the drought-baked grass in the front yard were closed tight, as were the curtains for the sliding glass door at the back of the house.

Earlier in the afternoon, Curtis had stopped home to eat lunch. She enjoyed his company. He was a great husband, always attentive to her needs. He had a good job with the City of Statesboro Water and Wastewater Department. His office was less than a half mile away, which allowed him to come home often and have lunch with her. She knew part of the reason he did it was to keep tabs on her mental health, and she appreciated his attention, but he had to get back to work.

Carly Sue leaned back on the couch flailing with her arms, fighting off the imaginary intruder without success. The man with the foul breath continued his aggression. Over and over, he tore at her blouse. The garment would tear, then it was whole again. She screamed at the top of her lungs and the man on top of her would cover her mouth. The scene repeated over and over.

Carly Sue yelled out, "Make him stop! Oh God, please make him stop!"

Arms engulfed her, stopping her flailing. The arms weren't groping her, but had a gentle quality. A voice said, "It's over. You're safe now. You're safe, Carly Sue, I'm here. It's Curt."

Curtis held his wife firmly but gently, keeping her arms pinned to her sides so that she didn't punch or scratch him. He had been through her episodes before and had the scars to show for his efforts. Over the past few years, he had learned to keep important body parts away from her fingernails and teeth. She had no idea what she was doing during a bipolar attack. Her doctor warned Curtis that, during an episode, she could be dangerous to herself and others.

Slowly, Carly Sue came back to reality, but it would be some time, maybe hours, possibly days, before she was back to a happy equilibrium. When a major episode occurred, the balance achieved by her medications was disrupted. While the doctors didn't like to make changes to her mood stabilizing drug regimen, once something caused a disruption in that balance, some patients required adjustments to their dosages.

"I'm here, baby. I'm here."

Carly Sue heard the reassuring words. She recognized the voice, and it calmed her. Her eyes began to focus again. She saw Curtis holding her arms with his hands, keeping her at arm's length. His grip was as light as he could make it while still keeping her under control.

"Oh God, Curtis. I am so sorry, so, so, sorry."

"No, no, no, there's nothing for you to be sorry about. Let me hug you, okay?"

He slowly and gently pulled her to his chest and put his arms around her, trying to comfort her without triggering more horrific images. She had told him on numerous occasions what she saw and felt during a bipolar episode. The images were always the same. Only the episode's intensity and the level of realism were different. She told Curtis that there were times she really believed she was back in that car with "that bastard."

"Keep your eyes open, okay. Look around the house. You're home, safe with me." He continued to hold her lightly, his arms around her shoulders and neck, but ensuring that her arms were no longer pinned by her sides. He didn't want her to feel confined and have a relapse. "Whenever you're ready, you can tell me all about it, but if you don't want to talk now, we can wait."

Her body started to shake and convulse into sobs. She knew that it was a good sign. Her mind was relaxing, the images fading away. She was almost back to reality.

* * *

At 9:00 PM, Carly Sue and Curtis finished dinner. She hadn't touched much of her chicken and rice casserole, though she did manage to eat some garlic toast and salad. Curtis treated her with kid gloves. He could tell she was struggling to keep her emotions stable. So far, it was working. He hadn't asked what triggered her episode, figuring that she would tell him when she felt up to the task.

Curtis finished the dishes, making sure that his wife was always within his line of sight, or at least within earshot. He initiated most of the conversation, mainly about his day at work. No heavy topics.

Finally, at 9:50, she said, "Momma called today after lunch."

There it was: Carly Sue's mother. She had been a thorn in their side since the day they started dating. She always looked at Curtis as if he was some kind of pervert and made comments about how he shouldn't be taking advantage of her daughter. He hadn't taken Carly Sue out on a serious date until she was nineteen years old. She had already been living away from her mother for three years, though, at the time, officially her residence was still Cypress Lake Trailer Park.

Carly Sue despised her mother. She blamed her mother for her bipolar condition. It might, or might not, be true, but

Curtis knew that she was to blame for the long-term abuse of her daughter by her string of loser boyfriends.

In a soothing tone, Curtis asked, "What did your ma want?"

"She wanted to borrow some money. And she asked if you were treatin' me right. I told her the truth. You're the best thing in my life right now. I think you always will be."

He smiled at her and said, "Thank you, Sweetheart." He paused, still smiling. He waited for her to continue.

"She told me about the body they found in the lake."

She made this last comment in such a quiet tone that it almost didn't register with him. Then he realized what she had said. He had a hard time keeping his face neutral. He asked, "Did she say where the body was found?"

There was a delay in her answer as her eyes began to glaze over. She said even quieter, "Yeah. Right across from the trailer park." She looked directly at her husband and said, "It's him." Tears formed in her eyes and she said again, "It's him, Curtis."

He moved closer to her and put his arms gently around her, but she squeezed him tight, as if he was her lifeline. He could feel her heart pounding against his chest and the moisture from her tears on his cheek. The passion within him began to rise, the heat of the moment intensifying, but Curtis wasn't sure what to do. He had been in this position before, where he thought the right move was to move their embrace to the next level, but that had been a mistake. It sent her into a downward spiral. He wondered if this time it would be different.

He whispered in Carly Sue's ear, "Darlin', I think we should schedule an appointment with Dr. Rosen."

Dr. Sheila Rosen was Carly Sue's psychiatrist, the one who had diagnosed her bipolar condition when she was fourteen years old. MaryJo hadn't agreed with her diagnosis and prevented Carly Sue from seeing her. When Carly Sue moved out of her mother's trailer at age sixteen, she sought out Dr. Rosen, who agreed to treat her free-of-charge, as long as she was a minor. Several years later, when she and Curtis were married, the doctor invited him to Carly Sue's sessions so that he could better understand his new bride's fragile condition. It helped Curtis manage her mental state and helped them avoid disastrous arguments.

Curtis Hardy was a God-fearing, patient, loving man. He held his tongue when most men would lash out. He loved his wife as if she was a queen.

But Carly Sue was stubborn. That bull-headedness, coupled with her mental condition, made for some difficult, sometimes one-sided discussions. Curtis had to temper his retorts with a lot of love and empathy. At times, his responses didn't have the desired effect.

Carly Sue pleaded with her husband not to call her doctor. She feared that she might be committed to an institution and that Curtis would leave her there forever. It was all because of her bipolar depression, but to her, it was as real as the couch where they sat.

"Please, Curtis. Don't call. I promise I'll be fine. I promise. Please don't make me go."

Curtis took a deep breath and said, "Okay. Okay. It's the weekend coming up. Let's see how you do tomorrow and Sunday. Maybe on Sunday we can say an extra prayer that this will all pass." He held Carly Sue a bit tighter, hoping that she would understand that he had no ill intentions. He was relieved when she loosened her tight hug and seemed to relax.

"Thank you so much. I love you, Curtis Hardy."

"I love you, too, Carly Sue."

* * *

By 11:00 PM, Carly Sue was fast asleep in their bed. Curtis slipped from under the covers and tip-toed to the family room on the other side of the house, then flipped on the television to Channel 3 News. He listened as they repeated the story about the discovery of a body in Cypress Lake. The anchorman provided an update, but it contained little in the way of details. The Bulloch County Sheriff did confirm that a weapon and some additional evidence had been found but would not elaborate on what was recovered.

Curtis saw the slime-covered Ford Tempo. It was a shot from earlier in the day, when the sun was still high overhead. The crime scene technicians were snapping pictures of everything. The camera panned to the Bulloch County Correctional Center inmates as they picked up trash along the shore. Curtis recognized Billy Ray Duke immediately, due to the white patch of skin between his eyes.

Curtis turned on the computer at the desk in the family room and waited as it ran through its startup procedure. When the system was ready, he brought up Internet Explorer and the website for the Bulloch County Corrections Center, and then selected Inmate Rolls. He searched on "Duke" and waited a few seconds.

The scruffy looking face of Billy Ray Duke filled the screen along with his most recent charges. *Public intoxication, disorderly conduct, indecent exposure.* A short narrative stated that the inmate was observed urinating in a public park, in full view of several civilians and a peace officer. He was given a breathalyzer test, which measured his blood-alcohol content at .21, far over the legal limit. Since this was his eighth offense, he was given thirty days in jail and his probation extended to five years.

Curtis cursed to himself. Billy Ray was there when the body was sent to the bottom of the lake, and again when the body was recovered. What were the odds? The million-dollar question - *Was he going to keep his mouth shut? Was there any way to make sure that he did? What were the risks versus rewards of making sure Billy Ray did not talk?*

His thoughts shifted to his crazy mother-in-law. Every time she called Carly Sue, it sent her into a tailspin. It was time to confront her and get her to stop interfering in their lives. They had moved on and they needed for her to do the same.

Curtis went back to bed but sleep eluded him. At least it was the weekend. With the new edict from City Council, he had to work in the morning. It should be an easy day, but with the continuing drought, no one knew for certain.

Chapter 8

As anticipated, Saturday was another hot, humid day, with no relief from the ongoing drought. Central Georgia residents were wondering if it would ever rain again. Since there was little grass to cut and no landscaping to manicure, many folks had free time on their hands. Very few fishermen were on the local lakes as the water levels were so low that boat launches were high and dry, away from the retreating shorelines.

The stores seemed busy, though people weren't spending much money. Wandering around in malls, or big box stores was just something to do to fill the void left by the lack of other normal summer activities. The fear of dehydration, or other heat-related maladies, caused the cancellation of a myriad of organized outdoor sports and games. Recess had even been cancelled at a number of schools as the end of the school year approached. Some schools with gymnasiums did allow physical education to continue as long as the building's air conditioners remained in working order. At least the stores had air conditioning, which provided some relief from the heat.

Tommy Alexander, his wife, Cheryl, and their two daughters, were just leaving the JC Penney Store at the Statesboro Mall when they heard a woman call out.

"Hey, Cheryl!"

They turned and saw Cornelia and Andy Pepperdine with their four-year-old daughter. They had a few shopping bags in hand, but, just like Tommy and his family, it appeared they were shopping just to escape the house for a spell.

When out in public, Tommy always expected to see people he knew from around town. When you sell insurance to a lot of local residents, you run into your clients in stores, restaurants, and church. Tommy just hadn't expected to run into Andy and his family.

When the Pepperdines met them by the fountain, the two women smiled, briefly hugged, and gave each other light kisses on the cheek. They were close friends and served together on a few community groups. The women would have liked for their families to be closer, but Andy and Tommy distanced themselves from each other. This seemed odd to the two women because their husbands had similar interests. They both enjoyed college and professional sports. They both golfed, but with other men, not each other. They both had families with children of similar ages who enjoyed each other's company.

A number of years back, Cheryl had asked Tommy about his attitude towards Andy. She knew that the two men had gone to school together their entire lives. She had even heard others in the community say that they were once best friends, hanging out together nearly every day.

Tommy had been noncommittal with his answer, saying that they had just grown apart, that there wasn't anything weird about it. He just said that Andy got busy with his family business, and he got busy learning the insurance business, so time was no longer available to carry on a close friendship.

Cheryl seemed to accept Tommy's explanation, though she did ask about it from time to time. She had asked Cornelia if she also wondered why their childhood friendship hadn't lasted into adulthood. Cornelia had said that she got a similar explanation from Andy, that life just pushed them in different directions. She did tell Cheryl that she also believed that there was more to the story, that maybe they both chased the same girl in junior high or something. Cheryl didn't believe any of the current explanations. It was always in the back of her mind whenever she saw Andy and Cornelia.

Andy and Tom shook hands, but kept their left hands buried in their pockets. Once their greeting was complete, they turned their heads away and looked around the mall, as if it was their first visit to the place.

The three young girls gathered on a bench by the fountain. They talked about their clothes and the jewelry that each wore. The women smiled at the girls, then turned back to each other.

Cheryl turned away from the girls and quietly asked Cornelia, "Did y'all hear about the body they found in the lake down the road from us?"

"Oh my word, yes. Is that scary or what? They're sayin' it was murder."

Cheryl nodded. "It must've happened a long time ago. The news said there wasn't much left but a skeleton. They don't even know if it's a man or woman. You know my brother, Dennis?"

Cornelia nodded. "The sheriff's husband, right?"

"Yep. He said they think the murder took place back around 2000 or so. That was about the time they were putting in our subdivision. The land around the lake was all rural farmland and woods. That trailer park was there, but that's just about it. They're startin' out with little to nuthin' to go on."

Cornelia frowned. "There could be a killer amongst us to this day and we wouldn't even know it."

As the women talked about the discovery of the body and the lack of evidence, Tommy and Andy stood by, their nerves kicking into overdrive. They made eye contact a couple times, then looked away, avoiding the discussion. Tommy pulled his hands out of his pockets and rubbed the scar on his left hand with his right thumb. He turned back towards Andy who was watching him. He got the message. *Not a word.* Andy looked away, irritated that Tommy thought he needed a reminder.

As the women's conversation droned on, Tommy's mind wandered back to the night in late August 1999 when he, Andy, Curtis, and Billy Ray helped a poor, crying girl bury the past. The longer Cheryl and Cornelia talked, the more vivid the image became. His muscles tensed as he imagined himself, and the others, push on the car's bumper, not making any progress. Carly Sue's constant cries of despair filled his ears. Fear that someone might hear her and come looking gripped him. Then the image of the dead man in the front seat materialized in his head.

"Isn't that right, Tommy?"

"What?" Tommy had not heard a word that his wife said for the last few minutes. He looked at Cheryl, a blank look on his face. He quickly shoved his hands back in his pockets. "Sorry, I wasn't paying attention. What did you say, Hon?"

Cheryl rolled her eyes. "I said the sheriff put Gerry Brannen in charge of the murder investigation, right?"

"Yeah, that's what Dennis said anyway." He paused. "Excuse me for a second. I'm going into Hibbett's for a few minutes. I'll be right back."

Before Tommy could get away, Cornelia turned to Andy and said, "Why don't you join Tommy. Didn't you say you needed some golf balls or some other golf stuff?"

"That's okay, sweetie. The courses are all dried up anyway. I won't be playin' much this year."

"Oh, go on. You two need to catch up."

Cheryl jumped in. "We're havin' a bar-b-que tonight. Why don't y'all join us? It's mostly family, but Dennis and Evlynn will be there. Maybe she can catch us up on the murder investigation."

Tommy said, "Sweetie, Evlynn won't be able to say anything about the investigation. You know how tight-lipped the police are about ongoing investigations. They can't say anything 'cause they'd get sued if they're wrong. Besides, it'll all be in the papers and all over the news soon enough."

Andy agreed. "He's right. Besides, we already have a commitment for tonight. Right, honey? Your folks are watching the kids and we have a dinner date."

"Oh, shucks. You're right. Sorry, Cheryl. Let's plan a get together soon, though. We haven't done that, outside of church activities anyway, for a long time. What do you say?"

The women looked at their husbands, who were speechless. They didn't know what to say. They knew that their wives were going to rope them into a get together whether they wanted to or not.

Cheryl said, "It's settled. We'll set the date and let you guys know when and where you have to be."

The women looked at the three girls playing quietly with each other. "Hey, girls, how about a party? Would you like that?"

The three girls yelled in unison, "Yeah!"

Cheryl said to Cornelia, "I'll call you and we'll get this party planned. We'll get the girls to help. That'll be fun."

* * *

The two families went their separate ways. Tommy went into Hibbett's Sporting Goods while Cheryl and the girls went into Belks.   Andy, Cornelia, and their daughter headed towards Bath & Body Works, Andy opting to remain seated in the mall.

He was irritated at Tommy. There was no need for him to purposely rub his palm. It was like a warning or even a threat. *If anyone needs a warning, it's Billy Ray.* Andy had been following the low-level criminal activities of their former friend. Billy Ray had been in and out of jail dozens of times over the last fifteen years. Trouble followed him everywhere he went. Or was it that he caused the trouble that usually found him. *Yeah, Billy Ray is the weak link here. No reason to threaten me.*

* * *

Tommy walked around in the sporting goods store, looking at new golf clubs, though his were only four years old. He looked at golf shoes. Again, his were only a year old. He picked up a putter, gave it a couple of quick test strokes, and put it back in the rack. He didn't need a single piece of golf equipment or apparel. He was just passing time and that wasn't a good thing. It meant his mind was free to wander, thinking of the past, and the present.

All we have to do is keep quiet. This will be over and it will go into the cold case file. Nobody will know or care in a year or so. I wonder why the heck Andy looked at me like that? He looked annoyed, like I was doin' something wrong. I just wanted to remind him that we have an agreement. But he isn't the one we got to worry about. If anyone's goin' to crack, it'll be Billy Ray. His life's a mess, drunk and doin' dope all the time. Yeah. He's the one.

* * *

The Bulloch County Corrections Institute was located northeast of Statesboro where the US 301 bypass met back up with US 301. The medium-security prison was on the same grounds as the Bulloch County Jail. The inmate population of around one hundred forty was mostly non-violent.

One of the advantages of being in Bulloch County Jail was that, if you were able to get on a work detail, your sentence was reduced. Any day an inmate worked knocked an additional day off their sentence. It was a bonus for the taxpayers because they got the surrounding county roads cleaned on a regular basis. It was also a good deal for the inmates for obvious reasons, though you could get a hot meal while incarcerated that most inmates said was better than the food they ate on the outside.

Billy Ray sat at a permanently mounted picnic table in the common area of the Cell Block C, minding his own business, reading the *Statesboro Herald* about the body found in Cypress Lake. There were few details of the discovery and no comments of any substance coming from the sheriff's office. He worried that he might not get out of jail before someone tried to pin the murder on him. As he read the story, written by reporter Eugene Morris, he saw the car's top in the water. Then he flashed to the night that he and his friends heard Carly Sue crying and went to her rescue. If it had been up to him, they would have left as soon as they saw the dead man in the car. It was Carly Sue's problem, not theirs. Hell, they weren't even sure if Carly Sue pulled the trigger, or if the poor bastard committed suicide. Or it could have been someone else and she just found the body. Any of those stories would do.

But none of the stories was true. He believed that Carly Sue had killed that man and he was pretty sure he knew why.

Billy Ray owned the trailer next to MaryJo Saxon. Back in 1999 he lived with foster parents at the trailer. He had inherited the trailer when his own parents died in a car accident. Somehow, an arrangement was made with the foster parents that they could live in the trailer as long as they cared for Billy Ray until he became of age. They left on Billy Ray's sixteenth birthday, not quite fulfilling their obligation, but they were tired of trying to keep tabs on the youngster who had developed a number of bad habits. Billy Ray's drinking was highest on their list of grievances.

Billy Ray was just ten years old when he noticed the parade of men going in and out of MaryJo Saxon's life. They all looked like shady characters and none of them lasted long. They'd show up one evening, stick around for a few days to a few weeks, then they were gone. The pattern was the same.

He noticed something else about that time. Carly Sue was becoming a woman. He wasn't the only one who noticed, either.

On the night before they heard Carly Sue crying, Billy Ray heard a commotion at Carly Sue's trailer. He snuck out of his trailer and went over to the patio next to Carly Sue's bedroom window. He found an old wooden step ladder, quietly set it up under her window, and began climbing. The steps creaked loud enough to scare Billy Ray. He hesitated, listening for any change in the noise coming from Carly Sue's room. When the commotion continued, he took another tentative step up. He was just high enough to peer into the window.

He couldn't believe what he saw. MaryJo's most recent boyfriend was in bed with Carly Sue putting his hands all over her. Carly Sue was trying to resist, but the man was much bigger than her. After a few minutes the man left. Carly Sue remained in bed, crying.

Billy Ray broke out of his trance when another inmate asked him if he could see the newspaper. He took one last look at the story and said, "Sure."

Billy Ray wondered when Carly Sue would pin the murder on him. He was a career criminal with no future – an easy target – and she was married to Curtis. He figured it was inevitable.

Chapter 9

Bulloch County Sheriff's Captain Gerald Brannen had enough years in the department to qualify for early retirement, but he wanted to stay on the force another three-and-a-half years until he turned fifty-five. He joined the sheriff's department in 1984 when he was just twenty-one. Back then there was only one other black deputy on the force. He had endured fierce discrimination during those early days, but came out a better man for the experience. He was even encouraged to run for Sheriff five years ago, and gave the suggestion some serious thought until Evlynn Adkins, a Statesboro Police Officer whom he had met a number of times, announced that she would run.

Evlynn Adkins told Brannen that she had no intention of running for Sheriff of Bulloch County, Georgia. She was content with her position, and her steady climb in the ranks, on the Statesboro Police Department. With six years on the force, she was in line for a promotion when the standing Bulloch County Sheriff announced he would not seek reelection. Immediately after his announcement, two men came forward and declared that they would run for Sheriff on the Democratic ticket. No Republicans expressed interest, and it appeared that a Democrat would be the new sheriff for the first time in nearly twenty-four years.

Brannen knew that Adkins was no patsy. She was outspoken, but not rude; smart, but not arrogant; and tough, but fair. Her ten years in the U.S. Marine Corps had transformed her life. She told Brannen how she came to be a police officer.

As a teen, she had no clear direction in life. Her parents suggested community college, but she believed that it would simply be a continuation of her high school classes, only labeled "higher education." She wanted something that would grab her, shake her, and shape her. One of her friend's brothers had just come back on leave from the Marine Corps. She remembered him from the time he was in high school. He had been a bit of a nerd, smart, not athletic, and not assertive.

When she saw him at her friend's parents' home, she hadn't recognized him. His appearance was completely transformed. He was in a tee shirt and gym shorts. He was polite, handsome, confident, and proud.

When he said, "Hello, Evlynn," she recognized his voice.

"Hello, Dennis."

She told Brannen, "From that moment, I knew that I wanted to join the U.S. Marine Corps. My friend, Cheryl Adkins Alexander, told me that we would fall in love. Darned if she wasn't right."

When she told her parents of her plan to join the Corps, they both expressed shock and fear. Initially, they said that they wouldn't support her, but over time, they realized that there was no stopping her. Before the end of the first week following high school graduation, she was off to basic training.

When she returned from boot camp, her parents were again shocked. This time, it was the transformation of their daughter from a wandering, aimless teen to a confident, self-directed young woman. She told them that she had passed all of the testing and been accepted to be an MP - Military Police.

Over the several years of their friendship, Brannen saw that the nine-plus years she spent in the Corps' Military Police made her tougher than most of her female peers. During her time with the Statesboro Police Department, she had kept herself in top physical shape. She had also taught women's self-defense courses. Despite all of that, she found the time to marry Dennis Adkins. They both had left active duty with the Marine Corps, and they both joined the Marine Corps Reserves.

Brannen knew both of the men who were running for Sheriff. They were long time employees of the sheriff's office. Both were out of shape, arrogant, and believed that they were entitled to the job due to their longevity. They believed strongly that the job was no place for a woman.

When Brannen heard the men make some disparaging remarks about women in law enforcement, he suggested that she run against them. She floated the idea by her husband, who smiled and gave her his blessing with a kiss.

She won in a landslide after a campaign that proved Evlynn was, by far, the superior choice.

Her start at the Bulloch County Sheriff's Office was a little rocky, but once the rank and file understood that, not only was she qualified, she excelled at her job, they quickly rallied around her. There were still a few holdouts from the "Good-ole-boy network," but they were near retirement and would soon be replaced with new blood.

The rest of the men and two women on the force didn't rely on word of her experience. They could see the way she conducted business day-to-day. She was a good cop and a great boss, supportive of her troops, but strict and tough when it came to conduct. She would bust balls when someone colored outside the lines. Public trust and image were important elements of the job, but officer integrity was expected and non-negotiable.

It was Saturday morning, 11:30, and Sheriff Adkins sat at the head of the conference room next to Captain Brannen. The room was twenty-five feet square with several rows of tables and folding chairs. There was a whiteboard, and a projector screen that could be lowered from the ceiling. The projector hung from the ceiling in the middle of the room.

The space could comfortably accommodate twenty normal-size people, but not twenty law enforcement officers in full gear. The air conditioning struggled to keep pace with the generated body heat. The officers were waiting for the meeting to begin, hoping that it would be short and to the point. It was one thing they liked about Sheriff Adkins. Her meetings had no fluff. She was all business and hated to waste time on what she called "chatter." She raised her hand to get everyone's attention.

"Let's get started so you can get out on the street. Captain Brannen is going to provide a brief of the murder at Cypress Lake. Before he gets started, I want you to hear it from me. This murder happened some fifteen years ago or more." She looked at the eyes of the officers, looking for any attitude amongst her deputies. She didn't detect any. "There is no statute of limitations on murder. There may be a murderer out there who thinks he or she has gotten away with it. We're going to make sure that they're wrong." Again, a pause for effect. "Any questions for me before I turn it over to Captain Brannen?"

You could hear a pin drop. Sheriff Adkins nodded to Brannen.

"Thank you, Sheriff." Brannen began. "A white 1990 Ford Tempo was pushed into the lake around the year 2000, give or take a year. It was discovered by an inmate cleanup crew…"

Brannen provided the facts as they knew them. He spoke of the drought exposing the car's top, the low lake level, the expanding shoreline, the gun and a bracelet found at the scene, and the bullet found in the bottom of the car. He described the skeletal remains and the bullet hole in the skull. The jawbone and dentures were intact, which may help in the positive identification of the victim, and a partial license plate number was visible on South Carolina plates. Again, being Saturday, they didn't expect anything back from the South Carolina Bureau of Motor Vehicles until Monday morning at the earliest.

"Most of you will continue with your normal duties. I will advise those of you who have specific duties associated with this case. The reason for this update is that we may have a killer out there. When they see the news broadcasts, which have already hit the news stations and the *Herald*, they may panic. If you get any reports that might remotely be associated with this case, do not be a hero. Work as a team and let's remove this killer from our streets. Your first order of priority is to protect the public. Second, protect yourself and your fellow officers. Are there any questions?"

One deputy raised his hand and asked, "Yeah, Captain. Is the lab working on the evidence today? Think we'll hear anything on the gun?"

"The lab's workin' overtime on this case. Just like any fresh murder case, the quicker we move, the better the chances we'll have of finding the murderer."

The same officer had a follow-up. "Any chance there will be some rotation of officers on and off the case? I know I'm not the only one who would like to get a crack at this."

Heads nodded around the room. Captain Brannen appreciated the enthusiasm and started to reply, but the sheriff put her hand on his arm, letting him know that she would like to respond. She smiled ever so slightly. "Captain Brannen and I will talk it over. I appreciate that many of you want to get involved in this unusual case. There's only so much manpower that we can apply to this without leaving the rest of the county vulnerable, so be patient and vigilant."

Captain Brannen asked, "Anything else?" There was silence. Captain Brannen said, "Dismissed."

As the deputies filed out of the room, Brannen pulled aside the men selected for the investigative team and asked that they take a seat again. Once they were seated, Brannen led the discussion. He laid out the initial plan. While the lab processed the car, gun, bullet, and bracelet, the team would question residents of the trailer park.

"Over the next fifteen minutes we want to get a standard set of questions for the tenants. First is, how long have they lived in the park. If they just moved in, ask them about gossip and any stories that they might have heard."

Brannen continued to go over their strategy. One thing he wanted to impress upon the team: work in pairs. Never approach a trailer alone. He reiterated that if the killer caught wind of the discovery of the body, they might feel trapped and try to run…or fight.

A deputy asked, "Are we planning to question the folks at the other houses along the lake?"

"We will after we finish the trailer park. We know the park has been there a long time. Most of the houses in the area have only been there a few years. We'll do a database search on the area around the lake and find out when those houses were built. We'll start with the oldest homes." He paused for a moment to allow for any questions. "We're hoping that someone remembers something from back then, but it's already been over a decade. Chances of anyone remembering anything are slim. We found the body in the driver's seat and the car in neutral. Somebody killed this guy and pushed the car into the lake. That had to make some noise. If we find someone who remembers hearing some commotion by the lake, and they can give us a better date, then we have a starting point. Our key is to get more pieces to this puzzle, quickly. Right now, we don't have much. It doesn't help that it's the weekend, but we have to play the cards we've been dealt."

Brannen picked the least experienced deputy to work with him. The other deputies would be the second team. He told them to meet at Cypress Lake Mobile Home Park in twenty minutes. Then they would decide which team would take which trailers. With that, the meeting ended.

* * *

At 12:25 in the afternoon, Captain Brannen and his partner went to the trailers to the right of the main road that bisected Cypress Lake Mobile Home Park. The other deputies approached the trailers on the left side of the road. The heat was oppressive, the sun punishing the barren, dry red clay of the park. Tall pine trees cast shade on some areas. The deputies were sweating before they took just a few steps outside of their cruisers. They hoped that some of the tenants would invite them into their air-conditioned mobile homes, but from first appearances, many of the ancient trailers didn't have working air conditioners.

The park had been surveyed with lots established in the early 1970s. Each mobile home site had its own septic system, but water was originally supplied by a central well. In 1994, the well was replaced by a rural water authority.

The first two trailer occupants that Brannen and his partner encountered said that they had lived in the park for less than two years. They were both younger couples, each with three young children. They didn't know anything about the murders except what they saw from the side of the road. They did mention that Millie Crider, the old woman who lived in the third trailer in from the main road, boasted that she knew all about the murder and even the identity of the victim. They said that most of the residents thought that she was crazy and that anything she said should be taken with a grain of salt. They also heard that Crider had lived in the trailer park for as long as anyone could remember. Their kids were afraid of her and wouldn't play outside anywhere near her trailer.

Brannen thanked both couples and moved on to Crider's trailer. As they approached her door, they were surprised when she opened it and said, "Y'all come on in. I been expectin' ya."

When they entered Millie Crider's trailer, the first thing they noticed was what looked like a gray sweater on the floor. When the pile moved, they realized that it was an old cat.

Millie looked at the cat. "Alright, Dusty. Ya already been fed. Just head outta here now."

Brannen was shocked at the mess inside the old lady's trailer. He and his partner could barely stand the musty odor, like a neglected nursing home.

In a hurry to ask their questions and move on, Brannen asked, "Ms. Crider, we understand that you were living here back in 2000?"

"That's right. I been livin' here since 1976. My trailer is the first one in the park."

He asked, "You've heard about the body found in the lake yesterday?"

"Yes, sir. That body's been in there since August 1999."

Brannen's brow wrinkled. That was within the timeframe that the crime scene folks guessed for the murder. The range was pretty broad, but how could a civilian know this? Maybe her neighbors had misjudged her.

Chapter 10

The two deputies on the second team finished the first two trailers on the east side of the park. The first resident had lived there for just three months. The only thing they knew of the murder was what they saw the day before. The second trailer was owned by Ginny Hardy. She had lived in the park for well over twenty years, but didn't remember anything unusual from that long ago. Her son, Curtis Hardy, had moved out about ten years ago when he married. She said that Curtis' father was never in the picture and was gone before Curtis was born. She stayed in the park because she couldn't afford to leave. Deputy Jones had asked her if she remembered anything unusual that happened around fifteen years ago.

"I don't know. That's an awful long time ago. Maybe my neighbor, MaryJo Saxon, can tell you something. You might want to catch her before she starts hitting the bottle." She pointed out the trailer next to hers as she spoke. After she finished, she looked away from the deputies, avoiding eye contact. She seemed nervous, but didn't provide any additional information. They thanked Ms. Hardy and moved on.

The deputies knocked on MaryJo Saxon's trailer door for nearly a full minute. When MaryJo finally opened the door, she appeared confused. She asked, "Whatchy'all want?"

Deputy Jones detected the odor of alcohol and noticed that MaryJo was staggering a bit. He asked, "Ms. Saxon, have you been drinking?"

Her smile was liquid. "Why, yes, I have, officer. Is that a crime?"

Jones and his partner questioned MaryJo Saxon for ten minutes, but they couldn't tell what was real or alcohol induced fantasy. They thanked her for her time and told her that they would be back another time. They were certain that she wouldn't remember them being there.

* * *

Captain Brannen and Deputy Jones sat across from each other at a conference table at the Bulloch County Sheriff's Office comparing notes from their trip to the mobile home park. The door was open so Chief Adkins walked in and pulled up a chair to listen.

Brannen rubbed his salt-and-pepper hair as he said, "The old lady, Millie Crider, said that she knew who the victim was, but she didn't know his name. She said she heard his car leave from the trailer across the main road from hers. That's MaryJo Saxon's place. She said the muffler was so loud that she heard the car turn onto the main road. Shortly after that the car's engine shut off."

Jones was thinking about MaryJo Saxon. "Ms. Saxon was drunk when we knocked on her door a little after 1:00. Who does that?" He paused. "Maybe someone under stress? Maybe she works the late shift and this is her time to unwind? Her neighbors said she's unemployed. They also said she has few friends and keeps to herself. One of her neighbors, a Ms. Hardy, said that she thinks Ms. Saxon drinks quite a bit."

Brannen listened to Jones' description of MaryJo Saxon's lifestyle. It matched what Millie Crider had said. He turned his attention back to Crider. "Most everybody in the park said the old lady's a card short of a full deck, but I'll tell ya, she seemed pretty sharp to me. She said that MaryJo has a daughter, Carly Sue, who was kind of a tomboy when she was young. Then she grew up into a pretty girl. She said that MaryJo's boyfriends started lookin' at Carly Sue with a little too much interest. Said she can't prove anything, but she thinks the victim was one of 'em who was getting' a little…too close."

Jones rubbed the stubble starting to form on his chin. MaryJo hadn't mentioned that she had a daughter when they questioned her earlier in the day, but she was three sheets to the wind at the time. "You think Ms. Saxon got protective of her little girl? Maybe a motive for murder? Could be that's something she wants to forget, but now the body's been found and she's worried that somebody's gonna remember something?"

"Could be. I think we better pay Ms. Saxon another visit. Maybe she's come down off her bender by now."

Chief Adkins listened to the exchange. She liked how her men were pooling their information and following up. She waited without saying a word, letting the men put the pieces in place. It wasn't much, but it was more than they had just hours before.

Finally, she said, "Maybe this Millie Crider's not as crazy as everyone thinks."

Brannen and Jones both nodded, then Brannen said, "I agree, Sheriff. I think she's been playin' this part for a long time, but she knows exactly what she's doin' and sayin'. She sure rattled off the answers to my questions, no hesitation at all."

"I'll let you two get going. Keep me informed. I'm stayin' late. I should be here until about 9:00."

Sheriff Adkins left the room. The two men took a few more minutes to discuss how to handle the visit back to MaryJo Saxon's place. They decided that just the two of them would go. Both men were big, imposing figures. They thought it might give them an advantage talking with a single woman in the relatively confined area of her trailer's living room…if she would let them in.

* * *

The Bulloch County Sheriff's car pulled into Cypress Lake Mobile Home Park and slowly pulled up to MaryJo Saxon's trailer. It was 6:48 PM on the computer that sat between the two deputies. The sun was still bright, the rays casting long shadows as it angled through the pine trees. As the men stepped out of the car, the heat assaulted them. Their dark uniforms, loaded with standard issue gear, didn't help, but they were both fit and shrugged off the uncomfortable heat. Brannen ascended the three rusted, metal steps, hoping that they were still strong enough to support his weight. He noticed that there was a thin space between the edge of the door's window and the curtain that hung on the inside of the door. He saw MaryJo sprawled out on her living room couch. She was close to three hundred pounds and looked as if she might fall to the floor at any moment. He looked back at Jones with a disgusted head shake.

He pounded on the door with three quick raps, looked past the curtain, hoping for some movement. The woman didn't budge. He watched for a few seconds, hoping to see any sign of life, and noticed that her chest was rising. At least she was alive. Again, he pounded on the door with the same results.

He turned to Jones and said, "She's in there on the couch. Looks passed out. She's alive, but even if she does wake up, she'll be a mess."

Jones said, "Let's leave her a card with a note to call us. If we don't hear anything tomorrow we can always come back early Monday morning."

Brannen nodded and reached in his wallet for a card. He pulled a pen from his pocket and scribbled a note. He tucked the card in the space between the door and the frame, then made his way down the rickety steps.

* * *

Curtis Hardy turned into the trailer park and immediately spotted the Bulloch County Sheriff's car parked at MaryJo's trailer. He cursed under his breath, wondering what MaryJo might be telling the deputies. Then he saw that one officer was still knocking on the trailer's door. He quickly pulled into his mother's driveway. She wasn't home, so he sat in the car, worry etched on his face.

Moments later the sheriff's car drove by, heading back towards Cypress Lake Road. When the deputy in the passenger seat saw him sitting in his car, he motioned for the driver to stop. Curtis saw the car stop, then the deputy exited the passenger side and walked towards him. Curtis opened his car door and slowly stepped out.

Curtis faced Deputy Jones and asked, "Can I help you, Deputy?"

"Maybe. Are you a resident?"

"No, sir. This is my mom's place. Just visiting. She's supposed to be home any minute."

Jones looked at Curtis for a moment, apparently trying to read his face and body language. After a few seconds, he said, "Okay, thank you."

He sat back in the cruiser which continued on towards Cypress Lake Road. Curtis let out his breath.

Time to get the hell outta here.

* * *

At 7:10 PM, the sun was coming in at a western angle, which helped keep Tommy Alexander's patio in the shade, providing some limited relief from the oppressive heat. While he took a pull on his longneck beer, he put the finishing touches on a dozen hamburgers that sizzled on his gas grill.

His wife, Cheryl, was in the middle of a group of their friends and family. The topic of the discussion was "the murder." Cheryl's brother, Dennis Adkins, was answering questions about the investigation because his wife, Sheriff Evlynn Adkins, was working late and could not attend. Dennis had little information that he could divulge to the group, beyond what was already on TV news channels or in the morning edition of the *Statesboro Herald*. He did assure everyone that the Sheriff's Department was working the case around the clock, as evidenced by his wife's absence from the barbeque.

There was some speculation within their small group that the murder was a body dump by drug dealers from Savannah, or gangs across the border in South Carolina. This was bolstered by the Ford Tempo having South Carolina Plates.

Before the discussion could go much further, Tommy hollered that the hamburgers were done and that anyone wanting cheese added should see the chef right away. He took another pull on his beer as he waited for anyone in the crowd to take him up on the cheeseburger announcement.

When Dennis came over and asked for American and Swiss cheese combination, he obliged. "I know you can't talk much about this murder thing, but have they even identified the body yet?"

"No. Evlynn said that they didn't expect anything until Tuesday morning on the ID. I will tell you this, there's an old lady in the trailer park who's lived there a long time. She claims to know who the victim is."

That sent Tommy's eyebrows up, making the lines on his forehead pronounced. His mind wandered back to the trailer park when they used to throw rocks at her trailer to spook her. *How could Millie Crider know? She was an old senile bat even back then.*

"Hey, Tom, my burger's burnin'."

"Oh crap. Sorry, Dennis." He snatched the burger off with a spatula and put it on the bun that Dennis held in his hands. "Pass me that plate, please. I'm going to clear these off the grill."

Tommy proceeded to stack the burgers on a plate. He motioned for his wife to come over. When she got there, he gave her the burgers. "Put these on the food table, please and get everybody to stop jabberin' and fix their plates."

She gave him a sideways glance that seemed to say, *Stop being so bossy.* He smiled, and kissed her on the cheek before she headed away with the plate. He turned off the burners on the grill and headed for the house. He locked the bathroom door behind him and stood, staring at his image in the mirror. He could see the stress lines on his face. If anyone asked about it, he could claim the drought caused his anxiety, but Cheryl would know that was just an excuse. She somehow knew there was more to his daydreaming and lack of focus. His routine had always been a systematic process, from the moment that he awoke until he went to bed at night. Even now, as he stood in the bathroom, his mind wandered to August 1999. He couldn't keep the dead man's image from his mind.

In fact, the vision seemed to grow more vivid with the discovery of the body.

A loud *bam-bam-bam* on the door made him jump. As the bathroom came back into focus, he asked, "Who is it?"

"The boogey man. You have a request for some hot dogs. I guess a couple of the kids would rather eat dogs than burgers," Cheryl informed him through the closed door.

"Tell the little rug rats I'll be right out."

There was a long silence. "Are you okay in there?"

He cracked a sad smile that he could see in the mirror. "Yeah, Honey. I'd be better if I could finish my business in private."

He heard his wife's steps as she headed back out to the yard to entertain their guests. Tommy knew that it was going to be a long night, talking about his mood and his lack of concentration. He wished he could avoid that conversation, but it was inevitable. Cheryl was too perceptive. Now he had to get his cover story perfected. That was going to be tough. He was a lousy liar.

Chapter 11

Carly Sue slept well Saturday evening into Sunday morning. To Curtis, it was a good sign that a change to her anti-psychotic and anti-depressant medications might not be necessary. There was still the troublesome knowledge that she would see the continued news coverage of the murder, which could trigger another bipolar episode. He was hopeful that he could keep her away from the television and newspapers all day Sunday. With any luck, by Monday, the constant barrage of coverage would be over, and the short attention-span of the television audience would move on to the next horrific life story.

Curtis and Carly Sue sat in an oak pew midway back on the right side of the First Presbyterian Church on Fair Road. The sanctuary was a wide-open space with benches on either side of a center aisle. Beautiful stained-glass windows rose high along the side walls of the church building. The altar was on a raised platform, with lecterns on either side. The tiered choir loft was to the left of the altar, facing the congregation. Of the ten choir members, all but one had gray or white hair, or no hair at all, their ages averaging somewhere north of seventy.

The opening hymn and greeting prayers, the first reading, Isaiah 6:1-8, and the second reading, Romans 8:12-17, were all complete. Pastor Jonathon Squire was just finishing the Gospel according to John 3:1-17.

"…but to save the world through Him. The Word of the Lord."

The one hundred and fifty or so parishioners answered in unison, "Thanks be to God."

All were seated as Pastor Squire made his way to the front and center of the sanctuary and said a brief, silent prayer for divine guidance. He wore a flowing green robe, wire-rim glasses, and a wireless microphone, though most folks in the congregation believed that the microphone was overkill. With his jet-black hair, most said he looked like a Supreme Court Justice instead of a Presbyterian Minister. He looked around the congregation with a smile. Then slowly, as he removed his glasses, his smile faded. In a clear, booming voice, he spoke, "For God did not send his Son into the world to condemn the world, but to save the world through Him. It seems like such a simple arrangement. All we have to do is accept Jesus Christ as our personal Savior, to be born again in the Spirit. It is free to all: a gift, a handout, the keys to heaven for eternity." He paused, the silence in the sanctuary dramatic in contrast to his commanding voice. He continued, becoming more animated, looking around at his flock, raising his arms. "And yet, we see the rejection of salvation all around us. We see murder…"

* * *

Carly Sue held Curtis's hand as Reverend Squire continued to preach the good Word. She barely heard the hymns and the greeting. She was staring at the back of the pew in front of her. She couldn't see anything in the church.

Her thoughts were halfway across town, late at night, in the passenger seat of an old Ford Tempo. She saw the clay road leading out of the park onto Cypress Lake Road. There was no traffic. The car turned left onto the road, then took a right onto a narrow path. The headlights lit up the shore of the lake ahead. It looked like a grassy field, abruptly cut off by darkness. The car bounced as it moved along the little-used path that led to the impromptu boat-launch used mainly for flat-bottom boats. Tall weeds scratched against the side of the car as it approached the lakeshore.

Carly Sue felt the .38 revolver press against her backside with each rut in the path. Her nerves were pinging, fear causing adrenaline to flow throughout her body. As her mental vision approached the lake, she gripped Curtis' hand harder and harder.

* * *

Curtis looked at his wife, his concern growing, as her grip on his right hand tightened. He could see by her expression that her mind was elsewhere. He leaned over to her and whispered, "Hey, sweetie, you with me?"

There was no reaction. Carly Sue continued to stare straight ahead, squeezing his hand, her grip tightening slowly but steadily. He saw the dark circle under her left eye. He couldn't see her other eye. Curtis hoped that Pastor Squire would keep his sermon short, but there was little chance of that. Squire was known for his lengthy, dramatic oratories, and it appeared that he was just warming up. Curtis leaned in close and whispered, "Hey, sweetie, you gotta come back to church now. Pastor Squire's not gonna like it if you interrupt his sermon. Okay? So, lighten up on my hand, dear. Okay?"

There was still no change. The knuckles on her left hand were turning white, her grip was so tight.

Pastor Squire's voice boomed again to make a point of the sin that surrounded his congregation, his city, and his state. His voice grew louder with each point, his fist coming down hard on his other palm. He took a step closer to his flock, looking around the sanctuary, making sure he had everyone's undivided attention.

A woman sitting behind Curtis leaned forward and tried to shush him. He didn't turn around or make any moves that might draw undue attention, but the woman's efforts drew the eyes of several people nearby.

Pastor Squire was in one of his dramatic pauses when an infant child from the back of the sanctuary cried in his mother's arms. The poor woman immediately began rocking the baby making calming sounds. An elderly man near the front of the congregation coughed and took out a handkerchief to contain the noise and the spew of germs. Curtis was grateful that attention was away from Carly Sue, at least for the moment.

Pastor Squire continued, lowering his voice for this part of the sermon. It was no less dramatic, as people leaned forward to soak up every word. Curtis turned again to his wife, hoping that she would break free from the mental anguish that consumed her, but she still stared off into nothingness, the grip on his hand as tight as ever. He was getting more concerned as the minutes passed. He didn't want to pry her hand loose. He feared she might interpret that as him abandoning her to whatever monster attacked her mind. He couldn't put his other arm around her. He leaned over to her and again whispered in her ear, "Sweetie, please listen to me. You're safe here. We're in church amongst friends." As he spoke, he lightly put his other hand across her hand. He did not squeeze, he just let his hand rest, in a way that he hoped would provide comfort. "I'm right here with you, darling. No one is goin' to hurt you."

The woman behind him leaned forward and gave him another *shhh*. He turned to the woman and calmly whispered, "Please stop."

The woman's glare could have melted ice, but she sat back and turned towards Pastor Squire who was quoting passages from today's readings, connecting them to current issues. His voice was again ramping up in volume and intensity.

In such a confined space, Curtis's options were few. He nuzzled closer to Carly Sue, hoping she would feel the warmth of his body next to her. He continued to allow her to keep her death-grip on his hand. He looked at her face, tense with fear. Whatever journey her mind was on, she was terrified. He hoped that she would not scream out in the middle of Pastor Squire's sermon, but something had to be done to break her spell.

* * *

From her seat in a pew several rows back and across the sanctuary from Carly Sue and Curtis, Ginny Hardy could see her daughter-in-law's tension rise. Her own anxiety level ticked up as the good reverend continued the crescendo of his sermon. Ginny feared that Carly Sue would leap from her pew and tell the congregation about her plight some sixteen years ago.

Suddenly, Pastor Squire's finger was pointed in her direction, proclaiming her to be a sinner. How could he know? There was no place to run. She couldn't breathe, but the good shepherd moved his finger on to the next sinner with the same proclamation. She glanced at Curtis and Carly Sue. They were still tense, clutching each other's hands.

* * *

The Preacher was nearing the peak, his arms flailing, his robe a flash of green. He looked from one side of the sanctuary to the other, giving random parishioners an icy stare. He pointed his finger at parishioners as he made his point, that all are sinners, and all must repent, and accept Jesus Christ as their personal Savior. His gaze and his pointed finger landed on Curtis and Carly Sue.

In his loudest proclamation of the sermon, he said, "You must cast off your demons and be born again in Christ Jesus, to gain entry into the kingdom of heaven."

"Amen," could be heard from several of the parishioners in attendance. The crowd was feeling better, feeling the moment.

When the first "Amen" rose from the crowd, Carly Sue's grip began to relax. Curtis was amazed. Could Pastor Squire have cast out Carly Sue's demons? Curtis was a religious man, but had difficulty believing that the priest had cleansed his wife's soul.

It took nearly a full minute, but Curtis could feel the blood return to the fingers on his right hand. He kept his left hand in place over his wife's, hoping to reassure her that she was safe. He looked at her face. She was not smiling, but the tension was gone. She looked exhausted.

Curtis exhaled. He realized that the church was as quiet as an empty cavern. Pastor Squire had completed his sermon and was preparing to continue the service. Suddenly, everyone rose to their feet and Pastor Squire began to lead the congregation in prayer. Curtis helped his wife to her feet. They locked eyes. Carly Sue's were filling with tears that spilled onto her cheeks.

* * *

When Ginny Hardy saw Carly Sue and Curtis relax at the conclusion of Pastor Squire's homily, she bowed her head and gave a personal prayer of thanks to the Lord. The walls that surrounded her began to recede. She could breathe again.

* * *

As they left the service, Pastor Squire was at the door bidding his flock farewell. When Curtis and Carly Sue attempted to pass unnoticed, Squire reached out and grabbed Curtis's hand. He asked, "Mr. Hardy, Mrs. Hardy, did you enjoy the service today?"

Curtis said, "Yes, Father, we did."

He was about to nod and continue out the door when Squire said, "If there is anything I can help you with, I am here." He looked from Curtis to Carly Sue, then back again. "If you call my assistant, she can schedule a time for us to talk." As he said "us" he put one hand on Curtis's shoulder and one hand on Carly Sue's. Curtis was waiting for his wife to jerk away. To his surprise, she smiled at Squire. Her smile was relaxed, trusting, and calm.

Curtis looked back at Pastor Squire. He simply replied, "Thank you, Father."

Carly Sue smiled, her face coloring, taking on a shy expression. It was like she had transformed into a completely different person. They left and headed out into the heat of the day. After sitting in the air-conditioned church, the walk to the parking lot was challenging. Their car was hot even though he had put the windshield guard up. He started the car as they stood outside waiting for the air conditioner to bring the heat down to a bearable level.

When they were safely in the car, outside of earshot from any other churchgoers, he asked if she was okay. She replied that she was, but with little conviction.

The drive home from the church was barely three minutes. When they had changed out of their Sunday church clothes, Curtis fixed himself a cup of coffee. He asked Carly Sue if he could fix her anything. She said no, that she would start lunch in a moment. Curtis took the opportunity to do a little careful probing.

"Hey, sweetie, you know that you kind of zoned-out in church, right?"

"Yeah, Curt." She looked at him and smiled. "I missed most of the service. I'm sorry."

"Sweetie, it isn't your fault. I wish I knew what set you off. If we could figure that out…"

"I don't know. One minute, we was just sittin' there and everything was fine. Pastor Squire was starting his sermon. The next thing I know, I hear him say something about expelling demons, and I see your face, all kinds of worry all over it. But I was fine, relaxed. I don't know what happened."

Curtis chose his words carefully. He asked, "So, are you comfortable with Pastor Squire?"

Carly Sue gave him an odd look, as if to ask, *What do you mean?*

He clarified his statement saying, "Would you be comfortable talking with him about what is bothering you, about your bipolar condition?"

She looked up at the ceiling, then all around the room, gathering her thoughts or maybe seeing where she could run. Curtis couldn't tell by her expression.

"I don't know, Honey. How much should I tell him?"

"As much, or as little, as you feel comfortable tellin'. He's a man of God. Whatever we tell him has to remain in confidence."

"I…I don't know. I can't really talk about much, because I don't remember much, except that creep's hands all over me. Then I remember crying. Then you boys helped push the car, and I went home."

Curtis sighed. "You don't have to decide now. Just think about it. If you don't want to, we won't. I don't want to push you."

She walked over to Curtis and kissed him on the lips. That took Curtis by surprise.

She said, "Why don't we go to bed and rest a bit before lunch." She bent over and kissed him again with passion.

They made love for half an hour, after which Carly Sue fell asleep. Curtis took advantage of the opportunity to make love to his wife because it happened so seldom. He felt content and relaxed but with just a twinge of guilt. He shook his head, telling himself that he shouldn't feel this way.

Then he thought about Carly Sue. He didn't know exactly what she had endured all those years ago, but he was certain that she saw much more than she admits to remembering.

Chapter 12

At the Trinity Episcopal Church, on the western side of Statesboro, Father Roderick Ransom's sermon maintained a similar theme as his Presbyterian counterpart, Pastor Squire. Unlike Reverend Squire, Father Ransom had a soothing, silky voice. He needed a microphone for his voice to reach the congregation. His manner was outwardly calm, relaxed in his position as the shepherd of his flock. He had been an Episcopal Priest for thirty years. He sported a few extra pounds, eating well, and not exercising enough, causing his robe to stick out a bit at his midsection. With his thinning, blond-gray hair, pale complexion, and rosy red cheeks, he looked more like an accountant than a priest.

In his calm, amplified voice, he said, "Remember what God told us all in John 3:17. He did not send his Son into the world to condemn the world, but that the world might be saved through Him.

"So, we have a great drought with no end in sight. Why are we looking at this cycle of nature with such limited eyes? God gave us the answer to weather such events, pun intended, in his holy Word. And what did he tell us? God instructed His people that when you have abundance, you use what you need and store the remainder for lean times. Well folks, here in the United States, we have abundance. Our stores are packed with food, so much so that we throw out packages of edible food simply because some random *use by* date tells us we must. Even if this drought lasts far into the future, there will still be far more than we need.

"We have withstood lean times before. For many of us in the United States, we have had an abundance of food for so long that, when we are challenged with a drought, we panic, we spread fear. We cry that the sky is falling. All manner of disaster will befall us.

"Look around you. Do you see anyone near starvation among us?" There was a pause in his sermon as his flock smiled at each other, some embarrassed that they were obviously consuming more than their share. "Look at me." He smiled. "I guess I have enough stored for several of us." He rubbed over his belly, exaggerating his own girth.

"So, I say to you, my brothers and sisters, if you have abundance, share with your family, your friends, your neighbors, and especially those in greater need than yourselves. If you are amongst those in need, ask and the Lord will provide, through the kind hearts of family, friends, neighbors, and all manner of religious, and civic organizations. No one need starve because of this drought. Though there is darkness now, this too shall pass, and the light will shine again.

"Remember, God did not send his son into the world to condemn the world, but that the world might be saved through Him. Smile. He's on our side. Amen."

Andy Pepperdine sat with his wife near the front row of the sanctuary. He preferred a seat near the back, but Cornelia wouldn't hear of it. As generous as they were to their employees and their community, especially their church, she believed that they deserved a seat close to the altar. Early in their marriage, Andy suggested that they didn't do those generous deeds for any heavenly return, or to gain prestige among their fellow man, but because it was the right thing to do. They shouldn't place themselves in the spotlight based on their philanthropy. She smiled and, as if he was a child, led him to the front pew. Over the years, they had moved back a few pews, but remained near front and center. They sat in the same spot for so long that other parishioners left the spot open for them every Sunday.

Andy looked around the sanctuary and noticed Tommy and Cheryl Alexander and their two girls sitting a dozen pews back. Tommy and Andy locked eyes for a moment. Without thinking, Andy began rubbing the scar on the palm of his hand, and his mind drifted away from church, to that dark night.

He saw his three young friends: Tommie, Curtis, and Billy Ray. They were still kids, twelve-year-olds, their faces looking like adults, standing around an eerie looking tree. The bark over most of the tree was peeling away, as if diseased. In one particular spot, it had been stripped away about six feet up from the ground. A gash was visible in the bare wood. The cut oozed a dark red stream of blood that ran down the full length of the tree and pooled at its base. Leaves rustled in the breeze. A gust of wind caused the branches to move, making loud, creaking noises. Andy looked up, watching the motion of the tree branches. They appeared to have a life of their own, like arms reaching out, ready to encircle him and his friends.

Cornelia grabbed his arm and whispered in his ear, "What are you doing?"

Andy came back to the present and looked around. The congregation was standing, responding to the prayers of Father Ransom. He realized that he'd missed several minutes of the service. He stood and turned to Cornelia and whispered, "Sorry. I was thinking about work."

"We're at church, dear. You don't bring that mess in here."

Andy noticed his daughter looking around her mother at him, a worried look on her face. She looked up at her mother, looking for assurances that Daddy was okay. Cornelia leaned over to her daughter. Whatever she said must have satisfied her curiosity. She turned her attention back to Father Ransom.

Andy shook his head and rolled his neck. He couldn't let the discovery of the body rattle him. He vowed to himself that he would concentrate on the here and now and forget about the past. There was no alternative until all this blew over.

He looked back at Tommy Alexander. Again, Tommy was looking at him.

There's no alternative. Here and now. Stay focused.
* * *

Tommy sat midway back in the sanctuary. He had a clear view of the back of Andy Pepperdine's head, though he tried hard to not look his way. His wife, Cheryl, had one arm hooked in Tommy's arm and her other arm draped over their youngest daughter's shoulder. She looked up at her husband several times during the ceremony, apparently trying to read his mood. He hoped that she didn't notice that he kept looking in the direction of the Pepperdine's.

Tommy thought back over the years since he and his friends pushed the car into the lake. Somehow, the four men had gone sixteen years without breaking the pact. They had all dealt with the pressure in their own way. He, Andy, and Curtis had become successful adults, concentrating their energies on achieving their goals. They managed to keep their minds free of the potential negative consequences should their deed be uncovered. At least, that's what Tommy believed.

Tommy wondered why Billy Ray couldn't stay sober, couldn't focus on something besides booze and drugs to take his mind off that fateful night. Maybe he wasn't mentally tough enough. Over the years, the anxiety associated with staying silent had subsided.

Then came the drought, and with it, the discovery of the body.

Tommy's own tension had skyrocketed to near the breaking point. He knew he had to hold it together for the most important people in his life – his wife and girls. He just had to remain focused, maintain things in perspective, make sure he had his priorities straight. The thing at the lake would blow over. All he had to do was keep his promise to remain silent about what he knew. As long as everyone else kept his part of the bargain, they were in the clear. *As long as they keep their mouths shut.*

But if he was feeling this much pressure, certainly the other three were, as well. And if Billy Ray was a train wreck, even in the best of circumstances, he had to be coming apart at the seams now.

* * *

Billy Ray Duke lay on his bunk reading a Stephen King novel from the jail library. He liked to read, something that he did as a young boy, but stopped when he turned twelve. During his first stint in jail, he began reading again, realizing that he had way too much free time on his hands. Even with trustee duties, the dead time was difficult to fill if you didn't have a hobby. Billy Ray found that, after a day of sobering up, his mind was clear, and he could focus on the storylines. It was one of the few positive aspects of his dismal existence.

If his old childhood friends saw him reading, they'd be amazed. He never told them that he read quite a lot when he was a child. He had been afraid that they would make fun of him. That didn't matter to him now. His friends were all successful. They had found ways to channel their energies, leading to their careers. He, on the other hand, had found the bottle to channel his energy, or in reality, pickle his brain. He drank to forget, but the more he drank, the more the memories invaded his mind. So, he drank more, and the cycle continued, until he found himself in a holding cell, hung over, not knowing how he got there.

After a time, he came to know the jailers. When he was sentenced to more lengthy stays, he would sober up and realize that he had to find something to do. He picked up the book of one of his cellmates and read it, cover-to-cover. Then he discovered the prison library and read as much as he could.

Now, when out of jail, he spent some time in the public library. It managed to keep him away from the bottle for a time. But without fail, his thoughts would work their way back to Cypress Lake. Once there, he fell back to the only relief he knew. The booze would take over and send him back down the spiral to the drunk-tank.

He was scheduled for release Monday at 1:00 PM. He had a meeting with a chaplain at the jail this afternoon. Never having been introduced to religion, he hoped the meeting would be short. He remembered his friends, Andy and Tommy, talking about church and how much they hated it. He asked them why they kept going, and they both replied that their parents forced them to go. He knew that they were now going on their own, making their kids go. Maybe there was something to it. Maybe they found God. *Well, it ain't for me.*

Billy Ray was worried. He was to be released from jail in about twenty-four hours. He had to find a job right away, something to keep his mind occupied. He couldn't go back to the bottle. He needed to keep his head clear in case everyone turned on him.

Would they do that? Would they make me the scapegoat, leave me to take the fall for a murder that none of us committed? One thing he had to keep in mind. They were once his friends. It felt to Billy Ray like a lifetime ago. That part of his life was history. He was the easy target. They could get together and plot against him to make sure their nice families and their good lives remained safe.

Will they talk or will they remain silent? I'll only find out that they talked when it's too late...when they come for me.

Billy Ray picked up his book and started on the next chapter. In the story he was reading, a man everyone thought was dead and gone for good had come back to haunt them. The entire town lived in fear of him, thinking that he could not be killed. Billy Ray wondered if his friends thought of him in this way.

Chapter 13

Eugene Morris cursed himself for waiting until noon to stop at the Cypress Lake Mobile Home Park. The sun was high overhead with no breeze and no clouds. Escaping the oppressive ninety-degree-plus heat was impossible. He wore a thin, collared shirt and khaki pants, no socks, and deck shoes. His *Statesboro Herald* ID badge hung from a lanyard around his neck.

Morris didn't mind working on Sunday. He was used to working the odd hours of a newspaper reporter. News didn't happen Monday through Friday, from nine-to-five so you had to be ready to answer the call. Over the years, he stopped waiting for official notification and ventured out on his own to track down the stories. When he was first hired by the *Statesboro Herald*, he bought himself a birthday gift – a new police scanner. Over time, he developed contacts inside the Statesboro Police Department, the Bulloch County Sheriff's Department, numerous city departments, and other street sources. Some of his sources were reliable, others were not.

One thing he determined to be effective was talking with people. Over time, he could sense who was telling the truth and who was embellishing the facts. He would observe their body movement, their attitude, and the look in their eyes. Finding the truth came down to one thing: talking with as many people as possible who were close enough to the action to provide an accurate story.

That was the reason, when Morris received the call from his boss at the *Statesboro Herald* suggesting that he snoop around the Cypress Lake Mobile Home Park on Monday and chat up the park's residents, he was already ahead of the game. By Sunday at noon, his car was parked next to a vacant trailer in the park. He had just completed walking around the neighborhood, getting the lay of the land and deciding where to start knocking on doors, when his cell phone rang. His boss made the belated suggestion to interview park residents. In years gone by, Morris would have made some snide reply about being way ahead of his boss, but after being reprimanded a number of times for his attitude and being stripped of his *Investigative Reporter* title, he held his tongue. In fact, he made his boss believe that it was his idea and moved on.

Two days earlier as the crime scene was being analyzed by the authorities, Morris had watched the crowd gathered by the lake. He noticed two residents in particular, whom he wanted to question. He didn't know their names and wasn't sure where they lived, but both would be easy to identify, if they answered their doors.

He started his rounds of the park at the trailer closest to the front entrance. As he approached, he heard a man shouting at his wife, something about a boyfriend, and that she had better not be sneaking around with him. Thinking that it might not be a good idea to get in the middle of that discussion, he moved on to the next trailer and knocked on the door. A young woman wearing a blue tube top and shorts answered. A waft of acrid marijuana smoke escaped the trailer and hit Morris in the face.

Morris showed the woman his press ID. "Sorry to bother y'all, ma'am, but I'm Gene Morris with the *Statesboro Herald*. I was wonderin' if you had a moment to answer a couple questions about the murder at the lake."

The woman hollered over her shoulder. "Jake, there's a reporter at the door. You wanna come talk with him?"

A voice from inside said, "Crap. I guess so."

The woman backed out of the doorway and let a barefoot, skinny man in blue jean shorts and no shirt step to the door. He looked to be about twenty-two with black hair, and a few days' stubble-growth on his face. In addition to the pot odor, he smelled as if he'd already had a beer or two. Morris decided that if the man had lived in the park back around the time of the murder, he would have been in elementary school. The man asked, "Who're you?"

"Gene Morris, from the *Statesboro Herald*. Can I ask you about the murder?"

The man's face scrunched up as if to say, *What do I care?* Gene took that as permission to ask away.

Morris asked, "How long have y'all lived here in the park?"

"You know, we tol' the cops everthang we know, which ain't much."

"That's fine. Sometimes reporters can figure things out that the cops miss, so if you don't mind, could you tell me what you know?"

The man scratched his head. Morris wasn't sure if he was deciding to cooperate or if he couldn't figure out what Morris had just said. A boy about three years old stepped up behind the man and put his arms around his leg. The man acted as if he hadn't noticed the child. "We've only lived here a little over a year. The only thing we know is what we saw from across the road the other day."

Morris figured as much, but he wanted to know if they had heard others in the park talk. He asked, "Have you heard any rumors from your neighbors, no matter how far-fetched you think they might be?"

"Well, all I know is that the old lady next door swore that she knows who the dead guy is. Don't know how she knows that since all they got was a skeleton, but she says it's a guy anyway. Everybody says she's half a bubble off, though, if you know what I mean." He raised an eyebrow, pointed his finger at his head, and spun it in a circle for emphasis.

"Anyone else in the park who might know anything?"

"I heard that MaryJo might know something, but I think that rumor came from Millie."

"Millie?"

"Yeah, the old lady." He paused and thought for a moment, then said, "I think y'all'd have a ball talking with her.

She's a real hoot. Tells all kinds of stories about this trailer park. She knows, too; watches everthang that goes on 'round here. Sits in her trailer, looking out the windas with her binoculars. Wouldn't surprise me if she had videos of everbody's comins' and goins'."

Morris had a hard time suppressing a smile. He had only asked one question, and the young man was rambling. He decided to let the guy continue talking. Maybe he had more information than he really knew.

The man continued. "Millie says that MaryJo – she lives in that trailer over yonder – was a real tramp. Always having guys over until they ditched her. Then she'd cry the blues until another one comes along. I guess this has been going on for years. I haven't noticed it much since we've been here, but apparently, this happened about fifteen, maybe twenty years ago. I guess back then she was a looker. Now she's kinda, well, fat and ugly. Not ugly, but kinda worn out. That's life, I guess."

"So, I didn't get your name."

"Bart. Bart Wilson. Tammy Lynn's my girl, one who answered the door."

"So, Bart, what does this have to do with the murder?"

"Oh, yeah. That's what we was talkin' about. You see, MaryJo has a daughter – older than us, maybe twenty-seven, twenty-eight. Well, apparently, some of MaryJo's boyfriends started makin' eyes at the daughter. This was back when the daughter was maybe ten or twelve. Millie thinks that the one that was killed did a little more than look, if you know what I mean."

A voice from inside the trailer shouted, "Bart, you shouldn't be spreadin' rumors. Let him talk to Millie. She's the one spreadin' the rumors. You should stay the heck out of it."

"Okay, sweetie, you're right." He turned back to Morris and said, "I can't say no more or I'm in the doghouse, know what I mean?"

"Yeah," Morris said. "You don't want to end up in the doghouse." He winked at Bart. "I'll head over to Millie's place and talk with her. Thanks for the chat."

Morris backed down the steps and started across the open space towards Millie *what's her last name?* The distance between trailers was about one hundred feet. As he headed that way, he looked across the road towards MaryJo *what's her last name's?* trailer. A woman was looking out the window of what was probably the kitchen. She was staring right at Morris. He thought about changing direction and heading over to her trailer when she abruptly closed the curtains. He thought *That curtain won't protect you, MaryJo. I'll talk to you in a bit.*

Morris was about to knock on Millie Crider's trailer door when the door opened. A stout, elderly woman was holding the handle. Surprise was written all over his face.

She said, "Don't just stand there. You're letting the cool air out. Get in here so I can tell ya what's goin' on."

Gene Morris stepped into the living room of the small, run-down trailer. His first thought was that she needed central air conditioning. It was no cooler in the trailer than it was outside. The only difference was generated by a small, oscillating fan on the counter between the kitchen and the living room.

Not only was the air stiflingly hot, it was stale and smelled as if she had a gaggle of cats. He looked around for any felines, then noticed a lone pile of dusty fur on an ancient lounge chair. As if on cue, his sinuses began to clog. He knew he had to get this interview underway before he suffocated.

Before he could identify himself, Millie said, "You're that reporter from the *Herald*, ain'tcha?"

"Yes, ma'am. I'm…"

"Eugene Morris. I read your columns all the time. You're the only one up there's got half a brain."

Morris wasn't sure that he had been complimented or insulted, but he decided to sit back and see what Millie… "Ma'am, I know your first name is Millie…"

"Crider. Millie Crider. Call me Millie. It ain't my formal name, but that don't matter. Nobody's called me Mildred since Momma died. You're here to talk about that boy they fished from the lake."

"Yes, ma'am…I mean Millie. That's my first question. How do you know the victim's a man?"

"First off, Eugene, he weren't no man. He was a sick bastard. And he sure as hell weren't no victim. He had it comin'. Sooner or later some little girl's daddy was gonna give that creep some street justice. It was only a matter of time."

Gene Morris intently watched Millie Crider's eyes. They were brown eyes surrounded by sunken sockets and loose, fleshy skin. The bags under her eyes were puffy. The skin on her face bore wrinkles that had been in place for a long time. Millie Crider appeared to Morris as one of those women who had been old as long as you could remember. But her eyes were clear and intense. She looked straight at his eyes when she spoke. There was no attempt to hide or deceive. She laid it all out as she believed it to be. The only question was whether what she told was fact or only what she believed to be fact.

"Millie, do you know who the victim…er…the man in the car, do you know his name?"

"No, but you can bet that that tramp over there knows." As she said the words, she raised her hand and, with her left thumb, pointed at MaryJo's trailer. "She was dating the bastard when he tried to get in her daughter's pants, the scoundrel. And he weren't the only one. A couple of her boyfriends was getting frisky with poor Carly Sue."

"I take it that Carly Sue is the daughter's name?"

She looked at him like he had a third eye. "Are y'all sure that y'all's a reporter? I woulda thought that was obvious. Anyway, he wasn't the first one eyein' up that poor little girl. And MaryJo would blame Carly Sue when them boys left. Poor thang. If that were my daughter and them boys started sniffin' around like they done, I woulda castrated 'em! Bastards!"

When Millie said "castrated," she jerked her arm with an upward motion as if she'd had practice. Morris winced at the mental picture. Sweat was already beading on his brow and pouring down his back and chest. His sinuses were clogged so tight he could barely breathe. When the oscillating fan moved his way, he tried to move his head in rhythm so he could get the most air flow possible. He had to wrap up the interview and move outside into the fresh air, regardless of the outside temperature.

"Millie, besides MaryJo, is there anyone else who might be able to identify the man that they found in the lake?"

"Yes. Carly Sue. She's married and lives in town now. Last name's Hardy."

"Okay. Good. Anything else you can think of?"

"Well, yeah. Can you look this up?"

She handed Morris a small scrap of paper. On it was a series of numbers and letters followed by "South Carolina."

She said, "That's the license plate number for that Ford."

"You mean, the car they pulled..." He stopped when he saw the disdainful look on her face. Of course she meant the car pulled from the lake.

"Thank you, Millie. You've been a great help."

"One more thing, Eugene. I think Billy Ray Duke might also know who that bastard from the lake is. He used to peek into Carly Sue's window at night. I think he liked Carly Sue. He was too young to know what he was doing, though. When he ain't in jail, he lives in the trailer on the other side of MaryJo."

Morris smiled despite his physical discomfort. Lots of people thought Millie Crider was crazy, but he could tell that she was sharp as a razor.

Chapter 14

Captain Brannen arrived at the Bulloch County Sheriff's Office early Monday morning to review all the information they had on the Cypress Lake murder. He knew there wasn't much to review, but, like with any puzzle, the more you studied the pieces, the better you would see how they fit together. In this case, most of the pieces were old and faded, making the puzzle that much more difficult. But Sheriff Adkins had made it clear – this case was a priority.

He sat in his office with a legal pad of his notes from his meeting with Deputy Jones. As he read through his own interpretation of the reports, it became clear that Millie Crider wasn't whacky. She may be a scary old lady to the kids, and a whack job to some of the neighbors, but she appeared to have a sharp memory. It was probably worth a second visit to pick the old woman's brain, especially regarding her neighbor, MaryJo Saxon. He planned to take Jones back to question Saxon this morning. He hoped they could catch her before she was hitting the bottle.

Out of the several dozen residents in the park, only a handful had lived in the park fifteen-to-twenty years ago. Crider and Saxon, then Mrs. Hardy and Billy Ray Duke. Jones had said that Hardy, Saxon, and Duke lived in three trailers across the main road into the park from Millie Crider. The three trailers were about one hundred feet apart with Saxon's trailer between Hardy's and Duke's. Saxon's trailer was also directly across the road from Crider's.

Brannen picked up the Sunday edition of the *Statesboro Herald* and saw the headlines. "Drought Uncovers Murder." The sub-headline read "Skeletal Remains Found in Shrinking Cypress Lake." The byline credited Eugene Morris. He read the story from start to finish. There were no surprises. Morris covered everything the two had discussed on Friday, leaving nothing out, and not embellishing the story in any way. He described the scene on the lakeshore where the car had been pulled from the water. His portrayal of the crime scene technicians and the grid search of the area near the lake with the metal detector were kept at a high level. He even gave credit to the chain gang for being the first to notice the car while still in the water.

He described the mob standing across the road as being mostly from the nearby mobile home park. To Brannen, the group seemed more like a group of nosey neighbors rather than anyone with information on the murder.

His attention was redirected by a knock on the frame of his open door. Justin Trembler, one of the deputies who was with the chain gang at Cypress Lake on Friday, stepped into his office and said, "Mornin', Captain."

"Mornin', Justin. What brings you in so early?"

"It's only ten minutes to roll call. It's not that early. I wanted to talk with you before everyone else started linin' up at your door."

This got Brannen's attention. "Okay. What's up?"

"Well, Captain, I was on duty with the chain gang at the lake. Right after that inmate saw the car in the lake, most everybody looked out at the lake to see what he was talking about. That is, except one particular inmate. Do you know who Billy Ray Duke is?"

"Yep. I busted him when he was just a fifteen-year-old kid. Hell, he's been in and out of the joint so many times, half the department knows him by his first name."

"Yep, he's the one. Well, when everyone else turned towards the lake, he turned away, looked anywhere but at that car. I thought that was kinda odd."

"How so?"

The young deputy thought for a moment. "It's kinda hard to explain. I mean, as soon as the one inmate pointed out that there was a car in the lake, everyone looked. The entire chain gang looked and locked eyes on the top of that car, like a magnet. But Billy Ray, he looked away. When he saw that I was looking at him, he started acting nervous, like he knew somethin', like he was guilty of somethin'."

"Well, he is guilty of being a drunk. Maybe that's all there is to it."

"That's not all, Captain. After a few minutes, we called dispatch, told 'em that we found the car, and asked for assistance. From that point on, Billy Ray stared at that car, even after we told the gang to get back to work cleaning the shore. He kept looking out at that car, as if he expected somethin' to rise up outta that lake. He looked…scared."

Brannen leaned back in his chair. What the young deputy just told him wasn't a crime. It wasn't even a good reason to question him, but it was enough to get him thinking. He knew Billy Ray lived near the lake in the trailer park. He also knew that he had lived there most of his life. He scratched his head, then rubbed his chin with his hand.

"When is Billy Ray scheduled to get out this time?"

"This afternoon, after lunch."

"Tell you what, can you tell Deputy Jones what you just told me, and let him know you spoke with me. Maybe Billy Ray needs a shadow for a few days."

"Yes, sir. I'll do that. Thanks, Captain."

* * *

At 9:40 AM, Monday morning, Captain Brannen knocked hard on MaryJo Saxon's trailer door. The entire wall of the trailer shook. He waited just a few seconds and knocked again with the same forceful hammering. Deputy Jones was at the base of the metal steps, smiling. After a moment, they heard the floor of the trailer creak as footsteps made their way from the back of the trailer to the living room. When the trailer door opened a crack and a woman peeked out, Brannen said, "Bulloch County Sheriff, ma'am. We need to ask you a few questions."

MaryJo Saxon appeared to have a terrible hangover. Her face was pale. The bags under her eyes were so dark that they looked as if she had been punched in both eyes. She asked, "'Bout what?"

"Ma'am, please open the door and allow us to come in and talk."

"Whatever."

The door was closed long enough for her to remove the safety chain, then it was opened wide. Brannen and Jones entered the dark living room and took a quick look around. The first thing that they noticed was the foul smell. A combination of stale beer, spilled booze, rotten food, and body odor assaulted their noses. Even at this early hour, the temperature inside the trailer was near ninety degrees. They were tempted to ask her if they could talk outside, but they thought that might draw the attention of the neighbors above and beyond the parked sheriff's car in front of her trailer. They looked at each other and Jones gave Brannen a rolling motion with his hand. *Let's get this moving as quickly as possible* was the message.

Brannen asked, "Are you MaryJo Saxon?"

MaryJo had plopped down in a chair that looked like the springs had failed years ago. When she hit the chair, a cloud of dust billowed into the air. "Yeah."

"Ms. Saxon, what can you tell us about the car that was pulled from the lake Friday?"

In an instant, her demeanor went from indifferent to hostile. "I don't know nuthin'. Is that nosey, old, bitch accusing me of something? She lost her mind years ago."

"Ms. Saxon, we're just askin' everyone in the neighborhood what they know. We're not accusing anyone of anything. So, what can you tell us?"

"I told ya, I don't know nuthin'."

"Back about fifteen years, did you have a boyfriend who drove a white Ford Tempo?"

MaryJo seemed to think for a moment. "That's a long time ago. I've had lots of boyfriends. I don't remember what they all drove."

"This boyfriend would have been from South Carolina, at least his car was. Does that jog your memory?"

"No, it don't jog nuthin'. What are y'all gettin' at? Y'all think I had somethin' to do with that mess by the lake?"

"Ma'am, we're just asking questions. Did you have a boyfriend who drove a white Ford Tempo that was registered in South Carolina?"

Jones was watching MaryJo's face closely as Brannen questioned her. He noticed her face getting paler. She looked like she might throw up at any moment. He was standing back, breathing through his mouth, trying to keep from getting sick himself. When she acted as if she hadn't heard the question, Jones leaned over and said to Brannen, "I think she's about to puke. Don't get too close."

Instead, MaryJo stood and moved quickly across the living room to the door. Before the men could do anything to stop her, she was out the door and down the steps, heading towards Millie Crider's trailer.

Both deputies were out the door, racing to get ahead of her. She was on the road half way to the old woman's trailer before they could get in front of her and block her path. Brannen ordered, "Stop!"

MaryJo tried to plow ahead, wedging herself between the officers, flailing her arms to try to make a path between them. She yelled, "Ya old bitch! Y'all quit lyin' about me! Ya got no right to accuse me of anything. Ya hear me?"

Brannen again ordered MaryJo to stop. "Ms. Saxon, stop now, or we're going to arrest you for disorderly conduct and assault on an officer. You back off now, ya hear?"

MaryJo yelled, "But she's tellin' lies about me! I'm the victim here, the victim of her lies! She's crazy…loony!"

"Ma'am, I'm not gonna tell you again! Turn around and go home!"

After a few more tense moments, she did. When they got inside, they made her promise that she wouldn't go over to Crider's trailer after they left. They also spent fifteen more minutes questioning MaryJo but got nothing new. After receiving a final assurance that she would not confront her neighbor, the men left and headed back to the sheriff's office.

On the way back, Jones wondered if they made a mistake leaving the neighborhood so soon after MaryJo's emotional outburst. He also understood that you can't babysit the entire community.

* * *

Billy Ray's session with the jailhouse Chaplain was interesting, far more so than he thought it would be. The priest with the Episcopalian Church in Statesboro, Father Roderick Ransom, had apparently taken some interest in Billy Ray's plight. He took the time to learn of his hobbies which, in jail, were few, but he did bring up Billy Ray's reading and that the jail staff believed him to be more intelligent than his lifestyle indicated.

Father Ransom asked, "Mr. Duke, who is your favorite author?"

The priest referred to himself as Father Rod. At first, Billy Ray was nervous speaking with him, but after a few moments, he became more relaxed, like he was speaking with a friend.

"I like Stephen King and John Sandford and pretty much anybody I can get my hands on in here. Oh, and Nicholas Sparks, too."

Father Rod smiled at his last response. Billy Ray's interest ran across quite a spectrum. He appeared surprised that a jail inmate liked authors ranging from horror stories to deeply personal, emotional tales.

"Mr. Duke…"

"Father, call me Billy Ray. All my friends do."

"Alright, Billy Ray. May I ask you a personal question or two?"

"That'd be alright, I guess."

"I noticed that you have a couple scars, one between your eyes and one on your left hand. How did you get them?"

Billy Ray thought for a moment. What would it hurt to tell him the truth? Father Rod was bound to secrecy, like doctor-patient confidentiality. The priest told him about this rule at the start of their conversation.

"My friends and I used to play in the woods near where I live. There's a tree that was kinda like our home base, like a clubhouse, but there's no buildin' or anythin' like that. Just a spot under the tree where we used to meet. One night, we was hanging out there, just goofin' around and we heard someone cryin' off in the distance." Billy Ray took a deep breath, becoming uneasy about breaking the silence. Was he violating their pact? Would this come back to haunt him and his friends?

Father Rod said, "If this is too personal, you don't have to tell me. You could just pray on it, you know, talk with God about it, then decide if telling me is a problem."

"Father Rod, I don't think I know how to pray. I ain't never done it. At least I don't reckon I have."

Father Rod paused for a moment, as if in thought about how best to instruct Billy Ray in the art of praying. He said, "You know how we're having this conversation?"

Billy Ray nodded.

"All you have to do is talk to God like you're talking to me. You don't have to talk out loud. You can just think about what you want to say. God will hear you, and if you're lucky, He'll answer you. It may not be in a voice like mine or yours, but He will answer."

Billy Ray wasn't sure if he understood, but he was willing to try. He said to Father Rod, "That night I was just talking about, that's when I got both these scars. We, my friends and me, was runnin' through the woods and I got whacked between the eyes by a tree branch. At the time, I didn't feel it, but one of my friends asked me if I was gonna bleed to death. Then I saw blood drippin' off my nose and got real scared. He told me I'd be alright, but I was still scared. Just after that, we made a promise, and one of my friends said that we had to make the promise in blood. He said we all had to cut our hands with our pocket knives and touch the tree with our bloody hands in the same spot. That way we sealed our promise with blood, and we can't tell anyone about the secret. That's how I got this scar."

Billy Ray abruptly stopped talking and rubbed the scar on his hand. Father Rod let the silence drag on, but Billy Ray would not open up and free himself from a lifelong secret that was tearing him up from the inside. He thought that Father Rod might be able to read his mind and know that this secret was the root of his self-destructive drinking. But as the silence dragged on, Billy Ray gained confidence that he should take the secret to his grave, just as Tommy and the others had promised.

Father Rod sat across from him, deep in thought, possibly trying to come up with a way to get him to tell the entire story. Finally, he asked, "Billy Ray, what if the pact was already broken by one of your friends?"

Billy Ray looked up in alarm. *Did Tommy, Andy, or Curtis already tell the cops what they saw? Were they listening to this conversation?* He was near panic.

Father Ransom noticed the fear in the young man's face and immediately went to assure him that he had no knowledge of any such breach of their pact. He held up his hands and said, "Listen, maybe keeping this secret was important, back when you were a young boy. But, maybe now, a pact made when you were eleven or twelve isn't that important anymore."

Billy Ray knew that Tommy and Andy went to Father Rod's Church. Could they have confessed to him already? Even if they did, is the pact broken if told in confidence to a priest?

Maybe I need to have that talk directly with God. What could it hurt?

Chapter 15

On Monday morning at 7:25, the sunrise was still young, but the day promised to be a repeat of the previous days: hot with no rain in sight. The air was trapped in a high-pressure system that simply would not move. The despair that gripped the collective souls of the community was bound to continue for at least the next several days.

Tommy Alexander stood at his kitchen window, staring out at his backyard. An untouched, lukewarm cup of coffee sat on the counter. His mind was again drawn to Cypress Lake. He was so far into his trance that he didn't hear his wife enter the kitchen.

Unconsciously, Tommy rubbed the scar that was a constant reminder of the pact made so long ago. For years, the pact had been at the back of his mind, always present, festering like a mild infection. Now the infection had come to a head, exposing the poison for everyone to see. If they couldn't hide the truth, there would be a price to pay. Of that, Tommy was certain. It was now a question of whether the secret would remain hidden, or if it would unfold for all the public to see.

"The girls are still getting ready for school. Just a few more days until…"

She stopped in mid-sentence when she noticed that her husband hadn't heard a word she said. She walked up behind him, as she had the previous Friday when he was in this same spot, staring out the window, the same worried posture, the same look of despair. She knew her husband was worried about more than the drought and wondered if there was another woman on his mind.

She was right behind him now. She said quietly, "Sweetheart, what's wrong?"

Hearing Cheryl's voice brought him back to the present. How long he had been in a trance, he couldn't guess. He turned to his wife and looked into her eyes. They were moist from the worry and loneliness that shown all over her, from her face to her body language. But it was the eyes that said it all. She was worried that their bond was weakening, that the love which brought them together was somehow not as strong. It tugged hard at his heart strings.

"Everything and nothing." He put his arms around her, held her close so she could feel his heartbeat, hoping that she could sense that what she feared, whatever had invaded her mind, wasn't the reason for his lack of focus on his business, his faith, and, most importantly, his family.

She looked up into his face and asked, "What can I do to make it right? I must be doing something wrong for you to be so…distant."

The desperate look in her eyes bore right through him. She looked vulnerable, afraid that her secure world was crumbling. He had to reassure her that everything would be fine, even if he didn't believe it himself.

He said, "I'm just having a hard time concentratin' on work right now, sweetie. I think this drought's got everyone…"

"You can't blame everything on the drought, Tommy. Everybody's facing the same thing." She paused for a moment, waiting to see if he had a response. He didn't reply. "Why are you and Andy acting so weird around each other when we get together, like there's some big secret between y'all."

There it was. Cheryl could see right through him. He might as well tell her the whole story. She and Cornelia were talking, and they were going to figure it out, sooner or later. He was thinking about the consequences of telling her the whole story when she spoke. With a serious look of concern on her face, in a near whisper, she asked, "Are you and Andy…lovers?"

The look of shock on his face must have been comical. He asked, "What?! Andy and me, gay?! Oh No, no, no...no, no, no."

With the pressure lifted, he began to laugh out loud. "Is that what you thought? Oh, sweetie, no. I'm not gay, and neither is Andy, as far as I know, anyway." He looked at his wife. She wasn't laughing.

"You both have that scar on your hands. I thought it might be some way that you two sealed your relationship way back."

So, she had noticed the scars. He wondered who else was taking note of the unusual "coincidence" of nearly identical scars on their hands. He had no idea how to explain the scars away so he remained silent.

"Well, then are you having an affair?"

His face turned dead serious. "Absolutely not. You are, and always will be, the only woman for me. Wild horses couldn't drag me away from you." He put his arms around her and pulled her in tight, hoping to erase her doubts. But now there was a decision to be made. The pact was causing problems in his marriage. Somehow, he had to keep it together better than he was doing now. He had to forget about the body, about the lake, about his friends, and about the fact that he was an accessory to murder. He didn't even know who the real killer was. From what he knew, it most likely was Carly Sue Hardy, but he didn't think she was the type to kill a man. But who else could it be? She was the only other person whom they saw at the lake. She was desperate to hide the body. All he knew for certain was that it wasn't him or any of his childhood friends.

He looked down at his wife. She had been watching him as he thought about his options. He had to tell her that she was right; something was bothering him, and it wasn't the drought, though the lack of rain played an unforgiving role.

Just then, he heard his daughters coming down the steps, heading for the kitchen. He realized that he hadn't put their lunches together so he kissed his wife lightly on the lips and broke free of her embrace. He whispered, "Let's talk later today."

She whispered back, "You bet we are, Mister."

"How about I come home for lunch today? I promise you we'll get everything on the table. But, Honey, I love you more now than ever. Don't you ever doubt that."

* * *

Captain Brannen spent most of the morning going over administrative paperwork for the department, trying to put that behind him so he could concentrate on the murder investigation. It wasn't working. He finally picked up the phone and punched in the number for the crime lab.

"Nikki Olsen."

"Hi, Nikki. Captain Brannen here."

"Calling for an update?"

"Yes. I know it's early, but what have you got so far?"

"Like, we don't have much to report yet, I'm afraid, but we have several tests in the works. And we're waiting on dental molds from the coroner's office. Like, we can run that through our databases and see if we get a hit. But the biggest thing we have so far is the gun and the bullet. We lifted the serial number from the gun and ran it through our state database. Unfortunately, we didn't get a hit."

"I thought you said it was the biggest thing you have."

"Well, like, it is in a way. The bullet was also not matched with any former crimes. Here's the thing. Like, if that gun has never been used in a crime, it might mean that the person we're looking for isn't a career criminal."

"How far back do your computer records go?"

He heard Nikki hit keys on a keyboard several times. She said, "Like, the oldest records are 2001. We're having college interns continue to add records, but right now, that's as far back as they go."

Brannen thought, *How much younger are they compared to you?* "That may not be back far enough. We're thinking that this murder may have occurred in 1999 or 2000, so that gun may have been out of circulation before your records even began." He paused. "What else have you got?"

"We did get a good DNA sample. It's being analyzed right now. We should have the results of the test this afternoon, then we'll compare it against Georgia's database. We can request South Carolina run the sample, too."

Brannen sighed. He had hoped for more progress but understood that testing and science and database searches took time. Like Sheriff Adkins, he was a big fan of accuracy, even if it required more time. "Okay, Nikki. Keep it up. Don't rush so fast that we make mistakes. This murder is old, so if it takes a little longer it won't hurt."

"Thanks, Captain. I wish I had better news. The remaining tests shouldn't take much longer."

Brannen was about to hang up when the technician said, "Oh, Captain, one other thing. In the trunk of the car we found a zipseal bag with some articles of clothing. It isn't normal clothes though. It's, like, gloves and booties."

"Gloves and booties?"

"They're, like, similar to ones used in hospitals or labs, but these are a little bit heavier than ones I'm used to seeing. And they're yellow."

"Yellow? What's the significance?"

"Yeah, like, I remember something from school about yellow being the color used for contamination protection. You know, radioactive contamination, but that was a long time ago."

Brannen thought, *You can't be that old. How long ago could it have been?* "So where would they use these types of gloves and booties?"

"I'm thinking, like, anyplace that handles radioactive waste. Power plants, hospitals that treat cancer patients with radiation, waste disposal sites. There may be others, but, like, that's all I can think of off the top of my head."

"Hmm. Okay, Nikki."

"One other thing, we're drying the algae on the car. We're trying some new techniques on the car's bumper to see if we can get some prints. It's a long shot, but some of these processes are pretty promising. The thing is, if we screw it up the first time, it destroys the prints. You, like, don't get a second chance. So, we're talking with the guy who invented the process to make sure we're following the instructions to the letter."

"Sounds interesting. Should I send one of our folks over to watch? Maybe do a show and tell with them?"

"If you can spare the manpower, it's fine with me, but it takes a pretty long time. Your call."

"I'll tell you what, if we can free up someone, they'll call and let you know. If you don't hear from us, don't wait. Regardless, call me with the results of your searches."

"Yes, sir, will do."

When he hung up his phone, Brannen thought about the car having South Carolina plates. Then he thought about the yellow booties and gloves. He remembered that the Barnwell low-level radioactive waste disposal facility was closed recently, but it was open for business back around the turn of the century. Could this guy have worked at Barnwell back then? If he did, that was good news. All workers in the nuclear industry were fingerprinted. They might have to get a warrant to access the database, but it was worth the trouble...if they could get a good set of prints. Now they had several avenues to identify the victim: DNA, dental records, the South Carolina BMV, and potentially, fingerprints. It was just a matter of which one was the quickest.

Relatively speaking, things were looking up.

Chapter 16

Tommy Alexander wasn't worried about the drought or the heat wave that wouldn't quit. He wasn't thinking about his customers or their problems. He wasn't thinking about his girls or that the school year was ending in four more days. He was on his way home for lunch, and he wasn't even concerned about what Cheryl had planned for their midday meal. He was focused on one thing as he pulled into his driveway: what was he going to tell the love of his life about his boyhood misadventures? That one night, August 26, 1999, and a snap judgment by a twelve-year-old boy, could spell the end of their lives as they knew it.

As he turned into his driveway, the garage door slid up, allowing him to park his car inside, protected from the scorching sun. With the car parked and the garage door closing behind him, he sat motionless, paralyzed by the task at hand. He thought about how easy it would be to leave the car running, open the windows, and just sit there until the fumes took over. But he wouldn't do that. He wouldn't leave his family like that, to face the disdain of their friends and the community at large. They would be left to search for answers to questions that they never knew existed. Why would he do it? What was so bad that he had to end his own life? Cheryl would be pitied, the woman whose husband chose the coward's way out.

The utility room door opened and Cheryl looked out. "Come on in, sweetie. Lunch'll be ready in just a minute."

He smiled, got out of the car, and headed for the kitchen, the fleeting thoughts of suicide left behind. He looked back at his car, smiled, and shook his head. *It isn't that bad.*

You've just been punishing yourself. Get over it. He bounded up the steps and met Cheryl in the kitchen with a short kiss.

"So, what have you got whipped up here?" he asked.

"Well, we had some steak left over from the barbeque, so I made some Philly Cheese Steaks, but with a little southern flare."

"Oh, I love the sound of that."

"You better taste it before you go tellin' everybody I'm the next Paula Deen."

"If it tastes anywhere near as good as it smells, it'll be fantastic. Anything I can help with?"

Cheryl smiled at Tommy. "Yes. Can you pour a couple glasses of tea?"

He did and joined Cheryl at the table. They said grace together, then arranged their napkins on their laps. The elephant was now in the room as the pleasantries were finished. After they each took a bite of their sandwiches and made the obligatory moans of satisfaction, Cheryl looked at her husband in anticipation.

Tommy looked at his wife and cleared his throat. He took another sip of tea as his throat seemed to close off and dry up. "You know, Andy and I were best friends back when we were in elementary school, right?"

"I gathered that by some of the stories your mom used to tell. Sounds like you were away from home more than you were there. Didn't you have a couple other friends, too?"

His wife had a great memory. There was no sense trying to hide the truth. "Yeah. Curtis Hardy and Billy Ray Duke. We hung out in the woods by this tree. It was kinda like our clubhouse. There wasn't a building, like a real clubhouse, but it was our secret place. We met there almost every day for a couple years."

"What kind of stuff did you do there?"

Tommy smiled. "You know, boy things. Stuff little girls can never know about." He frowned at his poor choice of words. "We played cops and robbers, cowboys and Indians, I Spy with My Big Eye. We told each other personal stuff.

Smoked our first cigarette. We even drank a beer...I mean, one single beer between all four of us. None of us liked it back then."

"That sounds like a great thing. Where is this tree?"

"Now that's a secret...or it was." He paused and realized that when he told her the location of the tree, she would put together the relevance to the murder. There would be no turning back. The time to break the vow of silence was upon him.

The lines on his face hardened. The light coming in through the kitchen window hit Cheryl's face, showing just how anxious she was to hear the rest of the tale. He took a deep breath and plowed ahead. "The tree is in the woods to the west of Cypress Lake Mobile Home Park. Billy Ray lived there. Still does. Andy and I were already friends back then. We were like nine years old and we rode our bikes everywhere. One day we rode out to the boat ramp on the lake. We used to catch tadpoles and frogs and watch the old, black men fish for carp."

Cheryl smiled as Tommy spun his yarn. She had never heard this story before, not from Tommy and not from his mother. She remained silent, coaxing him on.

"One day, when Andy and I were walkin' along the lake, these two other guys walked up and asked if we wanted to hunt for soda bottles, to make some money. We said, 'Sure.' That was how we met Billy Ray and Curtis. After that, we were all fast friends. Billy Ray said he knew a place that we could take all the bottles that we found and store 'em until we had enough to take to the store. That's when he led us to the tree."

"What's so special about this tree?"

Tommy smiled as he thought about the tree. Cheryl sat mesmerized by her husband's tale.

"The tree is at the edge of a clearing in the woods, a couple hundred yards southwest of the trailer park by the lake. The clearing is about twenty feet by fifteen feet. The tree stands alone in the clearing, but not in the center. It's kind of off to one side." He smiled with the face of a child. "The tree's main trunk was broken completely off about twenty feet above the ground. We don't know how. It was like that for as long as Billy Ray could remember. It had only two main branches off the main trunk: one to the left and one to the right. Those branches looked like arms, but one was angled higher than the other. Spanish moss hung from the branches like a gray robe. The branch on the left had another smaller branch that grew off at an angle that made it look like the grim reaper's sickle."

He looked at Cheryl. She was hanging on his every word. She asked, "Wasn't it scary meeting there at night?"

"Maybe for girls it would have been, but no girls were allowed." He smiled again, but his smile slowly faded. He was now at the point where he had to talk about the night of August 26, 1999. The story that had flowed so easily from his lips was now caught in his throat.

Cheryl noticed the change in his demeanor. He changed from a man telling a cute childhood story to a man having to deliver dreadful news. His eyes welled up. He took a deep breath. Cheryl didn't know what to expect, but suddenly she wasn't sure that she wanted to hear the rest.

Tommy sighed. "We were all at the tree on a Thursday night. We were having fun, but we were bummed out a little bit because school was starting up the following week. We knew that we wouldn't be having any late-night get-togethers at the tree during the week once school started. We heard this…"

The doorbell rang. Tommy stopped, looked at his wife, and asked, "Are you expecting anyone?"

"No."

"I can chase 'em off."

Tommy got up from the table and answered the door. It was Cornelia Pepperdine.

At first, he was a bit shocked, then quickly settled down, knowing that she wouldn't have any idea what he and Cheryl were discussing.

"Cornelia. Hi. Come on in." His tone was a bit too welcoming. "Cheryl's in the kitchen."

She walked past Tommy. "I'm surprised to see you home. Playin' hooky?"

"Nah, just stopped home for lunch with my dearest. How's Andy?"

She took a moment to answer. "He's fine, for the most part. I think he's got a lot on his mind these days, with the drought and all. A lot of our customers are havin' a dreadful time with crops and such."

"I understand."

As they reached the kitchen, Cheryl was already standing and greeted her friend with a hug and kisses on the cheek. "Hey, lady. What brings you out this way?"

"I was just in the area and was going to ask if you wanted to go out to lunch, but I see you already got a date."

Cheryl smiled at her husband and said, "Yep. We were just talking about old times. I think he needed a break from the office."

"I think Andy does, too, but he insists on working himself to death."

Tommy asked, "Since you're here and haven't eaten, can we fix you anything? I can whip up a southern Philly Cheesesteak. Cheryl already did the hard work."

Cornelia thought about it for a second. "Why not? Just make it half a sandwich though. I'm watching my weight."

Tommy rolled his eyes in an exaggerated manner. "Comin' right up."

Cheryl and Cornelia started talking as if Tommy wasn't even there, which suited him just fine. With any luck, he could escape the painful discussion that he planned to have about the pact, at least for now.

As he finished the sandwich and put it on a plate, Cheryl said, "Did you hear that, Tommy?"

"I'm sorry, dear. I was concentratin' on Cornelia's sandwich."

"Cornelia said that Andy is having a hard time keepin' his mind on his work. Keeps forgettin' things, and his mind is wanderin' a lot. I wonder what's goin' on?"

"Yeah, that's odd. He was always so focused. Has he said anything to you, Cornelia?"

"No, but he's goin' to. I plan to corner him tonight, after the kids go to bed."

Tommy took the opportunity to make his exit. He put Cornelia's plate in front of her, along with a glass of tea. "Hey, I'm gonna grab the rest of my sandwich and bag it up. I'll finish it at work. You two can catch up without me interfering."

Cheryl gave him a laser-like glare but realized there was no use fighting. Cornelia would be there for at least an hour, chatting about purses, clothes, their children, and their planned vacation for the week between Christmas and New Year's.

"Cornelia, let me walk my husband out to his car."

"Sure, sweetie."

When they reached the garage and Cheryl closed the door behind her, she turned to Tommy. "Nice move, Slick. But don't think for a minute that you're off the hook. You need to tell me the rest of your story."

All Tommy could say was, "Yes, dear."

* * *

Sheriff Adkins was at her desk, which was covered with notes on the Cypress Lake murder. She was hoping to put some of the puzzle together from pieces that were slowly trickling in. She was succeeding in only one thing: giving herself a headache.

Captain Brannen knocked on her door and walked in. "Hey, Sheriff. Got a headache?"

"How can you tell?"

"By the way you're rubbin' your temples. Like you're tryin' to poke a hole in the side of your head and pull the pain out."

She smiled. "It's getting' pretty bad. Readin' all this fine print isn't helpin' either. I see you got some more stuff for me to read?"

"Yes, ma'am. This here is from county records. The old lady, Millie Crider, owns all that land. It's been in her family for about forty-five years. She rents out the trailer lots through a management company. She ain't crazy, she's sharp as a razor, and crafty, too."

He handed Adkins the first piece of paper that he held. The sheriff looked it over for a moment. "That's a lot of acreage."

"We also checked her bank records and she sure don't need to be livin' in that run-down trailer she's in. She's worth over two million bucks. I was thinkin' about askin' her to marry me." He smiled.

Adkins cracked a slight smile through the pain of her headache. "While you're talkin' with your future wife, see if you can get her to tell you everything she knows about MaryJo Saxon and Billy Ray Duke. I have a feelin' that she knows what's goin' on here."

Brannen said, "I have a feelin' you're feelin' is right, Sheriff."

Chapter 17

The holding cell was more of a room than a jail cell. It was constructed of concrete block walls, a cement floor, and a solid plaster ceiling with a small ventilation duct. The room was quite cool, much more so than the general population area of the jail. The scent of industrial strength antiseptic cleaner filled the air. One wall had a large, one-way window. There were no frills. Three chairs and a single, round table, each anchored to the floor, were the only creature comforts. Since they were made completely of metal, they could hardly be called "comforts."

Billy Ray, already in blue jeans and a Trace Adkins tee shirt, sat in one chair facing the only door to the room. He was sipping water from a paper cup and reading the Stephen King novel that he had started the day before. The jailer in charge of the library told him he could take it and several others, if he liked. They had plenty of books in storage to replace them. Since he was one of the few inmates who actually read any of the books, he thought it was a good parting gift. Billy Ray showed genuine gratitude and took three others. He placed them in a bag with the large envelope that he was given containing his other personal belongings. One interview remained before his release…with Sheriff Adkins. He was told it might be delayed for about an hour. There was an emergent issue that needed the sheriff's attention, but they didn't want to put him back in the jail's general population. Billy Ray was content, sitting in the holding cell, reading Stephen King.

At the end of chapter seventeen, he paused, stood, and stretched. He saw his own reflection in the viewing window. He was twenty-seven years old, but he had lived a hard life.

The scar in the middle of his forehead looked like a white rectangle in the reflection. He laughed at his own image, thinking, *Who are you? You look like a beaten down, forty-year-old-drunk. Look at you. I don't give you ten more years.*

His mind was clear after ten days in jail without a drink, a toke from a joint, or any other drugs. He wasn't anxious to get out and face the real world because that world had not been kind to him since he was a child. Or, more accurately, he had never given real life a chance. Ever since he was eleven years old, he had been his own worst enemy.

Here he was, at another crossroads, one he had faced many times before. He had no confidence that he could thrive on the outside. Hell, he wasn't sure that he could survive, much less thrive. He owned the trailer at Cypress Lakes Mobile Home Park, free and clear. Somehow, there was an arrangement with the park's management that his lot rent was covered as long as he lived in the trailer. All the utilities and trash pickup, even a small homeowner's insurance policy was covered. He had no idea how it had come about. His parents were killed when he was just four years old. A young couple had cared for him in his parent's trailer until he was sixteen. They left one day and never came back, leaving Billy Ray to fend for himself.

His entire life was a blur. The young couple, his "guardians," were no more than glorified babysitters. By the time he was fourteen, he spent very little time at the trailer. He was always out in the woods, smoking cigarettes or dope, or drinking beer. He hung out at Cypress Lake, watching the old black folks fishing for their next meal. They were his friends back then. They shared their port wine and beer with him. In turn, he would bring them peanut butter sandwiches, and sometimes beer, if he could find someone of age to buy it for him. As the folks fished for food, he watched the lake, wondering if one of the anglers would latch onto a white car and drag it to shore. For months, he was drawn to the lake, like some telepathic command. His tension level would rise when one of the fishermen snagged his line and worked hard to either free it or pull in the offending object. He was sure that they would pull in a severed finger or an ear. He was mortified by that possibility, so he started to drink to forget. The more he drank, the more intense the paranoia became. So, he drank more and the cycle continued. Over time, he began to black out. When he did, his friends by the lake would watch over him until he could manage to get up and go home. One day, they thought he was dead, so they flagged down a car and asked the driver to call an ambulance. Instead of an ambulance, a Bulloch County Sheriff's Deputy showed up. The deputy was able to rouse him and he was charged with public intoxication. From there, he became a regular in the drunk-tank, first at the juvenile detention center, then at the Bulloch County Jail.

Whenever Billy Ray was free, he spent a lot of time at the tree. By the time he turned eighteen, he spent more time in the woods than he did at the trailer, unless he needed beer or dope. Then he would make the trek through the woods to his trailer, pick up his distraction of choice and head back to the tree.

The bare spot on the tree looked much the same as it did on the night of August 26, 1999. The bark was still bare and the dark stain remained, even after years of rain, heat, cold, and more rain. It still oozed dark, thick sap, like a wound that would never heal, like the scars on Billy Ray's mind that were ripped open every time he thought about that night. No matter how he medicated his brain, either with alcohol, weed, or pills, the scars wouldn't heal over.

What had Father Rod said? Talk with God. He will answer. But what will he say?

Maybe I need to talk with Tommy, Andy, and Curtis. But what if they've already spilled their guts and decided to pin this whole thing on me? What if Curtis already talked with Carly Sue? They never came back to the tree after that night. My friends...ha! They left me out there to fend off them demons alone, and look what it got me. Some friends. Maybe this has gone on too long. I think I need to talk to them. Tommy was always the one who made decisions for us. I'm gonna start with him.

Billy Ray was jarred from his thoughts when the holding cell door opened. Sheriff Adkins and Captain Brannen walked in. Both looked at Billy without smiling. They all knew each other from similar meetings in the past. Without a word, the sheriff and the captain took seats across from him.

This encounter seemed different than other pre-release meetings, which were at times very serious matters, admonishing Billy Ray for his public intoxication. Other times they were almost joking with him, telling him that they would see him soon, after his next binge. This time, they were solemn, almost like they were attending his funeral. Without a reason, their demeanor sent a shiver down his spine.

The sheriff put a manila folder on the table that probably contained his release papers. He had done this so many times before that he knew the forms by heart: details of the consequences if he violated his most recent parole conditions, where he should sign, where a representative of the sheriff's office would sign as a witness.

Sheriff Adkins looked right at Billy Ray and said, "We've been here before, Billy Ray. I'm not gonna waste your time and mine readin' over this paper. I figure that you're just gonna get out and do what you do best. That's get yourself all drunked-up and come right back and see us again. One of these days, you're gonna hurt someone other than yourself and there'll be hell to pay, but I'm not gonna lecture you. You've gotta figure that one out on your own. But there is one thing we've got to talk about before you leave us."

Billy Ray's eyes squinted as he looked from Sheriff Adkins to Captain Brannen. This was a new twist. He asked, "What's that, Sheriff?"

"Well, you were on the work crew at the lake when they pulled that car up and found the body. Someone told us that you seemed real concerned about that car when it was spotted. Said that, at first, you wouldn't look at it. Everybody else turned and looked. They said you acted like you already knew it was there. Then when everybody else went back to work, you stared at it as if the devil himself might rise up outta that car."

The sheriff stopped talking. She and Brannen stared at him, looking for any signs that might give them a clue as to what he might know. They knew about his rough life and that he lived in the trailer park since his birth. Half the deputies on the force had given him a ride back to his trailer after being picked up for public intoxication. It wasn't too much of a stretch that he knew something about the murder.

Billy Ray showed no sign of panic, no outward twitches or eye movements. He was rock steady, sober, and wanting nothing more than to leave the Bulloch County Jail. The silent standoff went on for nearly a full minute. Billy Ray stared at Sheriff Adkins. He didn't look at Brannen at all. He figured Brannen was just there to show a little muscle, maybe try to rattle him into admitting something that he otherwise might not say with just Adkins in the room. Billy Ray stuck to his guns and remained silent.

Finally, Adkins asked him point blank, "Billy Ray, do you know anything about how that car ended up in that lake?"

"No, ma'am, I don't."

That was it. Sheriff Adkins took out the forms and pushed them across the table. He signed and dated the forms. He pushed them back across the table to the sheriff who passed them on to Brannen who co-signed the papers and placed them back in the folder.

Adkins said, "Billy Ray, you are free to go."

"Thank you, ma'am."

Brannen walked Billy Ray to his waiting patrol car and told him to jump in the front passenger side. He was giving him a ride to the trailer park, unless there was somewhere else he wanted to go.

Billy Ray said, "Take me to Trinity Episcopal Church."

* * *

Billy Ray stood outside in the bright, hot sun at the front doors to the Trinity Episcopal Church. He was nervous but had no idea why. He had never been to a church in his life and wasn't sure if there was a procedure he was supposed to follow to gain entry. Father Rod told him that all are welcome, that God did not care what you had done in the past. *As long as you talk with Him and ask for forgiveness, and are truly sorry for your sins, you are welcome in His house.*

Billy Ray found it hard to believe that God was that forgiving. He didn't know any humans who were like that. Most people he knew were quick to point a finger and highlight your shortcomings. Father Rod was the only man who told him anything about God and religion.

During their talk back at the jail the other day, Billy Ray had told Father Rod that he tried to read the Bible once, but it was so difficult to follow that he stopped after just a few pages. The priest had smiled and said that he needed to read a version of the Bible that was interpreted by theology scholars. It was written in a language that was easier to understand. Billy Ray still planned to look for such a version.

The heat outside the church was getting unbearable. Taking a deep breath, he opened the large, oak door, surprised that it was unlocked, and walked into the vestibule. The door closed behind him with a dull thud which echoed inside the cavernous, empty church. He took eight steps and he was at the back of the sanctuary. Five more steps and he took a seat in the very last pew on the right.

Billy Ray looked around the church at the beautiful stained-glass windows, the beautiful wooden arcs in the ceiling, and the statues of various saints, a woman holding a baby, and a man nailed to a cross. It was all so new to him that he momentarily forgot why he was there. He sat in awe in the silence, then shook his head to clear the cobwebs.

It was peaceful and he felt calm, not threatened. He wasn't sure if he should talk out loud or if he should talk to God in his mind. He figured that no one was there to listen, other than God, so he said quietly, "God, I done some really stupid things in my life. I got the scars to show for it. But if I hurt anyone, I'm really sorry. Maybe I should'a come forward and told the police what we done back when we was kids. We just thought it best if we kept quiet. Maybe Tommy was right, maybe not. But we all agreed, it was what we were gonna do. And I ain't telling anyone about this…well, except you.

"I wanna do right, God. I wanna stop drinkin' too much. I wanna stop the pills and stuff, too. Maybe you can give me a hand with that." Billy Ray remained silent with his eyes closed for nearly five minutes while he thought about what he should do next. He said, "I should talk with my friends, clear the air. Maybe we won't have to talk about that night, but at least I can find out if the pact is still holdin' up."

When he opened his eyes, the sun was shining through one of the stained-glass windows. He looked down at his chest. The sunlight through the window was in the shape of a heart in the center of his chest. A warm feeling spread throughout his body and he smiled for the first time in years.

Chapter 18

By late Monday afternoon, Eugene Morris' first follow-up article to the Cypress Lake murder was nearly complete. The story asked more questions than it answered, but it was a good continuation of the initial murder report. It might give the Bulloch County Sheriff's Office more to ponder. There were just a few more interviews left before he e-mailed it to his editor. He would then fight to get the story on the front page. Sometimes when the initial story is front page news, any follow-on stories are relegated to the *Cops and Crimes* section. The story would be chopped to pieces, only a fraction of the article making it to print.

Morris turned into the Cypress Lake Mobile Home Park and parked in Ms. Virginia Hardy's driveway. As he approached the trailer's door, a woman looked out the window, giving her visitor a quick appraisal. She opened the door as he was about to knock.

He held his press badge for her to see as he said, "Ms. Virginia Hardy?"

"Yes. Call me Ginny. I see that you're Gene Morris. Come on in." As Morris stepped into her living room, she asked, "Can I get you somethin' cold to drink?"

"Would you happen to have some sweet tea?"

"Yes, I do. Comin' right up. Take a seat there at the table if you like." She pointed to a table in the eat-in area of the kitchen.

Morris looked around the tidy trailer as he sat. Ginny Hardy kept her trailer neat and clean, the curtains open, allowing light to spill in. She had central air conditioning which was doing a great job keeping the kitchen cool. Her trailer was far and away neater, cleaner, and felt more like a home than the other three trailers Morris had been in over the last two days.

He looked at Ginny Hardy and guessed that she was about forty-five years old. Like her home, she kept herself well groomed, tidy. She was slim, though she did carry a bit of weight about her hips. She wore a pair of light slacks and a white, button-up blouse. Her hair was dark, streaked with gray and up in a bun at the back of her head. A pair of reading glasses and a book sat on the counter, positioned so that she could grab them whether she was in the kitchen or the living room.

As Ginny Hardy set a glass of ice-tea in front of Morris she said, "I seen you walking through the park the other day. I thought you might stop by then."

"I planned to, but I got tied up with Millie. She's somethin' else."

Hardy smiled as she took a seat. "Yes, she is." She set her own glass of tea on the table.

Morris wanted to be cautious in the way he asked about her son, Curtis. He wanted her to open up. "I understand that your son is married to your neighbor's daughter."

Ginny stared at him for a moment as she took a deep breath. Her expression was neutral, not smiling, not frowning, almost as if she was resolved to not show any emotion. "Yes, he is. Curtis and Carly Sue have been married for ten or eleven years now."

"I'm sorry. I meant to ask, is there a Mr. Hardy?"

"No. I got pregnant with Curtis when I was in high school. Curtis' father never acknowledged us. He's never been a part of our lives."

"I'm sorry." He paused to let the moment pass. "How long have you lived here in the park?"

"Let's see. I've lived in this here trailer since about 1985. I got some advice that it would be a good idea to buy a trailer instead of renting an apartment. It turned out pretty good for us. It's been paid off for quite a while now. I just have to pay lot rent, which is a whole lot cheaper than renting an apartment. Overall, expenses are pretty low compared to what I reckon other folks face."

Morris thought that Ginny Hardy was rambling on a bit nervously. He decided to go right to the heart of the matter. "Do you know anything about the body that was pulled from the lake on Friday?"

She was apparently ready for this question. She said, "The police asked me already. I told them that I don't know anything." She looked at Morris as if she was going to continue, but was reluctant to say anything more.

Morris tried to prod her by saying, "But…"

"I'm not a gossip and I'm not a gambling woman. I think both are sins, but if I was a gambler, I'd put money on MaryJo being involved somehow."

Ginny looked down at her hands as if asking forgiveness for her loose lips. Her cheeks colored a bit and she took a quick sip of tea. Morris thought that she might be washing the bad taste of gossip, or maybe a lie, from her mouth.

Over the next few minutes they discussed why she felt that way. Ginny told him the stories, almost identical to the ones he had been told by Millie Crider, that MaryJo Saxon was a loose woman, but her men seemed more interested in her daughter than they were in her. That MaryJo blamed her young daughter for chasing her boyfriends away, even for seducing them.

Morris was beginning to believe that he was honing in on some important information and asked, "Do you get along okay with Carly Sue's mother?"

A frown momentarily flashed on Ginny Hardy's face. She started to reply, then paused to think. "MaryJo Saxon don't get along with no one. We don't speak. Even her daughter…" She stopped and looked down at her hands again. "I'm sorry. You should ask Carly Sue about her and her mother's relationship."

Morris stood and thanked Ginny Hardy for the tea and her time. He asked if she minded him leaving his car in her driveway while he made his rounds of the neighbors. She said that it was fine.

Morris looked at his watch as he stepped off the small patio next to Ginny Hardy's trailer. It was now 4:50 PM. He cursed that the trees in the park were so thin that they provided very little protection from the sun. The heat was still oppressive and sweat began to bead on his forehead as he took his first steps towards Billy Ray Duke's trailer. He had to pass MaryJo Saxon's trailer to get to Billy Ray's. As he walked by, he kept his eyes averted hoping that she wouldn't see him pass. He knocked on Billy Ray's trailer door and heard footsteps creaking on the floor. The door opened and a clean-shaven man with a pale looking scar on his forehead answered.

"Can I help you?"

"I'm Gene Morris with the *Statesboro Herald*." As he gave his spiel, he showed Billy Ray his credentials. "Are you Billy Ray Duke?"

"Yes, sir."

"Can I ask you some questions about the body pulled from the lake?"

Billy Ray's body visibly tensed. Morris could see in Billy Ray's eyes that he would rather not talk, but he said, "Yes, sir. Come on in."

When Morris got inside, Billy Ray shut the door behind him. Morris immediately noticed a dry, stale odor as if the trailer had been closed up for some time. A wall air conditioner was running, struggling to keep ahead of the assault by the outside heat. The kitchen counter was dusty, but clean dishes were drying in a rack next to the sink. An eight by ten photograph showed a happy, middle-aged couple posing for the studio shot. The colors in the photo were faded, a sign that the picture was from years ago. The man in the photo bore a slight resemblance to Billy Ray.

He said, "Have a seat. Sorry for the mess. I've been away for a while. I'm just gettin' started cleanin' up."

"That's alright. Mind if I ask where you've been?"

"I don't mind. You're a reporter. You're gonna find out sooner or later anyway. I was in the Bulloch County Jail for public intoxication."

Morris didn't make much of the revelation. He gave Billy Ray a look that said, *We all make mistakes.*

Billy Ray said, "What is it y'all want to know about the body they fished outta the lake?"

"First, how long have you lived in the park?"

"All my life. My parents owned the trailer." He nodded towards the picture that Morris had looked at moments before. "When they was killed, it was passed on to me."

Morris nodded. "Okay. So, you would have lived here when the murder took place back around 1999 or 2000?"

"Yep."

"Do you remember anything unusual that happened around then that might be related to the murder?"

"Nope."

"Are you sure?"

Billy Ray paused for a moment. "Yep."

Morris watched his eyes as he answered. There was very little emotion; no fear, no looking away as he spoke, no guilt. He waited, hoping to unnerve the young man, but Billy Ray remained silent and calm.

When the silence moved from awkward to ridiculous, Billy Ray said, "Mr. Morris, I just got out of jail. I went in drunk as a skunk; so drunk, in fact, that I don't remember being processed in. Right now, I am stone-cold sober. I am gonna try like hell to stay this way." He paused for a moment. "I don't remember what I did two weeks ago. I sure as hell don't remember somethin' from fifteen years ago." Another pause. "Do you know where I can get a paying job?"

The question surprised Morris. He wondered if Billy Ray was trying to change the subject or if he was serious? He said, "You know, there was a time in my life that I drank way too much. I needed help to get off the booze. I'm not a big fan of AA, but I've got to admit, they helped me. I still know a couple guys who go religiously." He paused again. "How serious are you about staying sober?"

"Very. I'm gonna die if I don't do somethin' soon."

"Do you want me to have them contact you?"

Billy Ray thought about this for a moment. "Yes. Yes, I do."

Morris took one more shot at trying to pry information from Billy Ray. It didn't work.

* * *

Eugene Morris was on the last leg of his journey into Cypress Lake Mobile Home Park. He back-tracked to MaryJo Saxon's trailer. Looking around at the clutter and junk outside the trailer, he was fearful of the things he would see if MaryJo let him into her home. There was an old charcoal grill that was rusted through the bottom and two beat up, rusted, metal trash cans that were overflowing with bags of trash. Shattered glass from at least one broken liquor bottle was scattered across the cracked concrete.

The steps to the trailer's door were rusted metal mesh. Morris took a close look before he ventured up the two steps to the equally challenged, four-foot-by-four-foot platform constructed of the same material. The whole thing creaked with each step. He knocked on the door, stood back, then heard movement in the trailer. When the door opened, Morris was taken aback by the woman staring back at him. She looked about sixty years old with bloodshot eyes, graying hair that was dry and frizzy, flat on one side, as if she had slept on it, and strewn in all directions on the other side. It was evident that she had been asleep.

"Whatdya want?" she asked in a hoarse, quiet voice.

Morris could smell the alcohol on her breath from three feet away. He was rethinking his plan to talk with MaryJo. He wasn't sure what to say for a moment.

"Whatdya want?" MaryJo asked louder and with more force.

"I'm Eugene Morris with the *Statesboro Herald*." He held his credentials up so she could read the badge, but he didn't believe she could read anything at the moment. "I wanted to ask you about the murder at the lake."

MaryJo's entire demeanor changed in an instant. Her expression became vicious, and she sneered at the reporter. She opened the door wide and pointed a curled finger at his face. In a guttural voice that sounded more like a wild animal's growl, she shouted, "I don't know nuthin' 'bout no murder! But I can tell ya who does! Them boys! Them boys who was always chasin' my daughter!" She took a step towards Morris, her finger still pointing at his face. "Y'all should go ask 'em! They was all at the lake! They was all tryin' to get in my little girl's pants! Just ask 'em! And when you see 'em, tell 'em they's gonna pay for that!"

Morris was shocked. He stared at MaryJo, afraid to take a step backwards, fearing that he might fall off the platform, or fall through the rickety wire mesh. He hadn't been able to take any notes because he didn't want to take his eyes off the crazed woman as she inched towards him, still shaking her crooked finger. He was trying to gather his thoughts and ask for the names of the boys she was talking about, but she beat him to it.

"Y'all can start with Carly Sue's husband, Curtis Hardy! Him and his friends know! Him and that Tommy Alexander, and Andy Peppin – or whatever his name is – and Billy Ray! They was all there! Y'all ask 'em! And you tell the sheriff to leave me alone! I ain't done nuthin' wrong. Nuthin'!" She looked down, dropped her arms to her side, and started to cry.

Morris was too stunned to feel sorry for the woman. He was about to ask if there was anything he could do for her when she looked back up and growled, "And you tell that old bitch across the way to stop spyin' on me and leave me alone!" She looked across the road and pointed her shaking finger at Millie Crider's trailer. She shouted, "I'm talkin' 'bout you, ya nosey bitch! Stay outta my life! Ya hear me?! Stay outta my life!"

When she finished her tirade, she stumbled back inside her trailer and slammed the door. The entire structure shook violently.

Morris stood there for a moment, his mouth agape, wide-eyed, staring at the closed door. MaryJo's sobs were loud, even with the trailer door closed. He had to take a deep breath, thinking, *What the hell just happened?* When he finally moved, he looked across the road at Millie Crider's trailer. He saw the old woman looking at him through her binoculars. Then he turned towards Ginny Hardy's trailer. She was looking at him from her living room window. He wondered if Billy Ray had heard MaryJo's rant, but thought anyone in the trailer park who hadn't heard her was deaf or dead.

Back to his car, he wrote down four names under the heading "Friends." Curtis Hardy, Tommy Alexander, Andy P., and Billy Ray. He thought, *I better talk with Billy Ray again.* Then he thought, *And Millie Crider.*

Maybe I'd better be more cautious with a killer on the loose.

Chapter 19

Though he had already worked for more than twelve hours, Tommy Alexander's long day wasn't over. At 7:30 PM he walked into the kitchen. The aroma of baked chicken and something with butter, onions, and sour cream filled the air. A smile glinted on his face, despite his tension.

The drive home was short, but his mind raced the entire trip. Earlier in the day, he had started to tell his wife that he and his friends helped push a dead body into Cypress Lake when Cornelia Pepperdine showed up. At the time, he thought the intrusion was a blessing. But his afternoon was consumed with worry. Would he still have the nerve to tell his wife about his part in a horrific crime? He still didn't know who the real killer was, though Carly Sue was obviously high on the list of suspects, at least in his mind.

Cheryl greeted him with a tentative, nervous smile and a short kiss on the lips. Quietly, she said, "The girls are with Mom and Dad at the movies. Can I get you a drink?"

Tommy smiled at his wife's forethought. She had cleared the house so that they could continue their discussion without interruption and without fear that their daughters would accidentally overhear their father's story.

He said, "I'd like a whiskey, on the rocks, and a glass of water on the side."

Cheryl smiled again. "Coming right up. Oh, and dinner's on the dining room table. I'll be in with your drink in just a minute."

When they were seated, the blessing complete, and their first, nervous bites behind them, Cheryl asked, "Are you sure you want to tell me the rest of that story? You looked like you lost your best friend back then."

Tommy looked Cheryl in the eyes, took a deep breath, and said, "I can't do it anymore. I'm the one who said we had to take the secret to our graves...but...I just can't." Tommy's eyes welled with tears, his body shook, and his voice choked on the last words. He set his fork and knife on the table and clenched his fists, looking away from his wife, first at the ceiling, then around the room. He picked up his napkin, covered his eyes, and put his elbows down hard on the table.

Cheryl waited, not saying a word. She felt her husband's pain, wishing she could hold him and will the pain away, but she knew he had to face this demon, to exorcise it from his soul. She feared what the next few minutes would expose.

After several excruciating minutes, Tommy's gaze finally made its way back to Cheryl's. He took a deep breath. "We heard her crying off in the distance. I heard it first. Then we all heard her. From our tree, it was real quiet and sounded like a cat crying or something. It didn't really sound human, but we knew it was. I told the guys to follow me.

"We made our way through the woods, crossed Cypress Lake Road, then down the boat ramp path. The closer we got, the louder the crying got. The girl was crying, saying, 'Help me, please, help me,' mixed in with sobs. We could tell something happened to her. She was so upset."

Cheryl sat perfectly still, listening as her husband told a story that had remained buried in the back of his mind for years. When he started the story, he had trouble keeping his thoughts together, pausing, taking deep breaths. As the story progressed, he seemed more relaxed, resigned to the fact that he was breaking his silence, that the pact was no more.

"When we got to the lake, there was a car there, facing the lake, right near the shoreline. The girl was sittin' with her back to the rear bumper. She was covered in mud. At first, she didn't see us walk up, and she kept crying for someone to help her. When she finally opened her eyes, she was startled to see us. She panicked. But I told her that we'd help her, but we didn't know what she wanted." Tommy shrugged his shoulders as if he was back at the lake, not knowing how he could help. "She said, 'Help me,' then she looked at the car. I asked her, 'Help you what?' She said, 'Push the car.' I scratched my head and asked, 'You want us to push the car into the lake?' The other guys laughed a little, like it was a joke, but she started crying again and nodded.

"We all agreed, but when we tried to push the car, it wouldn't budge." Tommy paused and took a deep breath. He was looking at a spot across the dining room but saw only the dead man with blood running down the side of his head.

Cheryl remained silent, holding her breath. She dreaded what came next, seeing her husband in such a state.

Tommy continued his monologue. "When the car wouldn't move, I figured that it was still in gear. Daddy taught me how to put a car in neutral if it had to be moved without starting the engine. So, I went to the driver's side door. The window was down. That's when I saw him." Tommy's body shivered involuntarily, and his eyebrows shot up.

Tommy stopped talking for so long that Cheryl wondered if he would continue. She feared that she knew what was coming next and asked, "Saw who, dear?"

Tommy looked at his wife like she had just appeared out of nowhere. His stare was still blank, but he was now facing her. "I don't know who he was. I'd never seen him before. All I know for sure is that he was dead."

Cheryl inhaled loudly, her hand quickly covering her mouth, her eyes widened in shock. In a near whisper, she said, "Oh my God! The body!"

The room remained silent for several seconds as Cheryl's shock worked its way from her brain throughout her entire being. A million thoughts collided, none making any sense. She realized that her body was shaking as she fought to regain control of her senses. After several deep breaths, she looked at her husband. He was calm, but his face was devoid of any emotion.

Tommy focused on Cheryl for the first time since starting the story and said, "We helped push that car into the lake and vowed that we'd never talk about it again, the rest of our lives." Tommy raised his left hand and showed Cheryl the scar on his palm. "We swore in blood on the tree."

Cheryl looked at the scar and remembered that Andy Pepperdine had a similar scar in the same place, on his left hand. She now understood why Tommy and Andy acted uncomfortable around each other. They had a secret that overshadowed everything.

But the secret was out. The drought forced their hands by uncovering evidence of an apparent murder, a murder that her husband helped cover up. She was just beginning to understand the gravity of his confession. How could he put his family in jeopardy like this? He knew about this crime for all these years. Then she realized that she was talking about a twelve-year-old kid who stumbled across a crime and was trying to do the right thing by helping a little girl. By the time he realized what he and his friends had done, it was too late to just walk away.

"Tommy, the girl, the one who wanted the dead guy pushed into the lake…?"

The unfinished question hung in the air. Tommy turned to his wife, his eyes focused. Without expression, he said, "Carly Sue Saxon."

* * *

Eugene Morris was still shaken by his visit with MaryJo Saxon. After leaving the mobile home park, he went home and plopped down in front of his computer. He was tempted to stop at the neighborhood bar but fought the urge, remembering his talk with Billy Ray Duke and the young man's struggle with alcohol. He knew it wasn't a good idea to consume even one drink. One usually led to another and he couldn't afford to go down that dark path again.

He pulled out his notebook and flipped to the page where he had jotted down notes from his discussion with residents of the trailer park. Thinking about his encounter with MaryJo, he put his pen to paper. Under her name, he wrote *"Frightening."* After taking a deep breath, he tried to concentrate on what the crazed woman had said. He looked at the four names that MaryJo had spat out during their encounter: Curtis Hardy, Tommy Alexander, Andy Pip-*something*, and Billy Ray Duke. She had accused them of trying to "...*get into my little girl's pants*." He wondered how Curtis Hardy felt about that since Carly Sue was now his wife. *Were the boys friends back then? How old were they? In 2001 they were what...ten to twelve years old?*

He thought about Ginny Hardy, Curtis' mother. She appeared to be prim and proper, a God-fearing woman. She was courteous and kind, well dressed in a plain pair of slacks and a white blouse, and kept her modest trailer clean and well maintained. Morris felt that she was nervous, possibly holding something back, but that might have been her desire to refrain from any gossip. She did reveal that Curtis was born out of wedlock, but many young girls make mistakes when it comes to what they believe is love.

Had Ginny Hardy and MaryJo Saxon, two neighbors for years, now related by marriage, always been hostile towards each other or had the discovery of the body ignited a long-simmering, hostile feeling? Was it true that MaryJo had no friends? Did she have other relatives besides Carly Sue? Was Carly Sue's relationship with her mother cordial, cool, or hostile?

Morris started writing a few notes, then switched to his computer, realizing that he would fill the notepad. He typed three full pages of questions and notes about the residents of the trailer park. Noting the family ties between Ginny Hardy and her son, Curtis, and Curtis' marriage to Carly Sue Saxon, MaryJo Saxon's daughter, he wondered if there were other family ties at the park. It might be worth a records search at the county. Then a thought occurred to him that maybe the sheriff's office had already completed the search. He looked at the time on his computer: 8:27 PM. *No sense calling the sheriff now. That'll have to wait until morning.*

Morris crawled into bed, but sleep eluded him. He went back to his computer, reviewed his notes, and typed out several pages with varying possibilities. All of the scenarios came back to residents of the trailer park, particularly MaryJo Saxon, Carly Sue Hardy, and Billy Ray Duke and his friends. He needed more pieces of the puzzle, but he was beginning to get a general picture in his mind. He reminded himself that this was a murder investigation regardless of how long ago the crime occurred. Someone, or several people, killed a man and tried to hide his body. Extreme caution was warranted.

* * *

At 8:15 AM on Tuesday morning, Eugene Morris pulled out his cell phone, found the contact number for the Bulloch County Sheriff and hit dial. When the phone was answered at the end of the first ring, he asked for Captain Brannen. In less than ten seconds, the captain was on the line.

"What can you do for me, Eugene?"

"Well, Gerry, that depends. Maybe we can do a little horse tradin'. I got some info that you might be interested in, but I need to ask you a question."

"I'm listenin'."

Morris hesitated while he thought how to phrase his question. "What can you tell me about these four names? Tommy Alexander. Curtis Hardy, Andy Pepp-something, and Billy Ray Duke."

Brannen was quiet for a few moments, either thinking about what information was safe to release or trying to recall the names at all. Morris believed that he certainly should know something about Billy Ray Duke and most likely Curtis Hardy. The other two may still be off the sheriff's radar.

"Eugene, I can tell you that we know Billy Ray real well. Hell, he practically lives at the jail. Most all the deputies know him on a first-name basis. Why the interest in the other three?"

"Well, I spoke to MaryJo Saxon at the trailer park…"

Brannen smiled and cut him off, "Ain't she a darlin'? Did you ask her out?"

"That's real funny, Gerry. I'm still traumatized. One scary woman. She was screamin' somethin' about them four boys always tryin' to get into her daughter's pants. Said they would know something about the murder, maybe even know the guy's name."

Morris heard Brannen shift in his chair and shuffle some papers on his end of the phone. Brannen asked, "Besides Billy Ray, what were the boy's names?"

Morris proceeded to tell Captain Brannen the names of the boys. "So, are you guys thinkin' that the killer or killers might still live at the trailer park?"

"I'll tell ya, Eugene, there sure seems to be a lot of finger-pointin' goin' on out there." Brannen paused for a moment. "I'm gonna tell you something that you need to keep under your hat. You'd figure it out on your own soon enough, but you can't say it came from me."

Morris' interest was piqued. "Y'all have my word, Gerry. Shoot."

In barely more than a whisper, Brannen told the reporter that Millie Crider owned the Cypress Lakes Mobile Home Park and the surrounding land and that she was worth in excess of two million dollars. Morris' eyes popped wide open. He had been in Millie Crider's trailer and she didn't appear to have two spare nickels to rub together.

In a skeptical voice, he asked, "Are you sure you're talkin' about the same Millie Crider?"

"Yup. I'm thinkin' that we could help each other out here. You find out all you can about ole Millie and let me know and I'll do a little diggin' about them boys...well, I guess they're men now. Deal?"

Morris didn't hesitate. "Deal."

As he was about to click off the call, he remembered that Millie Crider had given him the license plate number of the Ford Tempo. He said, "Hey, Gerry, you still there?"

"Yeah, Gene."

"When I spoke with Ms. Crider, she gave me a license plate number that she says was for the Tempo that y'all pulled from the lake." He flipped through his notepad as he spoke. When he found it, he read it off to Brannen.

Brannen replied, "The numbers match the partial plate numbers that we have. I'll follow up with the lab. Thanks, Gene."

Morris had thought that the trailer park was the epicenter of the investigation, now he had confirmation that the sheriff's office had the same inkling. He reminded himself of his earlier thoughts that he might be very close to the killer. *Time to be extra careful.*

Chapter 20

Early Tuesday morning, Tommy Alexander pulled off Cypress Lake Road at the trail that led to the makeshift boat ramp. He had driven past the turn-off three times before getting the courage to head back towards the lake. He was still conflicted, asking himself why he needed to visit the site. The internal argument had been going since the day the body was discovered. On one hand, the best that could come from it was more guilt and self-loathing for making a decision that would haunt him and his friends for the rest of their lives. On the other hand, he might be spotted by a passing sheriff's deputy and questioned about why he was there. He had no good answers.

The morning sun was to his right, beginning its trek into the sky. The weather's long term forecast gave a glimmer of hope that the next two-to-three days might have a chance of rain. It was only twenty percent on Thursday and forty percent on Friday, but that was the highest possibility of rain that they had seen in the past three weeks. The meteorologists on the *Weather Channel* said that a major change in the weather pattern was imminent. People were praying, crossing their fingers, and doing public rain dances, hoping to improve those odds.

Tommy pulled his car into a grassy area off the main path where law enforcement vehicles, the coroner's van, prison vans, news vans, and crime scene investigators cars had parked. The vegetation was flattened in a wide area from the automobile and foot traffic. He stepped out of his car and walked down to the lakeshore. Two ruts were gouged into the dry clay where a white Ford Tempo had been towed from the lake. Footprints were everywhere on the dried, cracked clay that had once been lake bed. Yellow crime scene tape still outlined the area that was considered off limits, but the tape had been torn and blown down in several places.

Tommy envisioned his friends standing in this spot almost sixteen years ago, bewildered by Carly Sue's cry for help. He could see the white, Ford Tempo, the five of them pushing on the bumper, straining to move the car. He remembered stepping to the driver's side of the car, believing correctly that the car was still in gear.

His heartrate jumped, his breathing becoming more rapid. There was the body, slumped down in the driver's seat, blood running down the side of the man's head. He saw the source of the blood: the small hole in his temple. Heat rose into his face, nausea began to build. He took deep breaths, trying to control his body's natural reaction to his rapidly rising anxiety. It worked, at least for the moment.

He had decided for the group that they needed to do what Carly Sue wanted. They had to hide the body in the only way that he knew. Andy, Curtis, and Billy Ray had always looked to him to make decisions for the group. They all had their place in the friendship pecking order, and Tommy, for whatever reason, was the unofficial leader. Back then, when he spoke on the important issues that twelve-year-olds faced, they followed his lead because they had confidence that the things he decided were correct. When his friends saw the body, they panicked, wanting to run away and leave Carly Sue to fend for herself. Tommy was the voice of reason even as his mind had raced, his own fear nearly paralyzing him to inaction. But he overcame that initial shock. He reached into the car past the dead body and put the car in neutral. With an air of extreme urgency, he told his friends to push with all their might. They nodded their heads and pushed. In that moment, his life, and theirs, changed forever.

"This is all on me. What have I done?" he asked rhetorically. He shook his head and turned, staring at the large, forested land across Cypress Lake Road. He started walking, crossing the road, looking for the path that had been there some sixteen years ago. It was all overgrown now and Tommy had a difficult time finding the tight opening that led back to their tree. But after moving a few branches and finding a few familiar trees, though they had become much larger over the years, he moved into the woods. As an afterthought, he pulled his car key from his pocket and clicked it two times. He heard the horn beep once, letting him know that his car was locked.

The morning walk through the trees was a challenge in dress shoes, a dress shirt, and khaki pants. Once Tommy had gone about one hundred yards into the wooded area, his shirt was getting whipped by branches. He stopped and closed his eyes, thinking back to the frantic dash down this path, remembering the cuts on his arms and face. He opened his eyes and continued walking. A few bugs were crushed on his shirt sleeves. He slapped at a bug that landed on his neck and he had nowhere to wipe the crushed guts, so he wiped his hand on a small tree trunk. The morning dew, what little of it that existed on the leaves of the shrubs, dampened his pants and shirt. He went another hundred yards and saw the clearing and the tree.

When he finally broke free from the undergrowth, he stood in a narrow beam of sunlight that angled through the trees. The clearing had shrunk in size, the bushes having grown larger, encroaching on the clearing from all sides. The trees surrounding the clearing were also larger, though they didn't look much different from when the four friends hung out.

But their tree, the one that looked like the Grim Reaper, the one with the missing main trunk twenty feet up, and the branches that looked like arms holding a sickle, looked as if it had not changed at all. Tommy looked up at the tree, amazed that even the Spanish moss that hung from the extended branches looked the same. Amongst the backdrop of green leaves from surrounding trees, it looked gray, dark, and imposing.

Tommy looked at the trunk at head height. The bare spot on the tree where, years ago, he had scraped away the bark to expose fresh wood, the spot where he and his friends had become blood brothers, where they had pledged silence forever…remained unchanged. Dark sap still oozed from the wound that he had inflicted on the tree. The wound looked fresh and angry. A breeze moved the branches and the tree creaked loudly, sounding betrayed and angry, a reminder of the horrors of that night so long ago. Standing on this spot, sixteen years later, fear embraced his entire body, his eyes welled with tears. He had demanded that he and his friends make a pact in blood, that all must remain silent, and that they take the secret to their graves. He had betrayed them all.

* * *

Billy Ray Duke sat under the stand of trees near the lakeshore, out of sight from the road, daydreaming about the same events that were on Tommy Alexander's mind. After Eugene Morris had left his trailer yesterday afternoon, Billy Ray got the itch to drink. He wondered if and when Morris was going to call his Alcoholics Anonymous friend. He hoped that he would get a call soon. His addiction was tugging at his brain. He thought that if he could make it through today and tonight without a drink, then he could make it until he got help. He'd been sober for ten days now, but that sobriety was forced by his incarceration. Beating the addiction while on the outside was far more challenging. He had read his Stephen King novel for a time last evening, and that helped. But even then, the urge to put the book down and pick up a bottle was compelling.

Trying to increase his odds of success, he decided to walk down to the lake as soon as he awoke. He thought that walking along the shoreline where he and his boyhood friends had once caught tadpoles would distract him. Maybe some of his old fishing buddies would be there, angling for a lunch of pan-fried crappie. That might not have been such a great idea since many of them drank port wine for breakfast. As it turned out, the drought had depleted the lake to the point where no fishermen were on the shore.

So, he sat behind the stand of trees, thinking about that night. Billy believed that it affected him more than his friends, but maybe that wasn't true. Now that he was sober, he was thinking more clearly and realized that he had been his own worst enemy. He was twenty-seven years old. Maybe it was time to get help. Could Father Rod be the one to open that door for him?

The sound of tires on loose gravel got his attention. He was surprised to see Tommy Alexander's Gold Lexus pull off the road and park. He half-expected his old friend to walk down to the lake and say hello, but Billy Ray remained out of sight while Tommy got out of his car and surveyed the area near the lake.

When Tommy turned and walked across the road, Billy Ray knew exactly where he was headed. The horn to Tommy's car gave a loud, single blast, startling Billy Ray. But the momentary jolt gave him a burst of adrenaline. So, he waited until Tommy disappeared into the woods, then followed at a distance.

Billy Ray had been back to the tree many times over the past sixteen years. He knew his way by heart even though the many paths to the clearing had grown over and would be difficult for the uninitiated to follow. He spotted Tommy ahead in the clearing, looking around, getting reacquainted with their former hangout. Tommy turned to the tree, which was away from where Billy Ray approached the clearing. He was looking at the tree with a trance-like reverence, mesmerized by its strange, eerie presence. It was a similar feeling that Billy Ray experienced when he was alone in front of the tree, as if the thing had its own soul, a spiritual life within, like it was reaching out to those in its presence.

Billy Ray walked to the edge of the clearing. Tommy heard the footsteps and turned with a lurch, frightened by whatever was approaching from behind. When he saw Billy Ray, he took a deep breath.

Tommy, though instantly relieved, realized that he hadn't spoken to his old friend in nearly sixteen years. He said, "Hey, Billy Ray." He paused. "Been a long time."

"Yeah, long time." Another awkward silence passed between them. "What brings ya out here?"

Tommy looked at the tree, at the bare wood at eye level. The sight of the dark sap had him tongue-tied. He didn't know what to say, since they couldn't talk about the night of August 26, 1999. But there was no doubt what was on both their minds.

"I wanted to see if our tree was still here." He waited to see if Billy Ray would say anything. When he remained silent, Tommy asked, "When did ya get out of lock-up?"

Billy Ray smiled. Just like Tommy. Hadn't changed a bit. Get right to the point. "Yesterday afternoon. Been sober for ten days now."

"That's great, man. You got a job?"

"Nah, but I'm tryin' to get into AA. I'm gettin' too old for this. It's gonna kill me if I don't get help."

Billy Ray was grateful for the small talk. It kept his mind off the eight hundred-pound gorilla in the clearing. He didn't want to be the one to break the pact. They all expected him to cave and spill his guts, but so far, he had been true to his friends, even through his binges.

Tommy asked, "Have you talked with Andy or Curtis?"

Billy Ray smiled. He figured that Tommy had already spoken with both and knew that he had not had contact with either of them in years – the same amount of time since he last spoke with Tommy.

"Nah. I ain't seen either one for ages. Seems like we all went our separate ways."

Tommy smiled back at Billy Ray, then said, "The reason I asked is Andy is involved with a lot of organizations that help people with all kinds of different problems. He probably knows someone who can help."

Billy Ray's smile changed from friendly to contentious. "Y'all don't think I can stay sober, do ya? I mean, y'all got your jobs and families, and new, fancy friends. I don't want to trouble y'all. And I sure as hell don't want to be anybody's project."

Tommy's smile faded to a look of guilt. "Look, Billy Ray, we didn't mean to...I mean...we had our own problems. I'm sorry we didn't help you back..."

Billy Ray realized that Tommy could not say what he wanted, because anything he said would lead to openly talking about that night, and that was forbidden. Billy Ray realized in that moment that their friendship was doomed the moment they placed their bloody hands on the tree.

Billy Ray was sure that Tommy understood their predicament. It was either they keep their promise and sacrifice their friendship, or they place their freedom at risk. Of course, he didn't know that Tommy had already violated the pact and broken his silence, if only to his wife.

Billy Ray, sorry that he had momentarily lost his temper, said, "Tommy, I miss you. And I miss Andy and Curtis and all our good times together. Them times here at the tree, they was the best times of my life."

With a serious face, Tommy nodded, but didn't say a word.

Billy Ray continued, "I'll get the help I need. You don't have to worry about me. I'll be fine. I'd swear on that tree again..."

He didn't finish. He stared at the tree for a long moment, then back to Tommy. Without another word, he turned and headed towards the mobile home park. He waved to Tommy over his head without turning around. He didn't want his old friend to see the tears that were blurring his vision.

Tommy watched Billy Ray disappear into the brush. His heart ached for his friend. The pact had protected them from the law, but at what cost? Had it destroyed their friendship forever? Was it worth it?

When Billy Ray was out of sight, Tommy took a last look at the tree. A cool breeze rustled the leaves on the surrounding trees. It felt good to Tommy as he stood in the clearing. Then he saw the branches of their tree sway as if reaching out for him. A chill gripped his spine. He took a deep breath, then headed down the path towards Cypress Lake, his own tears running down his cheeks.

Chapter 21

Visions of MaryJo Saxon, looking like a crazed psychopath, screaming, pointing fingers, and blaming everyone for her problems, kept Eugene Morris from concentrating on his breakfast. Her claim that four preteen boys knew about the murder seemed far-fetched. She even accused the boys of being at the lake when the murder took place. But were they there at the time of the murder or did they just hang out at the lake and catch frogs and tadpoles, and skip stones like young boys do? What motive would they have to commit murder? There were probably good reasons, but he could not think of a single one.

Had MaryJo actually said that Millie Crider knew who the killer was or had she just said that she knew something about the murder? He could not remember as he had feared for his life during her tirade. Her nearly three-hundred-pound frame, along with his own weight, on the rickety platform, were enough to push him into near-panic.

So, he had Millie Crider and Ginny Hardy accusing MaryJo of being involved, or at the very least, knowing some details about the murder. Millie went even further stating that MaryJo knew the victim, even said that she had dated the man. Ginny Hardy would only say that she would bet money that her crazy neighbor was involved.

The early morning sun was in his eyes as he drove east along North Edgewood Drive. All these thoughts bounced around his brain, trying to find a logical pattern so that one puzzle piece might interconnect with another. So far, nothing fit. Opposing accusations were flying around the little mobile home community. Clearly someone was lying; maybe everyone, to some extent.

He had to brake quickly as he nearly missed the right turn onto Holly Drive. The mature neighborhood had tall trees with full canopies. The homes, built in the 1960s to 1970s, were generally well kept, except that the lawns were crispy brown due to the drought and city-wide lawn-watering-restrictions. The neighborhood was still thriving, with owners who cared for their property. It felt like a neighborhood where people still looked out for one another.

Morris watched the mailboxes for 110 Holly Drive. When he noted the black mailbox with the correct numbers, he pulled into the driveway. There was no car in sight, but the door to the single-car garage was closed. Morris killed the ignition and headed for the front door; the heat already uncomfortable, even at this early morning hour.

As he rang the doorbell, he noted that all Curtis and Carly Sue's window shades were drawn. The air was stagnant and heating up, already into the high seventies. He could hear the central air conditioner running on the side of the house.

He was about to ring the doorbell again when the door opened. A man looked out and asked, "Yes?"

Morris noted the man appeared to be in his late twenties. He wore a light gray golf shirt with a City of Statesboro emblem and dark tan pants. Morris held up his credentials and gave Curtis Hardy his standard greeting. He asked if he could talk with him and his wife about the murder at Cypress Lake.

Curtis's expression showed a reluctance to let him into their home, much less answer his questions. He appeared to struggle with the decision.

Morris heard a female voice from inside the house ask who was at the door. Hardy turned and said, "Some newspaper reporter." He said it like reporters were as unwelcome as door-to-door salesmen.

The voice said pleasantly, "Well, don't make him bake to death out there. Let him in."

Curtis frowned. "Are you sure?"

"Yes." She had grabbed the door handle and pulled it open, then turned and headed back into the house. Curtis just stood there, partially blocking the entryway.

Morris didn't want to assume that it was okay to enter the house, so he asked Curtis, "Are you okay with this? If not, I can come back another time."

Hardy shrugged and stepped aside. "Might as well be now. I have about twenty minutes before I have to head out for work."

Morris opened the screen door and stepped over the threshold into a small foyer. To the left of the entry was a living room with a typical furniture arrangement. The house was neatly kept but definitely lived in. There was a book on an end table and the most recent copy of the *Statesboro Herald* on the coffee table, which sat in front of a full-sized floral couch. The newest issue of *The Family Handyman* was next to the newspaper. Apparently, Curtis Hardy knew how to fix and build things. Two other chairs, one matching the couch, the other an oak glider with cushions of a unique design were spaced around the room, angled towards the flat-panel television. With the curtains closed, the lighting in the room was subdued.

The young woman who had given permission for Morris to enter came into the foyer, smiling. She stopped several feet from Morris and introduced herself. "Hi, I'm Carly Sue Hardy, Curtis's wife."

"Eugene Morris, but call me Gene."

After a brief pause, Carly Sue asked, "Can I get you something to drink? We have fresh coffee finishing up right now, or water, or sweet tea."

"Water would be great, thanks."

The men made their way to the living room. Curtis directed Morris to the glider while he took a seat on the couch. They waited until Carly Sue joined them, delivering Morris's water and setting a cup of coffee in front of her husband while she settled in next to him.

Morris didn't waste any time. "As I mentioned, I'm doing a story on the murder at Cypress Lake. I spoke to your aunt, Curtis, and your mother, Carly Sue. I have to tell you, before we get too deep into this, that I'm getting conflicting stories from the residents at the trailer park." He watched for any reaction in Carly Sue's eyes. When there was none, he continued. "Carly Sue, your mother accused some of the neighborhood boys of...trying to take advantage of you." He turned towards Curtis and said, "Including you, Curtis. She said that y'all might be involved in the murder somehow? She mentioned the names..."

"Tommy, Andy, and Billy Ray. She blamed them, and my husband, for everything from knockin' over trash cans to startin' world war three. They was my friends back when we was in elementary school. I was a grade ahead of 'em. We used to play together all the time. And no, they never tried anything like that. Heck, they was too young to know anything 'bout that kinda stuff back then."

Morris took notes as Carly Sue spoke. When she was finished, he turned to Curtis. "This next line of...questions might be a little...um...difficult. Curtis, your mother said that she thought Carly Sue's mother might know something about the murders." He waited for a reaction, but all he got was a deep breath. He looked back at Carly Sue. "Do you know if that might be true, that your mother might know more than she's lettin' on?"

Carly Sue tensed. She was clearly uncomfortable with the question about her mother. Her mood appeared to darken. Morris noticed the change without reacting.

When Curtis remained quiet, Carly Sue answered, "Ginny's probably right. Mom spends all her time at her trailer. She can't never keep a job. She's always on a drunk. She's lived there in that trailer her whole life." Carly Sue's voice was rising, becoming more critical of her mother the longer she spoke. "And she's had a string of loser boyfriends who..."

Curtis put his hand on hers. It was apparent that he wanted her to settle down and maybe to not say something that might implicate her mother. Carly Sue stopped talking in mid-sentence. He gently folded his hand around hers. It was a loving gesture, so far as Morris could tell.

Curtis finally opened up and said, "It's possible that MaryJo knows something, but she isn't the type to murder someone, at least she wasn't back then. She wasn't as messed up as she is now."

Morris asked, "If you don't mind me askin', how long have you known your wife, Mr. Hardy?"

He replied, "We've known each other all of our lives. Heck, we lived next to each other since we was born. When Carly Sue got older, it turned into something more. We fell in love."

He squeezed her hand a little and she smiled, though the smile seemed a bit unnatural. She seemed anxious about something and Morris wanted to dig deeper.

Morris looked at Curtis and asked, "How do you know Tommy Alexander, Andrew Pip…" He paused because he didn't know Andrew's last name and made a show of looking at his notes.

"Pepperdine. Andrew Pepperdine owns the big farming supply warehouse west of town. Tommy, Andy, Billy Ray, and me have been friends since we was kids. Me and Billy Ray went to school together. We met Tommy and Andy by Cypress Lake. We ran into each other while me and Billy Ray was catching tadpoles. We showed Tommy and Andy how to do it. We just hit it off. Stayed friends for a long time."

As soon as he said it, he knew it was a mistake. He expected Morris to ask what caused their friendship to drift apart. To head off further probing about the friendship, Curtis announced that he had about five minutes left, then he had to leave for work.

Morris switched gears and asked Carly Sue, "Did your mother own a gun?"

"I don't never remember seein' one. She might have. If she did, she probably sold it for booze money."

Morris had one more question and it was the most difficult question of all. He asked, "Carly Sue, did any of your mother's boyfriends ever make advances towards you?"

Carly Sue looked directly at Morris. Her eyes welled up and in a shaky voice that was barely audible, she said, "No."

Curtis Hardy stood and looked towards the door. "Mr. Morris, I have to leave for work." It was a directive for Eugene Morris: time to leave.

Morris thanked them for their time and walked out into the heat of the morning. Once in the car, he reflected on Carly Sue's last answer. She had said 'no' that none of her mother's boyfriends had molested her, but he knew it was a lie. He could see the pain of abuse in her eyes.

* * *

Carly Sue was on the slippery slope to another bout of depression. She was doing well until the reporter's repeated references about her mother. Half the trailer park knew that her mother's boyfriends had tried to molest her. She might as well have been crowned the Cypress Lake Mobile Home Park whore. Her own mother had even called her a whore and accused her of trying to steal her boyfriends. Not a word of it was true, but she couldn't prove it either way. All her mother had to do was keep repeating it and everyone would believe it. Now that they found the body, everybody would assume that she killed him.

Curtis left for work just minutes after Morris left. He told Carly Sue that he wanted to stay with her for a while, make sure she was okay, but she insisted that she was fine. He couldn't afford to be late, even though he was the superintendent. He promised that he would be home for lunch with her favorite sandwich from the sub shop. That cheered her up for a few minutes.

After Curtis pulled out of the driveway, Carly Sue made her way back to their bedroom and dropped on the bed like a sack of potatoes. She left the curtains closed and the lights off. Her mind immediately went to Cypress Lake, late on a moonlit night.

She was in the front seat of a white Ford Tempo, leaning against the passenger side door, her mother's most recent loser boyfriend leaning against her, trying to pull her face to his. She was crying and he yelled at her to shut up or he would hurt her bad. She kept crying until he pulled her forward enough to give him room to take a swing at her face. The slap stung. From that moment on, she hadn't remembered anything...until the four boys showed up and helped her push the car into the lake.

After they watched the car sink, Tommy told her to never say anything about what happened that night and everything would be fine. She could see in his eyes that he hadn't believed it either.

Now, as she lay on the bed in her home, she plunged deeper and deeper into depression. The walls in her mind were closing in and there was nothing she could do about it.

Chapter 22

At 8:30 Tuesday morning after a call from newspaper reporter Eugene Morris, Captain Gerald Brannen finished reviewing the resumes of two prospective sheriff's deputies. As he walked into the common area outside of his office to refill his coffee cup, the fax machine hummed and spit out four pages. He ignored the incoming fax and picked up a glazed doughnut with a napkin. During the morning brief, he told Sheriff Adkins that they had interviewed all of the residents of Cypress Lake Mobile Home Park, and the residents in the homes surrounding the lake, but they had made little progress on the murder investigation. He promised that would change. Information from the crime lab on the bullet, the car, and the corroded gun were all expected today as was more information on the body, including DNA and dental work.

The fact that the murder was fifteen years old, or older, didn't matter to Brannen or Chief Adkins. He wanted to identify, and apprehend, the killer just as much as she did. They wanted justice for the victim, and they needed to demonstrate to the community that the Sheriff's Department was being proactive when it came to murder investigations. Statesboro's violent crime rate was higher than the national average. Adkins had made a campaign promise that violent crime would be reduced in the city, and Brannen knew she planned to keep her promise.

He took his coffee over to the fax machine, grabbed the four sheets, read the cover sheet, and headed back to his office. It was the report from the South Carolina Department of Motor Vehicles on the license plate number from the Ford Tempo. He compared the license number on the report with the one that Eugene Morris had given him over the phone just moments before. They were an exact match. *How had Millie Crider known the license plate number for the Tempo? This woman's full of surprises.*

He read the name on the report: Allen Jason Scott, born March 11, 1974, five feet nine inches tall, brown hair, brown eyes. His license should have been renewed during his birth month in 2001, but never was. The address on the license number was 412 Bay Street W, Allendale, South Carolina.

At least we have a name. Brannen took the fax and headed for the Chief's office. When he stepped in, he handed her the fax. "Our dead body is most likely Allen Jason Scott from Allendale, South Carolina. He was supposed to renew his license back in 2001 but he didn't do that, since he was probably dead. That's all we know at the moment, but we need to confirm with the ME's office that he's our dead guy. Having a name might help."

"This is a big step. Maybe things'll break loose now."

"I'll get one of the data guys busy searching different databases and see if we can find more info on Mr. Allen Scott. Maybe there's an old missing persons report out there or a relative who's waiting to collect on life insurance."

"Good work."

Brannen heard his phone ringing as he approached his office. He picked up after the fourth ring. "Brannen."

"Hi, Captain. This is Ginger Evans from the coroner's office. Dr. Malone is a bit under the weather, but he wanted me to get this update to you right away. We were able to get dental records from an office in South Carolina and match the records to your victim. His name is Allen Jason Scott. Last known…"

"412 Bay Street W, Allendale, South Carolina. We got the information from the BMV. Your report confirms the identity. Good job, Ginger."

"Thanks, Captain. One other thing. The angle of penetration for the gunshot was downward. Probably twenty-five degrees from the point of entry. We're not sure yet what that means, but we're thinking that he was shot by someone in the passenger seat, or someone standing outside the car. We're pretty sure that the gun used was a revolver; therefore, no shell casing would be left behind. That is just speculation, but the gun we found, if it was the murder weapon, was a revolver."

"Alright, Ginger. Anything else?"

"Nope, that's it."

"Thanks, and give Cedric our best. Hope he feels better."

"I'll pass that on, Captain."

Brannen disconnected the call and reached for his coffee, but the phone immediately rang. He answered, "Brannen."

"Captain, this is Nikki Olsen from the crime lab."

"Hi, Nikki. Got some good news for me?"

"Like, yeah. When I spoke with you the other day, I told you about a new procedure that we're trying on the car's bumper. It worked pretty well, better than I thought it would. We were able to pull some prints from the bumper, but the quality of the prints isn't super great. Like, there were some smudged prints, but we had some success. We're evaluating them now and we may have some partial prints that will be detailed enough to use in a comparison program."

"That sounds like good news. I think I hear a 'but' coming."

"Thing is, we have a bunch of prints to evaluate. It looks like five sets of prints."

Brannen frowned. "Did you say five sets, meaning five people?"

"Like, yeah. At first I thought that it was one person touching the bumper at different points, but after doing a quick evaluation, it is pretty clear that there were five individuals pushing the car. Hand sizes and individual prints didn't match up, so that's my conclusion."

Brannen thanked the young woman and hung up.

They had a name for the victim. Now they had fingerprints for five people helping to hide the evidence.

Brannen sat back in his chair, deep in thought. *Why would five people conspire to kill a man and hide his body?*

Could it be mob related? Maybe gang related? Drug deal gone bad? After sixteen years, is it even reasonable to expect that we'll find a motive for the killing?

He needed to update the sheriff. As he turned to head to Adkins' office, Deputy Jones met him at his office door. He said, "Hey, Captain. We got a name for our vic yet?"

"Yeah, we just got the fax from the partial plate number that we sent in and the coroner's office just called. Allen Jason Scott. You know the old woman, Millie Crider?"

"Yeah."

"She had the plate number written down, and she gave it to Gene Morris the other day. Morris said she pulled it off a notepad that she had sittin' on a shelf in her trailer. She knew exactly where it was, too."

Jones' eyebrows hitched up. "I think that old lady's got us all over a barrel, big time."

"Yeah. Here's another thing. I didn't bring this up at the morning brief and keep this close to your chest. She owns the trailer park and the surrounding land. She's rich."

Jones' jaw dropped.

Brannen said, "There's more, but I need to update the sheriff. Come on and you can sit in when I tell her."

As the two approached her door, Adkins waved a hand at her two guest seats just as she hung up the phone. "Gentlemen. What do you have for me?"

"Hey, Sheriff, I asked Deputy Jones to sit in so I don't have to go over this twice. Gene Morris from the *Herald* called this morning. He's been doing some digging on the murder. Millie Crider, the old lady from the trailer park, gave Morris a license plate number. It matches the plate on the car we pulled from the lake."

Adkins' eyebrows shot up, but she remained silent seeing that Brannen had more.

"Morris said she pulled the number off a notepad that she had sitting on a shelf. Apparently, this woman keeps track of what's going on in the park." He paused. "That makes sense since she owns the trailer park. But how did she get that license plate number? So, I get a fax a few minutes ago from South Carolina Motor Vehicles and the owner of the car we fished from the lake is one Allen Jason Scott. I just got off the phone with the coroner's office. Cedric's under the weather, by the way. His Deputy Coroner said they positively ID'd the dead guy using dental records and confirmed that our dead guy is Allen Jason Scott."

"Well, at least we know who our vic is. What else do we know about our dead guy?"

"He lived in Allendale, South Carolina. He may have been a medical technician or some kind of nuclear worker. We're checking the hospitals and other facilities that handle radioactive materials in the area. Barnwell waste facility looks like a good candidate. They were still very active accepting low-level waste around 1999."

Adkins asked, "How far is Barnwell from Allendale?"

Brannen said, "About twenty minutes, thirty minutes tops."

"Start there. I think these places that handle radioactive materials maintain good personnel records. If you need a warrant for the records, we can get one in short order."

"We're on it, Sheriff. One other thing. The lab performed that new technique on the car's bumper. They identified five unique sets of prints. So, a bunch of people wanted to hide that body."

Adkins placed her elbows on her desk, rested her chin on her fists, and took a deep breath. Tension showed in the lines on her face. Brannen and Jones sat silently as their boss sifted through the information in her mind. After half a minute, she asked, "Did the lab say how long it would be before they could do a fingerprint search?"

Brannen replied, "No, ma'am, but I can call Olsen back and ask."

"Gerry, you make the call to the lab. Jonesy, you call the folks at Barnwell." She looked back at Brannen. "When you finish with that, you and Jonesy go back out and talk with Ms. Crider and see if you can squeeze more information out of her on why she kept that license plate number. You don't just jot stuff like that down and happen to know exactly where it is sixteen years later, and know that, somehow, it belongs to a car that's been pushed into a lake with a dead body inside."

* * *

Tommy Alexander sat at his office desk still thinking about his encounter with Billy Ray. A picture of his wife and girls sat facing him. He wondered what the future held for them now that the pact was shattered – more precisely, now that he had broken his promise to his friends. A morose silence filled the office, interrupted only by the sound of the hum of the small refrigerator clicking on in the utility room adjacent to his office. Earlier he had been in the office bathroom cleaning the few crushed bugs and dirt from his shirt after his jaunt in the woods. He had also splashed cold water on his face, trying to clear his mind. He reached into his desk drawer and found a bottle of eye drops. He used them to clear the redness from his eyes after his brief crying spell. He had an open hour this morning. It was time to call an old friend.

He didn't have to look up Andy Pepperdine's number. He had looked it up so many times in the past that he knew the number by heart. The call should have been made years ago. Now it was inevitable. He had broken the pact by telling his wife their secret. He had to let Andy know before Cheryl told Cornelia and Cornelia, in turn, told her husband. He wanted Andy to hear it directly from him, not from the wife's grapevine.

With the receiver in his hand, he punched in the number for Andy's office. Andy picked up during the second ring.

Andy had caller ID because he answered in a voice that was filled with caution, "Hi, Tommy."

"Andy." A long pause followed. "We need to talk."

Andy took a deep breath. "Okay, Tommy, let's talk."

"Not over the phone. Can we meet over lunch?"

"Sorry, but I've got an employee luncheon, and I'm having dinner alone with Cornelia tonight."

Andy sounded as if the dinner with his wife wasn't going to be pleasant. He hoped that Cheryl hadn't yet poured out her heart to her good friend. It was more important now than ever that he and Andy meet as soon as possible.

"How about we meet for a drink right after your dinner date?"

Andy chuckled, the tension broken by Tommy's description of tonight's spousal encounter. Quickly becoming serious again, Andy said, "Name the time and place."

"How about Forest Heights. I'll reserve a small conference room for 8:00 PM."

Andy should have seemed surprised that Tommy wanted the meeting to be private, but clearly, he wasn't. He was ninety-nine percent sure that Andy knew this turn of events was inevitable.

"See you there. And, Tommy, is anyone else going to be with us?"

Tommy sighed. He knew that Andy was referring to Curtis and Billy Ray. "Not yet."

Chapter 23

Billy Ray Duke's five-minute walk through the woods, from the tree to his trailer, was a blur. He had walked this same path so many times that his body was on autopilot, but his brain was in a different place altogether. His emotions ran high off the charts, unchecked by the usual alcohol-induced fog. The scent of drying, brittle leaves caused him to sneeze numerous times. He rubbed his nose on his shirt sleeve, just as he would have done as a twelve-year-old. Initially, tears had clouded his eyes, running down his cheeks. After he regained control over his runaway emotions, random thoughts about his past collided in his alcohol-free brain. His mind was clear, but with so much information firing off at once, he found it impossible to manage his thoughts, to string them together in a logical, coherent manner. Before he knew it, he was opening the door to his rundown trailer, the hinges squeaking in protest, begging for a shot of WD40.

Sitting in his living room at 8:00 AM, immersed in his thoughts, the overpowering urge to grab a beer from the refrigerator was doused when he realized he had no beer in the fridge and no alcohol anywhere in the trailer. A sad smile graced his face at the hollow victory. He was a slave to booze and would be for life. His only hope was to get outside help, which he didn't see happening anytime soon.

Seeing Tommy at their tree brought back good and bad memories. But one unimaginable memory took over and remained at the forefront of his mind. He tried focusing on his friends and the good times they had, the things that most young boys from the country do while growing up. They smoked their first cigarette and shared a beer, then later, a six-pack. Andy had snuck that out of his old man's refrigerator. They had contests. Who could spit and pee the furthest. Who could kill the most birds with stones launched from the slingshots they made from tree branches. The time they tied Curtis up in the tree until late at night 'cause he told his mom about their hideout. He got a few mosquito bites and chiggers, but he survived okay. They were just starting to talk about certain girls at school and the way they seemed to be changing, getting' boobies and stuff, like Carly Sue. That was okay 'cause they didn't like girls much...yet. All those good times were a flash compared to the one bad memory that overshadowed them all.

Billy Ray spent three minutes thinking about the good times. Then the thought about Carly Sue Saxon sent him down the dark path and he wasted an hour worrying about what was going to happen next. *Stealing and drinking a few beers weren't nuthin' compared to...accessory to murder? What do them lawyers call it? Complicity to murder? Is that what we done? Hell, I didn't even know the dead guy. I sure as hell don't know who done the killin'. I guess that don't mean nothin' to a judge though.*

Just like the night back then, he could sense the coming storm. But this storm would do far more damage than any he had ever seen.

He thought back to his jailhouse discussion with Father Rod. The room had been cool and bright with fluorescent lights and smelled of disinfectant and industrial cleaner. The priest, kind and understanding, hadn't pressured Billy Ray to talk to him, but urged him to pray about it, talk with God. Billy Ray had prayed, or at least did what he believed was praying. Nothing had changed...yet. Not as far as he could tell. But maybe God was still thinking things over. Billy Ray guessed that He had a whole planet to watch over.

Looking around his trailer, it was clear that he had to find something to keep himself busy, to focus on anything but that dreadful night, anything to keep away from the bottle. Reading novels all day wasn't going to cut it.

Maybe Father Rod could help. The priest had said to call him anytime if he had questions or needed to talk. But, like God, the priest had a church full of people with problems that needed his attention. *Why would he abandon them to talk with me? Well, I need to talk to somebody right now.*

Billy Ray picked up the phone book and opened it to the yellow pages. With his index finger, he tracked down the church listings until he reached Trinity Episcopal Church. As he whispered the number to himself, his phone rang. No one ever called him. He looked at the phone as if it was a rattlesnake, coiled to strike. An irrational fear gripped him. He was so surprised by the call that he didn't answer until the fourth ring.

Slowly, he lifted the receiver to his ear and, in a shaky voice, said, "Hello."

The familiar, soothing voice of Father Rod said, "Billy Ray. How are you, young man?"

Hearing the pastor had a calming effect on him. He quietly replied, "Alright, I guess." He paused. "Well, maybe not so great. I was just thinkin' 'bout callin' you."

The call lasted less than five minutes. Father Rod asked Billy Ray if he might be free to help with some work around the church and maybe talk some more. He mentioned that it was a paying job. Billy Ray replied that he would be happy to help. The priest said that he would pick him up in fifteen minutes.

Billy Ray had *His* answer.

* * *

An impressive red brick structure with white columns and white trim originally built in 1894, the Bulloch County Courthouse was on the National Register of historic buildings. It had undergone multiple remodeling projects over the decades, both interior and exterior. The result was a handsome and functional office space for both the court system and county records.

The hall of records contained massive leather-bound books where land transfers, liens, deeds and foreclosure information was documented for all of the land in Bulloch County dating back to the days when the county was originally formed. The manual entry of data lasted up until 1999. Since then, all real estate transactions were recorded in a database and made available by electronic search. The entire database was periodically printed and signed by the county auditor so that an 'official hardcopy record' was maintained.

The electronic database didn't help Eugene Morris. He stood at a table in the hall of records, one of the large, leather binders opened in front of him. He was looking for the land transfer for the property on Cypress Lake Road. The clear and eloquent cursive strokes that filled the page were completely different than the computerized spreadsheets that were now used to record such transactions.

Manual searches, like the one performed by Morris, were time-consuming. If your transaction wasn't in the chosen book, you had to return the book to the service counter so that a clerk could return the volume to its rightful place and remove another. Since the books were about twenty-four inches tall by thirty inches wide and five inches thick, and weighed nearly six pounds each, it was physically taxing to select the wrong book. The massive books with their leather covers smelled a bit musty. They looked like a prop plucked from a Harry Potter movie, but they contained no wizarding lessons or magic potions. It was simply the official method of recording land transfers from one person or entity to another. The volume in front of Morris had obviously been handled countless times, the pages yellowing from age and the oils expelled from the human touch. But the ink was still clear, the information unmistakable.

Morris found the last manually recorded transaction for the land now known as Cypress Lake Mobile Home Park on Thursday, April 2, 1970. The purchaser was Miss Mildred Crider. He looked at the name of the seller. *Georgia Central Agriculture, Inc.*

Morris pulled out his cell phone and snapped a picture of the transaction. Then he wrote the identifying numbers for the records book on his notepad and returned the book to the clerk's desk. He stood for a moment, thinking about what he had just read. He needed two pieces of information. First, who owned *Georgia Central Agriculture, Inc?* Second, how much did Millie Crider pay for the land?

Morris went to the hall of records information counter where a man with small hoop earrings and light colored lipstick approached. His nametag said *Julius Holmes.* In a feminine voice with a strong southern accent, he asked, "How may I help y'all?"

After taking a moment to contain a growing urge to laugh, Morris asked, "Would you do a land sales search for me?"

"Why of course. Y'all know the records only go back to 1999, right?"

Morris nodded and said, "Yes."

"Good. Do you have an address or a legal description of the land in question?"

Morris handed Julius Holmes the top sheet of paper from his notepad with the trailer park's address. The clerk went to work on his computer and after thirty seconds said, "If y'all'll take a look at the monitor here, y'all'll see that the land was transferred about four years ago to the Cypress Lake Mobile Home Park, LLC. The seller was Ms. Mildred Crider."

Morris frowned. *Why would Millie Crider sell her property to some management company?* Then a light went on in his brain and the frown turned to a smile. *A shell company to protect her financially?* He would look up the principals in the company later, but he believed that he already knew at least one of the company's officers; Millie Crider. She was full of surprises and Morris was sure that this was just one of many.

Julius Holmes asked, "Is there anything else I can help y'all with?"

After shaking his head to clear his thoughts, Morris asked, "How do I find out the price that was paid for a piece of real estate?"

"Y'all have to contact the Tax Assessor's office. If you have enough information, that office can tell you the sales price." Holmes face lit up with a sly smile. "I have a friend at that office. I can help y'all with that. Is this the transaction that you'd like to know about?" He held up the paper that Morris had handed him.

Morris hesitated, then replied, "Yes. And the previous transaction to that one."

"I'll call. Do y'all plan to wait?" Holmes' smile was a bit flirtatious.

Morris paused then said, "Yes. Also, I'd like to use one of the computers to do a genealogy search. Is one free?"

"We have two computers available now. There's a fifteen-minute limit, but there's no one in line, so y'all can take whatever time you need. I can help with the sign-in." Holmes smiled.

The men walked over to a small desk that had just enough room for a computer monitor and a notebook. The keyboard pulled out on a platform just below the desk. Julius motioned for Morris to take a seat. When he did, the young man moved in behind him and leaned in next to his face, just a little too close for Morris' comfort, but he tried to concentrate on the monitor.

Julius instructed the reporter to click the mouse. When he did, the monitor came to life. A field for username and another for password were displayed on the screen.

Julius said, "Under the keyboard are the values that you need to enter for ID and password. When you click the Sign-in button, a screen will be displayed with all the legal mumbo-jumbo. You can just click 'Next' and continue to the next screen. The next screen will allow you to begin real searches. You first have to identify the type of search."

While Julius Holmes continued with his instruction, he seemed to inch ever closer to Morris. So close that he caught the minty aroma of the clerk's mouthwash. Finally, Morris said, "Thanks, Mr. Holmes, I've got it from here."

"Well, you just holler if you need any further instructions." The clerk smiled, winked, and waved his hand at the reporter in an overtly feminine manner, then turned on his heels and sauntered back to the counter.

Morris rolled his eyes, then turned his attention back to the computer. After a few seconds, he found that the search program was quite intuitive. He moved through several screens and found the one that he thought would help him get the information that he needed. He entered *"Crider"* in the "Last Name" field, *"Mildred"* in the "First Name" field and clicked "Next." In less than two seconds, a new screen returned the results.

There were two entries for Mildred Crider with basic information and a checkbox next to each line. After reviewing the limited information, Morris concluded that both names were for the Millie Crider at Cypress Lake Mobile Home Park. He checked the box for the first "Mildred Crider" and hit "Next."

A new screen filled with detailed information about Mildred Crider of Statesboro, Georgia, Cypress Lake Mobile Home Park, Lot #3. It listed her parents' names and had links available if the requestor wanted to find the parents' information. A horizontal line connected Millie's name to a field labeled "Spouse." The field was blank. Morris noticed a link next to the "Spouse" field which read "Previous Spouses." Morris hesitated, then thought that he could come back to this page and search for Millie's previous husband...*or is it husbands?*

Morris noticed lines from Millie's name reached below the viewable area of the screen. He used the mouse to click on the scroll bar and pulled the bar down to show the information below. In fields marked "Children," two names came into view. The first name was Cynthia Hardy, Date of Birth - October 15, 1968. The second was Virginia Hardy, Date of Birth - June 21, 1970. Morris' mouth opened in surprise.

He whispered, "I'll be damned."

He moved back one screen and clicked the link for "Previous Spouse." The screen again changed and displayed the name Douglas Hardy. Morris wondered - *Ginny Hardy's father?* He looked at the dates on the screen for the marriage to Millie Crider. They had been married from May 1974 until May 1986. So, Millie Crider and Douglas Hardy were not married at the time of Ginny Hardy's birth. Did he adopt Ginny and her sister? Where is Cynthia Hardy now?

Morris hit the back button to view Virginia Hardy's information. The "Spouse" field was blank and the link for "Previous Spouses" was gray, indicating that Ginny Hardy had never been married. He scrolled down the page following the single line to her only child. As expected, Curtis Hardy's name was displayed.

Morris clicked back to Cynthia Hardy. The name in the "Spouse" field was Randall Raymond Duke. He again scrolled down the page following the link for Cynthia's and Randall's children. There was only one child – William Raymond Duke.

His friends, and his cousin, Curtis, called him Billy Ray.

As Morris thought about the family relationships at Cypress Lake Mobile Home Park, Julius Holmes came up behind him and said, "That woman, Mildred Crider, must be family or she has some other connection to someone at *Georgia Central Agriculture.* She got the land free and clear."

Morris smiled. The woman was full of surprises.

Chapter 24

Millie Crider rocked back and forth in the decrepit rocking chair, the frame screeching in protest with each back and forth motion. Her just-as-decrepit old cat, Dusty, tried to jump into her lap, but she shooed the creature away. With a loud meow of protest, the ball of gray fur crept towards his favorite corner, made two complete three-hundred-sixty-degree turns, momentarily pawed at the ancient green carpet, then settled down in a curled-up heap.

Millie had just finished washing the dishes from a breakfast of cold milk and cereal and a cup of hot coffee. She needed the morning burst of caffeine, but she didn't need the internal heat that hot coffee generated, especially since the temperature in her trailer had not gone below eighty-two degrees in over three weeks. Even at 8:40 AM with all the trailer windows open, the little oscillating fan hardly moved enough air to make it worth the cost of the electricity to run the thing. The weatherman on Channel 8 News said the massive high-pressure system that trapped the summer heat was weakening and may actually move northeast within the next two days. But for now, the heat remained oppressive.

Millie thought about her dilemma. It had little to do with the current weather, though, indirectly, the drought had brought a long-held secret to the surface. She knew a lot about past events that others desperately wanted to know. With the discovery of the old Ford in the lake, the sheriff, that goofy reporter Eugene Morris, Ginny, MaryJo, Carly Sue, even the four boys knew bits and pieces, but they didn't have the whole picture. If she had anything to do with it, none of them would ever piece the entire puzzle together, at least not the true picture.

The bastard that they dredged outta that lake got what he deserved. His soul is planted firmly in hell with the rest of his ilk. No sense prayin' for him, I say. He was a waste of flesh and blood when he was alive. He dug his own grave. He's exactly where he deserves to be, fueling the fires of hell.

The telephone rang, interrupting Millie's thoughts. She cursed, struggled to her feet, and ambled across the living room to the ancient almond-colored, princess-model phone that hung on the kitchen wall. It was faded and stained an ugly brownish-gold from years of use. It was obsolete, but still worked.

She picked up the receiver and said, "Hello."

A nervous, whimpering woman's voice said, "Momma, I'm scared."

Millie was immediately both angry and disappointed. She had already discussed everything with her daughter, everything that she needed to know anyway. She was especially upset because she had told the young woman to never talk about sensitive issues on the phone. She figured that, these days, the government had all kinds of listening devices eavesdropping on everyone's private conversations. She had explained this to the woman on the line multiple times and thought that she understood.

Millie hissed into the phone, "You listen here young lady, you stop your cryin' and worryin', ya hear me? And not another word about bein' scared. Ya got nothin' to be scared of. Except maybe me if ya don't knock it off."

"But Momma, Billy Ray just went past, ridin' in some official lookin' car with a guy who looked like a cop. Him and Curtis are gonna talk, I just know it."

"I saw him. That was the pastor from Trinity Episcopal." Millie took a deep breath and squinted her eyes. She lowered her voice and took on a more serious tone. "Now listen, and I mean listen real good. First off, them boys don't know nuthin'. If they did, they woulda already talked to the sheriff. Hell, Billy Ray practically lives in the drunk tank.

He'd've spilled his guts a long time ago during one of his stints up there. And Curtis, even if he did know somthin', he ain't sayin' nuthin' that'll hurt Carly Sue." She paused again. "Pull yourself together, girl, and stop whinin'. I already told you that you're gonna be just fine. Didn't I tell you that?"

The woman was still whimpering but said, "Yes, Momma, you did."

"And if you listen to me and do as I say, everything'll be fine."

There was silence on the line. Millie thought that the call may have been disconnected, then she heard the woman's deep breathing. It was working. She was getting her emotions under control…at least for the moment.

Millie continued, "Now listen to me, young lady. We know that mistakes were made in the past and we dealt with 'em, right?"

"Yes, Momma."

"That's right. And we're gonna deal with this, too. Y'all trust me, right?"

There was silence.

"Come on, baby girl. You trust your Momma to protect you, don't ya?"

"Yes, Momma, I do."

"You have to help me so I can help you. The way you do that is by doin' and sayin' exactly what I told ya. You have to show them deputies that you believe every word that y'all are tellin' 'em. You have the upper hand darlin'. They's just grabbin' at straws. All they got is a…"

Millie realized that she was saying too much over the phone. She stopped the conversation in its tracks.

"Listen, sweetie, we can't talk no more right now. No more talk of this over the phone…ever. Why don't you come over when you get home from church? We can talk more then."

"Sure, Momma. I'll do that."

"And, Ginny, you keep prayin' just like you mean it, ya hear me?"

Ginny Hardy's voice became clear and serious. "Momma, when I pray, I do mean it. That's the God's honest truth."

Millie's smile was overlaid with skepticism. She replied, "That's real good, sweetie. Real good." She paused. "I love you darlin'. Don't you never forget that."

When Millie hung up the phone, she walked back to her Lazy Boy, but before she sat, she thought about her daughter and her very real fears. Maybe it was time to clear things up for Captain Brannen and the rest of the Bulloch County Sheriff's Office. It was time to get them nudged in the right direction.

She moved down the hallway to the first bedroom on the left and closed the door behind her. A small shaft of tree-filtered light angled through the partially opened draperies that hung from the wall, covering the three-foot-square window. The room, wallpapered in a bright yellow, sixties-era, flora pattern, held a single, narrow daybed and an old dresser that was painted with dark brown gloss paint. The only thing on the dresser was a small, round pedestal mirror which sat on an age-stained doily. A folded metal chair leaned against the end of the dresser. The hot, stagnant air matched that of the rest of the trailer, minus the benefit of the oscillating fan.

That didn't bother Millie. She unfolded the metal chair, set it down in front of the dresser, and lowered herself slowly onto the chair. She looked in the mirror on the dresser and saw a woman who, many in the trailer park say, hadn't aged in decades, but she could see the changes. Her face sagged a little more, the wrinkles were more pronounced, her eyes sunken into their sockets, and her skin's color faded to a light gray. There was no doubt, she was older. Some would say that she wasn't long for this earth and the discovery of the body was certain to add to her stress, aging her even faster. But she was determined to put her affairs in order before that time came. The drought just made that task more difficult.

Millie opened the middle drawer on the left side of the dresser. The drawer was filled from front-to-back, left-to-right with photographs in neat, perfect rows. The rows of pictures were divided by cardstock cut to the same height as the pictures. Four-inch by six-inch file cards with a tab separated the pictures by month and year.

Millie immediately went to the grouping behind the card marked 1999, then to the card with August. She grabbed a handful of pictures and tilted the August file card vertically to mark the spot where she removed the pictures. She placed the three-inch thick stack of photographs on the dresser and took a deep breath.

One by one, she looked at the pictures and placed them face down in a stack to the right of the initial stack. She found the four pictures that she needed. The rest of the pictures were returned to the drawer in the order that they were removed, minus the four that Millie needed for her plan.

This should just about do it.

* * *

Eugene Morris had been in front of the computer for nearly two hours. His last surprise about Curtis Hardy and Billy Ray Duke being first cousins fueled his determination to dig deeper into the lives of the tenants of Cypress Lake Mobile Home Park. His search seemed to hit a snag and no new information was unearthed, so he decided to shift gears and search for the owners of Georgia Central Agriculture, Inc. He thought for a minute, trying to remember the best way to search for the principals of a company, then remembered that the Securities and Exchange Commission maintained a database of corporations and their executive level officers called the Edgar database. He hoped that the county government computer would be able to handle the search.

He cracked his knuckles, took a deep breath, and typed in "SEC Edgar" in the Google search field and hit enter. A list of websites was displayed. He clicked on the first link in the list and he found himself looking at the official SEC Edgar database search page. He smiled. The instructions said to enter a company name in the search field. He typed *"Central Georgia Agriculture, Inc."* and clicked the search button. In less than one second, his search results were complete. *"No Companies Found."* His smile turned to a frown.

He sat back away from the keyboard and scratched his chin. *There has to be a listing for this company...if it still exists. Maybe they're no longer in business. Does Edgar's have an archive database?*

Morris clicked the back button until he was back at the Google search page. He typed "SEC Edgar Archives." A list of possible choices was displayed. His smile returned as he saw the second link on the page: the official SEC Edgar Archives link.

When he clicked the link, the archive search page looked much the same as the regular Edgar search page except that a warning was at the top of the page in bold lettering. *Searching the Edgar Archives without narrowing the parameters of the search may result in searches running for long periods of time. Use of limiting parameters such as Date Range, State, Type of Business, and others can help in shortening the response time of the search.*

Morris typed *"Central Georgia Agriculture, Inc."* Then he typed *"Georgia"* in the "State" field, and a date range of January 1968 to December 1975. He thought what other parameters he might enter, but none came to mind. He took a deep breath and hit the search icon. A circle icon popped up on the screen indicating that the search was underway. After ten seconds, he wondered if he should have narrowed the date range somewhat. After thirty seconds, he leaned back in his chair, thinking that the search might be the poster child for the need to add more limiting parameters. At forty-two seconds, the search clocked hesitated, then the results of the search appeared.

Morris bolted forward, looking at the screen. Georgia Central Agriculture, Inc. was incorporated in 1962. The corporate stock was not publicly traded. All shares were owned by Carl Pepperdine. On July 1, 1970, the company ceased operations and all corporate assets were transferred to Low

Country Seed and Supply Company. The owner of the new company? Carl Pepperdine.

In 1984, ownership changed hands from Carl Pepperdine to Marvin Pepperdine. Marvin ran the business until 2011 when the company again changed ownership. This time, Andrew Pepperdine took the reins.

Andrew Pepperdine, close friend to Tommy Alexander, Curtis Hardy, and Billy Ray Duke. This was getting interesting.

Why would Andy Pepperdine's grandfather's company give Millie Crider a large tract of land…for free?

Chapter 25

It was Tuesday, 3:10 PM, the fifth day following the discovery of the body. Captain Gerald Brannen sat at his desk, his face tight, tension slowly chipping away at his patience. His rattled nerves showed no signs of calming aided by six cups of strong, black coffee since lunch time. A little over ten years ago, he would have taken a smoke break. Not many years before that, he would have lit up right at his desk. He looked up at the bright, white ceiling tiles and remembered the days when those tiles were stained a sickly-yellow from the cigarette smoke in the office. Those days were gone for good. He knew his health was better for it, but, even to this day, his body ached for a hit of nicotine.

He and Deputy Jones planned to, once again, interview MaryJo Saxon and Millie Crider, but he had hoped more information would come in from the crime lab or from his database guy, before they faced the two women. The investigation appeared to gain some traction with the identification of the dead body, but the incoming information had come to a grinding halt.

Brannen promised the sheriff that they would make good progress and he hoped he could still deliver. Earlier in the day, he was confident they would get a break. It was just a matter of time, but as time passed, his hopes dimmed along with his mood.

He thought about the characters at the trailer park. Millie Crider played up the senile-old-lady angle to the park residents but showed a completely different side when he interviewed her. Eugene Morris had the same impression. He and Morris both thought the old woman was a little too slick to be ignored. Why did she live like a pauper when she had millions of dollars saved and invested? Why was she stockpiling money? The least she could do was put an air conditioning unit in her trailer.

She had that pair of binoculars handy and kept close watch on her tenants, one of whom was MaryJo Saxon, who wasn't fooling anyone. She was a few cards short of a full deck. What brain cells she had were pickled daily. At least she wasn't out on the road driving or, more accurately, there was no evidence that she was. She had never been arrested for driving under the influence or for public intoxication. She was a private drunk. From the encounters that he had with her, it was amazing that her liver still functioned. When they spoke with her, she was irrational, bordering on insane. Was she trying to drown out some awful memory, like a murder? Maybe she was a ticking time-bomb on the verge of exploding.

Billy Ray Duke had the same problem, as far as drinking goes, but he was a well-known commodity to the Bulloch County Sheriff's Department. He spent much of his time in jail. Common knowledge amongst the department was that Billy Ray wasn't a mean drunk. He just drank himself into a blind stupor.

His thoughts were interrupted by his ringing phone. He snatched the receiver from its cradle. "Brannen."

"Hey, Captain." It was Deputy Jones. "I've got good news and so-so news. Allen Jason Scott worked at the Barnwell Radioactive Waste Storage site starting December 1998. He was there for less than a year, then was fired."

"Did they say why he was fired?"

"Officially, no. I had to sweet talk 'em just to give me a start date and the fact that he was fired."

"Do I hear a 'but' coming?"

"Yes. Unofficially, he was fired for sexual harassment. He was 'inappropriately' touching young, female coworkers. He got written up several times before they gave him the boot."

Jones continued. "The man I spoke with said that we could not use any of this information in an official capacity, but since Scott is deceased, it didn't seem like much could come from it. He said Scott liked the younger girls and made some lewd comments to his male coworkers that made them uncomfortable. He said Scott had no friends and that everyone tried to stay away from him."

"Sounds like the guy had some serious personality issues." He paused to think. *If this guy was that odd in the open, maybe he was worse in private.* "Anything else, Jonesy?"

"Yeah. I have Templeton doing database searches in surrounding states. He's finished with Georgia and South Carolina. He has North Carolina and Tennessee running now. I'll call you as soon as we know something."

"Okay. I'll let you know if we hear anything from the crime lab. I'm hoping that they call soon. If I don't hear anything by 3:45, I think we should head back out to visit the old lady and her crazy neighbor."

Jones sighed loudly over the phone. "I'll be ready, Captain."

With the call disconnected, Brannen considered this new information. Maybe Scott was just a playboy and management believed he was causing an unsafe or hostile, work environment. Maybe there was more to the story. He didn't think it was worth reporting to the sheriff unless they received something concrete. As he began to wonder about Allen Scott's character, his phone rang again.

He answered, "Brannen."

"Hi, Gerry." It was Eugene Morris.

"Hey, Gene. What do you know?"

"A lot more than I did earlier this morning. Are you sitting down?"

"Yes, I am. Fire away."

Morris spent the next twenty minutes outlining the family relationships of the residents of the trailer park. By the time Morris was finished, Brannen had a pretty clear picture of the family tree: one that had some missing branches. Billy Ray Duke's parents were long gone, as was Curtis Hardy's father, and Millie Crider's husband. It wasn't clear if Crider's husband was Ginny Hardy's and her sister's father or not.

There were other questions, such as, why everyone despised MaryJo Saxon? Was it due to her drinking or was her drinking the result of the neighborhood's animosity towards her? Who was Carly Sue's father? How did Curtis and Carly Sue end up together? With such a divide between their parents, it seemed unlikely that a relationship would have much of a chance. Maybe the common thread was that they both had no father figure in their lives.

Brannen's head spun when Morris told him that Millie Crider hadn't paid a dime for the large tract of land that is now known as the Cypress Lake Mobile Home Park. It was acquired in 1970 from a company owned by Carl Pepperdine and his family. Brannen didn't know Crider's current age, but figured that she would have been in her thirties to early forties when she received title to the land. He also didn't know her financial situation back in 1970, but he did know that she was a single parent. If she was like other single parents in rural Georgia, she wouldn't have had much in the way of financial assets. How does a single woman with no financial assets acquire a large tract of land from a married man with a large, successful business? Some men can be charmed into giving a woman just about anything. Other men can be tricked. But most men who relinquish a significant amount of wealth to a woman, one who is not their wife, are blackmailed.

"Gene, did you find anything in your searches that would tell us why the Pepperdines gave Millie Crider the land?"

"No, but it sure sparks your imagination, don't it?"

"It sure does." *What did you do, Miss Millie?*

Brannen hung up the phone with Morris and was nearly out the door, headed for Sheriff Adkins' office, when his phone rang again. After being silent nearly all day, the thing was ringing off the hook. He turned, reached across his desk, and answered. "Brannen."

It was Deputy Jones. "Hi, Captain."

"I was just heading in to talk with the sheriff. What's up?"

"Templeton got a hit from North Carolina on Allen Scott. He was convicted on child molestation charges in 1996 and spent two years in prison. Before that, he was arrested in Tennessee and North Carolina, so they finally locked him up in the big house. But he got out and moved to South Carolina where he didn't report his previous convictions on his job applications. I think that's how he got hired at Barnwell."

"I wonder how he ended up at the bottom of Cypress Lake? You think some little girl's daddy did it?"

"If he had messed with my daughter, I reckon I woulda taken care of him. Bastard like that, let's just say he got his just rewards. This is all off the record, right, Captain?"

"Yeah, I guess. I'm a lot less enthusiastic about findin' the killer now. But I know the sheriff isn't goin' to let us drop it just because this guy was a sick son-of-a-bitch." There was silence on the line. "We're still gonna make the trip out to the trailer park and question them two women. How soon can you be ready?"

"Give me fifteen minutes, Captain. I'll meet you at your office."

"Don't rush. I still have to update Adkins. Like I said, she's not goin' let us slow down the investigation. If I'm not here when you get here, just wait. When I'm done, we'll head out."

"Okay, Captain."

* * *

On the way to the trailer park, Brannen told Jones about his update with Sheriff Adkins. She agreed that, being a child molester, he probably got what he deserved, but that wasn't the issue they faced. Someone murdered him. If people took the law into their own hands, the country would fall into chaos.

"She said we can't even give the appearance that we're slackin' up on the investigation. She pointed out that there were five sets of handprints on that bumper. That means that there're at least five people involved in the murder. She's right. This could be much bigger than an angry daddy out for revenge."

There was silence in the car for several minutes as they headed south, passing the Bulloch County Annex building on North Main Street in downtown Statesboro. The afternoon heat rose from the streets in waves. The air conditioner finally lowered the car's interior to a comfortable temperature.

Jones asked, "Who we talkin' with first? If we talk with the Saxon woman first, we might never get to Crider. That broad is slap crazy."

"That's true. But if we wait until much later, she might be passed out. This is the way we're goin' to play it. We talk with Saxon, tell her that we've identified the dead man and we know for a fact that she dated him. We tell her that he was a convicted child molester, which gave her good reason to kill the man – to protect her child."

"And you think she's going to break down and confess? You tell her that, and we best be ready to take her down, 'cause she's gonna go berserk. Honestly, I don't want to have to touch that woman." He paused and made a disgusted face. "How do we explain the five sets of fingerprints on the bumper?"

"We don't bring that up. We see how she responds to the accusation."

Jones smiled. "I already told you what she's gonna do. She's going to take that leap off the deep end. She's already nuts. If we push her like that, look out."

"What are you thinking we should do?"

"I say we talk with Crider first. Tell her basically the same thing, that ol' Allen Scott was a convicted child molester and see if she can fill in any blanks."

Brannen thought about it and agreed that it might be the better plan. If Millie Crider knew more about the murder and was just waiting for them to ask the right questions, it might add more pieces to the puzzle.

"Okay." A pause. "Alright. I like your idea. We'll start with Millie Crider and see where it takes us."

After the short ride on Cypress Lake Road, Brannen parked his car in front of Millie Crider's trailer. Before they stepped to her trailer door, it opened. "Come on in. I been expectin' y'all."

The air in the trailer was just as uncomfortable as it had been before, and Dusty, the cat, looked as if he hadn't moved since their last visit. In fact, the interior of the trailer looked exactly the same as it had on Brannen's last visit.

"Y'all take a seat at the kitchen table. I'll get us some iced tea."

Both officers declined, but Millie got three glasses of tea together anyway. The men didn't touch the ice-cold tea despite the oven-like temperature in the trailer.

Millie sat. "Y'all find out the name of that dead man yet?"

Brannen was tired of playing her off as a nut job, so he went right to the core of their visit. "You already know the man's name, don't you?"

Brannen thought he detected the slightest of smiles on Millie's face. He saw it in her eyes. She knew a whole lot more than she was offering. He suspected that was how she managed to extort a bunch of land from Carl Pepperdine.

"Well, Captain, I might. Was it Allen Scott?"

Chapter 26

At 7:50 PM, Tommy Alexander parked in the membership-only Forest Heights Country Club's north parking lot on the western edge of Statesboro. Even with the sun low in the western sky, he still had a clear view of the ninth and eighteenth greens and fairways, which were bright green, in sharp contrast to the dry, brown rough. The club was abiding by grounds-watering restrictions imposed by their water supplier, the City of Statesboro.

It was one reason Tommy hadn't played a round of golf in nearly a month. Being on the links normally meant an enjoyable, challenging, but sometimes frustrating day away from work, but since the drought transformed the course into green strips bordered by crispy, golden-brown weeds, he didn't take pleasure in the game. The condition of the course reminded him of the drought, which reminded him of his and his friend's current dilemma.

He walked into the clubhouse lobby and headed straight for the reserved conference room. Before he made it ten steps into the main room of the clubhouse, a man called out his name. He turned towards the voice as one of his elderly clients approached.

"Hey, Tommy. Haven't seen you here in a while. Come on over and join us."

"Hi, Stan." He looked past the man and saw a group of familiar faces sitting at a table in the bar area. He put on his best smile but with a twist of an apology. "I wish I could, but I've got a meeting at 8:00. Can I get a rain-check?"

"We might have a new client for you if you can spare a few minutes. My wife's brother and his family just moved here from Ohio. I told him you were the best agent in town."

Tommy looked at his watch and saw that he had about five minutes. "Let's go. I can spare a minute or two."

After introductions, broad smiles, and some pleasant but brief conversation, Tommy gave the man his card and said to call his office in the morning to set up an appointment. He was happy to help. As they continued light conversation, Tommy saw Andy Pepperdine enter the clubhouse and head for the conference room. With a smile, he took his leave from the group, followed Andy into the room, and closed the door.

The room was small, about eight feet on each side, with expensive vinyl wallpaper that sported a pattern that was supposed to be ornate. A small conference table in the center of the room held a computer keyboard at one end and a handful of gold coasters. A flat panel television hung from one wall. A small refrigerator sat next to a cabinet that served as a dry-bar on which sat a bucket of ice and several tumblers.

The two men faced each other, an uneasy tension between them. Tommy spoke first, his voice unusually tentative. "Thanks for coming. I…uh…I'm not sure how to start this…conversation. Do you need a drink?"

Andy replied. His own voice was filled with apprehension. "No, but thanks. Well, yeah. I'm gonna grab a water. You?"

"Yeah, water's good. Thanks."

Andy grabbed two bottles of water from the refrigerator and handed one to Tommy. They opened the bottles simultaneously and each took a big gulp. When they finished, each man instinctively looked at the other's left hand, looking for the scar. There were no more reasons to delay the coming conversation. As usual, Tommy took the lead.

He looked around the conference room, took a deep breath, then met Andy's gaze. "I got a confession to make. I think we both should sit down. This is going to be tough."

They sat, Andy waiting for his old friend to continue.

"Cheryl...well...there was no way I...uh..."

"You told Cheryl everything."

Tommy swallowed and nodded. "Yeah." A pause. "I did and I am so very sorry."

Tommy's eyes welled up. He fought the urge to cry in front of his childhood friend.

Andy cleared his throat. "Me, too."

Tommy's jaw dropped. "What?"

"Tommy, Cornelia may appear...naïve at times, but she's been gettin' suspicious ever since the drought started gettin' severe. I guess I'm not real good at hidin' my emotions. She can read me like a book. That's what our dinner date was about tonight. She all but threatened to cut me off. Maybe you didn't need to hear that."

The tension in the room drained away. The two men had come to the same conclusion on their own, with the help of their wives, at nearly the same time.

"Cheryl cornered me the other day. I went home for lunch and was about to tell her when Cornelia dropped by. She interrupted the story just as I was about to tell her about the..."

At that moment, both men realized that breaking the pact was the least of their worries. They still had a very serious problem. They were still involved in a murder. Neither man knew what to say next. They sat silent for a moment.

Andy broke the silence. "First, I want to say that I don't blame you for makin' that decision back then, you know, about stayin' quiet about what we saw. We were just kids, for cryin' out loud. We didn't know any better. At the time, it seemed like the best thing to do."

Tommy shrugged his shoulders. "I don't know, Andy. Seems like I should have thought things through a little more. But I guess you're right. We didn't have much time, or a whole lot of choices."

Andy nodded. "When the drought started to get bad, I knew that darn car was goin' to pop up. Heck, we were lucky we didn't get caught that night. Carly Sue was makin' so much noise." A pause. ". Do you think Carly Sue killed that guy?"

"You know, I've thought about that many times over the years. She really wanted to get rid of that body, but she doesn't seem like the type to kill anybody. You know what I mean?"

Andy smiled. "Anybody is capable of killin' someone under the right circumstances. But I know what you mean. She was a tom-boy, alright, but not creepy-mean. I don't think she did it. I'm just at a loss to think who could've done it. And if she didn't do it, why was she so intent on hidin' that body?"

Tommy nodded. "That's a darn good question."

They fell silent again, both lost in their thoughts about the night of August 26, 1999. Now that they could talk about it, they were immersed in their own thoughts.

Andy broke the silence. "Why do you think Curtis married Carly Sue? I would've thought that he'd stay as far away from her as possible, knowin' what he knows."

"Yeah. I always thought that was weird. How did they get together in the first place? I mean, they were neighbors, but Carly Sue's old lady would've scared me away. That woman is crazy mean. She was crazier than old lady Crider."

They both laughed, which knocked down the tension further. They both took a sip of water, then Tommy asked, "How about a real drink?"

Andy smiled. "Sure, why not. One drink won't kill us."

Tommy mixed up a couple whiskey and 7Ups and handed Andy his drink. They clinked glasses in a toast and took a drink.

The men sat down at the table again. Andy looked at Tommy and asked, "Have you talked with Curtis or Billy Ray about all this?"

"No. I wanted to start with you. I figured that Cornelia was going to hear it from Cheryl, that I told her everything, and I wanted you to hear it from me first. But we do need to talk with Curtis and Billy Ray. I did see Billy Ray earlier today. We spoke, but not about the pact or anything. Just some small talk."

"Where did you see him?"

Tommy hesitated for a second. "At the tree."

Andy's eyebrows rose dramatically. "At our tree?"

"Yeah. I went out there…I guess to get some kind of divine inspiration. Billy Ray walked up while I was there. He saw me go into the woods and followed." Tommy paused, thinking about the chance meeting. "He's determined to get his life straightened out. You know, he was on an inmate work detail at the lake when they found the car. He didn't tell me that, but I heard about it from Cheryl's brother."

"Tommy, I pray for Billy Ray every, single day. I feel bad that we didn't step in and help him, but that would have led to talking about…you know…and, well, you know, until now, that wasn't going to happen."

"Yeah. This stupid pact has been a real burden on us all and our families."

"Come on, Tommy. None of us knew any better. You can't keep blamin' yourself. I won't let you."

"I was thinkin' about Billy Ray, and how his life kinda fell apart after that night. We all seemed to be able to handle it better and move on, but Billy Ray…I guess we all got our ways of handlin' the stress."

"It wasn't his fault. We all had support. Stable families and all. Even Curtis, even though he didn't have a daddy, his mom seemed like she had it together. She is a bit of a religious fanatic, even more than most Baptists, I mean. But Billy Ray didn't have none of that. Remember those folks who was supposed to be takin' care of him? They ran off as soon as he hit sixteen. After that, he was on his own. What sixteen-year-old can handle that?"

They took another drink, then leaned back and looked at the ceiling, again lost in their own thoughts.

Andy spoke. "Where do we go from here? You and I both know that we have to talk about this with Curtis and Billy Ray. The pact is broken. We can't stay silent anymore."

"You're right. But let's talk between us some more, kinda figure out what we should do next. With Curtis married to Carly Sue, how do we talk about it without him gettin' all defensive. He might be tryin' to protect his wife from being charged with murder. Maybe he knows more now than we did back then. Maybe Carly Sue did it and she confessed to Curtis. Who knows?"

Andy rubbed his jaw, then took another sip. He was nodding his head in agreement. "Should we talk with Billy Ray first then? Or maybe get all four of us together, and lay it out, all at once?"

Tommy liked the idea of all four men getting together. But he and Andy needed to figure out how to tell their friends that they had broken the silence, but only with their wives, and absolutely no one else, and that their wives were sworn to secrecy, for what that was worth. But there didn't appear to be a good way to break the news to Curtis and Billy Ray.

Tommy was still not sure how to broach the subject. "Should we figure that Curtis has already broken the silence and discussed this with Carly Sue? Honestly, seein' as how she was the one who needed our help, and Curtis was one of the helpers, I don't see how they could keep from talkin' about it."

"Yeah. I see what you mean." Andy was thinking out loud. "Sure would be tough sleepin' in the same bed for all those years and not discussin' the most traumatic thing that's ever happened in your life. Let's put ourselves in Curtis's shoes. We help a twelve-year-old girl push a dead body in a lake. How do you ask her out on a date? Especially with her crazy mother. How do you even face her knowin' that she might be a killer? Or maybe he knew that she wasn't?"

A moment of silence settled in the room like a lead weight. Could it be that Curtis knew who the killer was, so he wasn't afraid of Carly Sue? Could she have confided in him, letting him know the identity of the killer?

Tommy tried looking at the meeting from this new perspective. Should they ask Curtis point blank if he knew who killed the man? Maybe Carly Sue did kill him but had a good reason. Even as a tomboy, she was such a sweet girl back then. He drained the last of his drink.

"Well, Andy, any other thoughts?"

"I'm thinkin' that we all should meet and get this out in the open, includin' findin' out what Curtis knows. Then we decide, all four of us, how we want to move forward. Maybe we keep talkin' but don't go to the sheriff. Maybe we go to the sheriff and tell him what we know. Whatever we decide, it has to be unanimous. You and me, we can't make that call without more information."

Tommy raised his empty glass. "I agree. Where do you want to meet?"

"Under the tree, tomorrow mornin' around 6:30."

Tommy took a deep breath. "I'll call Curtis and Billy Ray when I get home. If they agree, we meet under the tree, tomorrow mornin' at 6:30. I'll call you to confirm that we're good to go."

Chapter 27

Billy Ray thanked Father Ransom for the ride home and told the priest that he would be ready in the morning by 7:30. As the priest drove away, he turned to his trailer and rubbed his right shoulder, massaging the tightness in his sore muscles. Then he smiled. Working hard all day felt good; staying sober felt even better. The solid, twelve-hour day didn't leave much time to think of anything but the tasks that he had been assigned by Randy Ard, the Maintenance Supervisor at the church. They worked side-by-side, trimming hedges, cutting grass, blowing leaves, painting doors, and doing general cleanup. Randy said that the workload never eased around the grounds of the church and the rectory.

During their lunch break, Randy shared a glimpse into his life story. It was a sad tale of a broken home, punctuated by his father brutally beating his mother, his sister, and himself. He killed his father in self-defense, but only after the old man had beaten his mother so severely that she had suffered a severe concussion, sending her into a coma from which she never recovered. She died two weeks after being admitted to the hospital. Randy started drinking to excess, his life spinning out of control. It was a story that sounded eerily similar to Billy Ray's.

Then Father Rod stepped in. He gave Randy the job that he was now offering to Billy Ray…Maintenance Assistant. Randy credited the former Manager with his success at beating alcohol and drug addiction, and for keeping him out of prison. He told Billy Ray that he would help him as he had been helped if, and only if Billy Ray was serious about staying sober. There was no "maybe" or "let me think about it."

As Billy Ray stood in the driveway to his trailer, his smile grew. The heat of the day was slowly subsiding, dropping into the mid-eighties. He realized that he didn't even want a drink, except ice tea or ice water. It was a feeling of complete relief. Just how long the feeling would last, he didn't have a clue. He took a long, hard look at the run-down trailer. *It ain't much, but it's all mine. I guess I got it better than lots of folks.*

Once inside, he poured himself a tall glass of ice water, drank half the glass, and headed for the shower. He threw his sweaty clothes in a pile in the hallway, turned the water flow on lukewarm, and stood in the stream for several minutes, allowing the water to massage his back and chest and rinse away the first layer of dirt, grime, and salt.

With a lack of distractions, his mind wandered and settled on images of Carly Sue struggling against Allen Scott. He was mesmerized, transported back in time, standing on the rickety ladder outside Carly Sue's bedroom, thinking that he should do something to stop this creep from assaulting his friend. At eleven years old, he hadn't understood what was happening, just that Carly Sue was fighting back, trying to get her mother's boyfriend off her.

He opened his eyes and the images went away. He wondered if Carly Sue had it in her to kill a man in cold blood for what he had done to her. Surely, if she had killed him, it would have been self-defense. He had it coming, but, if it came right down to it, would her mother testify against her?

Maybe it was MaryJo. Maybe she made her way to the lake and shot the bastard, but not likely. Billy Ray thought that she was a piece of work, accusing her own daughter of seducing her boyfriends.

He turned the heat of the water up a notch. He was in love with Carly Sue back then: more like puppy love, or maybe infatuation. She was such a rough-and-tumble gal before she turned into a young woman. She never had a chance at a real life with her sorry excuse of a mother. Everybody in the trailer park hated MaryJo, especially Millie and Ginny. How did Curtis and she ever hook up? That must be some story.

Billy washed, rinsed, and dried himself, then dressed in shorts and a Lynyrd Skynyrd tee shirt. He downed the remainder of his ice water and refilled the glass. He looked out his window at MaryJo Saxon's trailer, which was in much worse shape than his own. He wondered how Carly Sue's mother lived with herself after what she put her daughter through. *Maybe she can't and that's why she drinks like I do...like I did. No more.*

The phone rang, jogging him out of his thoughts. He answered after two rings.

"Hi, Billy Ray."

"Hi, Tommy. I hadn't talked with y'all in years, now it's twice in the same day. What are the odds?"

Tommy had rehearsed what he was going to say to Billy Ray, but the words escaped him now that they were on the phone. "Yeah. Um...I heard you're working at the church. That's good, real good. Um...but that's not why I called."

"Kinda figured that, Tommy." He paused and waited for his old friend to get to the point. "What's on y'all's mind?"

"Can we meet in the morning?"

Billy Ray's mind was clear. "We" could mean any number of things. He pressed Tommy, "Who will be at this meeting? Just you and me?"

Tommy hesitated, and Billy Ray sensed that the two of them, Andy, and Curtis would be there, and he would know that the pact was broken. "All four of us...the old gang. You, me, Andy, and Curtis. I haven't called Curtis yet. Andy and I talked just a few minutes ago."

"When you say that you talked, you mean...?"

"Yeah, Billy Ray, you know what I mean. Can you save your questions for the meeting? I think all of us should be together when we talk about this."

"I guess you and Andy didn't think that was necessary. Y'all already talked, right?"

There was silence on the line for several seconds, which gave Billy Ray the answer. "It isn't like what you're thinkin', Billy Ray. There were circumstances…Cheryl, she was puttin' two-and-two together…If we can all meet, I can explain."

"Okay. Okay, Tommy. Alright. Only thing is, I have to work tomorrow morning at 7:30. How early can we meet?"

"I'm good with 6:30. I'll call Andy and let him know. I'm sure he'll agree. I just have to call Curtis. He doesn't know anything about this yet."

Billy Ray thought that Curtis might blow the whole meeting idea to pieces. His wife was at the center of the whole mess. "Okay, Tommy. Call me back when everything's firmed-up. Let me know where, too."

"I will. And, Billy Ray, you sound, uh, clear-headed. That's good, right?"

"It's good for now. Time will tell, but I'm gonna try like hell to stay this way."

After the call, Billy Ray thought about the meeting. He suspected that Tommy and Andy had already broken the pact and they were just making it official by having the meeting. It was curious that they spoke to him before Curtis, but it was clear why they did it. Curtis was most likely going to protect his wife at all costs. It was going to be an interesting meeting…if it happened at all.

* * *

Tommy sat in his home office with the door closed. He told Cheryl that he might be there for a while. The look on her face prompted him to tell her the truth, that the calls were related to the discussion that they had the night before. She nodded in understanding and left him be.

He took a deep breath as he looked at Curtis Hardy's telephone number, already typed into his cell phone. He paused before he hit the send icon, rethinking how to ask Curtis to attend a meeting where the topic of discussion might be whether his wife is a killer or not. The problem was that they couldn't leave him out of the meeting. If he found out about a clandestine gathering of his friends and he wasn't invited, he might feel that a plot existed against him and Carly Sue. There was no way out of the call. He made the decision years ago for the four of them to keep what they did a secret. He also was the first one of the four to break the promise. He had to man-up now, be the leader that they all believed he was back then, and get this mess under control again, whatever it took.

He hit the send icon and heard the phone ring in his ear. After the third ring, he thought about hanging up and trying later when he heard someone pick up. He was surprised when a quiet, female voice answered.

"Hey, Tommy."

"Hey. Carly Sue, I presume?"

She gave a short laugh. "Yeah. Long time, huh?"

"Yep. Too long. How'd you know it was me?"

In a joking voice she said, "There's this new thingy. Caller ID. You should look into it."

Tommy smiled in spite of his anxiety. "Yeah, Carly Sue. Funny." An awkward silence filled several seconds that seemed much longer to Tommy. Finally, he took a deep breath. "Is Curtis home?"

"What, you ain't goin' to ask how I'm doin'? I'll just tell you. I'm fine, Tommy. I wasn't fine for a long time, but I'm fine now."

Tommy heard a voice in the background asking who was on the phone. Carly Sue came back on the line. "Curtis is right here. And, Tommy?"

"Yeah?"

"Thank you."

After a pause, he asked, "For what?"

"For keeping quiet all these years. It was best…at the time, anyways. Here's Curtis."

At that moment, Tommy understood that Curtis had discussed the night of August 26, 1999, with Carly Sue and told her about the pact. As he, Andy, and Billy Ray suspected, Curtis had broken the pact already. Under the circumstances, he understood that it was impossible for them to not have discussed it.

Curtis's somewhat harsh voice cut into his thoughts. "What do you want, Tommy?"

"Hey, Curtis. We need to talk, considering everything that's happened in the last few days."

"I don't think we should talk at all, especially now. And don't you think that Andy and Billy Ray should be part of this?"

"We already talked and..."

"What!? You already talked to Andy and Billy Ray and nobody talked to me? You bastards are..."

"Curtis...Curtis, we haven't talked except to say that we need to talk...all of us...together."

There was silence on the line except for the sound of Curtis's quick breaths as he tried to calm down. He asked, "What do y'all hope to accomplish by talkin'?"

"I don't know, Curtis, but I don't want us, any of us, including your wife, to end up in prison. Can you meet with all of us tomorrow morning, early?"

"How early? And where?"

"6:30 at the tree, unless y'all have a better idea."

Again, silence engulfed the phone line. He thought that Curtis might be talking with Carly Sue, then he said, "Yeah, let's meet. 6:30, at the tree."

Tommy frowned. "Okay. I'll call Billy Ray and Andy and let them know. If they have a problem with it, I'll call you back. If you don't hear from me, then the meeting is on. Okay?"

Curtis's reply was short, almost terse. "All y'all just be there."

The line went dead.

Tommy thought for a moment. What did Curtis know about Carly Sue's involvement with the dead man? Did he know she killed the man or did she tell him who the killer was? Did she even know? How far would he go to protect his wife? Should he carry a sidearm with him to the meeting? He shivered. At one time, the four young boys were inseparable.

They told each other intimate details about their lives, as intimate as a twelve-year-old can get, and they had each other's backs. Now he considered taking a gun to a meeting with these same people. But they were adults now, essentially different people. They had made a pact and every one of them broke the silence...everyone except Billy Ray.

Tommy made the calls to Andy and Billy Ray. They both agreed to the time and location of the meeting, though Andy wasn't real enthusiastic at the prospect of seeing his childhood friends in the woods before sunrise. At least the heat wouldn't be too bad that early in the morning.

Chapter 28

Captain Gerald Brannen arrived home after 9:00 PM. His wife heated up his dinner of fried catfish, collard greens, and macaroni and cheese, and served it to him on a TV tray while he sat in his favorite chair in front of his fireplace. He had planned on having ice tea but opted for a bottle of Busch beer, mainly to avoid the caffeine intake.

There was no fire blazing this evening. The fireplace hadn't been in operation since back in early March, but he liked the ambience of the room. It helped calm him after a day at the Bulloch County Sheriff's office. He and his wife agreed that this was their "media free" room. There were no televisions or computers, video games or other electronics. He didn't even like to bring his cordless phone or cell phone into the room.

He did, however, take notes from work and reviewed them while he ate. As he maneuvered a forkful of greens to his mouth, he scanned his notes from the second interview with Millie Crider. She admitted knowing that the dead man was Allen Scott. How she knew that, Crider couldn't, or wouldn't, elaborate. But the big surprise happened when she pulled out four Polaroids that she claimed were of MaryJo Saxon leaving the trailer park, on foot, the night of August 26, 1999, and returning about half an hour later. It appeared that the photos were taken from Crider's kitchen window. She admitted that she took the pictures, with her own camera, immediately after Allen Scott and Carly Sue left MaryJo's trailer in his white Ford Tempo.

Brannen had confiscated the photos as evidence. He turned them over, one-by-one, and looked at the pen-written notes on the back of each one. The scribbles indicated the date and time that each picture was taken. The notes appeared authentic. The writing had blurred slightly, the ink appearing to bleed and fade, as it would over a long period of time. The notes indicated that MaryJo left the trailer at 10:06 PM and returned at 10:37.

Brannen and Jones were both dumbfounded. Brannen had asked Millie why she hadn't come forward back in 1999 with this evidence. She replied that she hadn't known that a crime had been committed, so why would she. He then asked her why she took the pictures. Again, she was ready with a quick answer. She replied that she kept tabs on what was happening in her neighborhood. They had experienced a number of break-ins around that time and she wanted to be a good citizen and keep the trailer park safe. Brannen wanted to ask her if it was because she was the landlord, but he wasn't ready to reveal that they knew about her ownership of the park and surrounding land. He was afraid that she would clam up for good.

The two lawmen had questioned Millie for nearly an hour, finally asking if she believed that MaryJo Saxon had killed Allen Scott. She had replied, "Yes, sir. Yes, I do. That woman has been off her rocker for decades. Y'all saw her and y'all know how crazy she is. She's a drunk and she goes into violent fits. Y'all seen it for yourselves."

Brannen flipped the photos back over and looked at the grainy images. The woman leaving and returning to the trailer park bore little to no resemblance to MaryJo Saxon, at least, not the one that he and Deputy Jones had encountered over the past few days. The photos showed a relatively slim woman with long, straight hair. They couldn't see the face in the pictures, so there was no way to know if the woman was, in fact, MaryJo Saxon. That was one reason they hadn't gone immediately to her trailer and arrested her. The other reason was that they had no physical evidence that she had a weapon, particularly a gun, on her at the time the pictures were taken. They couldn't tell if she was carrying anything at all. He wondered if the photos could be enhanced to provide more detail, but from what he saw, he knew it was a long-shot at best.

But the pictures, along with Millie Crider's eye-witness account, could prove that MaryJo was headed towards the lake at the time that her boyfriend had taken her daughter to the lake. He was a long way from declaring that MaryJo was a murderer.

The other troubling aspect of all the information that was coming to light was that Millie Crider appeared to be the sole source, and she seemed to have this information at her fingertips. Why had she kept quiet all these years? Only God and Millie Crider knew that answer.

Brannen finished the last bite of his dinner and washed it down with a swig of Busch beer. He sat back in his chair thinking that retirement sure looked appealing.

Brannen had let Deputy Jones know that, together, they would question MaryJo on Wednesday morning after they reviewed their notes of the Crider interview. They would plan their visit to MaryJo's for around 10:00 AM, before she had the chance to get totally sloshed. It was a good plan...so they thought.

* * *

At 8:45 PM, Curtis and Carly Sue Hardy finished cleaning up the kitchen from their later-than-usual evening meal. Curtis had lights on in the living room, dining room, and kitchen, trying to keep the atmosphere in their home as bright as possible. Her doctor had told Curtis that something as simple as the amount of light in a home could send his wife's mood up or down: the brighter the better.

Carly Sue had been feeling blue all day. She told Curtis to go ahead and eat without her, that she was going to lie down for a bit, but he wouldn't allow it. He told her that she had to eat before she could take her evening medications and that she had to take them in order for her to break out of her current doldrums. He tried his best to keep from using words that would send her deeper into depression. He felt as if he were tiptoeing through a mine field. It was a skill that he had mastered over the years of their marriage, but now, given all the publicity surrounding the body's recovery from the lake, it was even more challenging.

He was closely monitoring his wife's expressions without being obvious. She seemed to be weighing a heavy decision, her eyes looking at the floor, but seeing something entirely different. Carly Sue appeared to be in deep thought when she said, "Hey, sweetie, I need to tell you something."

Curtis's internal radar sensed that the coming discussion was going to be difficult, given her state of mind. His own anxiety tweaked up a notch. In a soothing voice, he asked, "Yes, dear?"

She continued to stare at the carpet, but her eyes were off in another time and place. Curtis recognized the look and knew that she had been reliving the horrors of that night by the lake, which accounted for her current state of mind. When she spoke, it was in an emotionless monotone, so quiet that he had a difficult time hearing the words. "I didn't kill that man, you know, the guy they pulled from the lake. Allen Scott."

Curtis's eyes bore in on his wife as she spoke. He did his best to maintain a neutral expression, but he was alarmed. In all the years since she was attacked, she had never spoken the man's name. They had many discussions about that night, about how she fought against "that man" or "that bastard" or a number of vile descriptions of the man. She obviously knew who he was, because her mother dated him twice. But Carly Sue's recollection of the incident always ended in her coming out of a defensive fight. She never said that she heard a gunshot, or saw anyone else at the scene from the time he parked the car by the lake until Curtis and his friends showed up. She remembered pushing the man's body off of her and seeing the man collapse against the driver's side door and the blood flowing down the side of his head. She even remembered crawling out of the car, looking around, trying to figure out what to do. She had described to Curtis how she tried to push the car into the lake, then collapsed at the rear of the car, crying for help.

She also remembered Curtis and his friends showing up and helping her push the car into the lake and the immense fear she felt when the car looked as if it wasn't going to sink. She also remembered Tommy giving her orders to go home and never talk about what happened. Curtis knew that she hadn't said a word to anyone else about that night, except him.

Their previous talks usually happened when Carly Sue was on the downhill slide into one of her bi-polar episodes. He prayed that she wasn't on that slippery slope now.

"Sweetie, I know you didn't kill that man. We've been over this."

"But, I remembered something, Curtis. I mean, I'm startin' to remember bits and pieces of that night. When I was layin' in that front seat, waitin' for...you know...he slapped me so hard. But, while I was layin' there, I saw a hand come through the window. I saw a flash, then...I don't know. That's as far as I can remember, except when I got outta the car, I remember panickin' 'cause I couldn't find momma's gun."

Curtis was silent for a stretch. He waited to see if his wife remembered anything else, hoping that she hadn't. When he spoke, it was in a soft tone, hoping to dissuade her from thinking about that night. "Sweetie, you know the doctor said that you might have dreams, thoughts that might not be right. She said your mind might play tricks on you, that some things might seem real, but that they really aren't." As he paused for effect, she looked at him with a pitiful expression, as if saying, *You don't believe me.* He continued. "I ain't sayin' that what you remember isn't right, I'm just remindin' you what the doctor said. She's the expert."

Carly Sue didn't reply, she just frowned and looked away. Curtis could tell that she was discouraged by his remarks, as if he had disciplined her for such crazy thoughts. He was trying to backtrack and soften the blow. "Sweetie, why don't you sleep on it and see what you remember tomorrow. If you are startin' to remember more, then this will come back to you and then some. I don't think it's healthy to rush to conclusions. We can talk more tomorrow mornin' at breakfast."

She nodded, but without conviction. Curtis's fears about his wife's memory were slowly unfolding, and there was nothing he could do about it, except hope that she would tell him before anyone else had a chance to question her. Then he would have a shot at steering her remarks in the right direction: at least what he believed was the right direction.

Chapter 29

The crystal-clear sky to the east of Cypress Lake showed a light blue-to-gray hue as the sun broached the horizon. To the west, the darkness began to lighten. Though another toasty, dry day was forecast for Wednesday, June 3, meteorologists for the major news stations in Statesboro were optimistic that more seasonal weather was imminent. They weren't making any promises, but rain was a genuine possibility within the next two days.

Tommy Alexander parked his gold Lexus in roughly the same spot that he had parked just yesterday morning when he met Billy Ray at the tree. At 6:20 AM, he was early enough that he could make the trek through the woods and still be on-time for the 6:30 meeting with a few minutes to spare, assuming he didn't get lost on the way. No doubt, darkness from the tree coverage would make the path more difficult to follow at this earlier morning hour.

As he approached Cypress Lake road on foot, another car passed the turn-off road, then slowed quickly. It was Andy Pepperdine. He backed up on the road and pulled onto the path, parking his blue Cadillac CTS next to Tommy's gold Lexus. The cars, like the men, looked completely out of place. Tommy greeted Andy with a tentative handshake and an equally uncertain, "Hi, Andy."

For his part, Andy appeared upbeat, smiling at his childhood friend and offering a firm handshake and a robust, "Hey, Tommy. Looks like we might get some rain, finally."

Tommy looked skyward. "It won't be today, but I guess the experts say in a day or so." There was a pause as the two men didn't want to say anything about the meeting without

Curtis and Billy Ray being there. Neither man wanted to be accused of plotting anything sinister.

Tommy said, "I think we better head that way."

Without saying another word, the two men made their way through the woods and arrived at the clearing at 6:26. Billy Ray was already there, squatting down in front of their tree. He rose when he heard the two men approach. Billy Ray spoke first.

"Hey, Tommy, Andy. Bright and early, huh?"

Andy smiled and walked up to Billy Ray. "Hey, Billy Ray. Been a long time. You look good, 'cept that big ol' scar on your head." He held up his hands and said, "I'm just jokin' with you about the scar, but I'm serious 'bout everything else, you look real good."

Billy Ray took Andy's offered hand and they shook, then hugged. Tommy looked on in surprise. When the two grown men separated, Tommy grasped Billy Ray's hand and shook it again.

A snapped twig caught their attention. They all turned to see Curtis Hardy standing at the edge of the clearing. He didn't move. He didn't say a word. He just stared at his three childhood friends. Tommy tried to read his mood, by the look in his eyes and his body language, without success.

Andy broke the brief, awkward moment. With a big smile and an extended hand, he closed the fifteen feet that separated them. "Hey, Curtis. How are you?"

Curtis took Andy's hand, but it lacked energy. It was a reluctant acceptance that he needed to be here, but really had no desire to participate. He let go of Andy's hand as quickly as possible. "Andy, Tommy, Billy Ray." In an accusatory tone, he asked, "How long have y'all been here?"

Tommy noticed Curtis's attitude. "We just got here, Curtis. Literally, within the last minute. Billy Ray was here, alone, when Andy and me got here."

"What, did y'all ride together?"

Andy decided he better step up so Tommy wasn't alone on the defensive. His tone was not harsh but pointed. "Curtis,

Tommy was parked by the lake at the boat trail. I saw his car parked there, so I parked next to him. He was already out of his car, walking towards the road. When he saw me, he waited. We didn't talk about anything but the weather. We, all three of us..." he pointed with his thumb at Tommy and Billy Ray, "...haven't talked about...that night. But I guess we're about to."

Curtis took a deep breath. He didn't appear completely satisfied by Andy's explanation, but was willing to move forward with the meeting. "Alright, let's get this show on the road. Who's leadin' this meetin'?"

Just like when they were kids, they all looked at Tommy. At first, he was hesitant, but his resistance turned to resignation. After all was said and done, he was the one who broke the pact by talking with his wife, though he suspected that Curtis had broken the pact years ago.

"Okay, okay. I'll do it." He took a deep breath, looked down at the leaf-covered ground in the clearing and began. "I know I was the one who said we needed to keep this to ourselves to the grave, but I broke the pact." He paused. "I was faced with a choice. Either tell my wife the whole story or let her suspect that Andy and me were lovers."

The three men took a half step back, then Andy exclaimed, "What?!"

"Well, you see, since the sheriff's office pulled that body from the lake, I've been in a fog, worryin' about what was goin' to happen to the four of us. I figured it's only a matter of time before somebody figures out what we helped Carly Sue do. Then we're all screwed. Well, she noticed I was actin' all weird and asked me if I had a mistress. I said no, then she asked if I was gay. She noticed that Andy and me got matching scars on our hands and she thought it was some kinda love symbol, so she thought that we was havin' a gay affair." A sly smile crossed his face as he looked at Andy. "I guess I coulda said yes, but I didn't think that you'd appreciate that."

"You're danged right about that. So that's why Cornelia ambushed me last night?"

"Yeah. I think that Cheryl told your wife that you had a secret and that you needed to be the one to tell her about it. Cheryl didn't tell her any details. Figured that you two should work it out."

"Well, she worked it out of me, alright. But I gotta tell ya, I feel better now that it's off my chest."

They turned to Billy Ray, who was smiling, and Curtis, who was turning red in the face. Curtis was obviously angry. He asked, "What, exactly, did y'all tell your wives?"

Andy went first. "I told her exactly what we did. You know, heard Carly Sue cryin' out, saw the body, helped push the car, and came back here. What else is there to tell?"

Tommy nodded. He said that he told Cheryl exactly the same thing.

Curtis turned to Billy Ray. "Who'd you tell?"

"I ain't told a soul."

Curtis looked skeptically at Billy Ray. "You mean to tell me that all them drunk days and nights, all that time in the drunk tank, and you ain't told no one?"

"Swear to God." Billy Ray was calm. He knew that all three of his friends feared that he was the weak link, that his alcoholism and casual drug use would lead him to blab their secret all over Statesboro. Here he was, the only one who kept the pact. He felt vindicated but didn't feel like gloating. He knew that the difficult discussion was ahead of them.

Billy Ray looked back at Curtis. "Did you tell anyone? Like, maybe, talk about that night with your wife?"

Curtis's face turned dark red. Then he snarled, "Yeah, we talked a lot. She's haunted by that night. That bastard was going to rape her."

Billy Ray said, "Did she kill that man?"

Curtis was livid. He started to yell, but realized that, in the still, morning air, their voices would travel a long ways. He lowered his voice and growled, "No. She didn't kill him."

Billy Ray said, "I wouldn't've blamed her if she did. He was molestin' her."

Billy Ray went on to tell them of the night he heard her struggling in her room and he put the ladder up to her window. It was the night before they helped her push the car into the lake. "That's why I thought that she did the killin', but I didn't think that she had it in her to actually kill a man."

"Well, she didn't do it."

Tommy and Andy had been listening to the exchange. They weren't surprised to hear that Curtis had discussed that night with his wife. How could he not discuss it? But to hear that Billy Ray had peeked into Carly Sue's window and saw the man molesting Carly Sue – at the time, she was their friend – that was a bombshell.

Tommy asked, "Why didn't you do anything about it?"

Billy Ray's face turned dark and sad. "Hell, I was just a kid. What was I gonna do against that goon? He'd a kicked my ass. Anyways, he got what was comin' to him."

Tommy turned to Curtis. "That sure is a good motive for murder."

Curtis growled, "She didn't do it. I know my wife. She didn't do it. She told me so."

Andy said, "Curtis, we believe that she told you that she didn't do it, but what did she tell you?"

Curtis paused, thinking about whether it was safe to tell them about his and Carly Sue's private conversations about that night. She claimed to not know much more than them until last evening. He was having a difficult time keeping his stories straight in his mind. So, he decided to keep it as simple as possible. "Carly Sue went to the lake with that bastard because he threatened to hurt her momma if she didn't. She swears that MaryJo didn't know the guy was molesting her. She was going to hurt the guy somehow, but when they got to the lake, he slapped her so hard that she blacked out. When she came to, the guy was dead. That's when she started crying, and then we showed up. She doesn't know who pulled the trigger. She swears. Look, y'all, she's in therapy for depression. She has bi-polar disorder. She still has nightmares about that night. But she didn't kill that man. All she's guilty of is the same thing we're guilty of…pushin' that dead guy into the lake."

They were all silent for a time, each trying to put the pieces together of the night that changed their lives. They each had the same basic pieces, but Curtis knew something that none of the others suspected.

Then Tommy asked, "If Carly Sue didn't do it, then who did?"

All four men were quiet until Curtis spoke up. "Besides my wife, the only one I can think of with a motive is her mother. Some guy that she was dating was molesting her daughter." Curtis looked at Tommy. "That's a motive. Carly Sue said her momma had a gun, a thirty-eight, and it came up missin' after the murder."

Billy Ray asked the obvious question. "So, what do we do next?"

Curtis was about to speak when Andy said, "We broke the pact, but only the four of us and our wives know. I say we don't tell anyone else. I'm sure our wives will go along with it. They – we all – have too much to lose."

Curtis looked at his childhood friends. He saw that they were thinking about the consequences to their families, their lives, and the ramifications of this going public. He saw Tommy and Andy nodding. He turned to Billy Ray, who was smiling.

Tommy spoke up. "I think I can convince Cheryl that it is best that we not say anything." He looked over at Andy.

Andy nodded. "Same here."

Billy Ray nodded that he thought it was best to continue their silence, with one addition. "I think we should talk with each other about this, when we need to talk, that is. We can't go on like we done over the last sixteen years."

They all nodded. Tommy put on a serious face and said, "Okay, y'all take out y'all's knives and…" He paused then smiled. "I'm just kiddin'. I wouldn't want to touch that ugly tree again."

They all looked up at the ugly scar on the tree that still oozed a rust colored sap and took a deep breath. They agreed to meet again if necessary, all the while hoping that it wouldn't be.

Chapter 30

Wednesday morning, the heat was already building, but with one difference. There were actual clouds in the sky. While there was still no rain predicted for the day, weathermen from all the major news channels expressed confidence that the southeast would get much-needed rain soon. The predicted shift in the weather pattern was taking shape and a storm front developed from the Texas panhandle to the northeast through western Michigan. The storms had a high probability of producing violent storms, but for now, folks in the southeast would take anything that produced precipitation.

The sheriff's car parked at MaryJo Saxon's trailer was already drawing onlookers as a number of residents stepped out onto their porches. With the murder discovery less than a week old, any law enforcement presence at the park drew everyone's attention. Millie Crider stayed inside her trailer, but watched as Captain Brannen and Deputy Jones exited their car. She figured that they couldn't ignore the evidence that she provided, though she knew that the pictures and her word wouldn't be enough for an arrest. They must have found additional information driving them to confront MaryJo. Maybe they weren't there to arrest the woman, but rather question her further, hoping to get a confession out of her. Millie smiled to herself. She had steered the investigation in the right direction.

* * *

Captain Brannen banged on MaryJo Saxon's flimsy trailer door. They were unable to rouse the woman, which only irked the lawmen. Brannen was getting frustrated with their inability to get straight answers from the crazy, alcoholic woman, especially since they now had evidence that she might be a material witness to the murder. With what they knew, she could be the murderer. She had opportunity – she rarely worked – and motive. One of her sick boyfriends was molesting her daughter. But did she have the means? Did she own or have access to a thirty-eight-caliber revolver? The plan was to make her feel as if they had the goods on her and see how she responded. They had hoped to present these facts to her this morning and get a confession for the murder of Allen Scott. Based on their past interviews with her, they expected a violent outburst, and an accusation that her neighbors were framing her.

Brannen banged on the door going on a full minute, then told Jones to take over while he walked around the outside of the trailer, looking for any other way into the old, rusted tin box. On the opposite side of the trailer, he found an old wooden, five-foot step ladder. It appeared to be unused for many years, partially buried in dead leaves. When he pulled it up, he thought that it might hold his weight. Shaking the leaves and dirt from the ladder, he set it up next to a window that would most likely give him a view of the living room. With the ladder creaking in protest, he climbed to the second step and peered through a section of venetian blinds that were broken off.

MaryJo Saxon was lying on her stomach on the floor next to the beat up couch. Her face was towards the couch. An open bottle of some kind of booze lay next to her head. From what Brannen could see, she wasn't breathing.

His anxiety spiked as he hopped off the ladder. "Jonesy, bust the door open and get in there!" As he yelled to his deputy, he scampered around the trailer as fast as he could. Jones was grabbing the door handle and kicking the side of the trailer near the door latch as he pulled with all his might. The door popped open, sending the deputy reeling backwards against the rusted rails of the porch. The flooring of the porch gave way under his right foot and his leg went through the wire flooring all the way to his knee. Brannen could see the gash on his leg as blood started to flow.

Jones yelled in pain. When he tried to pull his leg back up, the metal mesh that had failed pulled against his leg. Brannen forgot about MaryJo for the moment and told Jones to hold still. He reached under the porch and pulled the rusted metal back away from Jones's leg, allowing him to pull his leg free. The cut was deep and flowing red, but no major arteries or veins were affected.

Brannen looked up at Jones. "It's nasty, but not serious. Sit down here on the steps. Call the station for back-up and a rescue team. I'll check on Miss Saxon."

Jones winced several times. "Okay, Captain. I'll be fine. I'm gonna need a tetanus shot for sure."

As Brannen entered MaryJo's trailer, he was quickly reminded of the foul, stale odor that permeated the dwelling. He again wondered how anyone could stand living with such a putrid odor. There were new scents added to the air in the trailer, that of human waste. He moved towards MaryJo's body, looking all around as he went. MaryJo weighed in excess of three hundred pounds. Her flesh spread away from the center of her body. Brannen knew that moving her body, even for several people, was going to be a challenge. Her complexion was waxy white, the color of death, with the exception of the blood that had settled to the lowest point in her body. With no pumping heart to keep the blood circulating, the fleshy parts of her body that Brannen could see near the carpet appeared bruised. He had seen dead bodies many times before, and he never got used to it. Where there was once life, only a shell remained. He touched MaryJo's neck, just because he felt it was somehow required to validate what he already knew. MaryJo's body temperature was already cold.

He stood and slowly backed out of the trailer and headed for the porch. Jones asked, "What's the story in there?"

Brannen looked around at all the gawkers, then leaned in close to Jones's ear. "The Saxon woman is dead. There's an empty bottle next to her head. Most likely, she drank herself to death, but, given what's goin' on around here, we best call Cedric's office to make the official call."

"I already called for an ambulance and to get us some back-up. I'll call and have them contact the coroner's office."

"Yep. Looks like we got another long day ahead, but you need to have that leg looked at first. Whatever you do, don't go near her trailer with your leg bleedin' like that. You'll contaminate the scene. It looks clear cut, but you never know. Anything I can get for you right now?"

"Nah. Thanks, Captain, but I'll live."

"You should take the rest of the day off. I think that you're gonna need stitches and somethin' for the pain. That's gonna take a while to heal."

"Hopefully the EMTs will be able to give me something when they get here."

Brannen turned and headed back inside MaryJo's trailer. He tried to breathe through his mouth to minimize the effect of the foul air on his nasal passage. As he tiptoed back towards the body, he looked around for any signs of a disturbance, but remembering the chaotic nature of the trailer the last time he and Jones were here, it would be difficult to tell if anything was out of place, because everything was out of place. The trailer was in complete disarray.

The couch behind the body was dark blue, old, and worn out. It should have been replaced many years ago. Two mismatched table lamps with torn lamp shades sat on a pair of mismatched end tables, which were covered in dust. The surfaces had permanent rings from sweaty glasses or spilled cups of some liquid and the tables' edges were separating, the pressboard having been soaked over the years. The carpet was threadbare and stained in spots. A number of fibers were pulled up, causing long runs in several places. A few pictures hung on the walls, some in positions that were apparently meant to hide holes or other visible defects. MaryJo had apparently given up on hiding all the damage as several holes were visible in the walls around the living room and kitchen.

Brannen finally made his way to MaryJo's massive, disheveled body. She wore a white tank top, though it had yellowed with age, and a pair of light blue shorts. She had nothing on her feet and no jewelry anywhere on her body, at least none that was visible. The empty bottle by her head had once been full of Southern Comfort. Brannen looked for a glass or a paper cup or any indication that she was drinking from a container rather than straight from the bottle. There were none in the living room or on the counter that separated the living room from the kitchen, but he didn't think that mattered. As much as she obviously drank, she may not have bothered with a glass and opted to drink straight from the bottle.

Without touching anything, he looked closely at her body, then at the bottle by her head. He didn't see anything that would lead him to any conclusion other than an accidental death or a suicide. There was nothing under the couch, no lamps turned over or broken, and no signs of forced entry.

Brannen could hear sirens in the distance. It sounded like at least two vehicles approaching fast. The stench of the trailer was starting to overwhelm his sense of smell so he turned and headed for the door. Jones was sitting in the passenger seat of the sheriff's car with his legs extended out of the car. He had cut his uniform's pant leg so that the wound was visible. Blood still flowed and was pooled on the stone driveway. As Brannen stepped in front of his deputy, the rescue truck pulled up behind the sheriff's car. A young Asian-looking man in an EMT uniform exited the truck and headed for Jones.

In perfect, Midwestern English he asked, "What've we got here, guys?"

Jones twisted his leg towards the young man. "Got a little cut."

The guy smiled just as a black female EMT stepped to his side with a large medical bag. He said, "If that's your idea of a little cut, I don't want to be with you when something big happens."

The female EMT went to work, pulling out bottles of saline, sterile gauze pads, and other materials to help clean the wound and stop the bleeding. Brannen asked, "What's your names?"

"I'm Jason, that's Elle."

"Follow me, Jason, and be ready to hold your nose."

The men entered the trailer and the EMT saw MaryJo's body. "I see what you mean about the air in here." He looked at MaryJo's body, "No need to rush. She's been gone for a while. I'll call the hospital and talk with the on-call physician and get concurrence on time of death. Then I'll take a quick look over her to see if there's anything obvious that would point to other than accidental alcohol poisoning."

"You need my help moving the body?"

"If you don't mind."

Jason moved closer to the body pulled out a powerful penlight. He started at the top of her head and looked at her scalp. MaryJo's face was towards the couch, so he examined the back of her skull. He looked into her left ear then asked Brannen to help him turn her head. When they lifted her head to turn it away from the couch, her nose rubbed against the carpet. A dark, syrupy smear ran across her nose.

Jason frowned. He was in thought for a moment. "Let's lift her head for a moment. I'm going to look at the floor under her head while it's lifted."

"Okay. Ready?"

They raised the dead woman's head. The EMT used his flashlight to inspect the carpet. He frowned again.

"What is it?"

"I think we have blood on the carpet, but I don't see any wounds on her that would produce a puddle of blood." He moved the light up over MaryJo's head, starting with her face, opening her mouth, then looking in her right ear. "Ahh. Here's the source of the blood. Looks like her ear was bleeding. That's odd, but maybe it was pre-existing. The Coroner will take a look when they get the body in the morgue."

Jason went on to inspect her body and found nothing else of interest. The two men left just as the coroner's van pulled up. A very young, red-headed woman jumped out of the driver's door. Cedric slowly stepped out of the passenger side door.

Brannen greeted the two. "Busy week out here in the country."

Cedric smiled. "I guess my protégé here, will have lots of on-the-job training this week. What have we here?"

Brannen turned and gestured that they should follow him. "Ginger, we're going to have to help Cedric up the steps. Jonesy, my deputy fell through the decking on the porch. It really isn't safe, but it's the only way in."

The Deputy Coroner smiled. She turned to Cedric and asked, "You want to wait out here while I do the initial inspection?"

"That would be fine, dear. I'm still not feeling one hundred percent yet."

Ginger Evans performed the inspection of MaryJo's body and found nothing out of the ordinary except the victim's right eye was bloodshot more so than the left eye, but that might have been caused by the lividity. She also noted the blood that Jason pointed out, pooled in her right ear. She said they would know more when they got the body on the table. She took a preliminary body temperature – eighty-one degrees Fahrenheit.

"Based on the body temperature, the deceased died at least seven to eight hours ago. Beyond that, we can't say, at least until we do an autopsy. Cedric will decide if one is necessary."

Brannen did a quick calculation in his head. *Sometime around midnight to one in the morning.* He asked, "How are we going to get the body into the van?"

The Deputy Coroner said, "We'll back the van up as close as possible. We might have to get more help and maybe build a temporary platform. I'll ask Cedric what he thinks."

Brannen scratched his head. *I guess I'd better call for more help.*

Chapter 31

Eugene Morris pulled in behind the coroner's van at MaryJo Saxon's trailer at 9:02 AM. He heard the first reports of a dead body at Cypress Lake Mobile Home Park at 8:38 just as he finished brushing his teeth after showering. He listened to the exchange between the sheriff's office and the dispatcher describing a middle-aged woman, deceased in her home, no obvious signs of foul play, potential alcohol poisoning. Morris knew only one woman who fit that description.

When he stepped out of his car, Gerald Brannen walked up and greeted the reporter. "Busy week out this way, huh?"

They shook hands. "Hey, Gerry. What can you tell me? Is it that Saxon woman? I mean, it's her trailer."

Brannen looked around at the crowd gathered across the road from MaryJo's trailer. They seemed to congregate near Millie Crider's trailer because they could see around the coroner's van. It was the best view of the dead woman's trailer door. Morris could tell that some in the crowd didn't want to get too close to Millie's trailer.

"Yeah. Found her face down on the floor. By the way, these details are off the record, for now anyways. As soon as we get Cedric's report, I'll call you with the go-ahead to run with it."

"Okay, Gerry. I'm good with that. I have to get back to the county building anyway. I'm trying to locate old lady Crider's husband. I did some searching and I can't find out where he went when he left here. There's no trace of him staying in the area, but that was back in the seventies. Records weren't all that good back then."

"Why don't you just go over and ask her where he went?"

Morris smiled and asked, "You gonna provide police protection?"

The men quietly laughed. With that, Morris turned and headed back to his car. As he backed out, the crowd had to move so he could maneuver his car back towards the park's entrance. He noticed that Millie Crider was in her kitchen window, binoculars in hand, keeping a sharp eye towards MaryJo's trailer. Then he saw Ginny Hardy staring out her own kitchen window, hands clasped together, watching her neighbor's trailer. *What in the hell is going on here?*

***

The most recent excitement over, the crowd dispersed. Curtis Hardy pulled his white Ford Focus into Ginny Hardy's driveway just as a Bulloch County Sheriff's car headed for the park's entrance. He tried to avoid eye contact with the driver as the cars passed each other. The sheriff's car kept going without slowing down. In his rearview-mirror, Curtis saw it turn right onto Cypress Lake Road heading back towards town. He let out his breath, aware that his anxiety level was heightened just by the sheriff's presence.

He noticed the damage to Carly Sue's mom's wire deck, the rusted wire bent in different directions and a length of rope used to tie the trailer's busted door closed.

As he parked, he saw his mother staring at him through her kitchen window. She had her hands folded as if in prayer. He knew from experience that she was fretting over something, real or imagined. His request for her silence was bound to add to her worries, but it couldn't be helped.

He entered the trailer and greeted his mother with a hug. "Hey, Momma."

After they separated, she put a hand on his cheek and looked into his eyes. "Sweetie." After a pause, she asked if he wanted an iced tea or water.

"Tea, please, Momma." As she opened the refrigerator, he sat at the kitchen table and looked around. As usual, everything was in its place. He mentioned, "I just passed a sheriff's car leaving and I see MaryJo's trailer's torn up some. What's goin' on?"

Ginny Hardy paused as she hefted the large pitcher of tea onto the counter. "They were here to question MaryJo, I guess…you know…about the body. They found her dead."

In a voice void of emotion, "Oh my God! How'd she die?"

Ginny's voice quivered as she answered in a near-whisper. "Nobody's said, but you can bet she drank herself to death. That would be my guess. I'm sorry. I shouldn't be gossipin'."

Curtis was quiet, deep in thought when it dawned on him. "They'll be calling Carly Sue. She's next of kin."

There was silence until Ginny spilled his glass of tea on the counter. Curtis turned to his mother and noticed her whole body was shaking as she reached for a handful of paper towels. She started to clean up the mess on the counter when Curtis said, "Momma, sit down and relax. I'll get this."

Her voice was quiet and anxious. "No, no, I've got it, Curtis. I'll get you another glass."

Curtis was gentle and calm, but firm, a habit that he had developed while dealing with his wife's rapid mood swings. In a soothing voice, he prodded, "Momma. Just stop. Please let me handle this. I have to tell you something, anyways, then I have to go. I've gotta be there when they call Carly Sue. I don't know if this news will depress her or cheer her up. That don't matter I guess."

Curtis watched as Ginny sat down and stared at the table with her hands folded so tight that her knuckles were turning white. She appeared to be praying. He turned back to the task of cleaning up the spilled tea. There was silence in the trailer while he worked.

When he finished pouring himself a fresh glass, he sat down across from his mother and took a long, slow drink. He looked directly at her and asked, "Momma, do you have that necklace and matching bracelet that Grandma Crider gave you? You know, the real classy one?"

Curtis watched as his mother took a sharp, deep breath. Her eyes welled with tears. "I have the necklace, but the bracelet was stolen years ago. I think it was MaryJo who stole it. Probably hocked it for booze money."

They both knew it was a lie, but Curtis didn't care. All he knew was that she had to remain quiet and not answer any questions from the sheriff's deputies or that nosey reporter, Gene Morris. It was especially important now that MaryJo was dead.

"Momma, you need to give me that necklace right now. If anybody asks, it was stolen along with the bracelet. You understand me?"

Ginny nodded.

"And Momma, you can't say nothin' to nobody about that body...understand? You got to keep silent."

Ginny raised her puffy, red eyes from where they were burning a hole in her kitchen table. She kept her hands folded, as if asking for forgiveness from Curtis or God, or anyone who would answer her prayers. She whispered, "Which one, Curtis?"

The question puzzled him for a moment. What did she mean *Which one?* Was she serious? He meant the body pulled from the lake, but did she think that he meant MaryJo?

"That bastard they pulled from the lake, of course. If you stay quiet, everything will work out fine. Do you trust me?"

"Yes, sweetie, I trust you."

From the look on Ginny Hardy's face, any interrogator in the world would assume she was guilty of something. "Momma, y'all got to get yourself together. Stop lookin' guilty. When I leave, you go look in the mirror and convince yourself that you're goin' to be okay. If need be, go to church and pray and stay there until this blows over. Can you do that?"

"I'll do whatever you say, Curtis."

"Okay. I have to go see Carly Sue. Then I have to head back to work."

His mother had again lowered her head, this time closing her eyes completely. After a time, she stood, went back to her bedroom and retrieved the necklace. It was in an elegant box. Curtis inspected the piece, put it in a plastic shopping bag, and tucked it under his arm.

He feared that his mother was going to have a serious mental breakdown, if she hadn't already lost control. He wished he could stay and coach her more, but his wife needed him. He hated having to choose between his wife and his mother, but for now, there was no other way. Carly Sue was far more fragile than his mother, at least that's what he believed.

Then he had to deal with the pressures of work, and again deal with his childhood friends and their petty worries. With the drought ongoing, he couldn't take the rest of the day off. All time-off had been canceled. If he asked for time off, it would unleash a firestorm of protests from the union membership, not to mention the shit-storm that he would face from his superiors. He had a report to prepare for city council for the water department and he hadn't even given it any thought. It was going to be a tough couple of days.

***

Gerry Brannen had just finished briefing Sheriff Adkins and was trying to sit down at his desk for lunch when his phone rang. It was Nikki Olsen from the crime lab.

"Hi, Captain. I wanted to call you as soon as I could. Like, we cleaned up that bracelet that was found at the lake. Like, this is a really serious piece of jewelry. Like, I mean, the thing is worth serious bucks."

Brannen frowned. "How much are we talkin', Nikki?"

"Well, like, the bracelet is from Andrews Jewelers in Savannah. I called the store, and like, the sales people wouldn't even talk with me about it. They said the store's owner would call me back. So, like, he calls and asks for the serial number, and I give it to him. This bracelet was sold in 1970 along with a matching necklace. He wouldn't give me the name of the buyer. He said we would need a warrant for that. But, like, how does an expensive bracelet like that end up at a crime scene at a lake? I could see this being lost at an exclusive marina on the coast, but this is just, like, weird."

Brannen didn't say anything for so long that Nikki asked if he was still on the line. "Nikki, can you send me all the contact information for Andrews Jewelers and also send over photos of the bracelet. Include close-ups of the serial number and any other identifiers that make the piece unique. Did the store owner say how much the bracelet was worth?"

"Not exactly, but he said the bracelet alone was very expensive. With the necklace, the pair would be worth a whole lot more. He said if we got the warrant, he would cooperate fully, but he had to protect his client's privacy. Like, I can't argue with that logic."

"You get me the information and we'll get the warrant." He paused for a moment. "Anything else?"

"Let me think…not right now. Oh, wait."

Brannen heard Nikki talking with someone, then she came back on the line. "Warren, our database search guy, just said that they think they have a hit on the fingerprints pulled from the car's bumper. You know, like we tried that new process, and it kind-of worked. The thing is, the partial prints are just that, partial. So, there was just enough of a print…"

"Nikki…please. Do you have a name?"

"Well, like, yeah. William Raymond Duke. Does the name sound familiar?"

Brannen frowned. "Not when you say it like that, but when you say 'Billy Ray Duke,' now that's a very familiar name. Thanks, Nikki. This may be the break we need."

Brannen hung up the phone and stood. He headed for the sheriff's office to let her know about the break. Before he made it around his desk, his phone rang and he answered.

"Captain, this is Ginger Evans from the coroner's office."

"Hi, Ginger. You have some news for us?"

"Yes. Cedric said you needed to know this right away. MaryJo Saxon was murdered."

Brannen walked back around his desk and sat. "Ginger, say that again."

"MaryJo Saxon was murdered with a very thin, sharp object, like an ice pick or a thin barbeque skewer. My money's on an ice pick, but we can't conclude that without finding the object and testing it. When we did our initial examination, we didn't see anything too extraordinary. But we did an X-ray of the cranium and saw significant physical damage to the brain. We're doing toxicology now, and we're examining her organs. She did have damage to her liver. Most probably from heavy drinking, but she was definitely murdered."

"Thanks, Ginger. Please fax over your preliminary report as soon as possible."

"Sure thing, Captain."

Brannen headed for Adkins' office. When he got there, he said, "Sheriff, I have good news and bad news. The good news is we got a hit on the prints from Allen Scott's car. And we're closing in on the killer. The bad news is they killed again."

Adkins ran a hand over her face. "Okay, Gerry. Let's have it."

***

Brannen left Adkins' office with orders to obtain a warrant in Chatham County, Georgia, for all information related to the sale of a bracelet from Andrews Jewelers. She also ordered that Billy Ray Duke be brought in for questioning in the murder of Allen Scott.

Chapter 32

For the second time in the last three days, Tommy Alexander was going home for lunch. His mind had been occupied all morning with replays of his meeting at the tree with his childhood friends, and their decision to remain quiet. The pact was essentially renewed, but now included allowing discussions about the night of August 26, 1999 with their spouses. He needed to talk, just to unload the burden again. He thought that talking about it with Andy, Curtis, and Billy Ray would accomplish that, but he was mistaken. It only proved to distract him from business and daily life even more. When he called ahead to let Cheryl know that he was heading home, she was pleasantly surprised because it rarely happened.

As Tommy turned into the Irongate Subdivision, he noted the gathering clouds to the west. He said a little prayer hoping that the clouds would produce some amount of rain, if just to break the monotony of the ongoing drought. What they really needed, more than a thunderstorm, was a steady drizzle over several days. The news stations were predicting that rain was on the way. The clouds that Tommy saw weren't tall or dark enough to produce a lot of rain, but any rain would be a blessing.

As he approached his home, he instinctively clicked his garage door opener and slowed as he turned into his driveway. Billy Ray Duke stood at his front door, then walked towards Tommy's car as he pulled the Lexus into the garage.

As he parked, he wondered what Billy Ray was doing at his house. Crazy thoughts raced through his mind. Had he hurt Cheryl? Was he the killer? He quickly shook off his fears as Cheryl opened the door from the utility room to the garage.

When Tommy opened his car door, she told her husband that lunch was ready whenever he and Billy Ray were done talking. She said that she asked Billy Ray to join them, but he had declined. She smiled and told her husband to see if he could change his friend's mind.

He returned her smile as she closed the door, then turned to Billy Ray. "What's up?"

Billy Ray motioned towards the side of the house. When they were just around the corner from the open garage, he said in a quiet, calm voice, "Hey, Tommy. I had to tell one of y'all, then maybe you can tell Andy and Curtis."

"Tell them what?"

"I'm being hauled in for questionin'. Pastor Rod is giving me a ride to the sheriff's office in about ten minutes. I wanted to tell y'all in person though." He paused and took a deep breath. He had been sweating, his tee-shirt soaked, and he had dirt caked under his fingernails, like a working man's hands.

Tommy asked, "What are they questioning you about?"

"They got my fingerprints from the bumper of that car."

Tommy's eyes first showed shock, then fear. If they lifted Billy Ray's prints, surely they lifted the others. Billy Ray saw the change in Tommy's demeanor and explained, "You ain't never been arrested or been in the military, right?"

"That's right."

"Then you ain't got much to worry about. Andy and Curtis are the same. I don't think the city fingerprints their employees, so you three are safe. Same for Carly Sue. But, they got my prints all over their databases, I've been in jail so many times.

"I just wanted you to know that I ain't sayin' nothing' about that night. I'm gonna lawyer-up right away and plead the fifth. I know how this works. I'll only do that if they try to pin the murder on me."

Tommy's head was spinning while he tried to think of the implications of them questioning Billy Ray. The walls were closing in. It was more important now than ever, that they keep quiet. What could the police possibly have to incriminate them all? He turned to Billy Ray and was about to suggest that he tell the police that he had touched that bumper while it was parked at MaryJo's trailer when Cheryl opened the door to the garage. She hollered, "Tommy, you out there?"

Tommy and Billy Ray walked into the garage. "Yes, dear?"

"It was just on the news. That MaryJo Saxon woman was found dead this morning. They didn't say how she died yet, just that her body was taken to the coroner's office for an autopsy."

The men were shocked by the news. As they stood there, speechless, Father Rod pulled into the driveway to pick up Billy Ray and take him to his interview.

Tommy turned to his friend and said, "Do what you need to do, Billy Ray. I trust your judgment. I mean it. If there's anything you need, and I mean anything at all, you call me, alright?"

Billy Ray extended his hand, but Tommy closed the gap between them and gave his friend a hug. "God bless you, man. God bless you."

***

Tommy and Cheryl sat down for lunch. She had fixed grilled ham and cheese sandwiches with side salads and sweet tea. After saying grace, they talked briefly about MaryJo Saxon's death, how it was most likely alcohol-related. Then Cheryl asked what Billy Ray wanted.

He thought for a moment how to answer her question, then decided that the truth was the best option. He told her how they got his prints from the car and that they wanted to know how they got there. "Billy Ray's thinking about 'takin' one for the team.' He said he's going to take the fifth if they try to pin the murder on him. He's going to try to keep our names out of it."

"But if they have his prints, wouldn't they have yours and Andy's and Curtis's, too?"

"Maybe, but they don't have our porints on file anywhere. So, we're in the clear, for now."

"What did y'all talk about this morning at the meeting?"

"We talked about how it was impossible to not talk at all about that night. It created too much mistrust amongst us. We have to be honest with each other so that we can be comfortable knowing that none of us will talk to the sheriff."

Cheryl frowned. "Are you sure you can trust the other three? I mean, they're going to question Billy Ray this afternoon. You think he'll talk?"

Tommy paused for a moment. He knew that he couldn't be sure that any of them would remain silent. They had kept the secret for nearly sixteen years, at least, everyone but Curtis. As far as he knew, the only one he had spoken with was Carly Sue, and she was at the lake. She was the target of Allen Scott's repugnant advances. If they hadn't said anything to the authorities over the years, he was pretty confident that they would remain quiet now. "I can't guarantee anything, sweetie, but I'm pretty sure that they'll keep quiet."

"Are you sure staying quiet is the right thing to do? I mean, y'all were only twelve years old. I wouldn't think that you could be held responsible for a decision like y'all made back then."

"You might be right. But how about keeping it a secret once we turned of age? I'm not sure what a judge would say about that."

"Well, darlin', I hope we never have to find out. No matter what, I love you and I'm on your side. It's in God's hands at this point."

He smiled. "I hope he's on our side, too. With you and the Big Guy in our corner, we can't lose."

***

After leaving his mother's place, Curtis stopped at home to have lunch with Carly Sue and to be there in case the sheriff's office made the notification about her mother. They had just finished with a small bowl of vanilla ice cream when the doorbell rang. Curtis crossed the room and opened the front door. Two Deputy Sheriffs stood facing him, their faces solemn.

Curtis just stood there, knowing what was coming. The senior of the two men asked, "Is this the residence for Carly Sue Saxon Hardy?"

"Yes, it is."

"May we speak with Mrs. Hardy, please?"

From behind Curtis, Carly Sue's voice inquired, "Who is it, honey?"

"Sweetie, it's the sheriff's department. They need to speak with you."

When she reached the door and stood next to her husband, she asked, "Would you like to come in?"

Again, the senior man spoke. "That's not necessary, ma'am. You are Carly Sue Saxon Hardy, daughter of MaryJo Saxon?"

"Yes."

"Ma'am, I'm sorry to have to inform you, but your mother passed away earlier today. Her body is currently at the coroner's office. They will notify you when her body is available to you."

Carly Sue gave no response. Her expression remained neutral throughout the delivery of the terrible news. Finally, the senior deputy asked, "Is there anything we can do for you?"

In an emotionless voice, she said, "No. Thank you."

The men tipped their hats, both saying, "Sorry for your loss, ma'am."

With that, they turned and headed back to their cruiser. Curtis and Carly Sue watched them leave, then closed the door.

Curtis had to leave to get back to work within the next ten minutes. He asked, "Sweetie, are you okay?"

"Yes, dear. I'm fine." She took a deep breath, then asked in a forced, cheerful voice, "What would you like for dinner?"

***

The drive to the Bulloch County Sheriff's Office from the Irongate Subdivision was a cross-town trip. It would only take about ten minutes for Father Rod to get there whether they went through town or took the 301 bypass. The preacher opted for the bypass so that he could talk with Billy Ray without too much interruption.

"Looks like we might get some rain, finally, thank God."

Billy Ray was quiet for a moment. "You know, Father, I'm not really in the mood for small talk right now." There was silence, then Billy Ray spoke again. "I heard that, if I tell you somethin' in confidence, that you can't repeat it to anyone. Is that true?"

"Yes, Billy Ray, it is true. I am bound by the laws of the church and God to not repeat anything I am told in confidence. Is there something that you'd like to get off your chest?"

Billy Ray paused to collect his thoughts. He didn't have a wife to whom he could unload his burdens, like his friends did. He had to keep it all inside and allow the pressure to build. Now that he had a clear mind and had been away from the booze for nearly two weeks, he thought that lack of an outlet might be the catalyst that caused him to drink. It was the only way he knew how to stop the torment, but in reality, it only caused him more harm.

"Father Rod, when I was eleven years old, me and my friends…"

Billy Ray unloaded his history on the preacher. He told him the entire story about the boys finding Carly Sue by the lake, finding the body in the car, and how they pledged not to tell a soul. He also told him about recent events and their meeting at the tree and the promise of secrecy, at least among them.

"I'm plannin' to keep my promise again, and I ain't tellin' the police any of this. Am I wrong to do this?"

They had been sitting in the parking lot at the sheriff's office for fifteen minutes, talking about Billy Ray's dilemma.

Father Rod turned to his passenger. "I know we preachers are expected to have all the answers, but we're just men who have studied God's Word. So, I can't tell you exactly what you should do, except to pray on it and use your best judgment. You said that your friend, Tommy, believes in you. You should take that as a vote of confidence. You're clear headed now, you've had the strength to abstain from alcohol, one of the strongest addictions known to man, and you're winning. Let your conscience be your guide."

Billy Ray thought about what Pastor Rod said, took a deep breath, and gave the preacher a nervous smile. "I tried prayin' the other day. I think it worked. I feel at ease, anyways. I think I'm goin' to keep doin' that. It can't hurt."

"You're right, it can't hurt. In fact, let's say a little prayer together, right now."

Pastor Rod said a brief prayer for strength and forgiveness for Billy Ray, and that he would make good decisions during his interview. He closed the prayer and said, "You told me a bit ago of the demons that you've faced. This interview shouldn't be nearly so tough. God's blessings be with you. I'll be here when you're through."

Billy Ray nodded and thanked the preacher for the ride. He strode into the Bulloch County Sheriff's Office with his head held high.

Chapter 33

Captain Gerald Brannen had just finished briefing Sheriff Adkins on the interview that he and Deputy Jones had with Billy Ray Duke. The sheriff wasn't happy with the results, or lack thereof, but neither was Brannen. They had believed that MaryJo most likely was Allen Scott's murderer, given the photographs of her that Millie Crider provided. But that was some very thin evidence. It was hard to determine that the pictures were of a woman. If it was a woman, it was nearly impossible to verify that the woman was MaryJo. That evidence didn't fit any credible scenarios now with MaryJo being murdered.

Brannen was again trying to fit some original pieces of the puzzle into the big picture. Could MaryJo have killed Allen Scott? Yes. Even with her murder, it was possible. She may have had motive; her daughter may have been molested by Scott. They had no hard evidence that Carly Sue was molested, except that Scott was a known pedophile and had served time for molesting underaged girls.

MaryJo had the opportunity. The pictures from Millie Crider showed her, if it was really her, heading towards the crime scene, probably around the time of the murder, if Millie Crider's notes on the backs of the photos could be trusted. Did she have the means? According to Carly Sue, she had a thirty-eight revolver for home protection. But if she was Scott's killer, why would anyone now kill her, unless this new killer was a friend or lover of the deceased. Sixteen years was a long time to carry that much hatred.

Who else had motive to kill Allen Scott? Curtis Hardy was now married to Carly Sue, Scott's only known local, alleged victim. But, sixteen years ago, did Curtis have a thing for her? He would have been twelve years old at the time. If there was an attraction, it could be classified as puppy love. But twelve years old is a very young age to contemplate murder, much less plan and execute the murder. Did Curtis have opportunity? No one knows where he was at the time of the murder. Did he have means? Who knows?

During the interview with Billy Ray, Brannen asked the young man how his fingerprints ended up on the bumper of the dead man's car. Billy Ray replied that he had no idea. He did say that he and his friends played around the mobile home park all the time. Their fingerprints were probably on every flat surface in the place. They had been in most of the trailers in the park and had played Hide and Seek, Cowboys and Indians, Kick the Can, and countless other games in and around the park. So, finding his prints on the car didn't surprise him.

Before Brannen could ask another question, Billy Ray asked if they thought he had killed that man and if he needed a lawyer. When Brannen didn't reply, he asked for a lawyer.

The captain said, "Billy Ray, you can get a lawyer, but I'm not going to ask you any more questions. You just listen, I'll talk. Okay?

Billy Ray nodded.

"We've got your fingerprints on the car where a dead man was discovered. One of the deputies who was at the lake with the cleanup crew said you were acting awful strange when the car was discovered. That was before the car was towed ashore and before we discovered the body. After that, he said you acted even more tense, almost panicked."

Billy Ray didn't react at all.

"Now, I'm going to tell you something that only a couple people know. All of them work in this office. So, if I hear this from anyone other than those men, then I'll know you were the source." His eyebrows raised, his face took on a serious look. "We found a bracelet at the crime scene right near the gun that was buried in the mud. It was an expensive bracelet. We traced it back to a jewelry store in Savannah. The person who bought the bracelet was one of your friends' granddaddy. We suspect that your friend's fingerprints are also going to be found on that bumper."

Brannen watched closely for any reaction from Billy Ray, but he saw nothing, no signs that Billy Ray was concerned. Billy Ray had already told Brannen that his and his friends' fingerprints were all over the trailer park. Brannen thought that the young man would have had a great career as a poker player.

He continued. "We also know that the dead man was a child molester and that he may have had eyes for Carly Sue Saxon back then."

Still no change. Brannen remained silent for several minutes.

During the interview, Jones didn't say a word. He just glared at Billy Ray, trying to unnerve the young man, but it didn't appear to faze him in the least.

After the silence, Billy Ray asked, "Am I under arrest for anything?"

The delayed response was, "No, Billy Ray."

"Do you have any questions for me?"

"No, Billy Ray. Y'all's free to go. Anything you want to say before you go?"

"Nope."

Billy Ray left without another word and got into Pastor Rod's car. The car left the parking lot.

Brannen and Jones were frustrated. They hadn't been able to get anything out of the young man. For a recovering alcoholic, especially one who had just recently found sobriety, he showed no signs of frayed nerves.

So Brannen sat at his desk, still pondering all the bits of data that had come in regarding the Allen Scott murder, and now the MaryJo Saxon murder.

Under Allen Scott, he checked off each piece of information. He was a known child molester. He had a bullet hole in the skull. Billy Ray Duke's fingerprints were on the car from when he was about twelve years old along with four other sets of fingerprints from persons yet unknown. Millie Crider secretly owned Cypress Lake Mobile Home Park. She provided an accurate license plate number for the victim's car and pictures of, supposedly, a young MaryJo Saxon heading towards the crime scene on the right date and at the right time of the murder. They also had a rusted gun that was of little use and an expensive bracelet that was purchased by Andy Pepperdine's grandfather.

Under MaryJo Saxon, there was a contentious relationship between MaryJo, Millie Crider, and Ginny Hardy. Ginny Hardy was Millie Crider's daughter and Curtis Hardy's mother.

Who had a motive to kill the woman? Curtis was married to her daughter, Carly Sue, and Carly Sue may have been molested by her mother's boyfriend, but that had been some sixteen years ago. Could the discovery of Allen Scott's body have caused old secrets to surface?

What, if anything, did Billy Ray's other friend, Tommy Alexander, have to do with any of this? Maybe nothing, but the other three childhood friends had some tie to the murders either though evidence or family relations – or both.

Somebody at that trailer park knows more than they're lettin' on. We just have to ask the right person the right question. We're gettin' real close which means it's gettin' real dangerous.

Brannen's phone rang. It was Eugene Morris.

"Hey, Gene."

"Captain. Hey, I've been doin' more searches on family relationships for folks at the trailer park. You sittin' down?"

"Y'all about to tell me that this gets more complicated than it already is?"

"Well, yeah. I found MaryJo Saxon's mother. Her name's Clara Jean Saxon. She lives in Allendale, South Carolina."

Hearing Allendale, South Carolina, tickled Brannen's brain cells. Then he remembered that Allen Scott had lived in Allendale until he was killed.

"Hey, Gene, have you talked to this woman yet?"

"Just on the phone. Not in person, but I've got a meeting with her tomorrow morning at 10:00."

"Did you tell her that her daughter was murdered?"

"No, no I didn't. It's not my place. I told her that there were some things happening at Cypress Lake and wondered if she could answer a few questions about the park for me. Do you want her phone number so you can tell her about the murder?"

Damn. I sure don't need this. "Yeah, give it to me. Was this woman anything like her daughter?"

"We only spoke over the phone, but she sounded just as...how can I say it...uneducated as her daughter. But she wasn't disrespectful when we talked."

"You said you're meeting this woman tomorrow morning at 10:00?"

"Yeah. It's a little over an hour's drive, but I want to talk with her face-to-face. I can let you know what I find out afterwards."

"Okay. Sounds like a plan."

Brannen was about to hang up when he heard Morris say, "Wait, Gerry. That's not all. We know that MaryJo Saxon's only daughter is Carly Sue Hardy, right? Well, MaryJo's daddy is Douglas Hardy."

Brannen frowned, trying to get a handle on what this new piece of data meant. Then it hit him. Douglas Hardy was Millie Crider's husband...before he disappeared.

"Gene, you're telling me that Ginny Hardy's stepdad was MaryJo Saxon's biological father?"

"Yep. Not only that, about the time MaryJo was born, or actually, just before she was born, Doug Hardy disappeared off the face of the planet. I've done some searches for 'Douglas Hardy' and can't find a trace of him anywhere. Here's somethin' else to add to the mix: Clara Jean used to live in Statesboro. She lived at the trailer where MaryJo lived. Apparently, she moved away in 1981. That would mean

MaryJo was ten years old, but Clara Jean didn't take MaryJo with her."

"What the hell? How did that little girl survive with no parents?"

"Well, you know who knows everything that happens at the trailer park, right? I'd ask the Crider lady."

Shit. "That's a darn good idea, Gene. Call me tomorrow when you get done with the Saxon woman, will ya?"

"Sure thing, Gerry."

When Brannen hung up the phone, he added Clara Jean Saxon to his list of clues. *Why would a mother leave her pre-teenage daughter alone in a trailer and leave the state? Who took responsibility for the child? How did she pay for the trailer and utilities and food? Did Douglas Hardy have an affair with Clara Jean Saxon before he left Millie Crider? Did Crider kick him out...or worse?* It was time to talk with Millie Crider again.

***

Curtis Hardy left work and headed home. The necklace, which was worth more than four times his Ford Focus, was in the center console in the original box from Andrews Jewelers. Having the necklace right at his elbow made him so nervous that he nearly ran a red light. He took a deep breath and shook his head. He couldn't afford to get stopped with the necklace in his possession.

He briefly thought about pawning the necklace, but that would undoubtedly leave a paper trail that would lead right back to him. He thought about throwing it into Cypress Lake, but he thought about the car that he and his friends had pushed into the lake, hoping that it would never again surface, and how that turned out. He had to dispose of the necklace in a place where it would never again resurface. Or maybe he should put it where it could easily be found and point the law in the right direction, away from his wife and mother. That would mean going back to MaryJo's trailer. That was a huge risk.

Did the reward outweigh the risk? What other options did he have? He would have to decide tonight.

Chapter 34

The early morning sun was just high enough in the sky where it was no longer in Eugene Morris's eyes as he drove towards the city limits of Allendale, South Carolina. The outside temperature had already surpassed the eighty-degree mark. More clouds were visible in the sky as the humidity slowly climbed. All the prayers for rain had yet to be answered, but it looked like some drought relief was imminent.

Morris was following Clara Jean Saxon's instructions on how to get to her trailer. Her directions were a bit sketchy, but she said that her trailer was in a small, unnamed community just off Main Street. According to Morris's GPS, US 301 and Main Street were one-and-the-same as it passed through Allendale. As he approached the first curve, the earth-moving equipment dealership that Clara Jean mentioned came into view. She instructed him to make a right turn onto the gravel drive just before the dealership's parking lot. As he approached the drive, he understood why she cautioned him to turn in slowly. Rain, from before the drought, and traffic had eroded away much of the gravel at the turn, leaving deep ruts. There was no road sign, only a crudely, hand-painted piece of plywood that said, Rustic Valley Trailer Park. Morris wondered if the valley referred to the ruts that he was navigating.

He drove about thirty yards to a fork in the road. Another hand-painted sign had an arrow that pointed to the right, indicating that the gravel path was one-way only. Clara Jean said that she lived in the fourth "home" on the right.

Clara Jean Saxon's "home" was a 1950's era mobile home that hadn't had much in the way of upkeep. It eerily reminded him of MaryJo's trailer. A similar set of metal mesh steps, complete with rust and peeling paint, ascended to an equally challenged, six-by-six-foot deck.

Morris thought about riding past the trailer and heading back to Statesboro, but he noticed that Clara Jean was looking out the front window directly at him. She was waving. He had no choice but to stop and talk with the woman.

She already had the door open when he exited his car. The heat in South Carolina was no less hostile than in Georgia. Morris looked at his watch and saw that he was fifteen minutes early. He figured the sooner he got started, the sooner he could finish and head back home.

"Mr. Morris?"

"Yes, ma'am. Call me Gene. Ms. Clara Jean Saxon?"

"That's right. It's just Clare. Please, come in."

Despite the fact that Clara Jean looked like MaryJo's twin sister versus her mother, she had none of the hostility that her daughter bore. This woman was polite and soft spoken. She was a big woman but she weighed about one hundred pounds less than MaryJo had weighed. She wore a white tank-top and light blue shorts. In contrast to her daughter, her hair was neat and pulled up in a bun on the back of her head.

Once Morris was inside and seated, she offered him a glass of ice tea or some other cold beverage. She said she could make coffee if he liked. He accepted the offer of tea.

Clara Jean's trailer was in disarray. She wasn't much of a housekeeper, but the living room was comfortable, cooled by a working air conditioner. Morris also didn't notice a build-up of dirt on the carpet or dirty dishes in the kitchen. He did see two small bowls on the floor, one with dry food and one with water, so he assumed that there was at least one cat in the trailer. The air smelled fresh, though it appeared to be aided by air freshener. The windows were closed but the curtains on the side of the room away from the rising sun were opened, allowing indirect light to pour in.

Once they were settled, Clara Jean asked, "Well, Gene, what is it that you want to discuss?"

"I understand that MaryJo Saxon was your daughter?"

"I *am* her mother, unless there's something that I should know about."

Oops. "Um...well...yes, there is. Your daughter was killed, either yesterday or the night before."

The news didn't appear to upset his hostess. In fact, the only change to her facial expression was a slight dipping of her eyebrows. Morris figured he was about to find out why.

"Was it alcohol poisoning or did that crazy woman across the road kill her?"

Morris frowned. Why would she assume that?

She spoke before he could respond. "Gene, that old hag...I'm sorry...Millie had it in for me and my daughter. You see, she was jealous of my relationship with MaryJo's father, Doug Hardy."

Morris thought about asking her a question, but waited a split second to see if Clara Jean would continue, which she did.

"Doug Hardy was a handsome, hardworking man. He would come home from working the fields for a large farming company and he'd be bushed. All he wanted from her was a hot meal on the table and a little companionship once in a while. When she wouldn't meet his expectations, he would sometimes come over and lay all his problems at my feet. Me, being a compassionate, young woman, would listen and offer him words of comfort."

"I take it, *words of comfort*, wasn't all that you were givin'. Is that right?"

"Well, MaryJo is evidence of that fact. When I became pregnant with MaryJo, the old bag, I mean, Millie knew that Doug was the father. If Doug thought that he had it bad before she found out, he didn't expect the vile behavior that she put on after. She was a woman possessed. Then right before MaryJo was born, Doug disappeared."

"Did he tell you he was leaving?"

"No. Just the opposite. He said he was movin' out from Millie's and movin' in with me. Said he was goin' to do right by me and my baby. He and Millie had the two girls, Ginny and Cindy, but they was adopted. She couldn't have no kids, or at least that's what they suspected. So, when I got pregnant, Millie was hoppin' mad. Before Doug could get moved in, he disappeared. I didn't hear another word from him, ever. I asked Millie about where he went. She just gave me this evil smile. I'll never forget it. I thought that, maybe, she killed him, but I didn't have no evidence. I called the police and they treated me like I was nuts. Said he probably ran off."

"Did you live at the trailer park at that time?"

"Yes. I lived in the trailer across from Millie, with MaryJo." She looked out the living room window, but there wasn't really anything to look at. She was collecting her thoughts. "You never did tell me how my MaryJo died."

Morris took a deep breath. "She was murdered. Somebody stuck a sharp, thin object, like an ice pick, in her ear and it penetrated her brain. She may not have suffered, because the coroner said that she was pretty drunk at the time, maybe even passed out."

Clara Jean gave a weak, half-smile as if the news about her drunken state was expected. She looked back at Morris. "My daughter never had a chance in life. Part of it was my fault and part of it her own. I had to work to pay the bills. The jobs were all low payin', dead end jobs. I kinda set a bad example for her. I also set a bad example for relationships." She looked out the window again, her expression sad. "I was pregnant with MaryJo by the time I was fifteen."

Morris looked surprised. Apparently, Doug Hardy liked his women very young.

Clara Jean continued. "My mother left us when I was very young, so my older sister was forced to take care of me. That was tough on both of us. When I got pregnant, she clamped down hard on my social life. I had a child and no husband so she helped support us. I don't know how, 'cause she never had no job. But she always seemed to have plenty of money. She was seein' some rich fella from in town. He bought her nice clothes and stuff, but she didn't appreciate it.

Never wore any of the dresses he bought. Then he just stopped coming to see her. Even after that, she still had plenty of money for us to live on. Like I said, she took care of me and MaryJo. That was good for about ten or so years.

He was captivated by this woman's story and that of her daughter. As Clara Jean spoke, Morris was thinking about questions that he should ask her. Was she talking about Carl Pepperdine?

Clara Jean continued. "Then MaryJo went through the changes in life and started to get rebellious…like I was at her age. What do they say? The apple don't fall far from the tree."

He asked, "When did you move to Allendale?"

"1982, thirty-three years ago. I up and left and never looked back."

Morris did a quick calculation in his head. MaryJo would have been ten or eleven years old. "When did MaryJo move back to Cypress Lake?"

"Move back? She never left."

He wasn't surprised. He had figured this much out by his database searches. He had another question but wasn't sure how to ask. It was a long shot. "Did you know a man named Allen Scott from here in Allendale?"

She thought about it then said, "Wow. That's a blast from the past. Yes, I did. I met him at a nightclub back about fifteen, maybe twenty years ago. He was younger than me so he didn't interest me much, and I didn't seem to interest him. He had eyes for younger women. But we did talk a bit while we was at that club. He asked me if I had a daughter, so I told him about MaryJo."

"When was the last time you heard from him?"

"I only ran into him a couple times at that place, then he never came back in. Why are you askin' about him?"

Morris didn't want to answer yet. He sat trying to place this new information on the timeline in his head. He looked back at her as she was again deep in thought. He could see she was conflicted.

"Gene, I can see the question written all over your face. I didn't leave my daughter all alone. I left her with my older sister."

"Your older sister lived with you at the trailer?"

"No. My older sister lives across the road from MaryJo's trailer. I packed my bags, walked across the road, and told her that MaryJo was her problem now. Like I said, I left and never looked back. I didn't care about anything at that point. I was fed up."

Morris was confused. Who was this sister?

Again, she saw his confounded look.

"Didn't you know? Millie's my sister."

Morris was floored. The family tree that was already blurry just got even more complicated. As he sat thinking, he understood why Millie Crider had such disdain for MaryJo Saxon. She, the illegitimate child of her sister and ex-husband, was literally dumped in her lap. He wondered how Clara Jean could have simply walked away and never so much as inquired about her daughter. As hospitable as she was to him, she had to have an ice-cold heart buried in her chest.

He had one other question. "Clare, did you know that you have a granddaughter?"

Her jaw dropped. She raised her hands to her mouth, showing her first real emotion. She obviously hadn't known.

"And the reason you never saw Allen Scott again is because he was killed sixteen years ago. His body was hauled out of Cypress Lake just last Friday. He had a bullet hole in his head. MaryJo was a suspect until she was killed."

Clara Jean didn't know what to ask first. "Is my granddaughter doing...okay? I mean, is she normal, with a normal life?"

Eugene Morris had no idea how to answer that question. Carly Sue was far from normal, though she and Curtis put up the pretense of a normal life. They were both possibly tied to the murder of Allen Scott, though no one knew for certain.

And what happened to Doug Hardy? Did this woman have a clue? Did she even try to find out?

"Clare, did you ever find out anything more about where Doug Hardy went?"

She gave a half-smile again, as if she suspected something but didn't know for certain. "All I know is, one day he was there, at Millie's, the next day he was nowhere around. He had a car, but he didn't take it with him, assumin' he left on his own. Millie drove it to a car lot and had it sold. But Doug vanished. I wouldn't want to guess what happened to him."

Morris thanked Clara Jean Saxon for her time and headed for the door. Before he opened it, she asked, "Do you think my granddaughter would want to meet me?"

He thought for a second before answering. Knowing the circumstances, the fact that Clara Jean may have sent a child molester into his granddaughters' life, he didn't believe it wise that she make that trip. But it wasn't his place to say so.

"I really don't know, Clare. Maybe you should give it some thought before you drive down there and surprise her."

"Yeah, maybe you're right."

***

Gerry Brannen got a call from the Chatham Savannah Metropolitan Police. They had the report on one necklace and bracelet set sold by Andrews Jewelers to Carl Pepperdine. Andy Pepperdine's grandfather had purchased the set for $72,598.00 on May 12, 1970. Somehow, the bracelet ended up in the mud on the shore of Cypress Lake near a gun allegedly used to kill Allen Scott.

Millie Crider received all her land from Carl Pepperdine. Could he have also given her the bracelet? Was she at the crime scene? Could she have killed Scott? If yes, why, and why would she try to frame MaryJo Saxon?

There's no way around it. We have to question Ms. Crider again.

Chapter 35

Tommy Alexander finished his meeting with his fourth client of the morning, though he had a difficult time concentrating. The young couple had signed a contract on a new house and she was pregnant with their first child. They were nervous about the coming year and the changes that were on their horizon. They came in for advice on what changes they should make in their insurance policies. Tommy walked them through the options and recommended several policy changes that he believed would best protect them as their family evolved. He also suggested that they come in, annually, for the next couple of years to review their plan and make adjustments, if needed.

When they left, he quickly double-checked the policy changes that he had recommended, just to make sure he hadn't zoned out and given them bad advice. After confirming that he had pointed them in the right direction, he sat back at his desk, pondering the latest news from Cypress Lake.

He couldn't believe Carly Sue's mother was dead. Carly Sue had endured such trauma in her life. He wondered how much more she could take. She had Curtis to lean on, but what was going on with him anyways? *He was so defensive when we met at the tree, like he was hiding something. He couldn't have killed Allen Scott. He was with us. Is he trying to protect Carly Sue?*

Tommy thought about Billy Ray. He said he would keep their secret when questioned by the sheriff. He wondered if his old friend was able to keep his word. Then Tommy smiled. *Billy Ray was the only one of us who did keep his mouth shut. I guess I don't have room to talk. I'll just trust that he did what he said he would do.*

He wondered if he should try and get the four of them together again to see if Billy Ray learned anything during his interview. Was it possible that his friend would be arrested for the murder, or even for MaryJo's murder? What motive would he have for either murder? It was ludicrous to even think that they had any evidence implicating Billy Ray. Like Curtis, he was with them when Allen Scott was murdered. Maybe the sheriff was trying to scare him into providing information or confessing. Even Andy, Curtis, and he thought that Billy Ray was the weak link. That turned out to be a fallacy.

Tommy's thoughts trailed back to Curtis. If Carly Sue had killed Scott, then Curtis had good reason to do whatever he could to protect his wife, even though he legally could not be coerced into testifying against her. Tommy doubted it would come to that. Was it possible that Curtis killed MaryJo to protect his wife? But from what? Did he believe that MaryJo would sacrifice her own daughter in exchange for…what…her freedom? Could she have killed Scott for molesting her daughter? That was a good motive. She wasn't working, as best he remembered, the night they pushed the car into the lake.

It was time to get answers from Curtis, and they all needed to hear what he had to say. This was going to get settled tonight. This had gone on far too long already.

He picked up the phone and dialed Curtis's work number. He was going to demand that they meet tonight at 7:00 PM. Once Curtis agreed, if he did, then he would call Andy and Billy Ray. He was tired of the stress and he was terrified of not knowing the truth.

***

Captain Brannen had just unrolled the wrapper on his toasted Roman Burger sub, the aroma filling his office with a combination of beef, salami, lettuce, tomato, onions, and mayonnaise, when his phone rang. The caller ID said Crime Lab. He cursed, re-rolled the sandwich in its wrapper, and wiped his hands on a napkin. He took a quick drink of Coca-Cola and took a deep breath.

"Brannen."

"Hi, Captain. Nikki Olsen. We've found some things that you need to know right away. Do you have a minute?"

"Sure, Nikki. What have you got?"

"Like, we went through Ms. Saxon's trailer and we found a gun, a .38 revolver, hidden in the wall behind a picture. It was sitting on a piece of wood that was nailed in the wall, like it was put there for the purpose of hiding something."

Brannen frowned. He waited while Nikki continued.

"We, like, dusted the gun for prints and, like, we didn't find Ms. Saxon's prints on the gun, but we did find another set of prints. We don't, like, have an ID on the prints from the gun, but, like, this next part is weird. We matched the prints to a set of prints from the bumper of Allen Scott's car."

Brannen asked, "Are you saying that they matched Billy Ray's prints?"

"No. Like, they matched one of the unidentified set of prints. We put the prints that we found on the bumper into our database as John Doexxx, the 'xxx' being a unique identifier so that…"

"Nikki, I get it. So, the prints match one of the other sets of prints from the bumper?"

"Yeah. But that's not all. Like, we test-fired the gun and it matches the ballistics on the bullet that we found in the car." She paused. "So, like, the gun from Ms. Saxon's trailer is the weapon used in the Scott murder."

This confused Brannen. He thought that they had retrieved the weapon used in the murder from the murder scene. It was rusted and caked with mud, but it was the right caliber. Nikki had told him several days ago that there was no way to test fire the weapon, that it was too corroded. The discovery of the actual murder weapon changed many aspects of the case. Maybe Millie Crider was right. MaryJo could very well be Scott's killer. But why would the gun not have MaryJo's prints on it and why would another set of unknown prints be on the gun, especially prints from the victim's car?

"Captain, are you still there?"

"Yes, sorry, Nikki. I was thinkin' about this new evidence."

"Like, while you're thinking about it, here's something else. We have a clear serial number from the weapon. It was purchased back in 1997 along with two other identical weapons. Like, we're ninety percent sure that the weapon found at the lake, the really rusted one, is one of the other weapons bought at that time. So, there's still another .38 out there. Well, potentially anyway."

"Do you know who purchased the guns?"

"Yeah. Mildred Crider. I have a copy of the invoice right here."

Brannen's jaw dropped. "Nikki, can you fax me a copy of that invoice, immediately, please?"

"Yeah, like, sure thing, Captain."

***

Eugene Morris drove southwest out of Allendale, South Carolina, as the first raindrops hit his windshield. They were light and didn't inspire hope that the drought was over, but it was something. Maybe all the rain dances and prayers were starting to work.

He tried for the third time to call Brannen's office from the hands-free cell phone in his car. He was just about to give up when the call went through.

"Hey, Gerry. Talkin' with the wife?"

"No. Better than that. Nikki at the Crime Lab."

"Really? What did you find out?"

"They found the murder weapon for the Scott murder in MaryJo's trailer. It was hidden in a wall, behind a picture. But, get this: MaryJo's prints weren't on the gun. There was another set of prints on the gun that matched one of the sets of prints from the Tempo's bumper."

Brannen went on to fill in Morris on Nikki Olsen's report. He was shocked, and as he continued his drive towards Statesboro, he tried to fit these new pieces of evidence into their proper place. Then he told Brannen about his discussion with Clara Jean Saxon. Brannen suggested that they meet in his office as soon as Morris got back to town. Morris replied that he had a deadline for his latest story on the murders and Brannen countered that he should save the story until they solved the murder. He said he believed that it wouldn't be long now. Something was going to crack and he would have a front row seat when they made an arrest.

***

Morris shook the rain from his hair as he entered Gerald Brannen's office. The rain was still light, but it was welcome, nonetheless. He took a seat across from Brannen and pulled out his notepad.

"The more I think about it, Gerry, the more I'm convinced that Doug Hardy was murdered and Millie Crider is responsible. Hell, he disappeared before MaryJo was born. Like I said, I can't find any trace of him anywhere in the country."

Gene Morris and Gerry Brannen began by discussing Morris's interview with Clara Jean Saxon. Brannen had just poured two cups of fresh coffee and the aroma filled the space, mixing with the lingering scent of Brannen's Roman Burger sub sandwich. Morris had just finished reviewing his notes from the interview, feeling more confident than ever that Millie Crider's husband from years gone by was the victim of foul play.

"That's a pretty serious accusation, Gene. Maybe Doug Hardy just left the area and lives off the grid, so to speak. I mean, how hard is it to disappear in this country?"

"Harder than you think. Unless he changed his name, if he applied for a credit card or a loan, bought a car, got insurance, renewed a driver's license, and a whole lot of other transactions, he'd show up on some agency's database. I'm not finding anything."

Brannen rubbed the midday stubble that was starting to form on his face. "Clara Jean is MaryJo's mother and Millie Crider's sister. Clara Jean had Millie's husband's baby, MaryJo, when she was fifteen. MaryJo is a difficult child and Clara Jean Saxon dumps her ten-year-old daughter in her Aunt

Millie's lap. Then Clara Jean just leaves and doesn't come back. Can this get any more twisted?"

As Brannen talked, Morris scanned his notes again. It was clear that the trailer park was ground zero for the Scott murder. It was also clear that Millie Crider, if she wasn't the epicenter of the murder, was real close. She was pointing the finger at her murdered niece. That must have been a real contentious relationship. It may have been the reason that MaryJo was personally so messed up.

"Clare said that Millie treated Doug badly even before she became pregnant with MaryJo. After Millie found out she was pregnant with Doug's child, she said his life was a living hell. Then he just disappeared. He told Clare that he was planning to move in with her and help raise her baby. By the way, did you know that Ginny Hardy was adopted, that Millie couldn't get pregnant?"

Brannen shook his head. "Nope."

"Another thing that Clare said was that Millie never had a job, but she always had enough money for groceries and clothes for her and MaryJo. They didn't have to pay rent or utilities. It was all taken care of. I wonder if Millie was already workin' on a plan to get the trailer park and the surrounding land from Carl Pepperdine around then."

Brannen was again in deep thought. As much as Millie tried to point the finger away from her, the more the focus of the investigation seemed to point back at her.

Morris, who had been scanning his notes again, broke into his thoughts. "Last thing, Gerry. Clare said that, if Doug left the area, he hadn't driven off. He left his car at Millie's and she sold it. When she asked Millie what happened to Doug, she didn't answer. She just gave her sister what she described as an evil smile. I got chills as she told me about that."

"I'm goin' out to the park with Jonesy in the morning. We're goin' to question Millie again. There's just too much evidence and other information that points to her. I hate like hell to do it, but there's no way around it with the gun purchase, the family relationships, the bracelet and missing necklace, the fact that she conveniently had Allen Scott's car's license plate number at her fingertips."

"Don't forget the pictures of MaryJo."

"Yeah. Just a bit too convenient."

Morris turned and looked out Brannen's office window. Rain was now coming down in earnest. "Yeah, Gerry. I think you're closing' in. You guys be real damn careful."

Chapter 36

The rain from earlier in the day had soaked the brown lawn and washed away weeks of accumulated pollen from the roofs of houses, roads, parking lots, sidewalks, and driveways. The air smelled damp and refreshing. A break in the clouds allowed sunlight to heat up the ground. Water vapor rose from all dark surfaces as the late afternoon temperature reached near eighty-five degrees, the humidity rising significantly.

Curtis Hardy walked in the front door of his home at 5:15 PM, his mind occupied by the fact that he was hiding evidence from two murders in his car's trunk. He decided that disposing of the evidence was in everyone's best interest, particularly his wife's and his mother's. But he reckoned that others would also benefit.

As usual, all the curtains were closed, the living room was dark, with only ambient light piercing the blinds from the patio door in the dining room. The house, what he could see from just inside the front door, looked the same as when he left for work this morning. Not a single item had changed place. Yesterday's newspaper was still on the coffee table, his empty coffee cup was right where he had left it on the dining room table next to the plate and knife he had used for English muffins with butter and honey. Even his napkin was balled up on the plate. It was unusual for Carly Sue to leave anything out of place, especially dirty dishes.

"Hey, sweetie, I'm home." He expected that Carly Sue would walk into the room and greet him. When she didn't, he called out again. There was silence.

The house had the feeling of gloom, more so than usual. He walked into the dining area, through the kitchen, into the utility room, then headed down the hall towards their closed bedroom door. She never closed the door. Curtis tensed, fearing what he would find, knowing that his wife was already close to the abyss.

He took a deep breath. As quietly as possible, he turned the doorknob and pushed the door open, just a crack. Carly Sue was lying on their bed, eyes wide open, staring at the ceiling. The covers were in a pile at the footboard. She was still in her light robe. He wasn't sure if she had taken a shower that morning or not. At first, Curtis thought that she might be dead, but he saw color in her face and lips, then noticed the rise and fall of her chest as she took in air, then exhaled. She was in a trance-like state and Curtis feared that she had relived the worst moments of her life throughout the day.

He lightly stepped into the room, trying to decide how he should approach her, not wanting to trigger one of her episodes. He spoke as he eased himself onto the bed. "Hey, sweetie. Everything alright?"

She took a deep breath, but she continued to stare at the ceiling, then she closed her eyes and said, "Curtis, I remember everything."

Curtis frowned. What did she mean by *everything*? If she was talking about the night of the murder, that was bad news. For nearly sixteen years she hadn't remembered anything from shortly after she arrived at the lake until Curtis and his friends showed up. He had to know exactly what she meant. There was little time because he had agreed to meet Tommy, Andy, and Billy Ray at the tree in a little over an hour. He had to be there early so he could take care of a task that couldn't wait any longer.

Curtis used his most soothing, calming voice, hoping to keep his wife calm, and back her away from the edge of whatever ledge she was on. The words flowed, his voice smooth as silk. "Sweetie, tell me what you remember. And please, don't leave nothin' out."

She kept her eyes closed, took several breaths, then began to walk her husband through her nightmare, the one she had lived a decade-and-a-half ago. She began at the point that used to be the end of her tale, when Allen Scott had slapped her hard.

***

The roads in Statesboro were wet, but there was a break in the rain. Curtis was deep in thought in the car on his way out to Cypress Lake Mobile Home Park, or, more specifically, the tree just to the west of the park. Finding Carly Sue lying on the bed, distraught at what she remembered, troubled him. It was the first time in sixteen years that she remembered the horrific events of that night, including the murder of Allen Scott.

Carly Sue had remained prone on the bed, staring towards the ceiling, seeing nothing but the events as they unfolded. She had said that the slap from Allen Scott had stunned her. At that moment, she realized that there was no fighting back. Though he wasn't a big, strong man, he was much stronger than she, and he would hurt her badly if she resisted further. For several minutes, he roughly groped her.

Curtis thought about what the sick bastard had said to Carly Sue, the little twelve-year-old girl, after the sharp slap. *"I'll break your arms if you keep struggling and I'll cut your face. You'll be so ugly, no man will ever want you."*

While she was forced to lay flat in the front seat, he moved the seat back to give him room away from the steering wheel. He took his shirt off and pulled his belt off. He showed the belt to Carly Sue and threatened to choke her with it, then he threw it on the floorboard. As he unzipped his pants, she saw an arm come through the passenger window. She saw a hand with a gun and a wrist with a beautiful bracelet. Then she heard a loud pop and saw a flash in the dark, like a flame.

She didn't know how much time passed. It seemed like a long time, but Allen Scott's body slumped over on top of her. She panicked, pushing his limp body off of her, flailing as she did, squirming to get out from underneath him. Finally, she was able to push him over against the driver's side door. The blood was trickling down the side of his head. She was sure that he was dead.

She reached for the passenger-side door, threw it open and stumbled to her knees as she got out. The earth was muddy. When her knees hit the ground, her right knee hit something sharp. She looked down and saw the bracelet. Her knee forced it into the soft clay. She turned and started to run when she realized that she couldn't find the gun that she brought. It was no longer tucked into the back of her pants. It must have fallen out and was in the car somewhere. She quickly looked, but seeing the body scared her and she began to cry for help between bouts of sobbing, her body shaking with fear. Then, he and his friends had shown up.

There had been a moment of silence as he processed what she said. She saw the bracelet, but did she put it all together? She answered his unasked question before he could dissuade her from believing what she had seen.

Her eyes had remained closed. What she said next was obviously painful for her to say. "Curtis, that bracelet was your momma's. I seen her wear it all the time, she was so proud of it. She had a matching necklace that was so beautiful. I know it was hers because she let me try it on one time. She said it was a gift from her momma. That was before you and me got together."

She turned her head and opened her eyes. She appeared to have aged fifteen years since he left for work this morning. He knew that she had not wanted to tell him this, that he might stop loving her if she accused his mother of murder. She felt even worse since Ginny had saved her from being raped…or worse.

He thought about telling his wife that she was mistaken, that his mother was at church late that evening, or some other excuse, but there was no denying it. She knew what she saw. Her memory was obviously clear and the evidence supported it.

There were two possible paths that he could take. First, he could get his wife to agree to remain silent, to join Curtis and his friends in their new pact to keep everything between them. Second, he could try to convince her that lying, and saying that MaryJo was the shooter, would be the right thing to do. MaryJo was already dead and Carly Sue hated her anyway. She loved Ginny Hardy like a mother, and that woman had saved her from being sexually assaulted, unlike her own mother who had let her boyfriends molest her. Besides, that guy deserved to die, didn't he?

The only question was, should he broach that subject now or after he returned from the meeting at the tree? He had to make up his mind quickly.

In the end, he comforted his wife and told her that he had to go to a meeting about the drought at the city building. He would be back soon.

A horn honked behind him. He was in a trance at a stop sign. He raised his hand at the driver behind him and went through the intersection. It was 6:20 PM. It was only ten minutes to the Cypress Lake. He had time, but he couldn't afford to fool around if he wanted to bury the necklace and ice pick in private.

***

Tommy Alexander parked his car in Billy Ray Duke's driveway at 6:40 PM. He hadn't told Billy Ray that he planned to do it, but he thought it was a better idea than parking down at the lake. The path to the tree from the trailer park was shorter than the path from Cypress Lake. When he turned off the engine and looked up at the trailer, he saw his old friend pull back the curtains and smile. Tommy opened his car door and headed towards the trailer's steps just as Billy Ray opened the trailer door.

"Hey, Billy Ray."

"Tommy. You know, y'all's Lexus couldn't look any more out of place. I mean, if you plan to leave it here while we go to the tree, I can't guarantee that it'll be in one piece when we get back."

Tommy smiled. Billy Ray returned the smile. They closed the distance between them and shook hands.

Tommy looked his friend from his head to his shoes. He was still covered in dirt and sweat. "Still workin' at the church, I take it?"

"What gave it away? The saintly appearance?"

They both laughed, relaxing in the banter. Billy Ray asked, "You want to come in for a drink? I got water and cold water."

"Thanks, but I'm good. You want to head down to the tree? I know we're early, but maybe we can catch up some more."

"Yeah. We can do that. Let's go."

As they walked, Tommy asked if he found a sponsor for AA yet, to which Billy Ray replied no but that he was working with a recovered alcoholic and he was helping out while he looked for a sponsor.

They talked more about Billy Ray's work as they approached the clearing and the tree. Tommy put his hand on Billy Ray's arm to stop him. He saw Curtis through the leaves at their tree. He threw a shovel off into the brush away from the clearing. Tommy wondered what he was doing. He looked at Billy Ray who must have seen the same thing.

Tommy again moved towards the clearing with Billy Ray next to him. When Curtis heard their approach, he was startled. He turned towards the two and, with an edge in his voice, said, "Hey, Tommy. Billy Ray."

Just as Tommy said, "Hey, Curtis," Andy Pepperdine broke into the clearing from the path that led to the lake.

"Hey, guys."

As usual, they waited for Tommy to make the first move. Tommy was nervous, especially now that he and Billy Ray caught Curtis doing something suspicious. He noticed some ground that looked like it had just been disturbed. He casually walked in that direction, stopping within three feet of the freshly turned earth, and looked in the direction Curtis had tossed the shovel. The handle was clearly visible. He walked into the brush and grabbed it. When he turned around, Curtis's face was red with anger.

Tommy asked, "What are you hidin'?"

Tommy, Andy, and Billy Ray thought that Curtis was going to leap on Tommy, but he just stood there for several seconds, tense, with his fists balled. Slowly, his anger dissolved into defeat. He fell to his knees, his shoulders slumped, and his chin fell to his chest.

"I can't hide it anymore. I thought I could, but I can't."

Tommy walked over to his childhood friend and knelt beside him. Andy and Billy Ray did the same. They all sat, forming a circle in front of the tree. As they did, raindrops began to pound against the leaves above them. Soon, the drops made their way through the forest's canopy. They looked up at the place where they had once vowed silence. It oozed rusty looking sap, just as it had nearly sixteen years ago.

Tommy put his hand on Curtis's shoulder. "It's okay, Curtis. Let it out. We'll keep your secret if you want, but it might be time that it all came out."

Curtis spent the next half hour telling his friends the secret that haunted his family to this day. Their tears were mixed with the rain that soaked them all to the core.

Chapter 37

Friday morning at 7:55, the rain pounded against Captain Brannen's cruiser. The wipers had difficulty keeping pace with the torrential downpour. The roads were slick with water and accumulated gunk that hadn't been washed away in months. Brannen remarked to Jones that it seemed no one remembered how to drive on wet roads as the pace of traffic was too fast for the conditions. More than once, he had to brake for a crazy driver coming towards their car while passing oncoming traffic on Cypress Lake Road.

He and Deputy Jones were on their way to Millie Crider's trailer. "I'll ask questions first, then you can jump in and ask any follow ups that you want," Brannen instructed.

"Sounds good, Captain."

Brannen pulled the Bulloch County Sheriff's car into Millie Crider's driveway, but kept the engine running while he and Jones made sure they had all their equipment in place. They looked at each other and nodded. He cut the engine and pushed his door open. The rain had slowed to a drizzle, but the grounds of the trailer park were soaked, with pools of water everywhere. The standing water was

a clay-saturated, rusty red, topped with green pollen.

As the two men approached the trailer door, they heard a woman's voice wailing and crying. They couldn't make out the words. Another voice answered the first in a scolding tone. They easily recognized the second voice. It was Millie Crider.

Brannen held up his hand to stop their advance. He hoped that they might pick up the tone of the exchange, but he saw Millie look out the window. They stepped up on the porch as the old woman opened the door just a crack. The wailing from inside the trailer continued and she turned and told the person to hush.

Brannen spoke. "Ms. Crider, we have some questions that we'd like to ask you. May we come in, please?"

"Captain, this ain't a good time. We got a family matter that needs my attention."

"Ma'am, this can't wait. We can ask you here and now, or you can come with us to the county."

The wailing from inside the trailer grew louder. Brannen thought he heard praying embedded in the loud, uncontrolled screeching. He was gaining confidence that he and Jones had justification to enter the trailer without Millie's blessing, that a person needed assistance. He looked Millie in the eyes, a stern stare letting the woman know he meant business. "Millie, you let us in or we're comin' in without your permission."

For a moment, the woman remained defiant, then her resolve crumbled. Her shoulders slumped as she stepped aside and opened the door. Brannen and Jones stepped into the trailer just as a lightning bolt hit close by, followed by a booming thunder that shook the trailer. After a few seconds, the rain's intensity picked up and more thunder shook the trailer.

The two men turned and saw Ginny Hardy on her knees, leaning over the cushions of Millie's dilapidated couch. She clutched a crucifix and a bible together in her hands, her grip so tight that her knuckles were white. Brannen thought he could make out the cadence to the Lord's Prayer, but the words were indecipherable. She hadn't noticed the two lawmen; at least, she showed no sign that she was aware of their presence.

Brannen turned his attention to Millie. "Ms. Crider, we understand that you purchased three guns back in 1997." He told her the date, the store, and the purchase price for the three weapons. He had to raise his voice so that Millie could hear him above Ginny's continued wailing and the rain pounding on the trailer's roof. Another loud rumble of thunder shook the trailer.

"That's right. We had a series of break-ins here at the park. I bought three guns, one for Ginny, one for MaryJo, and one for me. This is America, ain't it? It ain't no crime to defend your family and your property."

"Were you aware that two of the guns have been recovered. Both were connected to Allen Scott's murder."

"Murder?! That sum-bitch was killed…" She stopped in mid-sentence. "Let's just say, his killin' was justified. He tried to rape my…" she didn't want to say the words, but it wasn't Carly Sue's fault that she was born into an inescapably horrific situation, "…grand-niece. He tried to rape that poor girl, Carly Sue."

Brannen didn't look surprised. He already knew that Allen Scott was a pedophile and that Carly Sue Saxon Hardy was Millie Crider's grand-niece. What he didn't know was what part Millie Crider played in Scott's death.

"Ms. Crider, did you kill Allen Scott?"

"No, sir, I did not!"

"Do you know who did?"

Ginny Hardy stopped her prayers and wailing and crying abruptly and screamed, "I did it! I killed him!"

Millie turned to her daughter and hissed, "You hush your mouth girl. You did not kill that man."

"Yes, I did, Momma. I did it! I killed that bastard! He was going to hurt Carly Sue! He was going to hurt her! I had to stop him because her selfish bitch-of-a-mother wasn't goin' to do nothin'. He had to die!"

Millie turned to Brannen and said, "She's outta her mind. She didn't do it." After a pause, Millie declared, "I did it. I got my gun and walked down to the lake and…"

"Momma, don't take my confession from me! I got to get right with God! I confessed my sin! You can't deny me this!" Ginny began to wail again, breaking into the Lord's Prayer.

Millie tried to calm her daughter. "Ginny, please stop."

Rolling thunder, this round quieter than the earlier blasts, indicated that the current storm cell had passed. Brannen looked at Jones and whispered, "We need to separate these two. You take Ginny and question her about that night. See what facts line up right. I'll talk with Millie."

Jones nodded and asked Millie if they could use the back bedroom. She fought the separation for a few minutes, but in the end, she knew she had no choice. It didn't take long for Jones to realize that Ginny Hardy knew facts that she could not have known unless she was at the crime scene. Likewise, Brannen poked giant holes in Millie's confession. When Brannen and Millie returned to the living room, Ginny was sitting on the couch still holding the Good Book and the crucifix to her chest.

Brannen said, "Millie, we recovered two of the three guns that you purchased. Where is the third?"

"You ain't got no right to take my guns."

"We're not takin' your gun, Millie. It's just that the one used to kill Allen Scott was found in MaryJo's trailer. The first one, which wasn't used to kill him, was found at the lake, just about where we think he was shot. We just want to make sure that the third gun wasn't involved in the shooting, too."

"Y'all go get a warrant and I'll give it to ya."

Brannen rubbed his dark face, then rubbed his close-cropped hair. He was getting frustrated with the old woman who seemed to be in the middle of all the action. He didn't want to arrest her, but he believed that she had purposely misdirected their investigation. He thought that an obstruction of justice threat might be in order.

"Ms. Crider, I truly do not want to arrest you, but I will. I don't want your gun. Do you understand me? I just want to see it so I can compare it to the other guns that we've found, to make sure that it is the third gun that you purchased back in 1997. Please, ma'am, don't push me on this."

Ginny Hardy had been quiet since she essentially confessed to killing Allen Scott. She spoke. "Momma, just go get the gun and show 'em."

Millie looked at her daughter with pity. "Sweet Ginny. Why ain't y'all helpin' me? I'm tryin' to protect ya."

"I don't need you to protect me, Momma." She hugged the bible and the crucifix tighter to her chest as she rocked back and forth on the couch. "God will protect me, no matter where I go. God will protect me."

"You really believe that, don't you darlin'?"

Ginny smiled through tears and choked out, "Yes, Momma, I do."

Millie sighed and said to Brennan, "Come on back, Captain. I'll show it to ya."

Brannen looked at Jones and nodded towards Ginny Hardy, silently ordering him to watch her and make sure she didn't try to leave, though he seriously doubted that she had any intention of fleeing.

Millie's back bedroom was small, the walls covered in the same cheap paneling as the rest of the trailer. It was similar in layout to MaryJo's trailer and likely built by the same manufacturer. The room was just large enough to fit a full-size bed, a small dresser, and a nightstand with a small lamp. A small drawer in the nightstand was cracked open. Millie told Brannen, "The gun's in the nightstand drawer."

Brannen made his way along the side of the unmade bed and opened the small drawer. It was empty except for some prescription pill bottles, a few cough drops, some lip balm, and a nail file. Brannen frowned, then turned to the old woman who was standing at the door.

"Ms. Crider, you need to stop misleading this investigation. Where is the gun?"

Millie Crider frowned. She appeared deep in thought. "Captain, the gun was in there yesterday. I saw it. Are you sure…" She stopped before finishing and put a hand to her mouth. In a near whisper, she said, "Carly Sue."

Brannen asked, "What?"

"Carly Sue was here yesterday. She wanted to talk about that night. She was remembering stuff that she ain't remembered in years. She said she had to use the bathroom, but she spent longer'n I thought she needed. When I checked on her, she was just coming up the hall. She might'a come outta my bedroom. If she has my gun, that ain't good. She was a might bit depressed."

"Was she in such a state that she might hurt herself?"

"I don't reckon so, but I ain't no doctor."

"Ms. Crider, we'll be back. Don't you or Mrs. Hardy go anywhere."

Brannen grabbed Jones on the way out. They were headed to Curtis and Carly Sue Hardy's house. Thankfully, the rain had stopped, leaving rust-colored streams of water on the sides of the park roads. The drought was over, but Brannen and Jones had other things on their minds.

***

After Brannen and Jones left her house, Millie went to Ginny and asked her to sit on the couch. She had to get through to her daughter, to save her from herself. There was a way that they could all escape incarceration, but Ginny had to be a willing participant. They sat side-by-side for several minutes. Millie put her arm around her daughter and rocked slowly and lightly side-to-side, trying her best to comfort her adult daughter. Outward gestures of love were not her strong suit.

She had never been an easy mother to please. She demanded that her daughters be tough-minded, independent, and willing to let their men go because they didn't need them. Millie had extorted the land and money from Carl Pepperdine years ago, and that fortune had grown. Millie may act like a crazy old woman, but she knew how to make money. She had help from Carl, then from Carl's money manager. Only a handful of people knew anything about her finances, especially her family.

"Ginny, my darlin' Ginny. You didn't do nothin' wrong, girl. Not in the eyes of the law, and not in the eyes of God. You protected your family from evil. That...vile animal was going to hurt Carly Sue...did hurt Carly Sue...maybe not physically, but she's damaged by what he did. She's damaged by what her mother did, too. MaryJo should have defended her daughter. It shouldn't have been up to you to keep her safe. That was her momma's job, and she failed."

Ginny began crying, a quiet, whimpering cry, with tears rolling down her cheeks. She asked, "Then why do I feel so bad, Momma? Why can't I be happy? I screwed up my life, my son's life, and MaryJo…"

Millie growled at her daughter with more venom than she intended. "You listen to your momma, young lady. You didn't screw up MaryJo's life. Her life was a mess from the start. Her momma was trash, and she passed that on down to MaryJo. There weren't no fixin' that poor girl so don't you go blamin' yourself for her problems. You did Carly Sue a good turn when you got her and Curtis together. It saved her life. Curtis has been her rock. Don't you ever forget that."

As Millie rocked back and forth with Ginny, she worried that Captain Brannen would be back and find her other gun, the one that she kept stored above the loose ceiling tile in the closet, the one she had used to kill Doug Hardy. She should have disposed of it long ago, but she figured that she might need to use it again someday, that some other man would betray her and her girls.

She was lucky that Captain Brannen limited the search by the lake to the area where Dennis Flippin used his metal detector to find the gun. He might have stumbled across old Doug Hardy's rotten carcass. Then she would have had more questions to answer.

Her only question was *Who killed MaryJo?*

***

Ginny continued to cry. Many years ago, she had urged Curtis to ask Carly Sue out as a favor to her. She wanted to know what the young woman remembered from that horrific night when Ginny took her gun and followed the noisy car down to the lake. It had been a good plan, except that Curtis fell in love with her. That wasn't supposed to happen.

She saw what was happening with every new boyfriend that MaryJo brought home and she knew it was only a matter of time before one of them was going to go after young Carly Sue. She knew because she had been molested by one of the boys at the trailer park before she was ten. At the time, she didn't understand what was happening, but after she grew up, she looked back, blaming herself for allowing her body to be used.

So, she killed Allen Scott. Shot him at near point-blank range and walked home as calmly as if she was on her way back from school.

Now, everything was falling apart...and she felt in her heart that it was all her fault.

Chapter 38

Curtis was up early Friday morning even though he didn't plan to be at work until 9:00 AM. The recent rains had lessened the concern for the drought even though they had a long way to go before the region completely recovered.

When he got out of bed to shower, Carly Sue was already up and in the kitchen. He smelled sausage cooking mixed with fresh coffee. His smile was sad. After his meeting at the tree with his friends, he knew the hammer was coming down quickly. It was going to hit him and his family hard.

The previous evening, under their tree and only after another vow of secrecy, he confessed that his mother had killed Allen Scott to keep him from raping Carly Sue that night. All three were sympathetic and believed that she was justified in shooting the pervert. They swore that they would have done the same thing, and they felt a little better about helping push the car into the lake.

The discussion came around to what Curtis was trying to hide and he told them that it was some evidence that would implicate his mother in the murder. They didn't condemn him for protecting his family. Again, they agreed that, under the circumstances, it was the prudent thing to do. After the discussion dwindled, they all felt a new wave of guilt. They had, after all, helped hide a dead body. Would they take the same course of action today, as grown men, as they had as twelve-year-old boys? They had no idea, but they had a lot more at stake, with families, and homes, and businesses or jobs, and futures to protect. Would they agree to remain silent?

Tommy had taken the lead and said that they needed to keep together on this new pact, and talk to no one but each other. They all agreed, shook hands, and left their tree.

Curtis had gone back and dug up the evidence and thrown the necklace and the ice pick into a different plastic shopping bag. He had put the evidence in the tire well of his Focus and headed for home. His nerves had been firing all evening until he was numb.

He called out from the bedroom. "Hey, sweetie, how long have you been up?"

There was no answer, so he walked down the hall into the dining area. She was sitting at the dining room table writing on a sheet of paper. He couldn't see what she was writing from where he stood.

She looked up and casually turned the paper over. "Good mornin', baby. Breakfast'll be ready when you get out of the shower. I just put the sausage in the oven to keep it warm. Holler when you're out of the shower and I'll start the eggs."

"Okay, sweetie. What you workin' on?"

"Nothing important. I'm just jottin' down some thoughts. Dr. Rosen told me to do this back when I was goin' to her regular, ya know. I just never did it much, but with everythin' that's happened, I thought I'd give it a try, see if it helps."

Curtis was surprised that she would try something new, but maybe the pressure was getting to her, like it was to him.

After breakfast, Curtis leaned over and kissed Carly Sue lightly on the lips as she sat at the dinner table. "Thank you for that breakfast. It was great."

He forced a smile. She stood and put her arms around his neck. She kissed him with passion, then pulled back. "I love you, Curtis. You are the best thing in my life, ever. Don't you ever forget that...ever."

Curtis was surprised by her declaration and her kiss. He wished he could talk with her more about what she had been through in her life, but those talks always ended in her spiraling down into a deep depression. He looked her in the eyes. There was the usual sadness and despair, but there was something more, something that tugged at his heart. His mind told him that he should call in sick or take a vacation day, but the ban on vacation days had not yet been lifted.

He held his wife at arm's length and told her that he loved her as well and that there was no way he could ever forget how much she loved him. They had a special bond that would never be broken.

In a sad voice, he said, "But right now, I've got to get to work. I'll be home for lunch and bring your favorite sub sandwich. Okay?"

Curtis recognized the forced smile when she replied, "Yeah, Curt. That'll be perfect."

He had an uneasy feeling as he turned and headed for the car in the garage.

***

Brannen sped up Cypress Lake Road, then turned south to catch Highway 301 towards Statesboro. He made good time since the storm cell had passed. The main roads were wet but were draining. Very few puddles remained. Jones thought that they should have arrested Ginny Hardy before leaving, but Brannen believed that Carly Sue's life was in danger. He was certain that Ginny Hardy was going nowhere unless her mother was able to calm her down and convince her that she couldn't rely on God alone. Ginny was an emotional basket-case. She truly believed that God was her savior. It didn't matter anymore whether, according to the laws of man, she was guilty or not.

There was the off-chance that Millie might talk her into recanting her story, but Brannen believed that they had enough evidence to convict her, assuming a grand jury would indict her. She did have a case, however remote, for self-defense, if you believed that she did it for the young girl's protection. Jones agreed that it was a stretch.

Brannen turned onto Holly Drive and accelerated towards Curtis and Carly Sue's address. Curtis was backing his

Ford Focus down the drive as Brannen pulled the sheriff's cruiser in behind him. He honked his horn to make sure that Curtis wouldn't crash into the cruiser. Brannen saw brake lights, then white reverse lights blinked off as the car was shifted into park.

Curtis sat in his car for a moment. Brannen and Jones exited the sheriff's car

, Brannen going to the driver's side of Curtis's car, Jones heading for the passenger side.

Curtis stepped out of the car as Brannen said, "Mr. Hardy, please keep your hands where we can see them and don't make any sudden moves."

Curtis looked from Brannen to Jones and back again, then put his hands and arms out, palms up. He asked, "What's goin' on, Captain?"

"Mr. Hardy, is your wife home?"

Curtis hesitated before answering. He thought that the deputies were looking for him for MaryJo's murder. They hadn't drawn their guns or asked him to place his hands on the car so they could search him. With a quiver in his voice, he asked, "What do you want with Carly Sue?"

"We need to talk with her, that's all."

"About what? I'm her husband. I got a right to know."

Brannen was getting tired of having to explain himself to everyone associated with the murders. He took a more authoritarian tone. "Mr. Hardy, we need to see your wife right now. Don't play games with us. We don't have time to waste."

Curtis motioned towards the door with his head. He took a couple deep breaths as he approached the front door. He said, "I'm getting my keys out of my pocket, okay?"

Brannen nodded.

Curtis unlocked the door and stepped inside, followed closely by Brannen and Jones. He called out, "Carly Sue, there's a couple of deputies here to talk with you."

There was no answer. The house was dead quiet and dark. The curtains and blinds were closed throughout. The morning sky still overcast with thunder clouds in every direction added to the darkness throughout the Hardy residence.

Curtis tried again. "Sweetie, where are you?"

The three men heard the sound of a throat being cleared. "In here, Curtis."

The men walked into the living room. They had a clear line of sight into the dining room and saw Carly Sue sitting at the far side of the dining room table. She held a pen which hovered over a few sheets of paper. Next to her hand was a small-caliber revolver. Brannen knew that it was Millie Crider's gun. Her eyes remained on the paper, a slight tremble visible as evidenced by the shaking pen.

Curtis's demeanor took on a completely different persona. When he spoke, his voice was soothing. Brannen looked at him and frowned. Curtis asked, "Carly Sue, what are you doing, sweetie?"

The young woman's eyes didn't stray from the paper. She addressed her husband. "I'm finishin' writin' you a note, Honey. I just wanted you to know how much I love you, and how thankful I am for everything y'all have done for me over the years. If it weren't for you, I don't think I'd've survived this long."

Carly Sue used her left hand to wipe the tears from her eyes, still not looking up from the note. Brannen and Jones remained still. Curtis took a step closer. "Darlin', I know how much you love me. And you know I love you, I always have. We helped each other through some tough times, ya know?"

There was a long period of silence. No one moved. No one made a sound. Brannen and Jones looked at each other, not wanting to make a false move and cause the young woman to do something rash, like grab the gun and start shooting. They couldn't judge her state of mind because she was so calm and they couldn't see her eyes. They didn't know if she planned to use the gun on herself or someone else.

Curtis finally broke the silence. "Sweetheart, can you push the gun away from you? These men need to relax, and they can't if you reach for the gun. Please, slowly push the gun away from you."

Carly Sue looked up from the table and looked at her husband. She tried to smile but fell short. Her face settled into a look of despair. "Curtis, thank you so much for trying to help me. My momma let me down so many times…I was always so scared…anytime one of her creepy boyfriends came over. She let them…well, you know. I'm sorry I couldn't be the wife you wanted me to be. I'm sorry."

"That ain't true, sweetie. You are everything I ever wanted in a wife. You are good and kind. It wasn't your fault your momma didn't do right by you. That's on her and she paid for it. She can't hurt you no more, Darlin'. So, please, push the gun to the middle of the table. That way we can talk this out."

"Curtis…I'm broken inside. You know that. Ain't no fixin' it either."

Her tears began to flow in earnest, down her cheeks, dripping onto the paper. She put the pen down next to the gun. In a smooth motion, Carly Sue reached for the revolver, put the barrel to her head, then said, "Goodbye, sweetie. I love you."

"Noooo!!" Curtis leapt at his wife. He reached her hand a fraction of a second too late as the hammer struck the cartridge. The bullet ripped into Carly Sue's temple at nearly the same point as Allen Scott's fatal wound. She was dead before her head hit the table.

Brannen and Jones moved towards Carly Sue as quickly as they could, but there was no chance that they could stop the young woman from taking her own life.

***

After the ambulance left the Hardy residence with the body of Carly Sue Saxon Hardy and the neighborhood crowd dispersed, Brannen and Jones escorted Curtis Hardy to the back seat of their cruiser. Officially, they were taking Curtis in for questioning, but the lawmen knew that he wouldn't leave the county jail again until his trial. Shortly after the EMTs let Brannen know officially what he already knew, that Carly Sue was dead, he and Jones questioned Curtis about the entirety of the events that led to his wife taking her own life.

Curtis confessed to the murder of MaryJo Saxon to protect his mother, thinking that MaryJo was the only one who could provide evidence that Ginny Hardy killed Allen Scott. Carly Sue had told Curtis that she saw her mother peek out of her trailer window as Allen Scott drove away towards Cypress Lake. Curtis thought that planting his mother's gun in MaryJo's trailer would seal the deal. With MaryJo dead, she wouldn't be able to deny being the murderer. All his mother had to do was continue her silence. He didn't realize how much the guilt was driving her crazy over the years.

He handed over the necklace that was a perfect match for the bracelet found at the crime scene along with the ice pick he used to murder MaryJo. She was already passed out, so it was physically easy to ram the instrument into her brain through her ear. In reality, it was much harder to build up the courage, or cowardice depending on one's point of view, to carry out the act.

Brannen asked if Curtis knew anything about the corroded gun that was found at Cypress Lake. He hung his head. "Carly Sue took her momma's gun with her when Scott took her to the lake. She was gonna threaten him, or kill him…heck, she didn't know at the time. She was a scared little girl. When Momma shot him and Carly Sue scrambled out of the car, the gun fell on the ground. She was so freaked out that she forgot about the gun until she got home, then it was too late to go back and look for it."

Brannen asked Curtis what part his grandmother, Millie Crider, played in either murder. Curtis replied that his grandmother didn't do anything except try to keep Ginny, Carly Sue, and him quiet. "And point y'all in the wrong direction."

Finally, Brannen asked Curtis if Tommy Alexander, Andrew Pepperdine, or Billy Ray Duke had any involvement in either murder. He mentioned that they had Billy Ray's prints on the bumper of the car along with four other sets of prints.

Curtis replied, "You know, we was little kids back then, playin' all over that trailer park. We touched most every surface in the park. We didn't have no part in that pervert's murder."

Brannen said, "Funny, that's exactly what Billy Ray said. Pretty much word-for-word."

Curtis gave Brannen a half-smile. He didn't say another word.

Epilogue
October 23, 2015

Tommy Alexander sat with Andy Pepperdine and Billy Ray Duke in the gallery of courtroom number two directly behind the defense table. The gallery was empty save for three other spectators and reporter, Eugene Morris, who sat in the back row near the entrance. He had contacted the four friends in hopes of interviewing each of them for a true crime book based on events at Cypress Lake Mobile Home Park. The men had declined the invitation.

The District Attorney, an overweight man in his late fifties with slicked-back gray hair, sporting a cheap, gray suit and cranberry tie, sat at the prosecution table. A young, brunette woman in a navy pantsuit sat beside him. She had a notepad and pen on the table, ready in case note-taking was needed.

The three friends had been in the courtroom for twenty minutes. They were there to support Curtis. Two days after Carly Sue committed suicide, his mother, Ginny Hardy, died unexpectedly from a brain aneurism. She had been praying fervently without a break from the time Captain Brannen and Deputy Jones questioned her at Millie Crider's trailer until her death. The stress of her imminent arrest for the murder of Allen Scott, and the heartbreak of Carly Sue's suicide, caused her blood pressure to spike and remain dangerously high until a blood vessel in her brain burst. Brannen and Jones found her body when they went to arrest her.

The next morning, Millie Crider was found dead in her own trailer. She had suffered a fatal heart attack. Her ancient cat, Dusty, was also dead, curled up next to his owner's body.

The courtroom began to fill with City of Statesboro employees. In all, there were seventeen people in the gallery by the time Curtis was led into the courtroom by a Bulloch County Deputy Sheriff. He was in an orange jumpsuit with his hands cuffed. He smiled a weak, sad smile at his friends, then the smile brightened as he realized that he had a large contingency of friends and co-workers from the city in the gallery. He turned back to his friends, maintaining the smile. All three returned the smile, uneasy at what was about to transpire.

The court bailiff announced, "All rise! Superior Court Judge Carson Williams, now presiding!"

Judge Williams said, "Be seated."

The judge went through the required formalities, then got right to business. "Will the defendant please rise." After Curtis was standing with his court-appointed attorney, Williams continued. "Curtis Hardy, you are charged with the murder of MaryJo Saxon in the first degree. How do you plead?"

Without hesitation and in a strong voice, Curtis declared, "Guilty, Your Honor."

The judge looked to the Court Recorder and nodded, making sure that she had recorded the guilty plea. He returned his gaze to address the court. "There is no reason to delay sentencing. So, let's proceed. Is there anyone from the victim's family or friends of the victim who would like to make any remarks?" When no one in the gallery rose, he asked, "Is there anyone from the defendant's family or friends who would like to make any remarks?"

Nearly the entire gallery rose. The judge's eyebrows shot up in surprise. He took a deep breath and said, "Okay then, one person at a time, approach the podium, state your name, and address the court. Please keep your remarks brief and to the point.

After nearly forty minutes of supporting remarks from the gallery, the judge had heard enough. The last three to comment were Billy Ray, Andy, and Tommy. Their confidence was bolstered by the comments from Curtis's co-workers. It appeared to have an effect on Judge Williams.

Finally, the Judge turned to Curtis and asked if he had any final comments before sentencing. Curtis said yes and rose to his feet. He slowly made his way to the podium, followed closely by the deputy.

"Your Honor, I know what I did was wrong and I am truly sorry for my actions. I take full responsibility for what I done. I killed MaryJo Saxon because of the torture that she put her daughter through all her life and because she didn't protect her daughter when she was most vulnerable, as a young child. If the court will allow me to, I'd like to read the note my wife left me before she committed suicide right in front of my eyes."

Williams said, "You may, and we will enter the note into court records."

"Thank you, Your Honor."

Curtis cleared his throat.

My Dearest Curtis, I ain't much of a writer, heck, I ain't much of a talker either, but I want you to know that you are, and always will be the best thing that has ever happened to me. You saved my life many times, many times more than you know. You have a way of telling me that I'm worth something, something my momma never could do. She told me that I was trash and a slut and a whore, that I wasn't worth nuthin'. After a while, I believed her. I was always depressed, thinkin' that I'd never get outta that trailer park, never escape from her treatin' me like her punchin' bag.

But then you come along and told me - no, showed me - that I was special. It took a long time, but I was finally startin' to believe you. The doctors and the pills helped some, but you, you were my rock.

Then that bastard's body got found, and all the nightmares flooded back. And my momma went crazy, worse than before. And I got depressed all over again. I hid it better this time, but I couldn't get the monsters outta my head.

I'm sorry I failed you, my love. You didn't deserve a burden like me. You are so kind and patient and caring and loving. You deserved a wife who didn't have all this baggage with my crazy momma.

I love you, but I can't go on. Momma's torture still attacks me every day. So I got to put a stop to it. All the doctors and all the pills in the world won't help.

I'm so sorry. I love you.

Yours forever,

Carly Sue

"Thank you for allowing me to read that, Your Honor."

Curtis wiped tears away from his face. There was dead silence in the court as Curtis remained standing at the podium. After nearly a full minute, Judge Williams said, "Mr. Hardy, please take your seat at the defense table."

When Curtis was seated, the judge pinched the bridge of his nose and remained silent for nearly two full minutes. He looked around the courtroom, then spoke. "I have decided on a sentence. Mr. Hardy, please rise."

After Curtis was standing, Judge Williams focused his eyes on Curtis. "Mr. Hardy, normally in a case this heinous, I hand down the maximum sentence. In this case, it would have been twenty-five years to life, with possibility of parole after twenty years. But there are extenuating circumstances that are, quite frankly, frightening. I noted that you have never before been arrested for any violent offense, or any offense, not even a minor traffic ticket. I am, therefore, sentencing you to fifteen years in the state penitentiary with the possibility of parole after nine years."

The crowd didn't know how to react and looked at each other in wonder. The judge continued.

"Further, you will be remanded to Coastal State Corrections Facility, a medium-security prison. I will note in your sentence that, with good behavior, you should be considered for review at seven years for accelerated parole. I hope that your time at Coastal will help in your rehabilitation. This court is adjourned."

***

On his ten-minute drive home, Tommy thought about his last visit to the tree, the night that he, Billy Ray, and Andy came upon Curtis burying the necklace that matched the bracelet found at the lake, and the ice pick that he used to end the miserable life of MaryJo Saxon. They confronted him about what he was hiding.

At first, he was in denial, until his three friends pressed him and promised to keep his secret. They knew it was serious, even life threatening, for him to take such drastic measures.

Curtis finally broke down. He told his friends everything that he knew from that first night when they helped hide a body, right up to that moment, when he confessed to them that he had killed his mother-in-law, MaryJo. Then he had said, "It wasn't my idea."

Millie Crider, the woman everyone thought was a senile, poor old woman, had orchestrated the entire thing, from the murder of Allen Scott, to planting evidence on MaryJo, to her murder. "She was trying to protect her family."

Curtis went on to explain, "You see, Millie hated MaryJo for what she was. Millie's husband was Doug Hardy, my step-granddaddy…Carly Sue's biological granddaddy. I didn't know that at the time we was datin', but it turns out that her grandmomma, Clara Jean Saxon, had an affair with ole Doug when she was just fifteen and got pregnant with MaryJo. Clara Jean is Millie's younger sister.

"Anyways, Millie knew that MaryJo was neglecting Carly Sue, lettin' her perverted boyfriends get too close, and blamin' Carly Sue for being too pretty. Millie told momma that they had to do something about it. That's when she bought all them guns and gave one to momma and MaryJo, only MaryJo's didn't work. Millie did somethin' to it so it wouldn't fire. So, when Carly Sue took that gun to the lake to protect herself, even if she got the courage to use it, it wouldn't of worked. God knows what would've happened if she had tried to use it."

By the time Curtis finished his story, his friends were awestruck. They couldn't believe that the old woman had orchestrated a complex web of murder and cover-ups.

With Millie Crider's and Ginny Hardy's death, Curtis and Billy Ray were in line to inherit her estate. In her will, she specifically disinherited her sister, Clara Jean Saxon, and Clara Jean's daughter, MaryJo. Billy Ray promised Curtis that he would hire a financial planner to handle the money and a property manager to run the trailer park. Andy offered to assist them and recommend a few reputable firms.

As Tommy turned into the Irongate Subdivision, it began to rain, continuing the new weather pattern that began the day before Carly Sue's suicide. The drought was officially over for central Georgia, too late for this year's crops, but providing a glimmer of hope for the future.

The drought exposed a secret that a young woman, four men, a mother, and an old woman prayed would never resurface. But secrets have a way of eroding away trust among friends and family and, once exposed, can have devastating consequences.

As Tommy pulled into his driveway, he vowed never to keep secrets from his wife, Cheryl, again. Then he remembered his vow of silence to Curtis, Andy, and Billy Ray and realized that some things were better left unsaid.

###

Other PJ Grondin Suspense Novels

All titles are available in trade
paperback and various eBook formats.

A Lifetime of Vengeance
McKinney Brothers Book 1

A Lifetime of Deception
McKinney Brothers Book 2

A Lifetime of Exposure
McKinney Brothers Book 3

A Lifetime of Terror
McKinney Brothers Book 4

A Lifetime of Betrayal
McKinney Brothers Book 5

Drug Wars
Peden Savage Book 1

Flash Drive
Peden Savage Book 2

Visit www.pjgrondin.com
pjgron@pjgrondin.com

Author Information

Pete 'P.J.' Grondin, born the seventh of twelve children, moved around a number of times when he was young; from Sandusky, Ohio to Bay City, Michigan, then to Maitland and Zellwood, Florida before returning to Sandusky, Ohio, where he married the love of his life, Debbie Fleming.

After his service in the US Navy, in the Nuclear Power Program, serving on the ballistic missile submarine U.S.S. *John Adams*, Pete returned to his hometown of Sandusky, OH where he was elected to the Sandusky City Commission, serving a single term. He retired from a major, regional, electric utility after twenty-six years of service.

Under the Blood Tree is his seventh novel. His other works are *A Lifetime of Vengeance, A Lifetime of Deception, A Lifetime of Exposure, A Lifetime of Terror,* and *A Lifetime of Betrayal* in the McKinney Brothers suspense series. *Drug Wars*, and *Flash Drive* are the first and second novels in the Peden Savage suspense series.